THE HAUNTING AND ELDRITCH MANOR

GARRETT V WARD

Second edition - Ward, Garrett (Jan. 2019). The Haunting and Eldritch Manor. Cover Design provided by Rob Williams.

Copyright © 2021 Garrett Ward

First Edition

Cover Design by: EVE Graphic Design LLC

Editing by: Oren Eades, Skyhorse Publishing

Formatted by: Miki N. Ward

Published by Miki & Mine LLC

Paperback ISBN-13: 978-1-949250-21-3

Hardback ISBN-13: 978-1-949250-25-1

Ebook ISBN-13: 978-1-949250-20-6

Published in the United States of America

WWW.MikiAndMine.com

Metaterre

A - "The Old Crow"
B - Grocery
C - Market
D - James's Home
E - Presley's Home
F - Eldritch Manor
G - Spanish Garrison
H - Police
I - School
J - Hospital
K - Library
L - "Below the Salt"
M - Docks

E
J
H
D
1 Mile
1 Mile
L
C
1/2 Mile
G
A
1 Mile
B
F
1 Mile
Cliff
M
Metaterre
Bay
Cliff
Sandy Beach
Deep Water
Deep Water
Deep Water

To Kathi, the only woman capable of forgiving my continual disasters while giving me the freedom to write.

NOTE FROM THE AUTHOR

TO MY READERS...

Thank you for purchasing this book! Authors make their living off reviews. So, please leave me one—if you like the book, or you like me, or you believe in *(insert your favorite activity)*, apple pie and America!

This book is the final book in the Mirrored Worlds Series. It also marks the first book of the forthcoming, The Eldritch Manor Series.

A Haunting and Eldritch Manor contains magic, a demon, a touch of gore, more fear, plenty of violence, and copious amounts of cussing—thanks to Davi. Honestly, I don't like bad words. I simply couldn't get her to shut the hell up! Oh, and there are plenty of funny parts...I hope.

Sincerely yours,
Garrett Ward

LEAD IN

In case you didn't know, neither breeze nor dawn exist in death. Nor do boredom, passions, daydreams, or even modesty. But powerful emotions do cross over from life to the other side.

As an example, my frustration with my tiny tormentor, Davi, was just as strong in death. Still the single most powerful emotion, love rules all others.

I'm certain most of you have already learned its power. Me? I only recently discovered its purest form. Unfortunately, it was just before I died.

Though something that absolutely shocked me was the abject terror I felt because of the demon named Genosqwa.

So, sit back and read on. I'll explain how, despite my murder, I fought to reclaim my life with my new bride, María, whom I've not met—much less married—while a dimensional-traveling murderous alien and a demon situated inside its self-shaped world try to stop me and exterminate all life on Earth.

Hmm…where should I begin?

I'm Captain James Byrne—well, I was James Byrne. Shoot, this won't work.

Let's go to the genesis of the mess where I got killed.

This, as with most messes in my life, began with a woman. Not just any woman, either. This redheaded beauty is my best friend Presley's wife. She's the real reason that murderer Riaan Dahl killed me, allowing the demon-monster to snatch my soul and drag it into its realm—a reality where my soul currently is, as Genosqwa is bashing its mammoth club into my crumbling defenses. Yes, this is all Kate's fault—mostly.

Danged gingers!

You noticed I said *crumbling defenses*, right? Yep, I sure did. As I recount this thrilling tale, the demon is trying to get to my soul. I figure I've got four, maybe five, hours to polish this turd of a plan, then execute it, before it gets through, stomps me to dust, and slurps up my soul like it was a bowl of potato-leek soup.

It began on August the thirtieth, in the year of our Lord, seventeen-hundred eighty-one. It was a chilly morning that carried a heavy New England mist. Today, it provided the perfect camouflage for our ship as we snuck through a British blockade.

This was the fourth time we'd navigated through the enemy siege and into the anchorage of my home port, Metaterre. It's a town of little importance northeast of the busy harbor of New York. So, the British barricade was meant to punish the people in my fine town, most of whom had nothing to do with the rebellion against the Crown.

Because of the Brits' heavy-handed treatment, I threw my lot in with the rebels. I didn't take kindly to them using their army against people who only wanted life, liberty, and the pursuit of happiness. I mean, who couldn't support those goals?

I guess reading Mr. Paine's book played a key role in my choice to turn coat and help the colonists. I wasn't a politician, nor a brilliant orator, or even a persuasive essayist. But I was a superb sailor. When I commanded a ship, even Davy Jones himself couldn't catch me. Besides, those Brits couldn't capture me if they were towing me about the harbor on their own anchor chain.

I owned and skippered the *Monarch of the Sea*, a swift, two-masted brigantine. On second thought, King George owned her, but I stole my butterfly when I quit working for that fat majesty and began capturing his ships and selling his cargo.

At this moment, the *Monarch's* holds were stuffed with supplies and munitions. Jolly ol' England himself sent these goods to resupply his army. I stole them and intended to sell them to my contact, who would deliver them to the forces of Washington. In compensation, he'd pay me a fee grand enough to make that farmer George blush.

Thankfully, we were a fortunate group of mariners. Because if the Brits caught us—well, the penalty for treason is death. Still worse, the redcoats would seize our assets and send the gold to the same crazy King we opposed. That would leave our heirs with nothing. If the savages sporting those stupid red coats let them live, that was.

Also, what idiot dressed that army? Red was a terrible choice for a uniform color. Just name one circumstance where wearing red ever helped an army. Go ahead, I'll wait.

Yeah, I couldn't think of one either.

My contact was Don Diego José de Gardoqui, a wealthy financier. He had purchased the last three loads of enemy cargo we had liberated.

Who is Diego, you ask? He's the financial intermediary between the Spanish Crown and the Colonial government. That role made him powerful in both Spain and America. It also helped that his beautiful sister-in-law held an influential position with the Queen of Spain.

Now my dear reader, read on as my story begins. Hang on and enjoy!

In death,
James Byrne

JAMES

The icy gale bit and drove freezing rain bulleting into the bare skin of my face and hands. I tugged up the collar of my coat and spun slowly, exploring the landscape.

A dense woodland surrounded me. I couldn't see much, but recognized the weald was pine, maple, and oak. The forest here was thicker than the well-logged region near my hometown of Metaterre in upstate New York.

I don't recall this place. In fact, I'm not sure how I arrived.

Around me, the tumult raged, beating the branches into one another. The rhythmic sound blended into a natural metronome.

Tick, tick.

Cloud cover blocked any ambient stars or moonlight. Except for a slight glimmer in the distance, the night was absolute. I peered toward the pinprick of light, hoping my eyes weren't playing tricks. Still, while the iridescence didn't persist, continuing outside in this storm was certain death.

Tick, tick.

My tricorn atop my head and my cutlass in my hand, I jammed my other fist into the pocket of my leather coat, lifted my shoulders, and slogged forward, bending my face away from the weather.

The creaking limbs kept time with my stride.

Tick, tick.

The luminescence of my target grew. Far behind it, lightning flashed. Rain fell harder.

After more than an hour of cutting my way through the thick foliage, I spotted a circular expanse hundreds of feet in diameter. At its center stood a Native man and black woman. In front of them was a blazing bonfire. Its warming flames soared several feet into the icy storm.

Tick, tick.

He was dressed in deerskin leggings, a woolen breechcloth, and leather moccasins. She wore a simple burlap tunic cut from an onion sack. Around her waistline, she'd wrapped a hemp twine. Despite the cold, she wore no foot coverings.

Regardless of their Spartan dress, neither shivered in winter's assault.

Tick, tick.

A surge of lightning lit the sky behind them. Its brilliant afterglow deposited crimson orbs two-dozen feet above the couple. These giant eyes, birthed by the tempest, faded while rolling thunder beat my breast like a drum.

Tick, tick.

My clothes were sodden from the relentless rain. I was shivering. My heart was racing and my breathing was rapid. I needed these people's help or I'd surely perish in this frozen assault.

Tick, tick.

"Hello. Can you help me?" I called out before stepping into the clearing.

Neither figure responded.

Tick, tick.

Another crack of lightning and the flaming scarlet eyes returned. This time, they didn't dissolve. Instead, they glared at me.

I advanced toward the pair and their warming fire while the rhythmic dance among the trees became more resolute.

Tick!

The man was older than me. His heavily scarred face and sickly gray hair counterposed his athletic frame. His black-as-coal eyes blazing with the fire of hate never wavered from me as I walked closer.

Tick!

Lightning flashed and the flaming vermillion orbs grew greater. Thunder replaced the woodland metronome.

Boom!

I heard a deafening snap. Behind the mute couple, a tree fell as if it had been shoved aside.

Boom! The ground rumbled from the impact.

"My name's James Byrne. I'm lost. May I warm myself?" I pointed to the flames near them.

Again, they met my plea with silence.

Behind them, tree after tree fell in a parade, crashing inexorably toward me.

Boom, boom, boom!

The black woman was young and pretty. Her ebony hair was tightly curled and cut short, though her cocoa-colored eyes were empty as they peered through me. Her arms hung limply at her side, and at her feet lay an empty thatch bassinet.

Lightning flashed anew, this time atop us. I dodged as the resounding thunder beat against my body.

BOOM!

From the gloom, the glaring eyes grew into a terrible, demonic monster. This dread behemoth, clad in gray stone armor, bore fingers as long as my foot. Its sharpened fingernails dripped a terrifying sanguine fluid. It traversed the clearing, lumbering *through* the pair as if they were mist.

The beast raised a club the length of a tree. Its vast misshapen mouth opened, creating a jagged blackened crater. The scream was terrible as it brought the massive weapon down onto my head.

I bolted upright as the frenzy of my dream wiped away the sleep.

As I clambered from my bunk, I dragged in a sharp breath and held it before slowly exhaling. My feet slapped against the wooden decking, and I stepped to the basin to rinse my face. Only now did I recognize my cabin on board my ship and my wet hair.

AS WE GLIDED into the small harbor that morning, I stood watch on the quarterdeck and proudly watched my professional crew as they docked my ship. I didn't involve myself in such mundane acts. They were skilled and were led by my capable executive officer, Kia Dawson.

"Kia, I told you I was the luckiest son-of-a-gun alive," I said.

Not only was Mr. Dawson my XO, he was a good friend.

He chuckled and shook his head in disagreement.

"No, sir, you're not lucky."

"Then a son-of-a-gun I am. That's four crossings without a single sail setting after us. I'd call that success, luck or not," I called out over my shoulder while making my way to my cabin.

I paid Kia generously, as I did the rest of my crew. As Captain, I took a fifty percent share of the profits for operating costs and my cut as owner. I split the balance among the crew based on their position. This gave me the best shipmates available.

"Mr. Dawson, see to it our supplies are unloaded and warehoused after we tie up."

"Yes, Cap'n. Would ya like me ta fluff ye pillow whilst I'm at it?"

"That'd be fine," I replied in a monotone and with a neutral expression.

JAMES

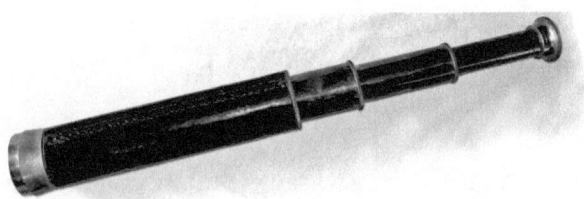

*I*t was mid-morning by the time we moored the *Monarch*. Remnants of the fog that had settled over the town had yet to burn away.

I departed the ship and picked my way along the steep path toward the market. As I walked, my wide, side-to-side gait marked me as fresh in port. It was as if I still needed to adjust for the rocking of the ship. This was typical for a sailor, at least for the first few weeks ashore.

I reached the road at the top of the rocky heights above the harbor, turned left, and began the mile or so journey to town. As the sun was still climbing, many more people were headed to the port.

Since we'd been at sea for nearly three full months, every person I passed called out their version of hello. From the riches to the poorest, I knew and liked them all. Most importantly, they liked me. I made it my business to remain in their good graces.

In truth, I'd admit to a modicum of ignorance about a small percentage of the townsfolk; but such unfamiliarity was often deliberate.

The unpainted shutters on *The Old Crow*, a diner, slammed open, sending a loud crack echoing into the morning mist. The busy eatery had begun its life as a house. Several shed additions later, it had been purchased by its old-goat proprietress, Susan Bond, and converted to its present use.

Passing the likable old restaurant marked the edge of the township nearest the port. To my left was the market and the bulk of the city, but if I continued my march, I'd reach my home nearly a mile further.

Hoping to skirt the market and avoid unwanted delays by hellos and how ya doins, I hopped up the steps of Susan's place and started down the boardwalk toward my home.

"Byrne. Dammit, James, I said stop!"

I did.

I turned to find the voice and saw a pint-sized beauty chasing after me. Her red hair flowed out behind her as she ran holding her arms across her, um, chest.

I stepped off the wooden walk to the edge of the roadway and waited the few seconds it took for my best friend's wife, Katherine Sue Varde, to catch me.

"If I would've known such a jewel would chase me, I would've come to the market sooner. Hello, Kate. How are you and Presley?" I asked as I spread my arms for a hug.

She puffed her cheeks and slowly let the breath seep out of her lips before she returned my hug, pulling my neck to her.

"Presley's fine. I didn't come for him, though; I came for me. James, I need your help."

"My help? What on Earth could I do that Presley couldn't?"

I let the double entendre hang for a moment before I offered her a ghost of a smile that had only one corner of my mouth slightly turned up.

Kate's my best friend's girl. They've been together since she found him eating lunch at *The Old Crow*. He told me she asked him to marry her the day after they met. A year to the day later, they married. They've been inseparable since.

She knew my word games and, most times, played along by giggling. Sometimes she even thought something I said was funny.

That she moved the conversation along now without commenting focused my thoughts intently on her next words.

"James, you know my grandfather, Charles. He's getting up in years, and, well, it's time we set his affairs in order. I don't want a mess after he passes."

"Alright, Kate. What can I do to help?"

"There are some..." She hummed the word, stretching it as she searched for what she wanted to say next. Finally settling, she continued, "...peculiarities at his home that I'd like you to investigate."

That lady never lacked in confidence. At least not publicly, anyway. When she cast those emerald-green eyes down and away, the hair on my neck lifted.

I should've answered, nope, not interested, left, and locked myself inside my house for the next two months.

Instead, I said, "Kate, we've got police for those types of goings-on. Besides, I'm a ship's Captain. What skills could I possibly bring?"

She examined me, searching my eyes. Her words were carefully chosen.

"Well, you *not* being police is the best part. They've looked into that mess loads of times and have found nothing."

"Fine..."

She interrupted. "Long after the investigators quit searching, you found that woman—what's her name, Breanne. You hunted where they said she couldn't be. Besides, everyone knows you never quit once you've set your mind. In addition, I'll pay you three thousand, five hundred dollars."

At that, my eyes shot open a full inch wider than they should have been able to open. Katie, her nickname since childhood, knew where to hit me. I hadn't become successful by lacking guile, though my sudden dry mouth and swollen tongue had me questioning that belief.

She must've noticed my unusual bout of doubt and pressed on.

"James, I know this is a lot of money. I don't want your help as a favor. I expect a great deal from you. In return, I'll pay you a year's worth of income, if Presley's guess regarding how much you make is right."

Having people know anything regarding my finances sent chills across my neck and my shoulders rose several inches. Still, he and I were in related professions. It made sense that he could make a reasonable guess, and I relaxed.

"Kate, why do you want me to look into that old place? You don't want to live in it, you've told me so yourself."

"Jim, do you know its history?"

I started nodding my head, but she interrupted, causing me to stop.

"I mean its genuine history, not the clothesline talk of these old gossips."

She tossed her head over a shoulder, meaning to encompass the townsfolk.

If Metaterre had a power, it was one that fed off rumor, innuendo, and whispers. Without a doubt, I knew what she meant.

"Katie, I only know what I've heard from the same back-fence talk, plus what you or Presley shared with me. If that doesn't cover it, fill me in. But first, let's sit."

I led her to a table that was setup outside the grocery next to the diner and pulled out a chair for her. I'd not give Presley a reason to chastise me for mistreating his lady.

"Alright, give me the facts," I said as I took my seat. I flipped it around backward so that I rested my arms on its back. My fingers tapped on the wooden chair back, strumming a marching tune I'd learned as a child.

Katie scraped her palms together, and then, folding them against her chin, she peered into my face and leaned forward.

"James, before I was born, my family was the wealthiest in the entire state. My grandparents lived in that old house. Then people started disappearing. True, that was terrible enough. But it got down-right terrifying when those stone figures first appeared. They're everywhere—in the copper mine, in the woods, inside the home. Everywhere."

"Kate, I don't know what you need me for. I'm not an investigator, and you seem to have a handle on what's happened," I said, palms up.

"Jimmy, some of those statues are as perfect as they were three decades ago. Others, created only a few years ago, are now dust." She sat back in her chair as if she'd checkmated me.

"I guess that's a surprise—"

I didn't get the chance to finish before she interrupted me again. Her eyes narrowed and color filled her cheeks. She raised a tiny hand and pointed her finger straight at my nose.

"James, my grandfather's old. That makes me the last in the Eldritch bloodline. I owe it to him to get answers about what happened to our family."

She refused to break eye contact.

I stared back as I answered, "Katie, my friend, I'm sorry. But with all the work I've got, you know, helping with these war supplies...I just don't see how...I'm sorry, I can't."

As I spoke, her shoulders slumped, and then her eyes cast down. Suddenly, she stiffened her back and popped up out of her chair.

"Thanks for listening anyway, Jim. I understand and realize how busy you are. You know Presley would be cross if I didn't invite you to supper," she said as if I hadn't just broken her heart.

"Let me get this cargo sorted. Then I'd love to come over."

"Great. Let me know when you're free and I'll cook up your favorite dish. Roast pig, is it?" She finished with a laugh as she turned and strode away.

"No pig," I called to her back. She knew my favorite was roast beef with diced potatoes, carrots, onions, and her homemade rolls. That little redhead could cook. I couldn't wait.

She called back, "Roast pig it is. You'll love it," and then disappeared into the crowd.

3

JAMES

I watched the diminutive redhead as she marched toward her home, tugging her dress up just enough to keep it clear of the mud in the road. Her home and mine were on the same side of town, but she could cut through the market and reach hers faster.

Still sitting in my chair, drumming my fingers on the backrest, I continued to fixate on her as she walked away. I stopped the beat when I saw her spin on her heels and stamp toward a growing commotion.

No one would confuse Metaterre with the bustling port of New York, but it still had its share of people passing through. Even so, a racket was uncommon.

The clamor was a confrontation between two people—a light-complected raven-haired beauty and a gentleman whom I recognized as one of the town's seven councilmen.

"You, sir, are an ass. How dare you speak to me like I am a trophy. *Yo soy* Lady María Pauleta Francesca Rose Pimetel de Rota! I am *not* some back-alley *puta* on display for some ancient, *entrometido, pendejo,* aristocrat!"

"Madam, it is no insult to advise a beautiful woman of her comeliness," the man stammered back.

No reasonable person would consider this man a fossil, yet he had at least two decades on the dark-haired beauty verbally sparring with him.

Her hair was blacker than coal and flowed in unison with her head as she jabbed a pointed finger at the unfortunate fellow's chest.

"Do you stop a man to tell him how well he is dressed, or comment unnecessarily on his appearance?"

She folded her arms and glared at him.

"Well, I...I wouldn't need to, would I? I was paying you a compliment," the chastened man mewled.

"No!" María exclaimed in victory. "Since you have nothing further to offer, *dejame en paz.*"

She then flicked her hand to shoo him away.

His mouth worked up and down like a caught guppy and he belched several grunts, vowels escaping his frantically exercising mouth.

The gussied-up gentry, unaccustomed to being dismissed, shuffled his feet forward, then to one side, before turning and striding away. His long steps searched for anywhere other than under the searing glare of Lady María.

Even provoked, this woman was stunning. If Helen of Troy were real, she stood in the streets of my city. I tended toward action, so my first impulse was to hurry over and introduce myself. Fortunately for me, Kate saved me a mortifying fate when I saw her striding to *my* Trojan doll.

María, recognizing her, smiled and opened her arms to the smaller woman.

"*Roja!*"

The tit-for-tat with the jilted nobleman forgotten, the amber-eyed stunner pulled the smaller woman to her.

"*Roja*, it is good to see you. I am going to the hospital. Will you walk with me?"

"I will. I see another man expounded upon your beauty," Kate said as a wide grin spread across her face.

"*Pinche boboso,*" María said, smiling equally prodigious at her friend.

"I'm surprised there's a man left on the continent who hasn't learned to keep his subjective appraisals private."

María took Kate's arm in hers and turned toward the hospital. They walked in silence for several steps. Her dark eyes squinted, and her brow furrowed.

"How is your grandfather?" María asked.

Her friend tensed, her back straightened, and her hand wrapped tighter around the dark beauty's.

"I am sorry, Katherine. I should not have pried," María said in response to the non-verbal clues.

"No, no. That's not it. I don't know how to talk about it. He's at my house. He's struggling both psychologically and physically, and it isn't safe to leave him for long. I came here to ask for help from a friend of mine."

"What can I do?"

"It's nothing, honestly. You need to get to work, and I must return home to my grandfather."

María turned to climb the steps to the hospital, where she worked.

"I will come to check on Mr. Doss later today," the black-haired demigoddess said.

Kate pulled the taller woman into an embrace before turning and marching toward her home. María spun and entered her workplace. The sting of alcohol filled her nose.

As soon as she entered, a graying doctor called to her.

"Young lady, I've been waiting on you for more than an hour. Please prepare this man for surgery. He has acute appendicitis, and we'll need to remove it."

As with all surgeries, this would be painful. María's job would be to clean and organize the needed surgical instruments. She would need to collect men from the street to help restrain this patient; the man was large, and she guessed strong.

After she had everything in order, including having provided the infirm a large quantity of whisky, she called the surgeon over.

"Doctor, we are ready."

María was a competent nurse who in some areas exceeded the knowledge of the physicians, although not one of them would ever admit it. They did, however, trust her with more and more of the work they'd do normally.

"Thank you, nurse. After I finish removing his appendix, I want you to stitch the incision. Can you do that?"

"Yes, Doctor," she answered. She'd already stitched so many wounds. This would be simple.

4

JAMES

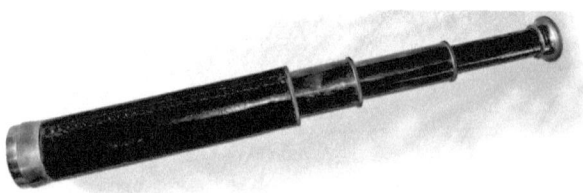

*A*ll the morning and much of the afternoon was gone by the time I had made my hellos and how-are-yous during my walk to my house. While some people may consider it an exhausting task, I relished it. Besides, I traded in knowledge. That information was gained from friends, who I generously repaid.

The sun was inches from its slumber when I reached home. My two-story Victorian sat on the town's southern edge. Its cinnamon-colored window frames stood out from the white trim and beige body. Kate had selected the paint scheme when I built the home last year. In fact, she'd ensured the decor was seamlessly coordinated throughout the newly constructed home.

I'd closed the half-round shutters before going to sea. I see now that someone else had latched them open, and had opened the windows on the ground and second levels, too. This created a draft, which removed my accumulated stench, as Mrs. Bond said.

Inside was cleaner than the day I'd left three months ago. A warming fire blazed in the smoke-stained hearth. A kettle of stew hung simmering on its edge. Its peppery scent permeated the air. My stomach rumbled.

I wasn't the wealthiest man in New York. I earned enough to pay for extravagances like cleaning and food preparation, but I didn't. That's one of the best parts of being me.

When I returned from abroad, I'd supply the grocer specialty food, wine, and liquor, usually from Spain or France, but sometimes from the far edges of the Mediterranean, where I'd purchased uncommon goods.

Supplying the town's grocer with these delicacies meant I never bothered with my pantry. He made sure foodstuffs arrived and were stowed away inside my larder before I returned home and on every Tuesday thereafter. The pantry would empty when I shipped out. I loved the magic of the system.

Susan Bond was caustic to everyone except me or those inside her establishment. Last year, I'd rescued her son from a redcoat impressment. Now, after every trip, she tidies up my place and prepares a meal, even though she refused to work as my maid. I know because I'd asked her many times.

"Ya's got to tidy up aft'a ye own self," she told me.

Besides, she was happy as the proprietress of her little restaurant near the town's market.

I was famished, so I gobbled a bowl of stew as soon as I arrived and another just before sunset. The salt now out of me, I retired to my bed.

A frozen zephyr had passed an hour before sunset. The north wind that followed grew teeth and chewed through the cracks around my doors and windows, though not enough that my fire didn't keep me warm. I hated night clothes, but tonight, I slept in my long shirt to ward off the nip.

Still, shutters rattled, and air whistled. Dead leaves climbed streams of air and ticked against diamond shaped quarrels of glass on my bedroom window.

After I blew out my candle, I plopped my head onto my soft, downy pillow. I breathed in, held it, then let it out, forcing my muscles to relax. I excised restlessness from my mind.

The leaves continued their *tick, tick, tick*.

I've always loved lots of blankets. Tonight, I pulled an extra on top. The wool itched, but I didn't care. I'd long since grown thick skin.

Sleep caught me.

Fog billowed around me. When the gale cleared the air, I was standing in the blizzard outside. Wind battered me. I glanced at my attire, my brow furrowed and my eyes squinted against the tempest. At some point, I'd dressed. Even though I wore my boots and coat, an icy blast knifed through me.

A lighted window shone maybe two hundred feet ahead. I tugged my coat around my ears and jammed my fists into my pockets. As I trudged, I realized the light didn't emanate from my home. Still, the gale bit hard enough that I wanted out, and the nearest exit was a doorway ahead.

As I neared, I recognized the rundown Eldritch Manor. But since it should've been miles away, the context was confusing. How did I get here? Even sleepwalking, which I'd never done, I shouldn't have covered this distance.

The seventy-year-old building was more crumbled than I remembered. Its once-pristine alabaster coating had deteriorated to a drab gray. Or had twilight duped my eyes?

The door opened with my push, hinges groaning. It was massive, even for this palatial residence. As I shoved through, a gust of wind drove snow behind me. The door's weight carried it into the stop, causing a crack to echo. My eyes opened wide, and my mouth formed a silent O in response.

Yellow light flickered through a doorway behind the upstairs balcony. Shadows danced around the bottom and corners of the walls, bouncing one direction before reaching for another.

"Mr. Doss, it's James Byrne. I had to get out of the snow," I yelled.

Charles Doss was Kate's grandfather and owner of this once-magnificent mansion.

A frozen draft blew across my neck. Goosebumps rose, and I shivered.

Using both hands, I closed the door. To finish the last inch, I pushed with my shoulder to latch it. Its warped frame no longer fit correctly into its paint-bare jamb.

Upon my about-face, I took in the breadth and scale of the chamber. It was the size of a barn, measuring fifty feet a side. No pictures decorated the decaying walls.

On my right was an empty hearth. The throbbing of the storm rattled inside its stone guts.

A great long-case clock guarded the blank wall to my left. Its ticking was distinctive even over the reverberations of the weather. Its wood was unstained, but showed no visible wear. It was dignified and well-preserved despite its age.

I startled at the sudden exclamation of its chime. It repeated three times. The hair on my nape rose as its ringing echoes died away.

"Hello! Is anybody here?" Only the ticking clock answered me.

At my front, wooden stairs curved upwards to a near-blackened balcony. In the past, something had crushed the railing near the middle as if a giant had mashed it. Pieces of spindles littered the floor, kindling awaiting a fire.

Since the stairs led to the only other source of light, I started climbing. I wasn't prone to trepidation. My feet were stone weights and dragged with each footfall through a halting progression. Each step caused a corresponding creak from the stair. The *tick-tock* measured my climb and turned it into a uniform march.

I reached the top and stood outside door of the lit room.

The gale outside gusted, shaking the house. I heard shingles being torn from the roof.

"Hel...lo," I cried anew. I wish my voice hadn't hitched.

Still no response. My gentle knock, then persistent banging went unchallenged, so I entered.

Besides massive spiderwebs brimming with crawlies, only three items were inside the chamber: a candle puddled inside a wall niche, a bronze spyglass standing near the window, and, at my rear, a mirror.

I didn't enjoy mirrors. I fancied them less when they had eight-legged arachnids jockeying for position inside the shadowed reflection.

But a spyglass was a different matter. I'd gathered a spectacular collection from around the globe. I strode over, pulled the glass to my eye, and saw nothing, which didn't surprise me, given the roiling ebony clouds.

The field glass was polished bronze and had strange graffiti or foreign writing on its largest section. Scrimshaw dragons, mermaids, and other fantastic creatures covered the three tubes below the largest. After examining it, I slid it back onto its mounting pin.

That damned ticking clock. The seconds clicked more loudly the further away I got. That couldn't be true. It was my imagination, right? I shook my head to regain my rationality.

This mansion had unnerved me, and I wanted to leave. I pivoted.

When I did, I faced the mirror. It'd grown several times since I first saw it, and now reached at least fifteen feet. That was taller than the wall.

I didn't see my reflection. Instead, a behemoth shifted within it. Great scales covered its granite-gray body. Standing over twice my height, it lumbered toward the front of the manor. As it stomped, it dragged a club the length of a tree.

I realized I'd been watching the beast from a window, not a mirror, inside of which I couldn't have seen that monster.

I broke for the stairs, skipping steps until I neared the end, halting three steps from the bottom. I froze.

The front door was ripped from its hinges as something crashed through it. The door fragmented as it spread across the floor. Chunks scraped gouges into the dusty wooden planks. Smaller pieces flew. I dodged away from them.

The giant burst inside, tearing away the door frame as it did. It glared at me, its fiery, unblinking eyes locked onto mine.

The clock began another series of knells.

Gong!

Had I been here an hour?

Gong!

What was I waiting for? Hope? Help?

Gong!

I swallowed the bile the terror had forced from my guts. When I vaulted over the broken banister, I dashed for the back door.

Gong!

A massive stone-hard hand grabbed me and flung me crashing into the wall. I fell, crippled, onto the dust-covered floor.

5

JAMES

I woke in my own bed as the sun rose. I wore only my nightshirt. I must have put away my boots and coat. Most importantly, I didn't recall the return trip home.

A cock crowed from a nearby barnyard. I startled as the shock of last night's terror again raised my bile to the point its bitter taste filled my mouth. I sat up and groaned in pain.

After removing my shirt, I found my right side, shoulder, and buttocks bruised. On my upper back were four lacerations lined up as if an enormous hand had clawed me. I didn't have time for this.

Outside, a few inches of powdery snow covered the ground. The zephyr that originally carried it was dead. The foliage on the large oak outside my window hung limp and brown.

I dressed, determined to find out more about that old manor house. I'd always been drawn to a mystery. Today, I had a fine one delivered by my best friend's wife.

I didn't bother to saddle my horse. The walk to Kate and Presley's home took only a few minutes. Besides, it'd take me longer to get Constellation, my stallion, outfitted and cleaned than three round trips on foot.

My breath formed a tiny fogbank in front of my face as I exhaled. I walked a path in the snow straight to their front door. I knocked a sharp *bang, bang* before I stepped back and waited.

When the door opened, it was Kate. She didn't hesitate before she said, "Jimmy, why are you out so early? Looking for a breakfast, I'd wager."

"Well, you know me. I'd be a fool to turn down a meal from the likes of you. May I come in?"

"Sure."

She opened the door further and swept her hand inside as a welcome. Breakfast was indeed cooking. I smelled the fat off the sausage first, but soon the smell of the biscuits browning beat it away.

"Where's Presley?" I asked.

"He had to go to the market. He'll be back in a bit. Jim, you didn't come here to eat, did you?" she said, hands on her hips. When she struck this pose, you knew she had read you, and you'd better come clean.

"No, I didn't. Last night, something happened. I can't explain it. But I want to talk to your grandfather if I can."

"You know he isn't well. His mind isn't working as it used to."

"I know, Katherine. If I get him upset, I promise I'll stop. Is that acceptable?"

"I know you love him too. I trust you. He's upstairs in the guest room." She pointed in the direction I was meant to go.

I'd stayed at my friend's home many times and knew exactly which room she meant. I knocked just loud enough not to scare the old man. I heard a grunt.

I opened the door and saw him sitting in a rocking chair facing the window. He turned his head enough to glimpse me out of the corner of his eye. Without so much as a hello, he turned back.

"Charles, it's me, James. You remember, don't you? I used to come over and help you with the chores when I was a kid." I bent down toward him, attempting to gain any acknowledgement.

He didn't respond.

"Mr. Doss, last night, I had a..." I struggled with what word to use and settled on, "...dream. Sir, have you had any odd dreams about your home?"

"I've had my share. They've plagued me many nights. Avoid four." He never wavered in his gaze outside as he spoke. But his speech was coherent and had much more vigor than I'd expected.

"Mr. Doss—Charles—have you ever seen anything odd outside of a dream?"

He quit rocking and sat still. The moments passed, and I was sure he'd forgotten my question.

"*Touye, lavi. Touye, lavi. Tou...*" He trailed off as he rocked forward in his chair, as if he meant to stand. Again, time trailed away. Nothing the old man said made any sense to me, so I gave up and decided I'd take the next step.

"Mr. Doss, may I have your permission to go to Eldritch Manor?" I had already told Kate I wouldn't, so I didn't know why I bothered to ask.

"If you are murdered, the stone will devour your soul and cast you into a waste," he said as he relaxed back. The squeak of the treads on his chair continued.

I went back downstairs to his granddaughter.

"James," a baritone voice boomed out.

My friend Presley strode to me, and we greeted each other as if we'd been apart for a third of the year. Which, come to think of it, we had.

"It's good to see you, my friend," I said as I backed out of the hug.

Breakfast was set and the three of us ate. Neither he nor I were brilliant conversationalists when food was on our plates, so Kate carried it for us.

After our meal, I asked my friend about visiting the manor.

"Yes," was her one-word answer. I caught a sly grin ghost its way across her face.

6

JAMES

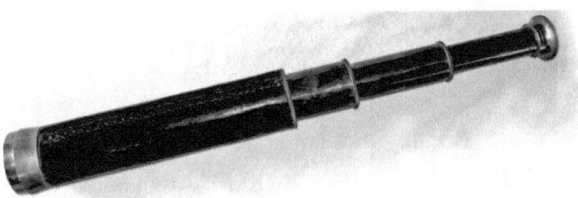

It was after four p.m. before I saddled my stallion, Constellation, for the ride to the old manor. Connie, as I called him, was an American Saddlebred steed as black as night. I'd had him for the last two years. Before I'd bought him, he was already comfortable with a rider, and had been with a person daily since his birth. Connie and I had grown comfortable with each other. He'd learned to trust me and I him.

Upon my arrival, I dropped his reins near a worn statue in the front of the old house. I didn't have to worry. He wouldn't wander away, even if spooked.

The front of the home looked just as it had in last night's nightmare—all except the door and light. The door was open, and there wasn't any light that I could see. In defense of my eyesight, the sun still hung above the frozen horizon.

Eldritch Manor had once been the hub of societal life in and around Metaterre. If you wanted to meet someone, you had better-than-even odds of finding them in this mansion at some point during any given week.

Today, it is a shell. It has virtually no furniture, and hosts more bugs and rodents than people by thousands of times.

As I reached the threshold, I learned why the door stood open—it was missing. The remnants of a single hinge remained. It was bent, contorted into a form only recognizable because of its location. The other hinges had been torn out of the jamb and were still attached to the door, which lay inside the manor. Something massive had smashed it into several large pieces. It had flung the door and dug huge gouges into the once beautiful marble floor.

I stepped across the remains of the wreckage and into the sunlit front room. A frighteningly familiar icy breeze blew across my neck and raised goosebumps.

Unlike my dream, inside the front room stood a human-sized figure of a woman. Presley had told me that the police determined she looked exactly like one of the Eldritch ladies who had disappeared almost thirty years ago. This statue was perfectly formed and as white as if it had just been completed.

"James, free us." The words were feminine, but were so softly spoken the sound couldn't have carried beyond my ears.

Startled and admittedly confused, I gaped. My mouth worked its muscles and my tongue bounced around inside my dry mouth. I stared, unblinking, into the face of the effigy. It stared back. Then it blinked.

This was the second time I had run from this place. Or was it the first? Did last night count, since I wasn't really here?

It didn't matter. I mounted my horse and rode away with what little dignity I could drag along in my fear.

No wonder the old man was a loon.

I rode Connie at a gallop until I reached the edge of town. No sense in causing a commotion, so I slowed him to a walk. I petted his neck. "Good boy."

He responded by tossing his head playfully. Good for him. He hadn't seen what I'd seen.

Now I had all the information about Eldritch Manor that I needed. As soon as I found Kate, I was going to give a resounding *no* to her request for help.

I stopped my stallion and jumped down to walk him the rest of the way into town. Hopefully, during the walk, my pulse and heavy breathing would return to normal.

Out of the general store on my left glided the same magnificent creature I'd watched eviscerate the poor fella yesterday.

I considered myself abnormally lucky with women. I had a talent for knowing what to say. In this case, I was certain I had a leg up, because I knew someone who looked to be her spitting image. I was surprised I hadn't recognized the similarities yesterday.

Unfortunately, I had made a terrible choice, as I was about to discover.

Not realizing the danger I was in, I confidently approached the beauty. The closer we moved, the more confident I became.

I *had* intended to walk straight at her, forcing her to stop and look at me. However, a step before my mark, I dropped one foot into a puddle of mud. I was so focused on Lady María, I hadn't seen the large quagmire of muck between the two of us.

She stopped and stared at me, mirth curling her lips.

I stood, one leg slightly shorter than the other. I pulled it out of the sludge to hover uncomfortably above the goo. Her brown eyes had me trapped. I recognized the playfulness in them as she spotted my predicament.

She took a step toward me and introduced herself. "Hello, my name is María."

She added a slight curtsy at the end that caused her ducked head to just miss my chin. I stumbled back a step and thankfully out of the hole. Which, I'd guess, was exactly what this dark-haired beauty had wanted.

"Miss María. Hello. I'm happy to meet you," I said, hoping I covered the effect she had on me.

"You are?" she questioned.

The smile on her ruby lips told me she knew exactly the effect she had on men, and, more specifically, me.

"You are the spitting image of another beautiful woman I know."

I'd used this as a line many times. But, in this case, it was true. She looked exactly like someone I'd met in Spain.

"We have never met. I was raised in Rota, Spain, and have been here for a few months. I have never seen you before, and would thank you for not bothering me further."

She lifted her chin and huffed before she flicked her wrist at me, just as she had the other unfortunate gentleman yesterday, and walked away without another look in my direction.

"Well, hasn't this been the perfect day," I grunted and headed home.

7

JAMES

The next day, I woke after an uneventful night's sleep. I dressed, had my morning meal, and left to see my friend. I hated letting people down, especially those I cared for. But that manor was a mess beyond what I could sort.

As I walked to Kate's home, I found myself wandering through the market, then to the front of the police offices. I stopped and stared at the front door. This was the long way to get to my friend's home, and I don't know why I took this path.

Bolstering my intestinal fortitude, I said, "James, walk in, ask a few questions, and tell Kate. That way, she won't say you didn't try."

Yes, I had a habit of telling myself things out loud. The thing was, I should've listened this time.

I glared at the doors as if I were angry for being there. I slumped my shoulders, stomped my boots, and went inside.

I didn't enjoy this building. The people working here had caught me misbehaving a few times as a lad.

The sweet cigar smoke that filled the air took me back to my sixteenth birthday. Dang, that was a day to forget. Not as bad as yesterday, but Presley and I had been grounded for weeks after that...

Despite not wanting to be here, I still had enough sense to have made many friends inside the building. In fact, a good friend of mine was the town's chief investigator. His name was Thomas Reagan.

"Hello, Thomas!" I exclaimed, pumping more excitement into the greeting than I meant.

"Jimmy!" he roared in return. At least with him, I always knew where I stood. This was his "you aren't in trouble and I'm glad to see ya" greeting. He was a giant of an Irishman. He stood a good six inches taller than me and outweighed me by at least a hundred pounds. It was solid muscle, too. Thomas wasn't one to pick a fight with unless you wanted to lose.

"My friend, I need some help today. I was hoping you'd talk to me for a few minutes before I go see Kate."

Even though Metaterre was a growing town, he and I'd run in the same circles in our youth, so he knew Kate and Presley. Me mentioning Kate was meant to predispose him to helping her, just in case he wasn't enthusiastic about helping me.

"Sure thin', Jimmy," he said as he slapped an enormous hand on my back and all but shoved me toward his desk.

After we sat, I leaned one elbow on the massive oak work top. The other hand strummed fingers onto my knee.

"Thomas, you've known me for a long time, and you know I'm not prone to exaggeration." I hesitated a heartbeat longer than needed between the words. It was as if I needed to drag them out of my throat.

"Sure. You're a bit of an arse. But nothin' I can't control," he deadpanned back.

I shot him a feigned-hurt expression before I asked, "Can you tell me what you know about the old Eldritch place?"

He sat up and didn't answer for a breath. "Jimmy, that place, she's a proper mess. You'd do well to jest stay away from 'er," he said.

"More than you know, my friend, I agree. But it's for Kate. You know I couldn't turn her down. She'd never feed me a proper meal again," I said, a broad, welcoming smile spreading across my face.

"Alrigh'. I know what yer sayin'—I canno' turn 'er down either. I suppose ya want'n ta know about them disappearances?"

I nodded my head.

"Jimmy, I've looked in'a that place several times. Always the same: nothin'. I've ne'er found a thing. No bodies, no blood, no clues. I can't ne'er find a connection to the disappearances eye'th'r." He pronounced either with an eye at its beginning.

Despite having lived most of his life in New York, he spoke with a thick Irish accent. Luckily, I'd been around his ilk long enough that I could understand his version of English.

He looked at me, silently questioning whether I wanted him to continue.

I nodded him on.

"The best I can come up with is the old man, Doss, done killed all those folks. And no, I don' know what's behind the statues, so don' ask." Irritation crept into his voice for the first time.

"Jimmy, the thin's I know for sure: Doss is a kook, an' all them who's disappeared did so in the cold." At that, he sat back in his chair.

I sank a bit. The burden seemed to weigh more than it had before I walked in.

"One last thing, Jimmy. That place, she's got a history as creepy as the ol' man. You need to check the papers at the library. It'll give you a better tellin' than I could. Talk to that old librarian. He's got more history-n 'em than me, anyway."

I stood, shook my friend's hand, and headed to the library.

Calling it a library was more aspirational than actual, though. We had our share of books and documents, and each of them was organized and catalogued. It's just that we didn't have many. The books filled the top four shelves of three whole bookcases.

We had less than two hundred books and several hundred periodicals and newspapers. I'd read each of the books more than once.

My favorites included *The History of the Decline and Fall of the Roman Empire* by Edward Gibbon and *Common Sense* by Thomas Paine. I even enjoyed re-reading Captain Cook's Journals.

One of my favorites was a French play called *Le Barbier de Séville ou la Précaution inutile*, or *The Barber of Seville*, written by Pierre Beaumarchais. It followed the story of a Spanish Count who, at first sight of Rosine, fell in love with her.

I wasn't a romantic of any sort. Still, the story interested me, and I loved reading French. It was the realism portrayed by the two lead characters while they sketched an unrealistic fiction that held my fascination.

Yes, I hadn't missed the obvious correlation between the Count and Rosine and my sudden real-life preoccupation with María.

I wandered through the aisles of periodicals, trying to avoid any information on the Eldritch place, which was the reason I'd come. A touch on my elbow caused me to turn in alarm. I didn't catch my breath before an extremely dark-skinned woman, who was now holding my elbow and pulling me close, spoke.

"Your actions at the manor will decide your world's future," she said.

"What?" It was not an intelligent question.

"What? Can you not fucking hear me? I told you what you needed to know. Your response is a single word. Why did you not just say, 'I am a fucking idiot,' instead?" she retorted.

The woman was quite pretty. Her eyes were icy-blue and her hair the most perfect color of blonde. She looked to be in her late teens or early twenties. But what a muck-mouth.

Her accent was from the Far East. I'd traveled far, and had visited India twice. Her inflections placed her from the region.

"I'm sorry—who are you?" I asked.

Now that I'm dead, I realize I should've run. Instead, I stood and waited for her answer.

"I am here to help you. I have helped guide for…well, longer than you could imagine."

"Guide? Why do I need help? Are you expecting me to go somewhere?"

Maybe she was seeking a job as my navigator on the *Monarch*. This conversation made little sense.

"I am not applying for a job, you dumb shit. I am here to teach you and keep you from fucking things up. Is that clear enough for you? Or must I fucking write it on a piece of parchment?"

Her voice echoed as it carried. The other people in the library stared.

I took a fresh approach.

"Miss, let me have your name, and we can go from there."

"Davi. My name is Davi. Do you understand everything now? No? I did not think so. Let me cut the bullshit. I am not from your world. I come from…well, it does not matter where. You cannot get there, so who cares? I have come…to…help…you."

The pauses she added after the words were a deliberate affectation meant to insult me.

I've been mocked by lots of people. Some were beautiful, blonde-haired, blue-eyed women, but those were women who I tried to seduce. Never—I repeat, never—had I been insulted so thoroughly by someone I'd only met. Well, there was that one woman whom I spilled my beer on, but she didn't count.

I looked back at the tiny blonde, weighing my response.

"Davi, none of what you said means anything to me. Are you sure I'm who you think I am?" I asked.

I hoped this was a case of mistaken identity.

"Of course I fucking know who you are? You are James Byrne, Captain of the sailing ship *Monarch of the Sea*. You are also a wizard. Do you fucking understand that?"

I didn't wait for her to respond. I grabbed her hand and marched out the door.

8

JAMES

Marching out of the library, I pulled Davi behind me, beside the market toward my home. She yapped the entire way. I didn't hear a word she said. My only goal was to get us inside my house before she said anything to get me killed, or worse.

Along the way, I tried to avoid eye contact with everyone. I failed. Of course, the primary failure was the beautiful, brown-eyed María. She'd watched my every move as I marched Davi down the steps of the library.

I slowed long enough to unlatch my front door as I got home, kicked it open, and escorted the still-muttering woman inside.

Once inside, I relaxed and asked her to sit. When she did, I pulled in a breath, held it, and then slowly released it. It usually worked. Not today.

"Now, let's start again. My name is James. Your name is Davi. Everything else you said is garbage," I said.

Her sigh was percussive.

"James, I know who and what the fuck you are. You sit. Let the grown-up in the room talk." She pointed to a chair across from hers.

I sat, only taking my eyes off her long enough to spin my chair around backwards and lean forward on it.

"Okay, spill it. Start with your last name," I said.

"You could not pronounce it. Besides, after everything I told you, I cannot imagine my last name is of any fucking importance."

She raised an eyebrow improbably high and leaned forward toward me.

"Fine. You tell me what's important, then."

I started strumming my fingers on the back of my chair, trying to burn off nervous energy.

"Here is what you must know. I am from a different world than you. An alternative Earth, if you will. My race had traveled the universes for millions of years before your kind dropped from the trees. Do you understand so far?"

"I hear the words. I don't believe a word you're saying. But I'll let you continue for a few more minutes. Then I'm tossing you out."

She laughed. It was as sweet as her mouth was vulgar. The two didn't belong together.

"James, what you must first believe is that you are capable of magic. If I have read things correctly, you are capable of tremendous levels of spellcraft. Second, I am here to help."

She put her hands out, palms up as an invitation for me to speak.

"Shoot." I dropped my head to the chairback, incapable of rational thought.

"James, I should spend months or even years cultivating a relationship with someone before even meeting them. We do not fucking have time for that bullshit. Someone named Riaan Dahl is coming, and you have to stop him. In fact, your bigger problem is that you have a demonic monster on its way too."

I was in real trouble.

"James, you must have known you were different. Your luck was better. You earned more money without trying," Davi said.

Her furrowed brow was the first hint she smelled the stench from the massive dump she'd just taken in my life.

"Luck differs from magic," I retorted, refusing to believe her.

"There is a terrible person coming, and he will fucking skulk his way through this town and murder everyone in it if you do not stop him," she said.

"Wait—you said you were here to guide me. Why won't you just tell me what to do to stop him?"

"You are right: I said, 'guide you.' I did not say I would fucking do the work."

I sighed and dropped my forehead onto the backrest of the chair again. When I raised it, she was still there. Well, my magic didn't include making her disappear.

She grinned. "No, James, you cannot make me disappear. Not yet, anyway. If you listen to me, you may learn how, though."

This time, her smile was conspiratorial and included me.

"Please tell me how this happened."

"When a man and a woman fall in love, they have intercourse. Sometimes, that union results in babies being born. You want details, or is the big picture fine?"

Talking to this woman was exhausting.

"How did I get to be all magic-y?" I replied.

I gritted my teeth as I spoke, my frustration growing.

"I do not know. Even amongst magical beings, their offspring are not always granted this gift. In your case, it probably came from your mother. She was very talented."

"Wait, you know who my mother was?"

"Is, James. I know who your mother is."

"Oh...okay. Too much information. Tell me about this person—the one who's going to kill everyone. Who is he? And where do I find him?"

"I said he was going to murder everyone in your town. I know, only a cunt-hair's difference. Where to find him, I do not know. I suspect he is not here yet. Besides, you are not ready. He would spank your ass into your last century if you met right now."

"Fine. Tell me what you do know."

"His name is Riaan Dahl. In worlds past, he was a powerful magician. I do not appreciate ethical comparisons, but in this one's case, I will make an exception. He is a morally bankrupt creature and nigh-irredeemable."

"Okay, so he's a bad person. What's he trying to do?"

"He is trying to get home. That is it. He cares about nothing else."

"So let's help him. That seems like the easiest solve."

"This is part of your problem. We only have a limited time before Dahl's arrival, and what you do not know will fucking kill you. It will also kill every living creature in your world."

The dark-skinned woman paused and puffed out her chest as she pulled in a cleansing breath—and held it. She stared at me like I was a toddler who wouldn't quit touching something. When I didn't respond, she rolled her eyes and exhaled.

"For fuck's sake, James, this is important. You could at least pretend to understand."

"Oh, I understand. I simply don't believe you. But you have a story; please continue."

Besides, her recital was so fantastical, it was impossible, though it'd give me an opportunity for a fine telling over a mead or beer with the boys.

Another roll of her eyes. This one involved her pinching her nose between her thumb and index fingers. You know the one when your teacher is trying to make a point and you decide to be clever? Yeah, that one.

She continued, "To reach you, Dahl will have opened twelve door-ways called portals. To get home, he will open the thirteenth. Therein lies your problem."

"Wait, that's the problem? I thought you said he'd kill—murder everyone. How can this doorway thingy be the problem?"

"By opening that gateway, he will also fling open the other twelve doors. James, those lead to dangerous places. Many of those creatures would find earth a smorgasbord of fine cuisine. You may as well ring a dinner bell. They will destroy sentient life on your planet, not just in Metaterre."

"Ok, what's a smorgas-thingy?"

Her mouth fell open and her eyes went wide.

"I just told you about how your world will end, and you are worried about my choice of words. I am amazed you survived childhood."

I squinted my eyes, scratched my head, and replied, "Good point. What do I do to stop him?"

I know I flushed at her comment, but I wanted to end this conversation, and the shortest path was to move on.

Davi answered, "Learn how to control your magic, make yourself a control device—your wand—and keep him from obtaining and activating an artifact."

"Many things are wrong with what you just said. But let's start with the artifact. What is it?"

"When it was created, it was a knife. A bronze knife."

My gut wrenched. I somehow knew what Davi was going to say.

"Thirty-one years ago, Charles Doss melted it and turned it into a spyglass," she said.

"I bet that explains the disappearances at Eldritch Manor," I deadpanned.

"James, you must stop Riaan Dahl from gaining control of it," she said.

"So how do I learn this magic?" I asked.

She pulled out a large hand-bound book. It was hundreds of pages thick and had indices cut into the pages. I flipped it open.

Amori was the first spell I saw in the book. Of course it was. That would be a complication I didn't need.

THAT NIGHT, I slept like a leaf in a cyclone. When I woke, I sat up and flipped through the spell book. I only glanced at a few of them. One strange thing was that the book seemed to be different every time I opened it. Spells that I thought I'd seen near each other weren't. Spells I hadn't seen were obvious.

The next morning, I dragged myself from bed. When I got downstairs, I found Davi sitting at the table. She was eating a thick porridge of some sort. No, I didn't ask her what it was. I didn't care.

"I need to tell Kate I'll do her job," I groaned.

"Just get your ass back in this house soon. We need to start your training," the diminutive woman said, then shrugged.

Kate wasn't at home. I wanted time to think, so I walked the long way. This meant I had to backtrack my way to the market. She has bright red hair, so she was easy to spot.

"Katie, I'll look into your peculiarities," I started. Before I could finish, she jumped into my arms and gave me a great hug.

Over her shoulder, I spotted María. She was watching with a slight incline of her head. I peeled myself away from my best friend's wife and headed to see the Spanish beauty.

I only casually heard Kate call out, "Thank you, Jimmy," as I marched toward María.

When I caught her, she watched me as if she were waiting on something specific. I hoped I was going to tell her what she wanted.

"María, I'm sorry about the way I came across yesterday. I was having a very stressful day, and you have to admit, you are quite stunning."

At that, she rolled her eyes and crossed her arms. I knew I needed to persist, because I wouldn't get another chance.

"Listen, I'm sorry if I insulted you. I didn't mean to. If you'd only give me a chance, I'd like to make amends."

The brunette tilted her head to the side and waited.

"I know you work at the hospital. What is it you do?"

She paused long enough that I thought she'd not answer.

"I am a healer," she said, then stared at me. In her eyes was a dare. I was sure I'd get beaten if I said something wrong.

I went noncommittal. "You must love it."

"Yes, I do."

I smiled at her and didn't talk. Her eyes darted around the market. It was obvious she was working her way around to asking me another question, so I waited.

"Why did you just hug Katie Doss?" she asked, one eyebrow raised.

"Kate?" I sputtered.

I got so caught up in the haunting at Eldritch Manor that I lost my ability to speak. I couldn't talk about it without sounding like a loon. Besides, Kate had asked me to keep it quiet. The last thing she'd want was more rumors. Also, I didn't understand their relationship, so I didn't want to say too much.

She stood there and watched me, waiting for me to finish.

When my brain reengaged, I remembered to say, "Kate's, my best friend's wife. She asked me for help, and I told her I would. That's all."

María considered my answer before asking me another question.

"Who was that woman I saw you pulling behind you yesterday?"

My brain went into full shutdown. There was nothing I could think to tell her that wouldn't sound like I'd lost my mind. I panicked.

You've got to understand my fear. Two nights ago, I'd slept through a nightmare, only to wake up and realize I'd lived it. Then I met a crazy, dark-skinned, blonde-haired, blue-eyed demon-woman who insisted I was a wizard. Yes, dear reader, you owe me a pass!

"Oh, she's my sister. I saw her with the neighbor...he's not of good moral character, you see..."

"Bullshit. I know something of the great James Byrne, Captain of the *Monarch of the Sea*." Again, the piercing eyes. Could she even blink?

"Listen, I'll explain it over dinner. Just give me a chance, will you?" In this, I put all my hope and luck. If I had any magical abilities, I could convince this young beauty to have supper with me.

We stared at one other.

I could intuit women and sailing. Well, lots of things. But I loved my friends and family, so it worked the best with them. I'd have to say women followed a distant second. Right now, my intuition was laughing. It was pointing its index fingers at me, dancing a jig as it did. I had no chance.

Except I did. I remembered that the first spell that stupid book had opened to was a love spell. In my panic, I forgot the spell.

Then it came to me. "*Amori*," I whispered.

I was triumphant. No more dancing intuition. My chest swelled, proud of my accomplishment.

Her face relaxed.

I had her. I was certain.

"No," she answered as she spun on her heel and left, her ebony hair dancing behind her.

I returned home deflated. My self-esteem took a further nosedive as I entered the well-lit entrance of my home.

"I told you to get your ass home at once. That did not mean you could stop and talk to every attractive girl. What kind of bastard are you?"

Davi stood with her hands on her hips. Her manner reminded me of my mother after I'd acted up in church and she was reprimanding me at home.

"Give it a rest, Davi. I came home as fast as I could. If Dahl wins because I stopped for five minutes, he's a bigger problem than I can solve. Besides, before we get started, I've got several questions."

"Fuck. Are you going to do an 'I'm going to ask her a million questions until her head explodes' routine?" she said.

When she said explode, I looked up in surprise.

"That can't happen, can it?" I asked.

My tiny tormentor stared back, eyes unblinking. You know the stare you get when you've said something especially dumb?

"Please tell me he is not this stupid," she said as she shook her head, looking toward heaven. Her expression was one of sadness.

"Okay. But you've got to admit you've told me several strange things. Never mind. Where did I get my magic? Tell me everything. Scratch that—just hit the highlights," I said.

While I spoke, I looked for a seat. We were in my kitchen, where I saw a new chair so pink, it nearly glowed. Its decoration was a repeating purple and yellow flower pattern with splashes of the darkest ebony I'd ever seen. The splashes were actually spatter marks, too. They covered elements of the smaller flower, having appeared to have dripped across the pattern—which, I noticed, never repeated in size or shape.

"You have a new chair?" I asked as I searched the print's detail.

In response, she raised an eyebrow, then plopped her skinny

bottom into her fancy armchair. She watched me, lifted her arms a foot, then flopped them back onto her chair's soft armrests. It frustrated her that I stood in the same spot. Her eyes darted from me to my chair.

I took the hint and dragged my comfortable wooden rocker to face her as she spoke.

She continued, "The highlights. Fine. You enjoy reading. Am I correct?"

I sat in my rocker, tilted back, and tucked my feet under the runners to hold it in place. I nodded my head at her, but remained silent.

She said, "There was a woman named Morgana. She was a Fae enchantress who had many lovers. One of them was your father, Geoffrey."

"Wait, the same Morgana of Arthurian legend? That was hundreds of years ago. How long do your people live?" I interrupted, shocked at this new revelation.

"We live longer than you and do not follow time in the same linear fashion as you. We have learned to manipulate it to an extent. Morgana could have left Arthur yesterday and opened the door to your world today."

"Um…"

"For fuck's sake, it does not matter. Just believe what I told you. We have more important matters to discuss."

"Okay," I replied, drawing out the word to annoy her.

"You need to know that an uncountable number of Earths exist. Do not use logic to understand. Just accept the reality that I tell you."

"Got it."

"I can travel between each of the Earth's versions. Also, I know the ones developing, like yours. In effect, I am skilled at time travel, or seeing a version of your past in a different universe. So I can perceive what happened—not an exact copy, mind you. But I can get close. It works in reverse, too. I can travel to many futures. These two allow me to learn what may happen with you. This explanation isn't perfect. The monkey living here should understand the basics."

I ignored her not-so-subtle insult and said, "So far, I understand what you're saying."

Davi continued to explain my past until my head swam.

"Let's stop with the history lesson and move on, shall we?" I asked.

"For fuck's sake, James, I was wondering when you would get sick of that shit."

The casual cursing was frustrating. She was beautiful; she shouldn't have a foul mouth. But she did, so my brain couldn't fit the two pieces together.

"James, I have until the end of October to teach you what you must learn to defeat Dahl. If you can, you will need to find a way to defeat the demon too. That gives you sixty-one days to learn what is necessary to destroy Riaan Dahl and a demon-beast."

My brain ignored her math and did it. It was September first, sooo…yep, she was right. Sixty-one days 'til All Hallow's Eve. Well, at least that part of my brain was still working.

"Are you done with the math?" she asked.

"How do you keep guessing what I'm thinking?" I retorted. This time, I was getting irritated, and pointed at her.

"James, you have one of the simplest minds of anyone with whom I have ever spoken. You cannot keep your thoughts off your face."

"I'm good at poker," I retorted.

"That is against this Earth's inhabitants. It does not count at the level we need to be playing."

She leaned toward me, eyes narrowed, as she finished.

"James, I do not have time to teach you how to make things float. You should have begun training at an academy when you were eleven. But here we are."

She pulled another book from a bag on the floor. Since the bag was bright purple, it surprised me that I hadn't noticed it. The book she handed me had a dark-brown cover and was an inch thick, but it was still much smaller than the last book she had given me. The publisher had indexed the pages with cut-in tabs. Its title, written in a lustrous gold, was *Down with Spells*. Beneath that, in the loudest red I'd seen, was *Your Condensed Guide to Spell-casting*. The last line, below that, read "by Professor Miranda Constance Goodwin, London's Magical Academy."

"What's different from the last book you gave me?" I spoke.

"If you could fucking read, this one is *condensed,* while the one I gave you yesterday was *unabridged.*"

I began a retort, then decided against it. Besides, I didn't care why she had given me two versions of the same book.

I was curious why I should've begun this training when I was eleven, so I changed course and brought it up.

"If you should've started training me when I was eleven, why did you wait another seventeen years before you came?"

"This is the problem with adults. They think they are smarter than they are. So they ask unnecessary questions. Dumbass. I did not say *I* should have started teaching you. I said you should have begun school at eleven. Enrolling you was your mother's job. You cannot expect the school to search you out, can you? If they did, fucking Jericho would not do anything but search for eleven-year-old brats," she said, shaking her head.

"Who's Jericho?"

She ignored me.

"The first spell you must learn is a protection spell. You must defend yourself against Dahl; plus, it will help guard you against the negative effects of any spells you fuck up."

"Can I use it to help other people? I mean, if this Dahl guy is trying to kill...ugh, or murder someone, I'd want to help."

"That's cute, James. No, you dumb shit. I want to teach you a spell to defend yourself. Protect yourself before you worry about anyone else."

Again, she shook her head. I almost laughed, as I imagined that if I asked her enough dumb questions, her head might shake itself loose.

"Fine. Before you teach me that protection spell, are there any spells I'm not permitted to use?"

"You can use any magic you want. But you will learn that casting dark spells comes with a cost."

"Where does magic come from?" I asked.

"It is the same as God…it is just here."

"Wait, you believe in God?"

"Of course I do. Don't be disrespectful. It is not the minor deity in your books. It is much bigger. Stop with the jibber-jabber. We must continue."

"Okay, just one last question: I know I need a wand, but what does it do?"

"Yes, you need one. Your wand does not create the magic. It only focuses and magnifies it."

"Where do I get one? Do you have a store where I can buy it?"

"You must build it yourself. It is a task only the user can perform. Trying to buy one would be the same as me making your hand. Your body created your hand while you were growing inside your mother's womb. Likewise, you must create your wand. We will get to that later."

"Fine. Let's get started."

She spent the next hour teaching me a basic protection charm. At the end, she said I was competent, but that she'd still cast her own for the time being. On top of the one I cast myself, that was.

"James, let us break away from protection spells. It is time you learn the effects of traveling between dimensions. This is tricky magic, and only a disciplined mind can use it effectively."

At that, she stood, grabbed my hand, and pulled me out of my rocker. This small blonde was strong. She pushed me away, holding onto my hands until our arms were straight out in front of us. She let go of my hands and continued to hold her arms out. I dropped mine.

Her "Ugh!" was percussive. I re-raised them.

She drifted away from me until our fingers no longer touched. When she dropped her arms, so did I.

"This spell will take you to a past version of Earth. You cannot fuck up your version by killing your own grandfather, because it is not *your* earth. It is developing comparably to yours, so will be related sufficiently that we can tell what happened in *your* past or future. Understand?"

"So far, so good."

"Step one is understanding the way the spell works. This spell will take you to the past or future that you feel first. But we do not give two shits about your feelings. We care about your thoughts because one has greater control over them. The problem is, you must learn to scour your feelings from your thoughts. Otherwise, this exercise is pointless."

"Got it."

"This spell will open a doorway. All you need to do is walk through."

At this, Davi closed her eyes and her face went limp, as if she'd fallen asleep. When she raised her hand, she was wearing a large golden ring. It had a red crystal stone surrounded by a circle of transparent crystal stones. I'd seen enough rubies and diamonds in my life to recognize them.

She moved her ring finger on each hand, alternatively touching and releasing it to her thumb. After a few seconds, she pointed all her fingers up, her palms facing away. Both hands moved in tight circles, her left clockwise and her right counterclockwise. As they whirled, I stared at her jewel. The color spun a crimson halo as it revolved. Before I realized it, there was a red-orange circle of light in front of me.

Abruptly, she made a fist, and the glow disappeared as if she'd wadded it up.

"James, that is how the spell presents. To make it work, memorize the movements of my fingers. That is how you activate this one."

It took her several times, but I memorized her finger movements. It impressed me—not Davi, though.

"James, before I let you try this yourself, I need you to know how it feels. You have seen it. Now you must experience it. We will travel through four different doorways to show you what you are dealing with. Do you have questions? No? Good."

Not giving me the chance to speak, she put her right hand in front of her. The large ring began its crimson glow, and within seconds, the large red-orange halo hung between us.

"James, this is only a doorway that I have opened. Now, I must concentrate on my target. Take my hand."

Davi stuck her hands through the glowing doorway. I reached through and took them. The hair on my arms stood as tingles moved over my wrists. I held her hands tight. She returned the grip. Again, the strength of this little lady surprised me.

"James, when I say, you will step into this doorway with me. Do not worry; we will not run into each other. Do me a favor and empty your thoughts. Otherwise, you will make this difficult."

I cleared my mind of everything other than the glowing door. And that a butcher was on his way to murder my entire town. Oh, and that a demon-monster was going to kill anyone Dahl missed.

I gave up and stepped through and into a large round chamber. Everything in the room, except the floor, carried a similar curve. A carved circular stone altar dominated the center, while wooden benches surrounded it in twelve concentric rings.

Two beings stood across from us. One was an old man. He was the type I might have seen walking through any colonial town. The other was far different. He was diminutive in stature, bent by either the weight of his life or nature. I couldn't tell.

"Can they see us?"

"No, because I cast a spell to keep us secret and safe," she said.

"I assume you'll teach me that too?" I asked.

"Of course, I will, dumb shit. Now shut up and pay attention."

I watched as the old man tied the smaller one to a scaffolding. The smaller man had dark tattoos covering his body. I marveled at his perseverance in getting them. There must be hundreds.

The older man said, "Riaan, did you eat your meal today without giving thanks to the four gods of weather?"

"No, master. I prayed as you've instructed: Rain, god of renewal, misery, and righteous rebellion, praise to you, for you gave us life; Wind, god of preparation, plenty, and scattering, joyful we sing so our life is manifest; Lightning, god of fire, redemption, and aching love, for through you, we are desired; bless the dread god Drought, demon teacher of suffering and deprivation—by your withdrawal, we've learned appreciation."

"Riaan, you have said the words. But did you believe them without hesitation?" the old man asked.

Sympathy and hate intertwined in a sick dance between the lines of his words.

Dahl's hesitation was trivial, but present.

"Master, I try to believe without questions. My mind doubts when I examine my motives," Dahl answered, his head bowed, resigned to his coming pain.

"Because of your admission, we will choose the lesser punishment––this time."

The old man removed a knife from a scabbard on his belt. He heated the tip to an orange glow, then dragged a series of cuts onto the insignificant creature's arm. They bled and blisters formed. The wounds were both immediate and painful. Dahl cried out, begging for forgiveness.

In front of me, Davi re-cast the spell to form the door. We stepped through. I was grateful to hear the end of the poor creature's torment.

The sympathy I felt for the wretched being disappeared by the time we reached the last of the four worlds. In each of them, he took pleasure in murdering his victims. It was always four creatures. He tortured each of them. The ravages lasted hours before Dahl granted them their wish for death.

We stepped through the last door. Relief flooded through me when I realized I was in my home again. Bile rose in my throat as I fought the urge to retch up my breakfast.

I hurried to my window and threw open the sash to let in the frigid air. There, I lost the battle and disgorged my morning meal. I hung my head, gulping in air until the nausea passed.

When I raised my head, I spotted María. Of course, she had seen.

9

JAMES

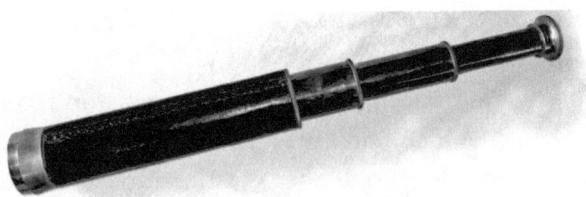

That evening, I left Davi to do whatever she did when I was not with her. I rode Connie to the home where I'd eat dinner. I had business to conclude with the home's master, and had been invited to dine.

His residence was a massive estate near the town center. I rapped with my fist and stood back.

A dark-haired angel opened it. Then her eyes shot open as she recognized me.

Lady María Pauleta Francesca Rose Pimetel de Rota stood in front of me, mouth open, blocking my entrance.

"Hello, m'lady," I said, waiting for a reply. Not receiving one, I added, "May I come in?"

I had arranged this meeting with her uncle, Don Diego. Of course, I contrived it to dine with her. She'd sunk her anchor into the deepest fathoms of my heart. No, this wasn't because she'd refused me twice. I could handle rejection just fine. Honestly, I couldn't even understand what pull she had on me. I'd never experienced these feelings before.

She searched my eyes, looking for the joke.

"Why? What are you doing here?" she asked. No, it was more of a demand.

"Diego invited me to supper. Your uncle, I believe." I maintained my meaningless smile and squinted my eyes. I didn't know why, but after my experience with Davi reading my expressions, I wanted to hide them from María.

She slammed the door in my face.

Inside the home, I heard someone—who I assume was her-- yelling. Then a male voice attempted to calm her.

The female voice said, *"Te atrevez,"* and, *"No pregunte."*

The male voice replied with, *"Mío,"* and *"Negocio,"* and then *"Por favor dejalo entrar."*

The door swung back open. The enchantress stood to the side and motioned me inside. She didn't meet my eyes and watched my feet as I stepped across the threshold. She shut the door, maybe too hard, as soon as I'd cleared its swing.

"James, my friend. Please, come in. Welcome to my home," Diego said.

His smile was as bright as the fresh snow and warm as his hearth.

"Don Diego, thanks for inviting me. Shall we conclude our business?" I asked.

I knew he'd decline. He followed proprieties. We'd have our meal, then discuss the cargo over cigars and brandy in his smoking lounge. His mansion was enormous. In fact, the only one larger was the old Eldritch Manor.

"No, no, James. Let's eat first. I hope you have plenty of room for food. We have a wonderful meal waiting. Come, my friend."

He motioned with his left hand as he held his right arm to my shoulder, directing me to the dining hall. It was a cozy setting for five. His wife, Juliana, and daughter, Christina, sat on either side of him, while María sat next to me.

She refused to make eye contact with me through the first half-hour of our meal. Finally, when I asked for the shaker of salt, she glanced at me. My fingers found hers as I took the seasoning. I'm sure I saw her blush. If I were thinking, I would've realized it wasn't a blush, but irritation.

The conversation was business-free, except for when Diego asked me to tell him about my crossing. As I described how we snuck by the blockade, even María leaned forward.

"I've been lucky in most ways. But I've worked to set up a loyal group of fishermen who have similar feelings for the Crown. Pardon me, I mean the British Crown."

Don Diego was an emissary of the Spanish Crown and María's uncle by marriage. I took care to stay on his good side. That included taking risky contracts when he asked. It benefited me when I needed a return for those risks.

"Mr. Byrne, you claim these men are your friends. How can you be confident?" María asked. I didn't know whether she was interested or leading me into a verbal trap.

"May I call you María?" I asked.

She nodded her head once, closing her eyes as she did. Damn, I could get lost in those golden orbs.

"María, these men have placed their family fortunes, even their very lives, on the line to bring me the information I need to navigate the blockade." I thought this answered her question.

"I understand, but you cannot know they will protect you," she said. This time, she raised an eyebrow, as if she had scored a point.

"I'm sorry; I misunderstood. A fair part of the answer is intuition. While I trust the men I work with, I pay them well. I also believe that none of these men would turncoat to help the Brits. Besides, if one did, they'd find an unwelcome reception from my friends—a list that includes everyone in town."

María watched, noncommittal. Her pouty lips had parted, a question forming, when her uncle stood.

"James, let us conclude our business," Diego said.

At that, the ladies stood to excuse themselves. I kissed the cheeks of Juliana and Christina. María stayed between and a full step behind the other two women; her arms crossed, akin to a shield covering her...chest. Dang it, I shouldn't have looked.

I peered into her eyes and spoke to Diego. "I wonder, my friend— may I have the honor of calling on your niece for a meal soon?"

Diego's eyes shot open and his mouth formed a circle as he let out an excited, "Oh."

His niece's eyes went wider, and she started shaking her head.

"That is wonderful, James."

Diego was close enough that he could touch both of our shoulders. As he did, the other two ladies beat a hasty retreat.

Thankfully, the dark-haired angel couldn't shoot daggers from her eyes. Otherwise, I'd be dead. Well, I'd have been dead sooner. She glared, those beautiful golden-brown eyes darting between me and her betraying uncle.

"James would make a wonderful husband...well, to another girl... not you. Although your mother asked me to keep an eye..." Diego stopped as he saw her expression.

Flames erupted from the maiden. Her eyes narrowed as she burned a hole through my forehead.

When her anger vanished, it was sudden. Her smile became the warmest embrace I'd ever felt from a woman.

"Uncle, I would be happy to dine with Mr. Byrne."

I should've become afraid of her quick turn in emotions. Unfortunately, I must've been thinking with what a doctor friend of mine called my abdominal-head. According to him, men had two centers of thought, one inside their brain, and another lower, near...never mind; it's not important. Still, in my defense, María had a blinding effect on me.

She left the room. I could see Christina lingering inside a nearby doorway. She took her younger cousin by the elbow and pulled her near.

"He's cute. Too bad you must return to Rota soon," Christina said as she shot me a conspiratorial smile.

I didn't take half-measures. Earlier that day, I'd spoken with her, and asked for her help setting up a chaperoned meal with María. Christina said she'd love to assist. Playing matchmaker was a pastime for her.

In that discussion, she'd told me, "Besides Jimmy, María wanted to learn more about you too. She only needed an excuse to ignore years of propaganda. Her mother claimed María's marriage should be arranged. It's one reason she left Spain. Besides, she loved your tortured looks when she let you down."

The target of my infatuation stole one last look in my direction. I'm sure it included a genuine smile too.

10

JAMES

I roused the next morning, comforted that I hadn't had another nightmare. The chill was sharp, so after dressing, I tugged on a woolen coat.

When I approached the downstairs landing, I saw Davi sitting in her floral-printed, overly padded armchair, eating her—whatever she ate.

Apparently, she wasn't a phantom of my imagination. I dipped my shoulders and plodded the last few stairs.

"Good morning, Davi," I murmured.

I used the corner of my shirt to grasp the heated kettle of water from the cooker. I turned to pour it over my coffee steeper in my mug, only to realize I'd neglected to get them.

"You could fucking give me a better hello than that," she offered, her perky giggle at odds with her obscene language.

I dropped the scorching pot back onto the stove, recognizing how hot it was only when it scorched my hand.

Clang! The impact was loud and rang in the spartan room.

An inch-long blister formed on my palm as I rubbed the burn.

My chin touched my chest, and my back hunched. Then I straightened and swung to face my tiny tormentor.

"I'm sorry. You're right. How was your night?" I asked, pumping energy into my expression while I continued to wipe my blistered hand on my trousers.

"Rising and setting suns do not have the same significance to me. Remember, I open passages through time. Besides, I am helping several beings in concert with taking care of you," she finished.

"Wait, what? What do you mean, you're 'helping several beings?'" I asked.

It astounded me the thrill the little blonde took in surprising me.

She waved her hand at me, flipped her wrist, and my hand quit hurting. A hot coffee appeared on the table. She also produced a plate of breakfast—her version of a morning meal. It was fruit and several vegetables. Among the legumes was one of the largest cucumbers I'd ever seen. Since it was safer to not quiz her about it, I remained quiet. Besides, she'd only twist it into a crude phallic joke.

"You fucking think I lie around sucking my thumb while you are not in the room? Or were you hoping I was pining away for you while I watched the door eagerly awaiting your return? You are a fucking moron if that is what you think."

"Huh, I just didn't think...uh," I finished, dumbfounded. Now I was certain she'd withheld information simply to unbalance my judgment.

"Well, for fuck's sake, that is the first intelligent thing you have spoken."

"What?" I choked out as the remains of a half-chewed quarter of an orange skidded down my throat.

You—yes, you, the dainty eater—shut up. Like you've never put too much food in your mouth. Besides, swallowing fast is an occupational necessity in my line of work.

"You said 'I didn't think.' I was complimenting you on the auspicious occasion of adding an intelligent comment. Congratulations. Now, shut the fuck up so we may begin," Davi said.

She raised both eyebrows and glared.

I twisted my fingers in front of my mouth as if I was buttoning my coat, then grabbed a couple of orange wedges and crammed them in before slamming my lips shut again. I grinned at her, my lips tight together and my cheeks bulging.

She shook her head.

"Remember, I cannot teach you the basics of spellcraft. I do not have the time. So get busy studying the texts I gave you."

Again, she raised her eyebrows. She also shifted her head, so her chin neared her chest as she glowered at me. It gave me the impression she was a teacher admonishing a small, dimwitted student. A remarkable feat, because I was standing, and she was a bitty woman sitting on a pink, puffy, flowered chair.

Although, I had just presumed her womanhood—from what I could see of her, um, anatomy. She had the...parts.

"James, you foggy-headed dimwit. Get your mind off my tits and *pay attention.*"

I shook the rest of the lethargy from my brain and concentrated, although I remained disturbed at how she could recognize my thoughts. I bit into the large red apple from my plate.

She continued, "Now we will investigate the dimensional transition skill that I taught you yesterday. Do you recall the movement?" She rose.

I nodded my head, but remained mute and gulped my coffee. This time, I drank too much, and it hurt as it cascaded into my throat. I didn't care, because her standing meant my breakfast was nearing its end anyway.

"Good. Here is the spell: *Deannix.*" She pronounced it Dee-annex.

The word, once uttered, produced a red-orange glow in front of her.

"You didn't move your hand and fingers and the door still opened," I said, challenging her.

"Yes. But it is only a door. It leads nowhere. I must cast it accurately to fucking make...it...work."

Her professional voice inflection was impressive. Especially considering I'm repeating this exchange from the wrong side of the grave. Also, hindsight may have taken out the sting. Nope. Never mind. I suppose it didn't. Moving along...

"I understand. But, since I don't have a wand, will the spell work for me?"

I sipped my coffee. Mmm. It was neither fiery nor frigid. I took a bigger gulp. Ahh...

"Before we do anything else, I will cast my protection and invisibility spells. Afterward, you will cast your protection jura. For a nitwit like you, that is shorthand for abjuration."

If I remembered correctly, abjuration had something to do with energy magic.

Davi cast her spells. When she stopped, she nodded for me to cast mine.

I stared at her, not knowing what she required.

"Um..."

"For fuck's sake, James, did you not read?"

"Well—" I started before she interrupted.

"It is called *Castellem*," she said. Sympathy clung onto her words.

I snapped my fingers together and said, "I remember! *Cast-tell-um!*"

She shook her head, eyes wide in disbelief. Nope, no kindness from Ms. Tiny-Grumpy-Pants.

"What?" I pleaded. Okay, perhaps I whined.

"We will get to it later. Now I want you to cast *Deannix*. Guide the door as I demonstrated," she warned. A disparaging smirk played across her face.

"I remember. I'll travel to what I'm feeling, unless I can fixate on my destination," I mumbled under my breath.

"Easy to say," I added as an afterthought.

I stood in front of her and moved my hand in the circle, then tapped my fingers together and recited the word. "*Deannix*."

The coral door opened, and we walked through. I was proud of my minor triumph. At least for a moment.

When the radiance of the opening cleared, I saw María. She was laying on a wide sandy beach––nude.

"You bastard, James. I should have realized you were a pervert," Davi said. The shadow of a smile teased her lips.

Horrified, I threw my hands across my face. Unable to help myself, I peeked through my fingers.

María rose from her blanket and walked toward me.

I stammered, "What now?"

"How the fuck should I know? *You* led us here."

"Get us out," I pleaded.

"Not my responsibility. You figure it out."

I did my best to wipe out the image of the nude woman. I slammed shut my eyes, then recast the spell. My traitorous brain didn't cooperate. Dressed or not, María was impossible to forget.

The second portal had barely disappeared before I saw the black-haired Venus again. At least she was wearing clothes this time.

Davi laughed.

"I don't…I mean, she isn't…my thoughts aren't entirely of her." My protests sounded foolish even as I spoke them.

"James, I explained how *Deannix* functions. Much like you, it operates one way. This young woman is foremost in your mind," Davi said.

"If she is, how can I travel anywhere else? I'll keep finding different versions of María," I carped.

"Try this." She waved her left hand across my face and said, "*Kinno Antim.*"

My mind cleared and I could focus.

"You should've tried that first," I said.

My voice rose with irritation at the mischievous little woman.

She shrugged, and her unfading grin proved she was guiltless.

"You should have read your book," she added.

I closed my eyes and envisioned Dahl. My mind leaped to the monster.

We stepped through the third portal.

The wind bit and snow blanketed the ground. I scanned the darkness for any recognizable landmark and detected none.

I glanced at Davi. She shook her head. Unsure of her meaning, I played it safe and remained silent.

A moment later, she nudged me. I swung to where she was pointing. Stalking through the snow-covered verge, leafless shrubs, massive maples, and imposing white pines were several scores of men. Their movements were silent, despite their numbers.

Each man was draped in nearly identical garb—a leather tunic, breechcloth, leggings, and moccasins. They had long hair, and many had various plumes and other adornments tied into their black braids. It was evident these noiseless men belonged to a native tribe.

"Algonquin," Davi breathed.

I shivered in the crisp pre-dawn gloom, despite my woolen jacket. The trees and underbrush were similar to my section of New York. I guessed we were north of Metaterre, perhaps into the wilds of upper New England.

I watched, mesmerized, as the men crept forward.

Crack! A branch snapped. The men froze. I jerked my head around, seeking the cause. There, I saw a second, smaller group of men.

A murmur whispered through the trees.

"*Soit silencieux,*" came a hushed command.

The smaller group was French. I recognized the order to be silent.

A bird cried. The men advanced noiselessly.

The Frenchmen wore light blue coats covering white shirts. Each wore red pantaloons and black boots. Many wore silver-colored metal helmets, and each carried a long musket. Some carried swords in hip scabbards, others pikes slung across their shoulders. Their clothing was obsolete by a century or more.

I scanned the colorful group to calculate their numbers—two score and four.

I stole a glance at my guide, who didn't return my look. She followed the men, captivated.

The joint army appeared to be hunters pursuing prey.

Another bird called. This one was further from my ear.

The army halted. Forward of the main body, a lone scout pointed. There, smoke from a campfire rose into the morning sky. Moments later, another bloomed, then a third. Soon, a dozen tiny columns rose into the frozen air.

"Kitchi, instructions?" asked a Frenchman.

I didn't have to guess the second word, because it was the same in

French and English. I assumed the first was the commander of the natives.

They'd discovered their prey.

Davi tugged my arm and recited the phrase, *"Kinno Antim,"* as her hand traveled across my face.

She nodded to me.

"Deannix," I said, and another doorway opened.

I focused on the encampment in the distance. Davi and I stepped through together.

When the glowing doorway faded, the sun had climbed above the horizon. She and I waited next to a fire, its smoke billowing into the morning sky.

Women and men sat singing and whooping nearby. They didn't recognize they were being hunted. I wanted to alert them, but realized I couldn't. Davi wouldn't let me. Besides, it was not my world, and I didn't know how to contextualize these events.

From a nearby shoreline, two men trudged toward a third, older man.

"Onondakai, Jakonsase, have you fixed the sacrifices?"

The man didn't speak English. Nor did he communicate any word I knew. Still, I recognized every pronouncement.

"Yes, Wáhta," one man confirmed.

"My friends, today we claim our triumphs. We will affirm the end of winter. Above all, we will instruct our captives: join us, or die," the hoary chief said.

"Iroquois," Davi added.

She must've seen this history, or some of it. She also should've prepared me for what I'd see. If so, I wouldn't have eaten.

Wáhta walked in the direction his men had come. They followed him. Davi and I shadowed the threesome, not keeping our distance.

On a sandy shore, near a vast body of water, four people hung by their arms. Onondakai and Jakonsase had prepared these four for their chief, Wáhta. They had lashed long poles together to build an X and staked them into the sand. They propped up the frameworks using a third pole wedged into the base where the poles crossed.

The victims' arms and legs neared dislocation. Their feet dangled inches from the ground. Their weight further distended their shoulders. It must have been agonizing.

Wáhta said, "One death for each sacred time of day. Remove their clothing."

I knew hate. This man despised those hanging before him. He sneered, his lips pulled tight against his bared teeth.

Onondakai began at one end and slashed off the victims' clothing. Jakonsase started at the other end. Neither man discriminated between raiment or meat. Blood, a vivid cerise, coursed in rivulets down the naked staked bodies, darkening the trampled snow.

Wáhta watched and listened to the screams of misery. He took a sick pleasure in torturing these men and women. His sneer turned to a wicked grin as the corners of his lips turned upward. Only when his accomplices had ripped free the last traces of clothing did he begin a deliberate walk toward his first victim.

As he strode, the fated to die hurled verbal abuse at the old warrior. He must've listened to these epithets before. He was untroubled.

"Kitchi will hunt you. He will slaughter your family," the youngest of the quartet called, his youthful muscles rippling as he spoke.

"May Chibiabos putrefy your spirit," cried a greying woman.

"Join me in combat, you coward," shouted a rotund man.

"A howling cur cannot shame stars or moon," Wáhta answered.

Each somebody spit their augury of hate, as malicious as it was impotent. All went on barking insults. All except one—a black woman.

"Where is she from?" I asked Davi.

She ignored me. Her lips were parted and her eyes wide, gripped by the developing scene.

"She is Tituba, a former slave, married to the Algonquin enemy," the diminutive Jakonsase told his leader.

"Sachem Wáhta, the new mourning-war captives claims she takes no name. She denies having earthly parents. Since we took her, 'The

Loa is my mother,' have been her only words," added the striking Onondakai.

This no-name female hung nude, facing west, fourth in the line of miseries.

"West is darkness and the path of change," Davi said after she nudged me in the ribs.

The slave's nudity had little effect on her. Her erect nipples were her single confirmation of winter. Her breathing was steady, despite torrents of blood trickling from her body. The rose of her life, freezing on the ground below her feet.

"This one's spirit—I will have it," Wáhta claimed as he pulled a golden dagger from his waist.

It began low. A moan grated through her throat as a dry bray. It built and, in a blink, became a blood-curdling screech. Tituba broke through the mélange shouted by the other prisoners. Her head swung forward, then back, as if thrown. Her execration called out a curious song in a dialect I didn't recognize.

Her voice, deep and melodic, stood in blunt opposition to her tortured nakedness hanging spread-eagle.

"Loa kadav mwen pral mannken ou. Depanse chalè li tankou yon dife etènèl pou konsome san mwen kòm ofrann. Loa epidemi sit sa a ak tout moun ki peche sou li. Loa frenn kè vanyan sòlda sa a ak madichon lam li yo. Mwen ofri nanm mwen yo dwe devore nan metal sa a avili, kòm yon oblasyon, nan ki pinisyon."

As she concluded, an English translation replayed across the forest wind, coming from nowhere and everywhere.

"Loa, my corpse will be your puppet. Expend its heat as an everlasting fire to consume my blood as an offering. Loa, plague this site and all who trespass upon it. Loa, spear this warrior's heart and curse his blade. I offer my soul to be devoured within this defiled metal as an oblation to that retribution."

The others in the macabre audience couldn't understand her message. In fact, I don't think any of them cared, especially Wáhta.

The woman continued her song.

"Touye, Lavi, Touye, La…"

"Kill, life, kill, li…"

In a single fluid motion, the Sachem's dagger flashed and opened the chanting woman from navel to neck. The glint disappeared as her gore covered it.

Before Tituba even noticed her own death, Wáhta reached into her splayed chest and ripped free her still-beating heart. In a fit of triumph, he bought it high above his head. Blood from the ruined organ ran onto his face and neck.

Wáhta's howl of triumph ended when an arrow tore through his own black heart.

Kitchi had ordered his Algonquin tribe and French cohorts to attack.

At the feet of Tituba's still-convulsing body, the cursed blade gleamed golden once again. It was as clean as if Wáhta had never used it. The blade had consumed the sanguine fluid of the witch as she became its mistress.

Wáhta fell, then lay abased at the witch's feet. His life pulsed a crimson stream from his destroyed heart. As the ichor spilled, it too covered the cursed blade, and Sachem Wáhta became the second tenant.

Inside the knife, Wáhta's spirit would endure. An eternity of misery awaited him as the slave of his last victim.

I didn't notice the swirling orange bloom, just that we were inside my home again. The sun radiated through the western window, while a clock chimed. It rang four times—or was it three? Hell, maybe it was six, and I miscounted. A dog howled at my window. I watched as he sat and stared at me.

My stomach churned. The demand to regurgitate my breakfast pushed acidic bile into my throat.

"Davi, why in Neptune's name did we see that wretched mess?"

My breathing came in brief gasps as I struggled to organize what I'd witnessed.

My mentor answered, "James, I cannot interpret it, although I predict we will soon find out."

She measured her words. Her eyes tightened and her brow furrowed. It was evident the horror weighed on her.

"That's enough, James. You must rest," she said. Her ending expression was a release of air blown through pursed lips.

"Not before you explain—that!" I exclaimed through gritted teeth. I wanted to yell at my guide.

"James, you face twin evils. The first was the monster. I have little doubt we witnessed its genesis. The second has just reached your reality."

"Who?" I asked, knowing full well who she meant.

"Riaan Dahl."

UNNAMED OMNISCIENT PRESENCE

*R*iaan Dahl awakened. This dawn was bleak, and a frigid breeze blew wisps of snow from the branches above him. Despite the wintry chill, perspiration formed on his gray forehead from the dread of his history.

The howl of wolves, a terror he remembered from an obscure past, was what spooked him from his slumber. Panic gripped him as his memory flashed to scenes of the giant beasts rising on massive hind legs as gore spilled from their great fangs. Was this wooded weald their haunt?

Riaan scrambled to his feet, his heart racing, and spun, searching. As his fear response subsided, he surveyed his surroundings. Granite blocks created a secluded patch of mossy ground under a craggy embankment. Small bushes blocked the sole entrance to this hidden lair beneath the strata of mineralized stone.

His pulse slowed.

Dahl struggled to recall how he had arrived at this location. His recollection was virtually barren, as only brief images lingered—a spinning yellow doorway, a knife, and running, lots of running... Dahl raised his hand and noticed the large obsidian blade.

A small animal jumped, and his heart quickened. His pointed ears near the crest of his bulbous head pivoted toward the noise.

Riaan did not know how he'd arrived in this exact location, but he knew he needed an exit into the surrounding forest. His spindly fingers clutched the trunk of the first bush blockading his way out. The shrub was a head taller than his stooped frame. Its wooden stem was as big as his wrist—or, in his case, as small.

He swung his dagger, severing the base of the shrubbery in a single stroke, then turned and shoved it into place beside the opening under his rocky escarpment. Once he cleared away more of the greenery, he would have a simple doorway leading into the forest outside his enclave.

Dahl wrinkled his brow. His enormous yellow eyes, made more obvious by his slate-gray skin, squinted as he worked to evoke his previous world. His first complete recollection was waking a few moments ago.

But his memories would come back. They always did. For now, they did not matter. He recalled the essential knowledge, the primal reason for his existence: find his artifact and return home.

Dahl retained few possessions. After the passage into this realm, all that he owned was a small wool blanket, pieces of tattered clothes, and his knife. To achieve his victory, he would require more, including shoes, a coat, and food.

His magic worked, but just. To discover the power of his sorcery in this world, he shaped a string of transmutation spells meant to transform himself. Even after enormous effort, he managed only slight alterations to his body. Once he learned the appearance of this world's dwellers, perhaps he could create enough slight modifications to fit in with them.

His illusion spell functioned sufficiently enough for him to catch a single furry animal. The capture exhausted his remaining magic, at least for a time. Dahl used his dagger to kill and skin the creature, then roasted it until its meat was charred.

"You are not worthy of a delicious meal," his priest had taught him.

When he'd asked for the reason, the priest beat him. The terrible tortures inflicted by those men flooded back to him, causing him to wince reflexively. Still, all that mattered was returning home.

After he fed, he cleaned the remaining gore from the hide, then fashioned cordage from a sapling before using it to draw the integument across the arms of a nearby bush. He would need to kill, stretch, and dry many pelts to produce shoes and a coat.

Tonight, Dahl would burn the reminders of his sins, including the murder of the animal, into his flesh.

The deranged fucker must always acknowledge sin.

12

JAMES

I ate breakfast with Davi the next morning—a meal where I would truly discover the deviousness of my tiny tormentor.

"James, I hope you had a night well-slept."

She picked up her teacup and sipped, set it down, turned the handle clockwise one-quarter turn, considered me, and then *smiled*. This wasn't one of her typical pasted-on mirthless grins, either.

"Um, yes, thanks," I said.

Jimmy, shovel in your food, then run. Save yourself, man. Her being nice can't be good.

"James, I understand you may feel aggrieved at being given this duty. Especially after what we experienced yesterday. You must accept your mental health is as critical as your magical and physical preparedness. I need to know how you are feeling today."

I stiffened at the prying question.

She took a spoonful of her…porridge, and it disappeared into her mouth. It was runny. Had I been eating it, I would have dribbled onto my shirt, but not her. She swallowed another bite before she slipped the spoon back into her steaming dish and lifted her pink cotton napkin, touching it to each side of her lips. After she examined the brightly colored fabric, she folded it and carefully replaced it onto her lap. The precision of her movements was mesmeric.

I couldn't evade this exchange. But I didn't have to disclose the abject terror yesterday's events had generated. This little woman had subjugated my life and bared my dignity to her derision. I wouldn't give her another reason to insult me.

"Nope, I'm great." I shook my head. I'd meant it as a reply, but it also worked to clear my brain of her hypnotizing gestures.

One eyebrow raised. She hoisted her spoon, ate, then set it back into the bowl. She gingerly lifted her teacup using her middle finger and thumb and blew across the hot liquid. Her pinky finger twitched, and the color changed from ebony to caramel as white spun through its center. She sipped, shut her eyes, and smiled, then set it down, adjusted its position, and looked at me.

Silence.

I'd watched men and even a few women die. Physical death was part of life. But I had never witnessed a ritual slaughter. Knowing that it had created the creature responsible for the turmoil at Eldritch made the carnage even more dreadful.

Last night, I had used Davi's words as a defensive barricade. That massacre happened elsewhere—*not here*. This allowed me to tuck it away in the secluded spot where I kept any other terrifying emotion, such as my first encounter with the demon. A fight I lost, if you recall.

I locked away those fears while ignoring their very real impact. Because if I spoke about their power, I could never hide from them again.

Still, as I replayed those incidents while hiding in the comfort of my own home, the hairs on my body tingled. Another wave of nausea swept over me. I gagged it back.

It's likely Davi recognized my conflicting thoughts. They must've danced across my face, over my furrowed brow and tucked chin. But I also didn't want her to recognize how deeply troubled I was, so I lied.

"Hey, death is the resolution of living. I've seen it happen before, and it's not a big deal."

Silence.

I spent the quiet time inhaling my food, not looking at her, although I was positive she knew I was holding back.

"Fine," she said, breaking the hush.

I switched the subject. "Davi, you taught me a protection spell."

"No. I showed it to you. You could not cast it without destroying this building," Davi said as she chuckled.

"What spells should I study first?"

I needed this lesson to be practical. Besides, I was tired of her calling me dumb. Worse, I was furious she was right.

"We do not have time to detail them. Besides, I hardly have time enough to help you grasp the few you require." She faltered, as if weighing her remarks, then went on, "Before you are killed, that is."

"Wait, what?" I demanded.

I really should've demanded we thoroughly discuss this issue.

She ignored me. "Let us agree you must grasp these five categories first: Conjuration, VIS, Protections, Charms, and Illusions."

Davi was as determined an individual as I'd ever met. She'd never discuss any subject she didn't want to. So, I moved on.

"Well, I should be able to remember the names. Except for VIS. What's that one?" I asked.

Davi dropped her head into her palms and shook it. Her shoulders trembled. Was she laughing or weeping? I couldn't tell. Besides, I wasn't sure it mattered.

"You are a dumbass, are you not? Worse still, you did not bother to study your textbooks. No, James, they are not names. Those are spell categories," she said, scorn dripping from every syllable.

I sighed. It was evident the nice Davi had gone off watch and the demon-Davi had reported for duty.

"I'm more of a do-er. Besides, you haven't defined VIS," I said, my frustration building. The truth was, I hadn't opened either book in two days. After yesterday's horror, I felt I'd earned a rest.

"VIS is the second most dangerous grouping. It encompasses everything related to energy," Davi said.

"Second most dangerous—what's number one on your list?" I quizzed.

"Charms is the most dangerous. An incorrectly practiced Charm can shatter a life far more simply than even a lightning bolt—a poorly worked Charms spell may induce someone to dedicate a life wishing for love from an unreachable target. That suffering is often worse than a swift death," she said.

Shit, she knew. I caught my breath and wavered between bites.

"Um—I need to find Kate and tell her," I said.

I needed to leave the room because I preferred Davi not learn I'd used *Amori* on María.

As an aside, I expected people to apply context when talking with me. In fact, during my last voyage, when I was on the *Monarch's* quarterdeck, without a preface, I'd said, "Mr. Dawson, we could do with a painting."

Since there was a work detail mopping the decks, my command had been explicit. Without hesitation, he'd ordered the men to scrape and repaint the stanchions and railing. In context, my random thought wasn't arbitrary.

Davi never contextualized my muddled remarks—ever. On the positive side of my death, I better understand her philosophy now. She had enough responsibility, and having my chaotic ramblings tossed in had to be aggravating.

"James, I am confident that, in that disorganized glob of goo where most humans have a brain, your words mean something. For me, they are meaningless jibber-jabber. So interpret them or stop speaking." She'd spoken without taking a breath, so she exaggerated her next intake of air.

Even knowing the demon-Davi was present, I still wanted to argue. I was a ship's Captain, and not accustomed to being spoken to so ignominiously. An immediate war launched inside my mind––"Don't talk to me like that!" versus *What is the point?*

My default when dealing with the evil blonde was to play it safe.

"Sorry, I meant that I need to tell Kate I'll help her with Eldritch Manor," I said.

"She is smarter than you. She knows."

"Um…"

"Perfect; tell her. Just bring your ass home so we can get on with your education."

I took the most direct route to Presley's home. I figured I should ask him about Kate hiring me to look into her father's home.

"Katie asked me to do some poking around at the manor. I came over to tell her I would. I also wanted to check with you to, you know, get your approval first," I said.

"Hell, Jimmy, you know better than asking me that. I trust you with my life—you think I'm less trusting with my family? Besides, you'd be smart not to let Kate hear you asked for my permission. She'd skin us both alive," he said.

"Yeah, you're right. Where's she at?"

"Purty sure she went to the market," he said, lifting his nose in the direction of town.

"Thanks, Presley. I'll find her. See ya later."

"After a while, crocodile," he quickly retorted. My friend had a hundred of these little quips that he used regularly.

I proceeded on to the market. It was a cloudless morning. The sunlight was warming, despite the crispness of the day. I had walked to Kate's, and it didn't make sense to trudge home, saddle Constellation, and then ride him to the exchange. So I walked there too.

On the trip, I saw a few people outside performing whatever task was indispensable to their day. But those milling about cried out their felicitations. I waved and smiled to each of them, but I didn't speak. If I answered, they may have construed it as an encouragement to converse. And Davi would eviscerate me if I didn't hustle back to her tender tutelage.

The town's hospital and police station bordered the market on the west. To the east was the grocery, and beyond was the bay. The school and library blocked the southern approach, while a fort garrisoning a company of Spanish soldiers defended the north.

From Kate's, I went between the hospital and police into the heart of the market. Spotting her, as ever, proved simple. Across the commerce, I saw a shock of red flow. With the lettuce and cabbages as a backdrop, her fiery hair drew my attention.

"Hello, Kate," I said.

I'd crept up behind her. It was unintentional, but natural, since she was vertically challenged. She couldn't see over the purveyor's stands, so she was easy to surprise.

She startled and recovered before she recognized me. Presley's wife was slight, but she was fearless. She was likewise one of the most perceptive women I'd ever known. She had a delightful smile, which she carried everywhere and offered freely to most everyone.

"Hello, Jimmy." Her grin widened.

"You already know why I'm here, don't you?"

"Oh, thank you," she said as she flung both arms around my neck.

She rose onto her toes and towed me to her. When she did, I saw María staring at the two of us. She veered toward a fruit stand near the grocery.

"Kate, I have to go. I have someone—" I peeled away from the tiny redhead.

"Sure—oh, Jimmy, I made a stew; stop by. There's plenty for you to take home."

She was glowing as she almost skipped away toward her home.

"Thanks, Katie, I will," I said.

Near the grocery was the sensational María. I called out as I hurried toward her. "María!"

She dipped her head, resigned, as if she realized she had no option but to speak with me.

Taking advantage was part of my personality. That's one reason I was a prosperous skipper.

"María, I'm sorry about coming to your home unannounced. I merely wanted you to speak to me. I shouldn't have—"

She grabbed my hand and hauled me behind an enormous pyramid of crates behind the store. Her eyes darted. Then she grabbed my shirt with both hands and tugged me to her.

Her mouth was as sweet as I imagined. Her tongue met mine, then traced my lips before she pulled away. She peered into my eyes and backed away a wee bit. She seized my gaze and held it for a lifetime. The waves crashed on the rocks below the cliff near us. The salt spray filled the air with its briny hotchpotch of smells. I reveled in the moment.

Then my lecherous mind turned to my *visit*, when I saw this Spanish Rose laying on the beach. My natural reaction was prompt and…uncontrollable.

She peeked down and smiled victoriously. Suddenly those glorious orbs shot to a corner, up and away from mine. Her raven hair bounced as she shook her head from side to side. She shrugged, whirled, and strode away.

I stood there, my mouth wide, my arousal suddenly snuffed out by her evisceration of my kiss. I lingered, too astonished to react. When I regained my senses, I dashed after her.

"Lady María, please," I called to her back.

She stopped and spun to confront me. Her face was fiery, and she punched her finger into my chest as I reached her. She fired her words as if they were a shower of arrows. Every one was Spanish. They pummeled me with their rapidity, and the only ones I could understand were profanities.

"Listen, María, I apologize for dropping in at your house. Well, maybe not for that. But I'm sorry for asking your uncle to see you. I should have asked you."

She relaxed. Her shoulders loosened and dropped slightly, and she looked down. Her hand dropped to her side and away from my chest. Then my mouth betrayed me.

"In my defense, you—

Wrong tack. She fired off another verbal flurry. I was going to have a bruise from her finger pounding my rib cage.

I raised both hands. "I'm sorry, I don't understand you. My French is decent, but my Spanish—except for the swearing…" I chuckled, thinking she'd join me.

She did.

"María, just give me a chance. Please have one meal with me. If you're worried, I can cook. I'll prepare a feast," I added.

I held my arms out, palms up in supplication.

"You are bold, Mr. Byrne."

"I'm a sailor. A sailor must be doughty!"

She grinned, but shook her head.

"No. It would not be proper," she said.

I was getting a read on this Spanish enchantress. She fought customs and scrupulously observed them. I'd have to watch my step with her.

"Post police at the door. One yell and they'd be at your side," I appealed.

"I will go to a communal establishment. And my cousin, Christina, will dine with us."

She peered at me. Her eyes sought settlement instead of scurrility.

"Aye, that's...*esta bien*. How about tomorrow night?" I proposed.

I used the Spanish term for that's okay. It was also the only non-profane Spanish that occurred to me.

"You are a peculiar man, Mr. Byrne."

She inclined her head, watching from the edges of her amber eyes.

My heart should have been racing. It wasn't. I knew she'd agree. She simply required space to arrive at the same conclusion.

"Deliver the preparations to my uncle's," she said.

She nodded and left, stepping with the grace of a goddess toward the grocery.

When she disappeared inside, I fled. I didn't trust my luck. So I marched home without speaking to another soul. My head and shoulders tucked, my collar up, and my hat tugged tight, I traversed the distance in only eight minutes—much quicker than I'd ever done.

I slipped in the front door instead of my customary side entrance. Straightaway, I saw a puzzling iridescence on my jacket lapel. The luminescence was delicate, and I only noticed it because of the feeble lighting. I tugged it loose and held it high. Only then did I recognize it as two filaments of hair, black as midnight.

"Davi, what do you make of these?" I asked.

I shuffled into her sphere as I held them out.

"Do I look like a fucking encyclopedia? Put those away. If you keep playing with them, you will go blind," she said, before adding, "Keep them, they may be essential."

Not wishing to argue, I shrugged and trudged upstairs. I folded the hairs into a small silver box from my bookshelf. Then I returned to the kitchen, to Davi and whatever insults she had developed for me.

"You took long enough."

Her insult didn't carry the same sting. I had a date with Lady María. Besides, I had become accustomed to them—a little.

"I'm here; let's get to work," I replied to prevent added ridicule.

"James, marry that young woman," Davi said, as if announcing, "The moon is full tonight."

Her nonchalance threw me off. She didn't even bother to glance at me when she spoke.

"What woman? Why? Who?" My mind raced. Did she know I'd cast the love spell, *Amori*?

"The black-haired belle," she said.

Still, she didn't make eye contact.

"I need better information. There are loads of them. And why must I marry?"

I struggled to purge *Amori* from my thoughts, sure Davi could read minds.

"Her name is María."

She finally looked at me.

My heart sank. She'd caught me. I had taken unfair advantage of the target of my affection when I cast that spell on her. That type of leverage was as unfair as it was dishonorable.

"James, while you have been dilly-dallying about, I have dedicated my morning visiting possible futures. You can win if you two marry."

"First," I said to give myself an extra second to think, "it'll be a frosty day in hell before she marries me. She scarcely tolerates me. She all but accused me of having an affair with Katie and you!"

My voice climbed in pitch and volume as I wound up.

"Are you and the Eldritch girl, mmm… familiar?" She asked.

"Hell no. She's my best friend, Presley's, bride," I said.

"She is a genius," Davi said.

"Kate?"

"James, sometimes I cannot tell if you are pathetically dim-witted or only pretending."

This woman was cluelessly duplicitous. It was maddening she could savage my lack of context when she was as guilty.

"So, María's smart. What's your point?"

"So, dumbass, she does not treasure her looks. She cherishes her intellect."

My shoulders rounded, and I tucked my head. Where was a pit when I needed one? I'd caused this woman to abandon reason —for me.

"I cast a love spell over her. That's why she kissed me," I blurted out.

"She kissed you? Well, for fuck's sake, not because of that pathetic *Amori* you cast. Your hand motion was shoddy. Besides, without your wand, it evaporated as fast as you cast it. As unthinkable as it sounds, this young lady is interested. Your meeting at her home offered the excuse she required. Now she can attribute any troubles to her uncle."

I sank into my rocker and shook my head. The more I thought I knew, the less I did.

"So, you are interested in love spells, are you?" Davi asked me after a ridiculous pause—time she spent laughing.

I still counted the win.

13

JAMES

avi and I finished the morning reviewing spell basics. When I say basics, I mean it. She'd press me to utter a spell name over and over until I wanted to puke. My inflection had to match hers, or she'd order me to restate it.

"James, every form of spellcraft is important. Your hand movements, your voice inflection, even your head and eye position may be critical," Davi said.

"I understand, but—

"Not possible, or you would have ended after, 'understand.' So, hush and do precisely as I do. Otherwise, quit wasting my existence. I have actual sentient beings who need my help."

"Got it," I responded, recognizing she was right and only struggling to help me.

Nevertheless, her constant insults were exasperating.

Davi taught me a separate invocation from each of her five sections and only began a different one after I'd mastered the present one—incantation after incantation.

The relentless repetition had me reliving Ms. Hildebrand's English recitals from my teen years. This study should be mystical and riveting, yet Davi had transfigured it into a yawnsome activity.

A knock at the door provided a much-needed interruption. I opened it to see Kate holding out a cast-iron Dutch oven.

"You forgot your stew," she said with a much-needed smile.

"Thank you, Katie."

I took the kettle as my friend turned climbed into her carriage and drove away, then hung the container near the fire to warm.

As if there had been no interruption, my tiny tormentor returned to her lesson. The drilling continued into the early afternoon and was only interrupted by the echo of my stomach roaring for food.

By this point, every eye-flutter, head-thrust, and enunciation had relinquished all precision. Lest you think I'm a complete dullard, my latest try was a tough shield spell. No matter how often I performed it, I couldn't make my intonation error-free.

You try it. "Chee-ell-ee-epsilon-tea-um-a."

It's not easy, is it?

"James, let us rest for lunch," my tiny demon-tormentor-teacher suggested.

In truth, her words really formed a long-winded diatribe focused on my lack of intellect. It likewise included many carefully chosen and inventive expletives. Davi had improved her invectives to an art form. It honored me to witness such verbal knifing, even though I was the recipient.

I didn't bother to rebut her. Instead, I pushed the Dutch oven full of the stew Kate had made me deeper into the flame. As I bustled through my galley, Davi watched me, an enigmatic grin traced lightly across her lips.

After I'd warmed my meal, I scooped out two large ladles from the cast-iron pot and into my bowl. I looked at Davi and held up the serving spoon as a question.

"I would rather eat pig shit," she retorted, although she was smiling, so I don't believe she meant the insult.

I slid my dish across the table, then dropped a little too hard into my chair in front of it.

"What, was it too fucking heavy to carry?" Davi giggled as she talked.

I ignored her, shut my eyes, said a brief prayer, and started eating. Davi watched me, drawing on that same cryptic grin. I considered asking about her faith before deciding I had enough headaches.

"I should be ready to cast my own spells soon," I said instead between bites.

Despite the way the lesson had ended, I'd successfully mastered a dozen spells today, so I calculated this should be an innocuous topic. Besides, I might hear something worthwhile. I also wouldn't see her eyes roll as I squinted out the window as I chewed.

"Dumbass, before you can prepare a proper incantation, you must build your wand. Without one, your spells will have scant effect and will barely last a second before being reclaimed by oblivion," Davi said.

"Okay—tell me how to make one. What is it made of?"

"Each wand is different," she shrugged.

"How's that possible? Inevitably, magic folk would have to incorporate the same, um, pieces."

She raised her shoulders as she drew in a considerable breath and held it. She emptied the full breath before taking in another. and answering.

"This is why training you is so tedious. You are remarkably unintelligent. But, since I must eventually explain it, I may as well do it now. Besides, the more I speak, the fewer idiotic statements you can make."

"Um, thank you."

Yes, I recognize it sounds as if I was thanking her for reminding me of my ignorance. No. I was being clever. I *was* referring to her finally explaining wand construction. That's my story.

She rolled her eyes and continued. "We create wands from four different ingredients: wood, metal, something from your truest love, and a magical element that will offer itself to you at the proper time. These items are special, even idiosyncratic, for each wand's maker."

I considered it amusing that Davi continually derided my intellect, but believed I was smart enough to know what idiosyncratic meant. The irony! Oh—it meant my wand would serve only me. I think.

"You said I need ingredients. Where do I find them?"

"How should I know? It is different for everyone. I discovered everything I required in a heap at the foot of my bed. I would not expect that to happen for you. But you never know," she said as her shoulders rose, then fell.

"I understand. Give the attitude a rest now, will you?" I asked.

"James, wand construction does not follow defined rules, except for the magical element. That piece, you cannot control. You will not receive it any earlier than required.

"The wood will be something treasured. The metal will be an aspect of your essential nature, or character, if you prefer. For example, for you, it will be dense and nearly impenetrable," she laughed.

I rolled my eyes.

"We both realize you have discovered the part of your truest love." She smiled shrewdly at me, akin to a mother excited for her little Jimmy and his first kiss.

"Ok, I have to find wooden and metal segments. The wood will be something I treasure," I said as I pondered. I scooped the last bite of stew into my mouth and dropped my spoon back into my bowl.

"James, since you have finished eating, I need to return us to an important subject. We must understand the creation of the spyglass."

"Why?" I asked. I'd seen its beginning. I also realized Charles Doss had transformed the blade into a spyglass, which began the disappearances at Eldritch Manor. Besides, something I never wanted to see again was that ritual murder.

"Your success depends on your understanding of the formation of that demonic realm," she said. "Otherwise, you have no hope of dismantling it."

My chin fell to my chest, and I shook it. I knew Davi was right. Still, I hated the idea of re-watching the murder of an innocent woman. Even more upsetting was knowing she would turn into a monster I'd have to destroy. At risk was the destiny of my entire world.

I took a deep breath, lifted my head, and smiled.

Davi cast a protection spell, *Serverbaris,* and invisibility, *Key-see-us,* over me before she cast *Deannix*. Once again, I never saw her put the ring on her finger, but her hand circled and an orange flare, the shade of a pumpkin, started spinning into a brilliant vermillion. Seconds later, the colors blended, then blossomed into a large disk-shaped gateway. Davi stepped through first, and I followed.

For the second time in as many days, I endured the gore as Wáhta dissected the witch, then tore her beating heart from her chest. At least she died quickly. With a sense of righteous vengeance, I watched as the arrow pierced the murdering Iroquois's heart.

Either reliving the event had boosted my senses, allowing me to pore over each moment, or Davi had somehow slowed time. The knife tumbled from Wáhta's hand and the ichor covering it disappeared, absorbed by the blade.

The knife thundered as it fell. I recoiled at the detonation. It stabbed into the ground, a doomed attempted murder of the earth itself. Then the Iroquois Wáhta collapsed, interring the dagger with his body, concealing it from my view.

I stared at his frame as his life was carried away by the rivulets of blood flowing from his barely pumping heart. I struggled to stay a detached witness, but I only wanted to retch. Then the native's body disappeared.

After the battle, the victorious Algonquin stripped the dead Iroquois of their valuables. A young Algonquin boy, scarcely a teenager, tucked the cursed blade into a strap at his waist.

Time quickened, and the sun jumped from one position to another. Scenes that had once flowed became a sequence of paintings held one by one in front of my eyes. Soon only bodies littered the ground and darkness fell. The last portrait was the perfect moon and a magnificent white stone sculpture standing where the cruel Iroquois had fallen. Snow blew from the pine branches onto the casting.

"Davi—"

She spun another door and we stepped through together.

The blackness of this place was complete. It was absent all light. I expected my eyes to adapt and discover the slightest gleam. When they didn't, fear gripped me, and I wanted to run. But escape to where? I wasn't anywhere, so I had no place to go. My heart raced and my breathing came in fierce gulps. I reached out my hands in search of something to steady myself and fell. As I stumbled forward, something caught and supported me.

"Careful, James—steady yourself. Squat, it may help."

The slight woman had perceived I was falling and had arrested my stumble. Her speech was steady and carried none of the fear I felt.

"Yeah, thanks."

I recovered my stability, bent both knees, spread my feet to shoulder width, and waited. My racing heart kept the time. The rapid beating led me to conclude we'd been waiting for several minutes. Eventually, I decided Davi had made a giant mistake. I awaited an orange glow coiling into a red blaze, opening an escape passageway.

Instead, her ring went white. After experiencing the utter darkness, this was so intense, I turned away. As I did, I saw Davi grab the light with her other hand, then toss it above her. It floated higher and higher, a kite caught on the breeze, until only a twinkle remained. Then it erupted. Unlike a chemical explosion, this outburst didn't abate.

As the region morphed from inky black into innumerable shades of drab grey, it grew into a Stygian wasteland that widened into a universe of shadows and broken geometry. As quickly as I saw a structure develop, it dissolved, then reappeared in another position. Eventually, I decided those features were a style of a three-dimensional wall.

I watched the darkened void evolve, frightened but unflinching. I concentrated on a single individual barrier and watched it move. Its motions, precise and regular, formed a rectangular pattern, shifting eighteen times before repeating. Each shift took a full second. I picked another bulwark. It fluctuated in the same frequency and pattern.

Through the eternally shifting obstacles advancing as if an invitation to climb, I decided we had to be near a slope. I wanted to know if I could see any overall feature at its summit. I turned and lifted my foot. When I did, Davi held her hand against my chest. I froze and replaced my foot, ensuring it settled where it began.

She gestured to a spot on the *ground* several feet ahead and on our left. At first, I recognized nothing odd. Then I saw a change. This differed from the barriers in that it neither had dimension nor reflected light. These blanks shifted like the walls, but were less plentiful. The edges were sharp and uneven, as if they were shark's teeth waiting to tear into flesh. I shuddered to imagine what would happen should I tumble into one of these.

"Davi, where are we?"

"Ah, James, here you will discover the true monster haunting Eldritch Manor," she said.

A smirk stretched across her delicate lips. Her grin was feral and her teeth bared. She was ready for an attack and seemed ecstatic at the prospect.

I'd never cowered from a fight, but this place was unlike any I'd imagined. Still, Davi had brought me here to prepare me to battle a demon from Hell itself. I'd faced it several days ago, and knew it was the most destructive power I'd ever encountered. I stiffened my back, relaxed my shoulders, and pulled out my blade.

"Put that away, dumbass," she said. "You cannot kill *this* beast with that tiny proxy penis."

No matter the situation, this woman still found the energy to insult me.

"Fine," I growled. "Now tell me where the devil we are," I urged as I tucked my blade into its scabbard.

"We are viewing the witch's domain, inside your world. This is what she created inside the knife. She's what supplied energy to this artifact, and why Riaan Dahl wants to own it."

"You said it's not a world, but a domain. What's the difference?" I asked.

"She created this space inside your universe. It is a bubble inside your bubbled universe," Davi answered, as if she were advising me that blood is crimson.

She must've seen my confusion, because she continued, "It is like a room on your ship."

I understood.

"You said, 'viewing.' Is that different than what we were doing before—you know—when we saw her get murdered?" I asked.

"Yes, James, it is very different. I do not have the power to actually bring us into this realm. Tituba created it for her. The only way to actually get inside is through death."

You know those times in your life, when, looking back, you realize you should have done something different, or even acted differently? Yeah, well this was one of those times. Again, I should have run away with my hands over my head screaming. Only I wouldn't realize it until much later.

After a hesitation, she started walking, and I followed. She scrupulously bypassed the pitch-black cavities to nowhere. Without reference, I didn't know where she was heading. But Davi seemed to know.

After a time, she spoke. "Stop; listen."

I crossed to her left, keeping her away from my sword hand. Regardless of her assertion, my sole weapon was my sword. I drew it from its scabbard and held it in front of me.

Davi shook her head.

In the distance, somewhat below us, I noticed the slain woman. She stood, centered inside a giant six-pointed star. Her arms gesticulated in grand sweeping actions. Each point of her star was lit by a blood-red candle, creating a dome of crimson light over the witch.

Outside the light, beating one point of the star near a lone candle, was the murdering Indian. He swung an enormous fat knife in one hand and a hatchet whirled in the other. He screamed an unintelligible roar with each blow. The light itself deflected each of his strokes. The only noticeable effect was a rapid brightening before it returned to its original intensity.

"This is Kaysan, my house of blood. You do not belong," the witch said.

"I am Wáhta, leader of the Iroquois. We are first among people. I am first among Chiefs. You will return me to my people, or I will destroy you."

The witch laughed. "You have no power here. Here, I am ruler. I am Tituba, and you are my slave."

The lighted barrier fell, and Tituba charged her executioner. Each struck blows. None landed.

The geometric hedges shifted faster and faster until I couldn't resolve them individually. Where walls had once shifted, rectilinear shapes and vast chasms formed instead—rectangles built inside one another, forming giant pyramids and massive walled enclosures. Cavities to nowhere formed, collapsing structures near them before disappearing and reforming in new locations.

Fire erupted from Tituba's outstretched hands and was deflected by the Native. Lightning flashed from his knife and hatchet before being dispersed by the witch.

Without the sun rising or sinking, I had no actual grasp of time. It was Davi who advised me that the battle had been raging for many decades.

Other souls appeared, following either Tituba or Wáhta. As they did, one side forced the other into a smaller part of Tituba's Kaysan. But no matter the strength devoted, neither force could conquer the other.

Throughout the struggle, Tituba and Wáhta persisted as the strongest. They also learned to leach energy from the others, consuming several of them. There was one, more intense than the others and unaffected by these attacks. This one finally opened an exit and escaped to an unknown place. After that light fled, the others became immune to leaching. Only new souls stood in peril. They remained at risk until the others showed them how to defend against the abuses of Tituba and Wáhta.

After this, the war transformed into a three-sided battle. The two most powerful continued fighting one another. But they had to fight to reclaim power over the weaker souls.

In a respite between the eternal battles, exchanges between souls explained that someone brandishing a dagger had murdered many of them. Others claimed they had only fallen asleep and were dreaming a night-terror.

The battles flared anew and raged, then abated, then flared

without any end. Eventually, Tituba and Wáhta retreated, meditated, and spoke with their gods.

The less-powerful huddled together.

Davi led me nearer the pointed star and crimson barrier and waited.

Tituba again stood within the center of her six-pointed star. She understood the call of supernatural energies struggling to thwart one another and her, and exposed her teeth in a savage sneer.

"I built this space. None can conquer me without its ruin. Wáhta, I have become tired of this eternal battle with you. Come, entreat with me. Let us regain power over these others inside this arena. Then let us recapture our mortal being," the witch said.

"Why should I? Are you afraid?" the dead man countered.

"Why should I dread what has happened? I cannot fear death. It is what I have become. You will find common ground with me, or I shall destroy this domain. You know I have that authority."

"Then withdraw your boundary and *let--me--in.*" His evil punctuated every syllable.

Tituba yielded, and for the first time since before their death, they stood as equals, not thrall or master.

"We must join and collect the feeble. Together, we will draw their strength," she said.

"I will give our creation form. It is neither demon, beast, nor superstition. It is death and dread and unbeaten," Wáhta said.

"Come, my ally and brother. Let us combine to reclaim our freedom."

The two mighty creatures joined hands. As they did, they blended into a single arm on two bodies. They embraced, and one body incorporated into the other, creating a single being.

Its spindly, foot-long fingers unfolded on hands the size of a platter. Sharpened fingernails dripped blood onto the formless ground. Its arms rose to the height of a man. They lifted its heavy hands above the grotesque head of the beast. Great grey scales covered its misshapen and crooked form. Legs the size of trees bore the great armored

figure. The creature's head elongated and expanded to the propor-
tions of a goat. Its eyes blazed red inside a blackened orb. Its teeth,
pointed and dagger-like, were clearly visible inside its lipless mouth.

The shriek, an auricular explosion of gore, rushed through the
void. The remaining souls trembled in dread. It was not fear for life,
for they were already dead. Their terror was abject panic over the loss
of their eternal souls, for that which now stalked their formless home
was far worse than death.

"It is called Genosqwa," Davi yelled over the shriek.

Davi opened a portal to Metaterre. In my haste to escape this
horrid place, I ran through.

14

UNNAMED OMNISCIENT PRESENCE

*R*iaan Dahl climbed from under his rocky overhang into the bright azure-and-white morning of the snow-blanketed forest. He'd spent his time hunting rabbits, squirrels, and other small animals to murder. Since his arrival, he's captured and murdered dozens of the hapless animals.

Dahl needed each murder as preparation for a journey. On this quest, he had one task. This task was all that mattered: find an artifact with enough energy to open his final gateway home.

He pulled the hide from the last animal, a fat beaver, and cast the carcass aside. Later, he would smoke the meat for his trip. But for now, he scraped clean the hide. When he'd finished removing the bits of fat, muscle, and other tissue, he crushed the animal's skull and removed its brain. He ground it into the hide, then stretched it across a framework made from small saplings and allowed it to dry.

His leather was ready after a day in the frigid sun. He stitched together several hides into a cloak. Others he shaped into boots and a hat. He could not fully transfigure his body, but he'd done enough that the cloak, boots, and hat could cover what his magic had yet to reach.

As the day ended, Riaan didn't forget to repent his sins. For each animal he'd murdered to steal their hide, he branded another tattoo onto his own. Thirty-nine new lines over the last two weeks.

Riaan Dahl was finally prepared to begin his search for his artifact. He was ready to go home. Though tonight he would sleep.

15

JAMES

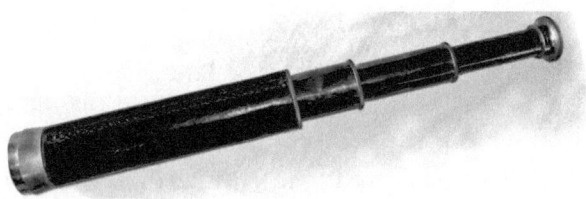

*D*avi and I stepped through the portal and into my kitchen, leaving behind the behemoth Genosqwa. My skin tingled and my heartbeat thundered in my ears. The clock chimed, hammering its distinctive four tones, rising three and a falling fourth, marking the quarter-hour. My breaths came in gasps as I strained to understand the implications of what we'd seen.

The night outside was as black as the demon realm we'd just left. A gale beat a single shutter against my house, pounding as it sought refuge from the frigid rage.

When the final chime faded, the gateway surrendered the last of its shimmer. The only light remaining was a mock afterglow, staining my vision with spotted swirls of vermillion and orange as they held tight to my memory.

Again, her ring blazed. She tossed the luminance into the air. This time, it didn't explode as it had inside Tituba's room, but settled on the ceiling and spread out until the whole of the ceiling glowed.

I re-lit the fire in my brick firebox, taking great breaths and blowing life back into the hot coals buried by dust of the burnt logs. Within minutes, a raging fire warmed the room.

The silence was as oppressive as the thoughts of the demon

monster Genosqwa haunting my dreams. The silence grew loud, rivaling the raging storm outside, and only broke with a final crash of the shutter.

Davi flicked her wrist and the banging ceased.

The clock chimed the half-hour; the tone rose and fell twice. This time, I glanced at it: seven-thirty. Had half the day passed, or was it several days? Maybe it was weeks.

"Did we watch Tituba and Wáhta merge into that...monster?" I asked.

"Yes, James. That is exactly what we saw."

She stared through the window at the storm raging. I could only see her reflection, as if she were peering in from the tempest outside my home. Her eyes narrowed, and tiny wrinkles folded across her brow and the top of her nose.

I examined every facet of her expression as she gazed out, searching for any nuance, any insight into her knowledge. Davi had explained many times that she'd *guide* me. I'd discovered that meant she didn't tell me everything.

"James, I must search your past and future histories to better understand what we just saw," Davi said.

"Fine; you spin the doorway, I'll follow," I answered.

"No."

This time, she was firm, and didn't hurl any of her usual invectives.

"James, I may visit places only seconds before shifting again. If I must wait on you, this will take me ages longer. Be a good boy—go to bed and let the adult do her job. Okay?"

I was wrong. She hadn't saved her insults.

"Got it," I replied.

Besides, she was right. The few transitions I'd done today had drained me.

Davi waved her hands, shooing me up the stairs and into bed. She didn't spin her gateway until I had the covers pulled up near my ears.

Tituba's murder looped through my nightmares that night. Visions of her evisceration, his perfectly timed death, and the gore spilling from both bodies kept my mind racing in their dance with death.

Several times that night, I awoke fighting a storm of nightmares. I'd experienced my share of death while fighting pirates on the British man-o'-war, and hadn't developed terrors from those experiences. Watching Tituba's murder and Wáhta's immediate fate had seared a fear into my dreams unlike any that I'd ever known. My gut wrenched.

I gave up the attempted sleep just after midnight. I took my spell book and opened it at random.

Depergeo: Cleanses a target's mind. Will also act as a minor mind-eraser, expunging the previous five-minutes from a target's memory.

Effect: When properly cast, this spell will allow the target to sleep peacefully. The effect degrades steadily, but cascades after six hours. Target must wish to sleep or it will function as a minor mind-eraser.

Casting time: Less than one second.

Movement: Form a circle using the smallest finger and thumb. Extend your remaining fingers as you move your hand from your left to your right across the target's eyes.

Warning: if the caster moves her hand too near her own eyes, this will cause a minor mind-eraser, despite the movement being the incorrect direction.

I'd already suspected this book had an ability to understand my needs. In my desperation to meet María, the first spell it had presented was *Amori*.

That this book *felt* I needed to learn this incantation was disconcerting. No, it was downright terrifying. Still, I'd have to remember to ask Davi about it.

I continued turning to random pages to read spell forms. In school, I'd been good at recitals, so these incantations proved easy to learn. Also, since Davi had cast her protection jura over me, and because I hadn't constructed my wand, I felt safe in casting, or attempting to cast, almost every spell.

Until I found *Disevocation*. Professor Miranda Constance Goodwin of London's Magical Academy said, "The *Disevocation* spell is one of the most dangerous spells known to the magical world. If cast correctly, this spell will disentangle all energy contained within the volume of the radius of the caster's wand movement." (Goodwin, M. C., 1492, 213,660.)

I've always been excellent at math, and did a quick calculation. The formula $V = 4/3\pi r^3$ is used to calculate the volume of a sphere. If I drew a circle with a diameter of eight inches, its volume would be near two-hundred sixty-eight cubic inches. That's not a massive volume to...disentangle—whatever that means. At least, it didn't seem large. But if I made a large circle, the volume would explode. Hopefully not in the literal sense, though. This was clearly a spell I'd need to examine cautiously.

I'd remained so engrossed in my reading I didn't notice the sunrise. But when the rooster crowed, I heard the hen call from downstairs.

"James, get your ass downstairs. We need to talk," Davi yelled.

I didn't bother answering. I only washed my face and dressed. When I arrived, Davi appeared rested, unlike what I knew I looked like.

"You bellowed, your Ladyship?" I quipped.

I decided that from now on, I'd give as good as she gave.

Davi's eyes widened, then narrowed. The edges of her lips curled upward, and her dimples appeared. The humor appeared and disappeared so quickly, I wondered if I had imagined it.

"So, you have grown a spine, have you? Well, it does not matter. Pay attention; we have work to do."

I offered her a two-finger salute, touching them above one eye, and dipped my head.

"Riaan Dahl wants that spyglass. Fortunately, he can only take possession if the owner gives it to him, or—it has no owner. Do not ask me why, because I have found thirteen different reasons so far. Do you know who controls it?" Davi asked.

"If I'd have to guess, it's old man Doss. I saw it at the Eldritch Manor in a dream. At least, I think it was a dream."

"Good. That is what I found too. You need to take ownership," she told me.

"How?" I asked, my eyebrows arching high in wonder.

"Typically, in this realm, it is done through a purchase agreement."

"What do you mean, 'in this realm?' Is it different in other realms?"

"Sure. There are places where you can claim ownership only if you steal it and brag publicly. Others do not have the concept of ownership. But, in your case, I meant you must purchase the manor," she said.

She stated this as if she'd told me to buy a loaf of bread.

"Even as rundown as it is, it's still worth more than I have. There's no way I could afford it," I retorted.

"Find a way."

"Can't I just buy the spyglass? It must be cheaper," I asked.

I only bought stuff I needed, or what made me more money, like better cannons for the *Monarch*. I'd gained quite a reputation for being frugal.

"No. Dahl could quickly trace it back to you. You must hide the change of ownership for as long as possible. Otherwise, you will not have the time to acquire the skills necessary to defeat either him or that monster inside the spyglass."

"Great—now I have to buy a haunted manor from an insane old man who's my best friend's father-in-law. Nothing to worry about working through that," I said as sarcastically as I could.

"Glad you understand your job," Davi said, straight-faced.

I pulled out my copy of *Down With Spells* and flipped it open. On that page was *Disevocation*.

"Davi, every time I open this book, things are in different places. I can't tell, but the spells seem to reorder. Also, it knows what I want. No, it knows what I need, and falls open to that spell."

"Very nice, James."

I searched for the mirth in her tone. Nope, she was genuinely excited at my revelations. "Okaaayyy," I responded.

"You have gotten this far; do not expect me to give you the rest of the fucking information. Start figuring out bits of this yourself. Otherwise, the other kids in the class will think you are the teacher's pet and may become jealous."

"Smarty-pants," I said.

She shrugged and giggled.

"I'd guess it has an enchantment causing the spells to reorder. Maybe one that can decide what I want?" I said. My tone increased as I went along and tinged higher on the last word, making it more of a question than a statement.

"Yes, and no. At least you are not a complete fucking moron today. The spells do reorder themselves based on your perceived need. Besides, that book cannot hold them all. If it contained every spell known to the magical world, it would be sixteen feet thick and printed so tiny, you could use your dick as the quill. It has a charm to present only spells that might interest you when you first touch it. Over time, it will learn your preferences and give you better choices."

Davi smiled as she finished, folded her hands in her lap, and waited on me.

"It doesn't have a brain?" I asked, not completely serious.

"I take that back; you are a fucking moron."

We spent the rest of the day in repetitious learning, starting by rehashing the spells I'd mastered yesterday. I guess she wanted to verify I could recall them exactly.

An hour before dinner, I called a stop to clean up for my almost-date with María.

16

JAMES

I met María and her cousin, Christina, at *Below The Salt*, a restaurant near the police station, renowned for its smoked, baked, and stewed meats and its…unorthodox proprietress, Melodie Saddler.

Mel was another fiery redhead from Ireland living in our township. We had collected our fair share. I'd first met her five years ago, in January 1776, when I was Executive Officer onboard *HMS Lively*. This was when I still worked for that fat King George. I hired her to oversee the *Lively's* galley. She was tough as a beaver and didn't take grief from the crew. Invariably, a person wouldn't fancy shipping with a woman, or took offense, as she preferred women. But she'd just remind them she had more dates than they did. That stopped their lip.

Mel became family during a storm off the coast of Italy that February. We were trying to reach Sicily when we saw a tartan fishing ship foundering in the heavy seas. The captain had called all hands on deck to help evacuate the smaller ship. A rogue wave swept me from the dinghy as we rowed to the survivors. Mel didn't hesitate. She leapt into the roiling ocean and tied me to a line.

In this storm, Mel met the captain of the fishing ship, Ingrid Santini. They shared many commonalities, and soon became inseparable. Ingrid paid my Captain to allow her to stay on board during our return to New York. The captain didn't have patrons, so he was always amenable to a bribe. That gold went straight into his pocket.

After that voyage, I'd taken command of the *Monarch* and asked Mel to take charge of my galley, but Ingrid insisted she give up her seafaring. Acquiescing, Mel started her restaurant. From the day she opened, she'd had a line of customers. But no matter the line, she always found a table for me.

I'd invited María and her chaperone, Christina, here because the food was amazing and Mel ensured my privacy.

My heart jumped and sweat beaded on my forehead when María glided into the room. I stood as the pair walked toward my table. She took my breath away every time I saw her. My heart beat ten times for every step she took. By the time she arrived, I was breathless.

"Hello, María. Hello, Christina."

I dropped my voice into its deeper range and was thankful when it didn't hitch.

"Hello, James," María said at the same time Christina said, "Hello, Jimmy."

I pulled out Christina's chair first. The whole time, I never broke eye contact with the dark-haired beauty. She held the smile of an angel and blushed when I slid her chair out for her.

"I hope you two are hungry. This place has the best meats," I said as I rubbed my hands together. This was deliberate, as it let me burn off nervous energy.

"It has always been my favorite since we moved here," Christina said helpfully as her cousin remained silent.

Okay, she still didn't trust me. I needed to make sure she understood I was interested in more than her looks.

"María, every time I tried to talk to you before, I said everything wrong. If you'd give me a chance, I'd like to begin again?" I paused and raised my eyebrows at her, tilting my head to make it a question.

She didn't speak. But she dipped her head slightly, which I took to mean, "You're on thin ice. But I'll give you one last chance."

"When we met, you told me you were from Rota. I'm sure I knew your mother some years ago."

That comment had an impact. "How could you know my mother?" she sputtered.

"My ship needed repairs after a battering in a storm near Sicily. Your mother offered us anchorage until we repaired the damage. She was stunningly beautiful, too."

María rolled her eyes and folded her arms across her chest. I ignored her. It should only take me a bit longer to make my point.

"She was also kind, intelligent, and interested in relationships to help her city. I was an idealistic Executive Officer on the British ship *HMS Lively*. Your mother believed helping us meant we'd leave her ships alone."

Both women stared at me expectantly.

Continuing, I said, "When we first met, I should've explained how alike you two are. She places a great weight on her intelligence. She relishes praise heaped on her because of her attractiveness. Or she lets men believe the flattery works. In reality, I don't believe it does."

We paused our conversation, looked over the Bill of Fare, and placed our orders. María and I both ordered a filet of beef and fried cabbage with onions, although I requested a double order of meat. Christina ordered the prairie-chicken with pickled carrots and cucumbers.

Satisfied that our culinary needs would be met, we continued our conversation.

"I will acknowledge you understand my mother. Why are you drawn to me? I doubt you would speak to me if I were ugly," my pseudo-date said.

"I guess. I couldn't be sure. What I know is that your mother told me about you. She spoke at length of your intelligence and dreams for your life. She's known for many years that you don't want to live in Rota as a royal toady," I replied.

"That is correct. I did not know she was aware, though," María said.

"Your mother is an exceptional woman. She believes you are her superior in nearly every way," I said.

I held my drink and swirled it as I gauged her reaction.

"That can't be true. She always…" Her mouth moved as she struggled to find the words.

"She valued her intelligence too," I said.

Our meal arrived. The filets still sizzled on the cast-iron pans Mel used during the preparation, and Christina's prairie-chicken steamed under its crispy brown skin. I was starving after having survived the day with Davi. María even offered me her final few bites of steak, scraping them into my pan without asking. She winked a brown eye. My insides melted.

Both ladies declined a dessert, but insisted I have one. Mel had a freshly baked apple pie with a cinnamon crust. How could I turn it down? They sipped their coffee and spoke together, including me enough that I felt a part of their conversation.

I paid the bill and escorted them outside. Within seconds, a carriage I'd stationed nearby stopped in front of us. I never underprepared. My date raised an eyebrow as the driver hurried to offer his assistance.

"James, how long have you had this poor man waiting for us?" she asked.

"For as long as it takes you to give me another opportunity to spend time with you," I replied, as if I'd known she would ask the question.

"Tomorrow for lunch, then?" she replied smoothly.

"Tomorrow, then, my lady," I said, offering her the slightest bow before helping her into the buggy leaving the driver to wonder why he jumped out to assist.

Then I turned to our chaperone and said graciously, "Christina." I offered her my hand, which she took before she climbed in after her cousin.

I looked at the driver, touched two fingers to my hat and said, "Driver, report back to me at my house after you've delivered these ladies home. Do you understand me?" I wasn't severe in my tone, but I made it plain that these women were under his protection.

"Yes sir, Cap'n sir," was his cheerful reply. He was one of my deckhands.

I never under-prepare.

17

UNNAMED OMNISCIENT PRESENCE

*D*ahl set out from his encampment on the morning of the fourth of September. Like a magnet, he was pulled to the spot where the artifact had gained its power.

Dahl was an expert at reading energies, but it still took him two full days to find the location.

Despite the decades that had passed, he knew many men had died here. He relished it as their pain washed over him. Later, he knew he'd have to punish himself for those sinful thoughts.

"*Osteaendo!*" Dahl exclaimed.

At his feet, a glow shaped similar to a large dagger or small sword appeared. Leading away was a trail of golden dust. He followed it. The golden trail wasn't terribly bright in the sunshine. But it stood out on the blanket of snow clearly enough.

He walked long after the sunset. Only once, when a group of snarling wolves decided he would be their next meal, did he deviate from his course. A well-placed blast of flames sent them scurrying away.

Near dawn, he found another hiding place inside a thicket of brush. He carved out an area to sleep. Sleep found him quickly, but

Riaan Dahl was incapable of proper rest. In fact, he didn't remember his last genuine sleep.

Tonight, his dreams took him to a home as large and opulent as his temple overlooking an ocean of water. He had seen massive bodies of water before and understood the power they contained.

Rain pounded the old house; lightning lit its exterior. Outside, a giant monster, terrifying even to him, stalked the grounds. Dahl watched as it pounded on the manor doors, searching for an entrance. Its fury never diminished, but it didn't so much as scratch the worn paint.

18

JAMES

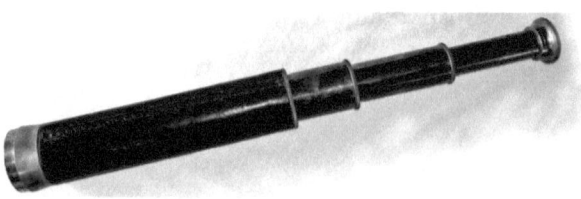

I got up early to find Davi in her chair. Her bowl of porridge steamed in her lap.

"It doesn't matter when I get up. You're always in that seat and your food is constantly hot?" I declared, expecting she would recognize it was a question and not an observation.

She didn't. "Your proclivity toward the obvious is breathtaking," she answered. Sarcasm dripped from each syllable.

"Finally, a compliment." Playfully, I bowed to her, extending one leg behind me and curling an arm across my belly while letting the other extend out behind me. I may have held the pose for a beat too long.

She quipped, "You are a fucking idiot."

Again, her head shook, and her fingers squeezed the bridge of her nose.

"Seriously, how is it you're in nearly the same position every morning when I get downstairs?" I asked.

"I am a many-thousand-year-old woman who has studied you longer than you have been conscious, and you do not believe I can decipher your breakfast schedule?"

Her voice trailed up, making it an implied question and an indictment of my lack of logic before I spoke.

"Good point. So, let's get to work," I said, wanting out of the latest verbal mess I'd created.

"Fuck no," she blurted.

I've got to admit, it's tough to surprise me. Yet women in my life routinely do. My mouth flapped open, but I couldn't speak.

"For fuck's sake, James, you are a dumbass most of the time. But if we begin before you have had your coffee and breakfast, I would be wasting my time."

I shrugged my shoulders and got busy cooking breakfast. Today, I went all out and made scrambled eggs, hashed potatoes, and a generous slab of salted-and-smoked ham that I cooked until the fat became crisp. Once again, Davi was correct. My meal thoroughly energized me.

It lasted for the next twelve and one-half seconds.

"Davi, if I need a wand to cast a spell properly..." I stopped and pointed a finger at her to keep her from interrupting before I went on. "...aaaannnddd you are the one actually performing the spells I'm casting, how is this helping me improve? It makes scant sense."

"It need not make *sense*, James. Did you forget that this...is... magic?" Again, she adopted a condescending and stuttering delivery to drive home her point.

We devoted the morning to protection juras. She said I needed to concentrate most of my time to studying these types of spells, at least until I could cast one to defend myself and others.

By lunchtime, I needed a rest.

"Alright, Davi, I've got to visit someone before lunch. Do you want me to bring you back something to eat, or will you conjure it?" I asked.

I meant my question as a joke, because she'd already instructed me that witches or wizards couldn't produce energy. They simply borrowed it. I assumed creating food needed as much magic as it transformed into energy, so most mages didn't bother conjuring the

ingredients, though, they were masters of taking those same ingredients and creating delicious feasts.

"First, it is not, 'I've got.' I hope you are a better ship's captain than
you are at using your native vocabulary. Second—no, James. I will
provide lunch for the two of us. It will be ready when you return."

Since she was right about my vocabulary, I chose not to be
offended. Still, her answer was so casual and lacked her typical
sarcasm, I almost asked if she was okay. Lucky for me, I took hold of
my tongue before it betrayed me and led to another five minutes of
taunts.

"Okay, I'll come back soon," I announced as I slammed the door
behind me.

I rushed to the hospital, keeping my head down to fend off any
unneeded conversation along the way. It was unlike me. I loved chat-
ting with people; that was how I learned the details I employed to
avoid British ships and foot patrols. Besides, this town was full of my
friends. I enjoyed their company.

But today was special. I was on a mission to see my brown-eyed
girl. Well, she may not be *mine* yet, but after last night's dinner-date, I
was confident my luck with her had changed.

I saw her well before she saw me. She was bowing near a small
child. His dark-as-night skin contrasted with her delicate coloring. I
watched as she pressed the boy's abdomen before quickly releasing
the pressure. The child moaned in pain and pulled his bare legs
toward his belly and his arms across to cover the area.

She bent and kissed his forehead. It didn't matter that his parents
were impoverished. To her, this was an individual deserving of
dignity and mercy.

Her bottomless amber eyes were scintillant; her streaming black
hair spilled over one shoulder, an impenetrable midnight. If love were
pearly iridescence, I'd vow it twinkled in her eyes as she delivered her
comforting words to the boy.

She glanced up and spotted me watching her. Her smile was spontaneous and welcoming. I was afraid I'd fallen far harder for this
magnificent creature than I imagined possible.

She sauntered to me. The warmth from her grin remained as she wafted in my direction.

"Hello, James. I did not expect to see you. Most men assume I will call on them after a first date. That has never happened." Her giggle made my toes tingle.

"Hello, María. I realize you're busy. How is the child?" I asked seriously.

She stared at me, looking for a hint of deceit. Her many previous suitors had misused this poor woman. She knew to watch for ploys to gain her favor.

After reassuring herself, she explained, "He has appendicitis. I will have to remove his appendix in a few minutes."

"Wait, you're a surgeon?" It shouldn't surprise me. But at her age, it did.

"No, but the doctors have seen enough. They depend on me to do some surgeries. This is one I have undertaken several times."

"I won't take much of your time, then. I only wished to express how much I enjoyed our supper last evening."

"I didn't want to go. My cousin is the one you should thank. She feels a remarkable affection for you. You must have comported your-self well with her, because she is not one to pay compliments. But I am glad she persuaded me to go. I too enjoyed myself. You have a richer personality than I first believed."

She inclined her head as if she were finishing the punchline of a joke.

I enjoyed her trivial levity in the fashion she meant and was over-joyed we had reached this stage. I hoped we could relax even more with each other.

"María, may I escort you home? I mean, after you finish at the hospital? Or, I'm sorry if you have plans; I can..."

She saved me from rambling. "Yes, James, I would enjoy walking with and speaking to you. Maybe I can catch you being authentic."

She blushed, and I guffawed. "You'll have to try harder than that to catch me," I replied, lifting my chin to the sky and slamming my fists to my hips.

Her squeak was slight, but it was there. I kept my hands on my hips and peeked at her. She burst out laughing. Giant waves of giddiness washed over her. Tears fell, and her hand reached out and took my arm as she struggled to keep her footing.

I swore to Davy Jones and his minions, I'd never wash that arm again. Tingles of excitement danced on my skin where she held me.

When our laughter subsided, she said, "Be here at five o'clock sharp."

I agreed, spun on my heel, and left.

I practically floated home. The strength of my joy must have been noticeable, as virtually every person I passed called out a gleeful welcome to me.

JAMES

*D*avi had me working the entire afternoon on two protection spells, *Castellem* and *Serverbaris*. The former meant fortress and just protected me. The latter meant safeguard and defended those over whom I cast it.

"James, these are advanced magic. They will not be simple for you to master, and you will wear messy clothing for several days."

Her maniacal chuckle meant little to me because she was continually disparaging my capabilities. Or, more to the point, my lack of capabilities.

Davi spent several minutes explaining *Serverbaris*, the safeguard of another person spell.

"James, you must gain a measure of expertise by shaping the spell away from you before you decide to cast the other upon yourself." Her dialogue continued, but my thoughts drifted out the window and disappeared into the cobalt-blue sky.

"James, have you been paying attention to me?"

"You know you don't have to call me James every time you speak? We're the only ones here. I realize you're talking to me."

"I will begin with chucklehead, or maybe *dummkopf*, or how about, *el más tonto?"* she asked, a "quit wasting my time" look written in vivid lettering across her face.

"Nope, James is fine."

"Cast your spell, then."

"Serverbaris," I shouted as I turned my hand and arms in the specified form.

I heard a raucous crack, and then a flurry of wind rushed around me. I glanced at my clothes. My shirt was backwards and mis-buttoned...behind my back. My pants were inside-out, and my shoes were on the wrong feet. But at least they were tied.

Davi laughed uproariously. She leaned forward and slapped her hand on her leg. *Smack.*

"James, you recall me saying there will be effects for miscasting a spell, don't you?"

I nodded as I held my arms away from my sides like a flapping penguin while I examined my attire.

"Well, this," she said, her hands gesturing from my head to my feet, "results from your loss of concentration. Now, try again."

I adjusted my clothes and smoothed my hair back into its perfect coif. I had hoped Davi would fix the mess for me, but no such luck. After a couple of minutes of effort, I was ready.

This time, I prepared and placed *Down With Spells* in front of me with the page opened to *Serverbaris.* Then I cast *Kinno Antim.* I'd practiced looking at my spell book at once after casting the mind-clearing spell. Since it didn't erase my memory—well, most of the time it didn't —I only needed my spell book as a backup.

"Serverbaris," I called as I closed one hand over the other fist, then pulled them open and thrusted my arms at Davi, ending with my fingers together and pointing at her.

Crack. I saw a hint of purple surround her. When I checked my attire, only my shoes were unlaced.

She nodded her head approvingly. "Not terrible, James. You have your mother's gift for abjuration."

"Abjuration?" I queried.

"Oh, I forgot. I'm talking to the human dodo. How many fucking times should I repeat myself? This is the grouping of protection spells. Is that better?"

"All new, remember? I've hardly been doing this for a couple of days. I'll get it right," I declared.

"You had better. If you do not, you are only jeopardizing the survival of everybody you love," she said.

"No pressure on me," I replied sourly.

She cleansed herself of the spell, and I cast it again. After performing this single spell for more than an hour, she ordered an end.

"James, I suspect you are getting worse. Let us turn to another spell for you to butcher. This one is *Castellem*. It is a fortress spell and shields you. From now on, you must cast it before you undertake to protect another. You cannot help them if you perish because you were too dumb to shield yourself first."

"Why?"

"Because their protection, as with every other spell you shape, will end upon your death," she said without emotion.

"Got it."

I turned to the next spell in *Down With Spells*. Again, the book realized which spell I'd need and opened to *Castellem*.

This one worked much like the last—it would cast at my first thought. So I needed a clear sense of what I was doing before shaping it.

The hand movements were vastly different. This one began with two fists meeting at my chest. Then my fingers opened as if I were dropping an orange. One hand rotated face up, the other face down, fingers together, palms flat. The palm-up hand moved past the top of my head, the other pushed down toward my feet hard, like I was trying to force something into the ground. Which, according to Davi, was exactly what I was doing.

Apparently, the result of miscasting was the same as *Serverbaris*. This time, my clothes wound up in worse condition. When I saw my underwear on the outside of my pants, I flashed back to the Shellback Ceremony the first time I sailed across the equator. That was a memorable day.

Dang, no wonder I kept making mistakes, with my mind drifting like it does.

After another hour of practice, I better understood the movements and started casting it correctly, although Davi was quick to point out my mistakes.

"James, you did not move your hand up to the top of your head. You stopped midway through your face. I doubt anything worth saving exists in the space above your eyes. Still, no need to take a chance. So take the split second and move your fucking hand above your head. Okay?"

At four-thirty, I halted the practice. "I'm going to change clothes."

Looking at my wardrobe, I'd tied together my shoes and my pants were on backwards—again. Several buttons had popped off and littered my floor.

"Do not trouble yourself." At that, she gyrated her middle and index fingers in the air as she pointed them at me. With another rush of wind, my clothes turned inside out and changed colors. In moments, I was wearing a fresh crimson shirt and cobalt pants. My boots were gleaming black, as was my belt. I carried a sprig of lilac and sunflowers in one hand, and in the other, a brand-new tricorn hat that matched my trousers.

I looked in the mirror that she'd materialized and that floated in front of me. I had to admit, Davi had hit the mark with her choices. Well, except for the flowers.

"Davi, you made me adjust my clothes every time I messed up a spell. Why didn't you fix it for me if it was this simple?"

"You remember, I am your guide, not your mender? It's also fun to watch you struggling to tie your shoes correctly."

It wasn't worth the effort to argue with my tiny tormentor, so I ignored her insult and focused on what she did that helped me.

"Thank you for the change of clothing. The flowers are out of place, though. It's November, and we've not had flowers for a couple of months now."

She wrenched them from my grip with another flick of her wrist and replaced them with a small wooden box filled with chocolate truffles.

"Again, thank you very much." I didn't know what else to add, so I reached out to offer her a hug.

"If you fucking touch me, I will blast your balls into tiny scraps," she said, although her tone was mirthful and contained none of the malice I would have expected.

I hugged her. She stiffened before she brought one hand to my shoulder and patted it once.

"You are welcome. Now get your fucking hands off me."

I did.

I had to give it to Davi. Her choice of clothing was impeccable. I rarely considered my attire. In fact, I owned many copies of the same shirts—mostly a light golden tan with gold braiding near the cuffs.

As I hustled to see my perfect María at the hospital, I stepped higher, more confidently. Nope—my feet didn't touch the ground. I floated the entire distance. Along the road, I waved and called out dozens of hellos and afternoons. I doffed my cap as many times, and even said a hurried hello to Susan Bonds.

When I arrived, I removed my cover, tucked it under my arm, and confidently strode through the open doorway. After all, today I'd be escorting perfection, a date with my destiny. Which was odd for me to consider, since I'd never fancied marriage.

Most of my friends, except Presley, had pushed me to find a wife, especially Kate. I suspect Presley's disinterest in my romantic life had more to do with Kate's wish to find me a partner than any real indifference on his part. She'd arranged no less than a half-dozen ladies for me to marry—yes, marry. While each had been pleasant, none fired my passions, nor bewitched my bones the way María did.

I paused inside the doorway and looked around. Across the room, a nurse glanced in my direction. She patted her patient on his shoulder and, after holding a hand up to me in the recognized "wait" gesture, spun and shuffled away.

My eyes accompanied the young nurse across the hospital and recognized María with her back to me. She turned and greeted me with her exquisite smile. My heart leaped, and my breathing came in pants as she sashayed toward me. My vision blurred as if something had trapped me inside a tunnel and María were the only light. Even in her smock, I couldn't take my eyes off her. Each stride was seductive, each arm swing inviting.

As she neared, I reflexively held out the box of candies. She never looked at it, but received it with one hand before tucking it under her arm. Unfortunately, I'd been so captivated by her approach that I hadn't noticed my expression, a fact I only recognized when she reached up with her other hand and touched the bottom of my chin, pushing my mouth closed.

I brightened as the blood flushed my face. She laughed, but didn't break eye contact.

I hauled in a sharp sigh and extended her my arm, and she rewarded me with her touch.

"Hello, James. May I call you Jim?" she asked.

Most everyone called me James. The guys on the *Monarch* used Captain. A few shortened it to Cap'n. But I enjoyed being called James. It was one of the Apostles' names.

"Hello, María. And of course you may call me Jim. I only let certain people use that, you know?" I said.

"Really? Why is that?" she asked coyly.

"Well, James is what I used growing up, and it stuck. Your cousin and my best friend's wife call me Jimmy, I suppose because I've known them most of my life. Plus, have you ever argued with either of them? Even if I told them to call me James, they'd refuse out of spite."

"Yes, they can both be stubborn," she added with another giggle.

We shared the laugh as we walked from the hospital. Her uncle's home was on the far side of the market. We should have passed its edge near the township's border. I wanted to spend more time with her, though, so I led her through the fruit market. She noticed.

"Do you always roam around the melons to get to your peach?" she questioned, looking up at me from the corner of one eye, a sly smirk touching her lips.

"It usually results in the greatest satisfaction," I replied smoothly. Mirth filled her giggle. My insides turned to jelly.

"Jim, you said you were helping Kate Doss. With what?"

On one hand, this topic was strictly off-limits. Alternatively, María is logical, analytical, and inarguably a genius. If I ever needed to be grounded in facts, it was dealing with Eldritch Manor. Besides, she'd asked, and if a beautiful woman asks for personal details, you give them. That's a rule of temptation and chemistry––just in case any of you guys wanted my advice, which you should. I'm just saying.

"What do you know of the history of Eldritch Manor?" I asked.

"Only rumor and conjecture. I have never visited," she said.

"It's as creepy as you've heard. But I bet you didn't know that many of those who've disappeared have almost identical statues of them in odd places throughout the grounds. A few of the latter ones have deteriorated into powder; while others, many decades older, appear as if something chiseled them yesterday."

"Are they made from the same stone? Because if they are not..." She didn't finish as she slipped into thought.

"The stone is the same. Besides, each base survives, and every one is still flawless. No, it's not the material or construction. There is something, though."

A few moments of silence passed with only the gelid breeze gliding past, raising the dust in our path. The brilliant sapphire sky remained, despite the lateness of the day.

"María, Kate asked me to figure out the odd occurrences out there. Her father is growing old. I agreed I'd do my best to present her an answer. You've got a brilliant mind. I could use your logic and scientific approach. What do you say?"

She didn't respond, and we continued to wander. I kept the pace slow. Even if she ruled against helping, I loved breathing her air.

"What could I offer? I do not believe in the supernatural. Logically, there must be a cause. It simply needs to be discovered," she said.

"I'll take that as a yes," I retorted, and pulled her to me. She laid her head onto my arm before turning and searching my eyes.

"Yes, Jim. I will help you."

"You know, it's a short walk from your uncle's house. I could escort you and show you the grounds, and then we could discuss what we see over dinner."

"Okay," was her simple answer. She took a quicker stride. I had to adjust mine to stay with her. She'd determined her destination and tugged me to follow.

20

UNNAMED OMNISCIENT PRESENCE

*D*ahl had been steadily walking south, following the dim golden pathway. Along the way, he murdered three foxes and a rabbit, for which he paid his simple penance, burning another scar and a fresh tattoo for each victim.

After a while, his route took him to a worn, potholed road. He avoided roads. Roads meant people, people meant exposure, and exposure meant he'd likely have to execute someone.

The woman who approached him was ancient. She trudged forward, bowed by age and fragility. She leaned heavily on her walking stick. As she approached, her silver-topped head tipped up and her olive eyes engaged Dahl. She froze and reached out a gnarled and shaking hand for her equally ancient companion. She missed several times and only just grabbed his coat, drawing him to a stop. The elderly man tugged the reins of the mule he was leading. The creaking wagon stopped as the beast halted.

She pointed an overlong finger at Dahl and shrieked, "Demon!"

Dahl's eyes widened, but not in fear, for he no longer feared. This was rage at the pointing biddy and resentment for this forced action. Dahl remembered being named Demon years ago. He'd never forget the terrible beatings at the hands of the temple priests after each accusation.

The man scowled at Dahl and reached for something inside his coat.

The aged woman, following his movements, pleaded, "Give ta road to the creature. Lets 'im catch t'other!"

Dahl would later recall the tired woman throwing herself in front of her companion as the heavy stone he had levitated crushed them both.

He hid their remains, then struggled to stash the crimes inside a vague fantasy. Forgetting didn't work. He couldn't forget. No matter how deeply he buried the memory, some aspect of him compelled him to replay each death, a terrible repetition that grew with each homicide.

"Didn't she call me Demon?" It didn't matter.

"She cast her vile accusation, right?" It didn't matter.

"Is this another dream?" It didn't matter anymore.

He'd just add it to his lengthy register of sins. A file that confirmed his filth as a being.

These two were part of the price he had to pay to return home. Besides, Dahl needed their mule. They had to die. Yes, their deaths were unavoidable because he needed their animal.

As darkness grew, so did his appetite for the artifact. So strong was its pull that its light spoke to him.

Dahl rested and meditated. Inside his meditative dreams, he discovered a mind, brilliant and inflamed by the fire of intelligence.

He cast his enchantment.

21

JAMES

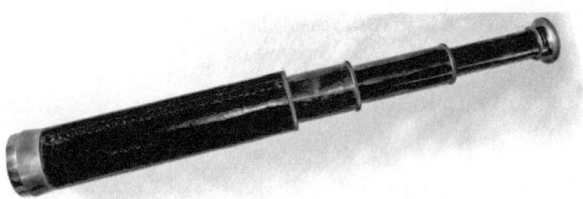

María and I strolled to the old mansion. As we approached the property, she paused, then examined several of the disintegrated statues. At each, a simple plinth, unaffected by deterioration, survived.

"James, this place rests on a precipice above the ocean. It shouldn't be surprising that stone would yield to the ravages of salt, rain, and wind."

A breeze gusted, and I held onto my hat. The wind lulled, but grew. On the horizon, lightning flashed, and clouds darkened the ocean.

"Let me show you something inside the house," I told her.

I'd grown wary of my visits here and wanted her out of the weather.

"Okay." Her tone had lost the sureness it had as we walked here.

The manor maintained the bones of its former opulence, but age and neglect had turned it into a decrepit bower. At its front, a circular carriageway was bounded by a U-shaped colonnade of Greek columns. This was where the wealthy had arrived--decades ago. We followed the gravel passage. Sounds of rocks crunched underfoot, and the wind whistled.

The heavy door to the mansion appeared repaired. It was exactly as it had been when I visited it the other day. I saw no indication of repair, let alone damage.

"I expect you won't believe this, but I saw this door get shattered. I guess it was in a dream. But I watched…" I trailed off.

"How could you have witnessed it?" she asked, doubt filling her manner.

I tugged open my tunic, revealing the lacerations on my shoulder.

"Jim, that wasn't a dream," she admonished as she studied the cuts. "Why didn't you come see me? You should have had these washed and sewn."

A flash, brighter than the previous one. One, two, three…I counted to seven. I felt a drop of rain. Maybe it was ocean water whipped up from the whitecaps near the base of the cliff.

"If you recall, you weren't talking to me," I needled. "Besides, it must have been a dream. I remember going to bed and—what else could it have been? Still, it seemed real, though I couldn't have seen the…"

I trailed off, not wanting to unnerve her needlessly. Searching her eyes for common ground, I discovered the dread I'd hoped to avoid.

Several flashes…two, three, four. The roar of thunder was deep, the kind that causes butterflies in your gut.

"María, I need to get you inside the manor. I don't have time to take you home."

"It will be fine, Jim. We will wait inside for the storm to pass," she responded, her confidence renewed.

I shoved the door, which was as large as I remembered. Unlike my dream, there were no lights inside to keep us from stumbling. Fragments of wood littered the floor. We remained near the door as our eyes adapted to the dim interior.

Long ago, I'd learned always to be prepared for any scenario. I spotted an Indian clay oil lamp in an alcove near the door. I had traveled to many parts of the earth, including the Far East. While there, I'd found sticks that produced corn-kernel sized flames. The merchant called them fire-inch-sticks. I carried three, each inside its own small box, with tufts of cotton stuffed onto the top to protect them from accidents.

Removing a fire-inch-stick, I scraped it against the wall. It burst into a flame, which I used to light the oil lamp.

"James, how did you do that?"

"It was a handy trick, wasn't it? I've got a few others, and when I take you home, I'll explain them to you. You'll love it." I preferred she ignore the strange storm.

The meager light of the oil lamp offered little luminosity to the room. The bursts of lightning grew more frequent and displayed more. Still, the tiny flame was sufficient to keep the gloom at bay.

The fireplace was located where I recalled. I picked up splintered wood from the floor and started a modest fire. Its light produced a glow enveloping the hearth, but this chamber was enormous. The blackness surrounding the distant wall and ceiling only faded into a deep gray.

A clock, as carefully preserved as I remembered, ticked on the far wall. The noise wasn't as noticeable as in my dream.

A flash. One, two, th...*BOOM!* The windows rattled before they returned to playing with the gale.

The clock chimed the top of the hour. *Gong!*

I watched my accidental guest. She stood ramrod straight, as if made of steel. She was scanning the gloom.

"That clock over there." I pointed and waited while she followed my finger.

Gong!

"It was in that same dream. It's just as I remember. But the stairs... and the railing's intact."

Gong!

"In my dream, something had crushed it."

I stopped before I gave her too much detail. I caught her side-glance before I shrugged.

Gong!

"It looks like a common clock, and the railing doesn't look repaired," María said.

"Agreed. But how could I have known? Unless I dreamt about it."

Gong!

"Jim, you have been a family friend for your lifetime. You simply recalled it during your dream. That isn't odd. Well, except for your pitiful logical leaps. They could be an issue."

She concluded by punching me playfully in the arm. I noticed she took care to avoid the shoulder where I'd shown her the scratches. I reveled in her playfulness.

"Alright, in my…"

Flash. *Boom!*

The clock had finished its chiming.

"…dream, I climbed the stairs to the room at the top. Inside, on the left is a niche."

This time, I pointed to the nook where I'd found the oil lamp.

"Inside were the waxy remnants of a candle. A mirror was leaning against the wall nearest the door. Right of the door was a massive spiderweb. And straight ahead as you enter was a window behind a bronze spyglass mounted on a stand."

She stared at me, wide-eyed, before following my arm as I indicated the top of the darkened stair.

"Let us have a look, shall we?" She started for the steps and climbed four of them before I realized she was really going.

I caught up, taking care to place my hand in front of the flame to protect it from the breeze generated from me hurrying to catch her. The treads groaned under my weight. She moved up the stairs with grace, her steps barely enticing the softest squeak.

Flash. *BOOM! BOOM!* Rain fell in giant drops. They were heavy and patted against the hard-tiled roof.

Small amounts of plaster flaked off the ceiling and fell onto the steps in front of us. The floating dust gained new allies.

We reached the top and I walked directly to the room, holding my light in front. On my left were the remnants of the dead candle. To my right, several spiders scurried from the light as others watched. I barely noticed the mirror. Its contents were a secret I wasn't ready to share with her yet.

To my front was the window. It was open, and the wind was blowing sheets of rain through, drenching the floor. I walked to it, fighting with the wisps of curtains, and slammed it shut.

The tripod stood as I remembered. But it was empty.

Wind wailed at the walls of the once-great manor. Glass hammered against its wooden casements. The lightning flashed, brightened, dimmed, and repeated. It was nature's perpetual motion and enchanting.

Past the empty tripod out the glass window, I saw movement. I stared. Not again.

Another flash. I was deaf. The red eyes stared back at me. The great maleficent beast continued its march. It never blinked and never looked away. I didn't need to watch it, because I knew where it was going.

"I need to get you to safety. You need to trust..." I turned as I spoke, struggling to rip my eyes from the glass. When I did, I found myself alone.

"María?"

She hadn't followed me.

22

UNNAMED OMNISCIENT PRESENCE

*D*eep in his meditative trance, Dahl watched a dark-haired woman walk along a balcony into a darkened corridor, turn right, and continue walking. She traced a finger along the wall as she moved through darkness. He knew where she was. Finally, he had arrived.

At the end of the hall, she entered a suite. Its only contents were a meticulously tidy bed, pillows placed with mechanical accuracy, a worn rocking chair that faced giant glass doors to a terrace, and finally, a dusty crystal cup resting on a deteriorated and crooked nightstand.

Outside, another flash of lightning burned a wrinkled line across the sky. In that light, a monster moved. It was large and had grey plates imitating scales, covering its entire body. It turned and looked at her. Malevolence poured through its red eyes. She looked away, unconcerned.

The booming thunder had become musical. It played as if it were leading soldiers into battle.

A third doorway excited to an anteroom. Inside was a relic pretending to be a baby crib, its bedding old and moth-eaten. A small toy boat lay in the middle of the bed, its paint as brilliant as if it were new.

The woman didn't recognize the room's discontinuities, but he did —he saw the torn curtains, counterposed by delicately papered walls, and the freshly waxed floor neutralized by a cracked ceiling and missing trim.

She was after an object, but she was uncertain what it was. She would have to explore. Then it called her.

"*Touye, lavi.*"

"*Fluye de la muerte.*"

She shoved the crib aside. It screeched, then collapsed as it banged into the wall. It was out of her way, though.

"*Touye, la...*"

"*Fluye de la muerte!*"

She started tearing at the wall, ripping loose chunks of plaster and lath. If any piece resisted, she beat her fists against it until it broke loose. She pulled off the baseboard, then began digging at the floor.

BOOM! Lightning streaked, burning daylight into the storm.

A shadow skulked into the chamber and crossed the bed. Another flash. Now the shadow stood against the wall in the anteroom. It disappeared as the bolt faded.

23

JAMES

I knew where María was, and ran after her.

"María!" I yelled into the unnerving blackness.

Since I couldn't carry my tiny flickering flame as I ran, I dropped it. Its small fire extinguished before it even reached the floor.

The clock chimed the quarter hour.

The beast from my dream was here. Was it after me or María?

I didn't care. I had one mission: save the woman I adored. She was the only one I ever loved. I barely knew her. Still, I'd always loved her.

Doors banged. I raced toward the racket. At the end of the hall, I bounced off the wall, and, pivoting off my shoulder, I turned right and shot toward the noise.

Lightning lit the hallway. I followed two tracks, one on top of the other. One was a shorter foot than mine and carried a narrow gait, dragging a path in the dust between strides. A second, larger print ghosted over the first. It reminded me of impressions my feet formed in the snow when I wore my fur-covered boots. My mind couldn't reconcile the two prints, one on top of the other. Why would anybody go with her and match her stride for stride?

At the end of the corridor was a heavy ten-foot-tall oak door. After they went in, the last person had shut it behind them. Whoever it was had locked themselves inside with María.

I flung my weight against it, crashing hard, repeatedly. The great oaken door groaned, but held. I braced myself against the edge of the hall. With one foot planted against it, I launched myself at the wooden obstacle. The casing near the latch creaked before it tore loose.

As the door banged open, I heard a second crack. Excruciating pain stabbed into my right shoulder, and I crumbled to the floor. My arm went numb and hung limply at my side as I pushed myself to my knees, and throbbing pulses of pain shot from my shoulder to my fingertips as I stood. I had to ignore the torture and find my love.

After a few seconds, I could feel tingling from my fingers. While I stretched my hand, rotated my wrist, and bent my elbow, I searched the darkened room. The blackness inside was total, and only broken by flashes of lightning strobing their dazzling brilliance across the once-alabaster walls. After several flares, it was obvious she wasn't here.

Two doors remained for me to explore. There were ten-foot-high glass ones that allowed access to the terrace. This balcony overlooked the broad carriageway at the front of the residence. Lightning flashed. The veranda was empty.

Inside the room, I swung to the smaller wooden door—small compared to the ten-foot entry. Still, it was eight feet tall and three feet wide, and, like the other, built from oak. Peeling paint covered the bulky wooden casing. Feeling that going through it was the fastest, I flung myself at it with my left shoulder. This door, as strong as stone, was unyielding as I hit it.

The clock chimed the half hour.

I ended my ineffectual attack and hunted for something to beat it open as lightning flashed repeatedly. I flew to the glass doors opening to the balcony, threw them open, and ran outside into the storm. Five feet off the terrace was a single window that opened to María.

Five feet may as well have been five miles. My shoulder wasn't working, and a small stone ledge was the only foothold, while the thin wooden window casing provided the only handhold.

Still, it was my only way in. I shinnied onto the stone ledge, rain and sleet wetting my hands and feet. As I climbed, I held onto the stanchion, anchoring the railing with my left hand, and forced my aching right arm into the air to grab the wooden casing above the window. The grinding in my shoulder was matched by a painful stabbing. Ignoring pain has saved my life on two occasions. This time, I hoped I could save another.

Through the gale, I heard rising and falling tones as the clock marked the three-quarter-hour mark.

I swung my left arm up, grabbed the small handhold, and held on tightly until I regained my inner stability. I inched my fingers across their slippery hold and slid my feet across the slick stone ledge. One fingerbreadth at a time, I edged toward the window. After several agonizing minutes of stabbing pain, pelting rain, blinding lightning, and roaring thunder, I reached the middle of the window, smashed through the glass, and rolled onto the dusty floor.

María was frantically prying floorboards free and tossing them aside. Her manic movements caused her to appear as if she were digging a pit into the wooden floor. She seized a sizable chunk of wood and wrenched it with both hands. It broke free, and she dove for the opening.

Lightning flashed again. I saw the giant beast's shadow on the wall behind my love. It stooped its colossal frame over her.

I lunged, grabbed both of her hands, and pulled them to my chest as I rolled her away from the hole.

I heard horrifying screams, partially from María and partially from something else. It was as if hell had opened, spewing forth the lamentations of the cursed.

"James..." was all she said before she went limp in my arms.

Inside a box under the floor, its lid torn free, was the missing spyglass, gleaming in the bursts of lightning. I left it.

I moved her near to the fire in the vast chamber at the bottom of the stairs and settled her in my lap until she woke. She had shredded her fingers and hands from digging at the floor. I dressed her wounds as best I could.

The clock rang at the top of the hour, tolling six times.

The storm abated, then passed. As it weakened, María strengthened.

"James, what happened? Who was that man?" she pleaded.

"There wasn't a man. We're the only ones here. I found you inside a room at the end of the hall. You went when I tried showing you my, um, dream."

"I remember a man. He asked me to get him something—a knife, I think. He said it was stolen from him and hidden in the room," she said.

"María, Eldritch Manor is unusual. Many oddities have happened here. Remember, that's why we came? I'm just grateful you weren't hurt worse."

She lifted her bandaged hands to her face and examined them. "How did I hurt my hands?"

"You were prying open a hole in the floor. It looked like you had tried several spots. I found you as you tried to pull a board free."

She stared at her hands; her mouth hung open as if she wanted to speak. Then she closed it and cried.

I pulled her close and held her until she stopped sobbing.

"I need to get you home before another storm blows in," I said.

24

JAMES

*T*he next day, I roused and stomped downstairs. Davi waited in her armchair, hot porridge cooling on her lap and a cup of tea steaming on the dinner table in front of her. She peered up at me with that annoying, inscrutable smile.

"Hello, James. Did you have a pleasant evening?" she asked without shifting her smirk.

"You bloody well know how my evening was," I answered as I worked to manage my temper.

"Please, James, describe precisely what transpired. It is essential."

In an instant, her smirk disappeared, dislodged by wrinkled brows and pursed lips.

At least she pretended my information was important. My temper ebbed, and I shifted from *fire a broadside* to *man the cannons*.

"Either Dahl or that monster played with María as if she were a marionette. She shut herself behind two locked doors inside the master's chamber, then started digging at the floorboards. I found her as she was attempting to snatch something hidden under the floor."

"What was it?" Davi asked as she leaned forward, eyes wide in anticipation.

"Again, you know precisely what it was. Don't you?"

My temper flared white hot. Without awaiting her reply to my rhetorical challenge, I pressed on. "Tell me what would have happened if she grabbed that thing."

I slapped my palms onto the table and leaned toward her. The impact sent searing pain shooting through my shoulder. I grimaced and clenched my right arm, cradling it to my chest. I bent my head away from her, hiding the pain emblazoned across my face.

To her credit, she didn't blink at the crack of my rage. Her eyes never left mine, but there was an unmistakable shift toward understanding. She considered me for several seconds, keeping her ambiguous smile, as if it were both a shield and a sword.

"James, I cannot answer with perfect certainty," Davi said.

"That's blooming rubbish, and you realize it. You don't have to be one-hundred-percent confident. But, by gosh, you will tell me what you think. Otherwise, you can get another bobolyne for your game!" I howled.

I was angrier than I'd been in years. Yes, I realized I barely knew María, but I adored her, and I'd do everything to defend her. And what had happened to her scared me nearly to tears.

"The domain created by Tituba may have consumed her. But I am sure Dahl charmed her, giving her enough protection to carry the artifact to him." Her description carried much more zeal than it should have.

I hung my head. Either Davi didn't realize the danger María was in, or she didn't care. "If you put her in danger or allow her to be placed in harm's way again, I'll quit helping you. Do you understand?" I demanded, watching the fireplace instead of my so-called guide.

"James, you are not helping me. I am helping you. Besides, I did not control last evening's events. You chose to take her to Eldritch. Also, I suggested steps you must take to safeguard her. Unless you completed your wand without notifying me, you still have that little milestone to carry out."

She was correct, and I realized it. She had outlined how to protect María, and high on that list was finishing my wand.

"You're right. I'm sorry. I let my passions get the better of me. So,

I've got two goals now: finish my wand and buy Eldritch," I acknowl-edged, pillowing my injured right arm with my left.

"James, your first task is to purchase the manor. You must put as many barriers between it and your friend Kate as you can," she intoned without a hint of scorn.

My misplaced anger spent, I had no choice. I had to beat Dahl and that demon. Last night showed me I hadn't been working hard enough. I decided that had to change.

"Right. I'm off to visit Kate."

"No," she commanded.

This surprised me. We had just agreed on what steps I needed to take. Thankfully, she recognized my confusion and spoke.

"I do not fucking have time for your body to heal. Besides, you are awfully dumb and unlikely to fix it yourself."

Oddly, I was pleased her usual snark had returned. She placed her porridge bowl––still steaming, by the way––on the counter and rose. She brought her hands through a complex pattern and launched a ball of green energy at me.

As the jade ball touched my shoulder, the pain dissolved. I relin-quished the vice-like grip of my left hand holding my right arm in place and tried moving the injured joint. The pain was gone. I whirled through its complete range, thrilled at the swift renewal.

"Now you can fucking go," Davi said as she slid back into her armchair and plucked up her dish of steaming porridge. She smiled cordially, satisfied with her skill.

"Davi, I don't mean to sound ungrateful, but can you fix María's hands?" I pleaded.

"I healed them while she dreamed. She will not recall the injuries," Davi said.

I exhaled a giant breath I didn't realize I was holding. "Thanks, Davi. I'll be back."

I scampered for the door and ran to Kate and Presley's house. On the slim chance Kate would go to her grandfather's house, I had to hustle.

Kate was accustomed to me knocking on her door for breakfast. I had dined with her and Presley as often as I ate at my house. When I thumped on her door, she only smiled as she opened it.

"Is Presley here?" I inquired.

He was. I had heard him shuffling around upstairs, and was only making polite conversation with the question.

"Yes, he is. Now, get on with it, Jimmy. What is it you want?" she asked.

I laughed and looked at my feet before gazing straight at her. I took in an audibly deep breath before I spoke. "Ok. I want to buy Eldritch Manor from you. It's been a trouble for ages. I haven't figured it out. The further I've looked into it, the more alarmed I get. Kate, I've got to own it so I can manage what takes place. With Presley gone as often as he is...well, I'll be able..."

I spoke rapidly and didn't breathe in. I only quit speaking because I ran out of words and because I didn't really have a compelling reason to buy it. At least, not one that didn't include magic, monsters, or a homicidal trans-dimensional being bent on returning home at the cost of all life on Earth.

I stood at the bottom of her steps, my mouth still hanging open, staring at her. Kate took pity on me. "Jimmy, stop! I understand. If you need it, you can have it. Give me $750 gold, drop your investigation fee, and keep me advised of your progress. If you quit working, I'll take it back," she said and stuck out her hand.

"Kate, you're letting me have it for far less than it's worth. The land itself is worth five times that."

"Not to me. Not to my family. You have forgotten what it has done to my entire family." At that, tears brimmed in her green eyes and threatened to spill onto her freckled cheeks.

"I'm sorry, Katie. My attorney will draw up the paperwork," I said, hoping to thwart her tears.

"I trust you, Jim. That's why I pleaded for you to help and not the police." She perked up, stood straighter, and beamed. "Now, do you want breakfast?"

Only a fool would turn down Kate Varde's cooking. She's a wizard in the galley.

When I returned home, I explained my agreement with Kate to Davi. You'd think she would congratulate me on finishing one of her important tasks. You would be wrong. Nope, she perched on her chair as if I'd reported my cow farted.

"Good. It is about fucking time."

My mouth gaped.

"Close your mouth or flies will fly inside and devour what inconsiderable brain matter remains inside your thick skull," she said.

I did.

"James, tell Miss Doss never to visit that house again."

"Ok, why? And her last name is Varde now. She married Presley more than a year ago," I answered, adding the last part to annoy her.

"That is irrelevant, and nobody gives a damn. The land and house are unsafe. So why the fuck are you asking me? You whined that your precious María was in danger less than an hour ago."

"Good point. Charles, her father, has lived there his whole life."

I stopped speaking when I saw her eyes sparkle. Tears filled them as the edges of her mouth sagged. She stood and turned her back to me. Her hand lifted to her eyes before she faced me.

"I appreciate that what I will say will sound heartless, James. I do not suggest it without concern for the consequences. Mr. Doss is a venerated man, but that relic has debased him. Trust me when I say he must return to Eldritch again." As she spoke, her tone softened and became compassionate.

"Why?" I asked, nervous I wouldn't like her answer.

She rolled her eyes and answered. "Because Dahl must conclude he is executing the landowner. I have reviewed Mr. Doss's will. After his death, it sets forth that his estate '...will pass to all who have gone before.' Charles Doss has willed Eldritch to every member of his family who have already perished."

She spoke haltingly, like a mother explaining to little Billy why he can't have a sweet, mistakenly believing if the lad only understood her answer, she could avert his tantrum. It was patronizing and altogether proper—unfortunately.

"Okaaay," I hesitated, confused about how she knew what was in Mr. Doss's will.

"James, do not attempt to understand why. It is magic —remember?"

I expect she left out "dumbass" by accident.

She continued, "You must warn Miss Doss—Varde—not to notify anyone you have acquired the estate. She must record it on the day required, no earlier. I have read your county charters, and that date is October 31st."

"Fine. I still don't understand how this will help us," I said, implying a question I purposely left dangling between us.

"Holy shit, you can be fucking dense sometimes. Dahl can only take it if we give it or if it is unowned. He tried to force María to recover it for him. Also, you need time to create your wand and learn the magic to thwart him."

"All I have to do is let my best friend's father-in-law get murdered," I replied dryly.

She didn't acknowledge the bait and kept talking.

"We must prepare for our battle with Dahl and that beast inside the relic. After Mr. Doss has passed, your enemy will await the reading of Charles's will. It will make clear that Ms. Varde does not control the manor. Dahl will not have another target, gaining us precious time."

"I don't like it. There should be an alternative," I repeated.

"James, you do not get to have your fucking way in everything. Your task is defending those around you, so put your big-boy pants on and stop the jibber-jabber. Besides, he is drawing closer, and we are running out of time."

My shoulders slumped in disappointment. Davi was right, and I despised myself for it.

We finished the morning and worked into the early afternoon practicing protection abjurations and several illusion spells. One of them was a charm Davi said I should place on the artifact to obscure its whereabouts from Dahl. But, since he was a powerful sorcerer in his own right, I couldn't completely mask it, so she taught me another to help mislead him. Using it, I could charm dozens of common items to shed the same energy as his artifact.

I hoped he couldn't force anyone to bring everything to him.

25

JAMES

*T*he clock in my living room chimed the half-hour. It was three-thirty. My head and arms hung limp with exhaustion. Even though I wasn't physically exerting myself, I was as drained as I'd ever been. I normally delighted in outworking everyone else, but spellcasting consumed my energy more surely than any manual labor.

"James, you have magic inside you. You utilize it to cast spells. When you do, it drains your magical reserves. Those reserves must be replaced from the magic held inside your world. Also, we do not call it magic reserves; we say manna," Davi said.

"So, I can empty my magic—I mean manna?" I asked.

"Sure. For you, it is easy. It will grow more difficult after you have your wand. Its manna reserves will be accessible for you to spend. Plus, the more you exercise, the larger your manna reserve will become."

"Kind of like using regular muscles, then?" My voice trilled up to a disguised question.

"Absolutely."

"Is this why you have me practicing…" Banging on my door interrupted my question.

"James, we must speak." Fear seeped from each syllable. But the voice of an angel carried that panic to my ears.

A sudden burst of energy rushed through me. I gaped at Davi, my eyes flashing to the stairs. I hoped she'd accept my hint and hide upstairs until María left. She rolled her eyes, a physical idiom she used repeatedly in our interactions. Still, she forced herself out of her cushioned armchair and slipped to the stairs.

"Coming," I yelled as I lingered for the tiny blonde she-devil to ascend the stairs.

I scuffed my way to the door, smacking my knee into my rocker as I did. "Ouch!" I growled under my breath.

"Dumbass," was the retort from the top of the stairs.

When I reached the door, I hesitated before tugging it open. I used that briefest delay to pull in a cleansing breath and rub my knee. Slowly, I exhaled, then opened the door. As I held it with one hand, I blocked her view inside with my frame. I didn't trust that little demon, Davi. Knowing her, she'd cheerfully turn this into a disaster for a laugh.

My Spanish beauty wasn't waiting for me to welcome her inside. She dodged under my outstretched arm and bumped her way through. After she passed through the doorway, she jerked me inside and slammed it behind her.

"James, what took place at Eldritch Manor yesterday—what happened to me? Why can't I recall it?" She asked her questions hurriedly, her eyes wide and her brow tight. She gripped my shirt with both hands, a threat and pleading intertwined.

I put my hands onto hers and peered into her eyes. She relaxed and freed my shirt. I recognized her fingers and palms were healed, and I glanced toward the top of the stairs and Davi.

"Let's sit, okay?" I asked, gesturing to the chairs in my galley. She took my rocker, the one I used when Davi was scolding—I mean teaching—me.

First, I considered the pink armchair, decided against it, and then tugged a chair from the dinner table, flipped it around backwards, and sat.

"María, I can't explain precisely what happened because I'm not sure. Do you remember following me upstairs?"

"I saw you enter the spider-room. Then…" She wavered, touched both closed fists to her temples, and flared open her hands like she was explaining an explosion. "…nothing until I woke beside the fire," she finished.

"Okay. Let me tell you what I did."

She nodded, rocked forward with her palms on her knees, but didn't speak.

I sighed—again—before continuing. "I stepped inside the spider-room. Rain was streaming in by this time, so I tugged the window shut."

I hesitated, expecting her to speak.

She remained stone-faced, wide-eyed, and mute. She blinked, then her eyes narrowed and she sat up straighter and spoke.

"When did the rain begin?"

"Oh, I'm not positive. I heard thunder before we came inside. But the lightning was on the horizon. It got to us fast, though. The rain was torrential by the time I closed the window. The lightning was close too. I shut it, spun around to say something, and you were gone. I raced after you. You…"

"Wait, where did I go?" she interrupted again.

"To the master's chamber at the end of the hall. Well, a room beside it, but you had to go through the master's bedroom. I guess you used the flashes of lightning to find your way. They were coming fast by that time."

María stared at me, her lips spread, her eyes twinkling in the firelight.

I paused, partly because she drew me into her big brown eyes, and somewhat because the balance of this tale was impossible. Unfortunately for María, I'm a talented liar. As Captain of a privateer and rebel turncoat, it was an essential skill. It was likewise suitable for gambling, which I also enjoyed.

"Well, I found you laying there. I brought you downstairs, lit a fire, and you woke. Nothing odd, except you couldn't remember what happened," I lied. If I had any magical skill to conceal my lies, it didn't work.

"Bullshit. *Mierda. No te creo.* Do not deceive me, James Byrne. You started the fire before we went upstairs," she declared.

She wasn't angry...yet. But she plainly hadn't bought an ounce of what I was peddling.

Then, a white robed, blonde-haired, blue-eyed demon strode confidently down the stairs and inserted herself into the heart of my life again. When she paused on the landing three steps above us, I swear her blonde hair waved away from her face as if caught in a delicate breeze.

"Dang," I said, and I dropped my forehead to my forearms, which rested across the backrest of my chair.

"Your sister? Right," María said, scorn dripping from each syllable.

"Well..." I started before Davi interrupted me.

"I am Davi, and an acquaintance of James, nothing more. I am here to aid him with a problem. María, that old mansion carries a secret. If I expressed it publicly, you would say I was mad, so I only speak of it with James. I am sorry, María; I will not allow him to speak with you further without your guarantee that you will protect, as secret, all you learn. This mystery you must bear to your grave."

Davi stood stock-still, hands locked onto her hips, staring at the eventual mother of my children. She had made her position clear, and either María would agree or she wouldn't. Davi didn't seem to care.

María was an equally determined woman. She stopped rocking and leaned forward in her chair as if she were preparing to escape both from it and my life. My eyes darted to her, then back to Davi.

One painful lesson I'd learned was that when two women are arguing, I should stay the heck out of it. Fortunately, I listened to my experience and remained mute.

"If you explain what is happening at that manor, I agree." Then she looked at me. "If you lie..." She trailed off, leaving the threat hanging by a thread, kind of like my hoped-for relationship with the amber-eyed beauty.

"Deal!" I blurted before Davi could interject.

Aaannddd that was a mistake. You know that expression on your mom's face when you've farted in church? Yep, that's the one Davi gave me. The daggers she threw in her frown would've wilted most men.

Luckily, I wasn't most men. I'd found what I wanted: a raven-haired lass standing, mouth parted, lips wetted by her tongue.

"*I agree*," Davi said, including exaggerated stress to the sentence as she returned her attention to my future bride. Well, at least I hoped she would be my future bride. They continued to glare at one another.

Davi spoke first. "James holds you in high regard. I consider him a fucking idiot most of the time, but you are a brilliant young woman. I have learned about you by listening to him drone on eternally, and my own observations."

The slightest smile danced across María's lips. I only spied it because I couldn't take my eyes off her.

Davi continued. "Energies exist in your world that you could not conceivably explain. María, I am not saying you couldn't understand. I have stipulated your brilliance. But in this, you lack the context to understand. Even when I offer context, your logic will insist I am mistaken."

Davi raised her eyebrows, bowed her head, and peered at María through the top of her eyes.

"Okay, so you will describe a poltergeist haunting Eldritch Manor. You're correct; I don't believe in ghosts. There is a rational explanation. Always."

María didn't believe in phantoms and wasn't ready to accept their truth.

"Oh yes, you are correct, my dear: there is no ghost. It is much more frightening. It is a demon contained, at least partially, within an artifact. I expect you were searching for it," Davi said, taking a breath.

"What kind of artifact?" María asked.

I could tell she remained unconvinced, but at least she still spoke English. When she broke out her Spanish, I expected trouble.

"It is a spyglass. Once, it was a dagger used to butcher a witch. She has been slaying the Doss family for many decades. Now, she has bonded with her executioner and created a giant stone monster named Genosqwa." Davi finished looking at me from the edge of her eyes.

María was glaring at me, too.

I must have looked real smart as my mouth flapped open and I replied, "Uuuummmm…"

Yep, I had this entire conversation under control.

I instinctively grabbed my shoulder and felt for the lacerations before remembering the end of the nightmarish final visit to Tituba's realm and the creation of the monster.

"If you have nothing useful to add, kindly shut the fuck up," Davi said mirthlessly.

I peeked at María and said, "Don't worry, insulting me is her favorite hobby. I haven't discovered if she's serious or not. But the risks are so great, I don't care."

"On that point, he is correct," the tiny demon deadpanned, not revealing which part of my remark she agreed with.

"Then this monster, Genosqwa, was trying to murder me?" María asked.

"It does not literally want *you* specifically. It wants any soul. That is how it becomes stronger. It formed the stone statues of the missing Doss family and laborers. Once it removed every essence of their humanity, merely husks remained. Those husks amalgamated following its excretion from Kaysan, its demon realm," Davi said, including the technical processes to spark María's inquisitiveness.

"I am not suggesting I believe you," she said. She wavered, glanced at me, then back at Davi, and then persisted. "If Genosqwa did not…"

She halted, grappling for the appropriate concept. I watched her give up and settle. "Who did?" she asked.

"You are a perceptive woman, María. You are correct: Genosqwa did not attack you. But something used you. This entity is far worse than the stone monster. His name is Riaan Dahl," Davi said.

We were in troubled waters. I was now worried María might warn the township of my madness after telling me my ship had set sail without my mind.

"I realize I may regret this, but here goes: Why is Riaan Dahl so dangerous? What do you mean when you suggested he used me?" María asked.

"James, you could learn a thing or two from her. Her questions are pertinent." Again, she looked at me over the top of her non-existent glasses, eyes narrowing ever so slightly.

"My dear, I must now explain far-more-unusual events. These explanations will not agree with your understanding of mathematics, astronomy, or even religion, and you cannot unlearn them. Are you sure you want to know?"

María didn't respond. She was at war with herself. On one side was her cool intellect, and on the other, her recent encounter, merged with Davi's stories.

I love watching people decide. Often, you can see it take place: their shoulders loosen; most have some facial change; their eyes widen, and they may grit their teeth.

María relaxed into my rocker in defiance, implying, "I'll listen—for now."

"Alright, speak. On my honor, I will keep your mysteries."

"Okay, my dear. Here it is: Riaan Dahl cast a spell on you. He sought to have you retrieve the spyglass for him. It is he who is coming. It is he whom we must prepare for," Davi said, expressionless.

"Spell?" María questioned.

"She mentioned it would be tough to believe. But I've seen events I can only describe as supernatural. A few days ago, I didn't accept her blather either. But she proved truths that shouldn't be imaginable. María, I believe Dahl is deadly to everyone. Davi and I are working to stop him, and I could use your help," I said. I threw that last bit in as a do-or-die bet. She craved helping others. Now, I counted on her wanting to help me.

I watched my Spanish princess wrestle with the knowledge Davi and I had provided. Her calm, rational intellect was warring over our information and the odd event that had happened…to her. Even as I followed her struggle, I didn't know which side she'd embrace.

Then Davi spoke. "James, have you told María you two must marry?"

I glanced at Davi, then back to María, too startled to speak. My mouth dropped open and moved up and down. I only hoped I wasn't creating any noise with my deplorable reply. My eyes ricocheted between the two women. The humor in Davi's face was counteracted by María's astonished expression.

My future wife rose, cut across the galley, and punched me in the face. "*Estúpido!*" she blurted before stalking out of my house.

"Was it something I said?" Davi asked, snickering.

I was so exasperated with Davi, I couldn't yell at her. I feared saying something cruel, causing her to quit helping. Besides, stopping Dahl and Genosqwa was much more important than telling her off, and according to her, stopping them was the sole path to saving María. Instead, I stomped my way upstairs without glancing at my tiny tormentor.

Unfortunately, my night wasn't any better than my afternoon. I slept badly, and what sleep I got was marred by giant monsters shredding my friends. Giving up on rest, I sat up and flipped through my intelligent spell book.

When I saw the sun beginning to color the horizon, I padded my way downstairs. The sunrise was peeping through my kitchen window and––as expected––Davi was already there.

This time, instead of relaxing in her printed, overstuffed armchair, she was perched in a smaller wooden chair at my dinner table. There, she had her steaming dish of porridge aligned perfectly in front of her, and to her left, a folded pink napkin with two identical silver spoons centered on the cloth. Seriously, who needs two spoons at once? I owned several for guests, but I used the same one every day.

To her right, a cup of tea for herself sat, while another cup sat across from her, steaming. I glanced at it hopefully.

She bent her head to it and said, "You are less stupid after you have had your first cup of coffee."

I smirked, acknowledging the tease she put into the insult. I accepted the offered cup, parked my backside in a larger wooden chair across from her, and waited for her to speak. She remained mute, peering at me.

A realization dawned: this would be one of those discussions. You know, like the one with the school dean—he understands his point, while you have no clue and only discover it before he delivers your swats. Swats that you didn't deserve, because it was Forrest who dipped Katie's pigtails in the ink. He absolutely framed you.

Not that it ever happened. This was an example. Never mind. The point is, you get the conversation I was expecting.

So, when Davi reached across the table, grabbed my hand, and said, "James, this will be difficult to accept, but I was helping you," even with the beatific tilt to her head and her cryptic smile, I wasn't convinced.

"You telling a woman I hardly know that we need to marry is 'helping?' You knew I'd fallen for her. So, you weren't helping me," I insisted. Yes, I used air quotes to exaggerate my scorn for her announcement.

"I have experienced many generations, and I have examined all forms of love. My friend, I *was* helping you," she countered.

"Friend?" Yes, that's the best comeback I had.

"For my part, yes. But we have more meaningful matters to discuss. How is your wand construction going?"

I deemed little more worthwhile than my contact with my Spanish princess. But, sadly, Davi was right—we needed to discuss more critical issues.

"It's not. I only have a couple of strange glowing hairs. Hardly intimidating."

My progress discouraged me, and I wasn't ready to be insulted, so I buried my eyes as I dropped my chin and swung my head.

"Monkey nuts! James, you must complete it. Otherwise, you will not be useful to anyone. And you will be dead." Her head bobbed side to side as if she analyzed the ramifications of my death, including what it meant for her plans.

She went on, "At least you have your spell book. Maybe when you have a wand, it will become useful."

"Got it. I need a wand. Give it a rest, will ya?'" I intoned.

"Just remember, you have until Dahl learns you own that manor. Your drop-dead date is October 31st if Ms. Varde records it properly."

"Nice choice of words," I replied.

"They were deliberate. Now, do I have to continue busting your balls, or may we begin?"

"Let me eat breakfast." I'd stood to cook myself ham and eggs when I received a nudge on my chest and stumbled back into my seat.

Davi said, "Sit the fuck down. I do not have the patience to watch you meander around like a muttonhead who cannot recall he can perform magic."

Then she waved the hand with the crimson ring and a prodigious breakfast filled the table. Eggs, scrambled and fried, cut and fried potatoes, a ham steak, bacon, fresh buttered biscuits, sausage gravy, and blackberry jelly filled the table.

My mouth fell open and started watering as the smells blended, creating an olfactory feast before I ever tasted a morsel.

"Close your mouth or flies will burrow. Now eat. We have work to do," she said.

I wrinkled my brow as I remembered an earlier conversation. "Didn't you tell me we couldn't use magic to create food? Something about how it took more energy than the food provided?"

"I will give you partial credit for misremembering. I said we do not typically create food for our own consumption. In this case, I have created your breakfast from my mana reserves. In other words, I am using my magical energy to provide you with physical energy, dumbass."

"Okay," I mumbled, chastened.

After I stuffed my belly, she wielded her hands again, and food, dishes, and utensils disappeared. My cup of coffee, however, stayed hot and never ventured below two-thirds full.

"Okay, where do we start?" I asked, rubbing my palms together.

"Today, I will explain destruction spells, starting with *Spaceum Deleo*. It is powerful and can consume the entire domain that Genosqwa inhabits," she said.

"Wait, what about the innocent souls trapped inside?"

"Do not fucking get ahead of yourself, dumb-dumb. I am teaching you what you need to learn, not what you must use. See the difference?" she asked derisively.

"Moving on..." I said as I rolled my fingers in a circle, imitating a wheel spinning.

"*Mortus Exerptum* will give you access to the energy of the deceased. You can transform it into a myriad of energies with differing effects. *Vis Indi* will allow you to return energy to them," she said.

"Why?" I interrupted. I'd prefer not to steal energy from lost souls. They had already been through too much. Genosqwa had executed them, after all.

"*Soporium* will cause your target to sleep," she went on as if I hadn't spoken.

I guess it didn't matter. After all, I didn't have to use a spell I didn't like.

Whenever she said a spell name, *Down With Spells* opened to the appropriate page. Davi allowed me less than ten minutes to read and perform each spell before she went on to the next.

"*Stingeu* and *Extingeu* are the same style, but have remarkably different effects, depending on how you apply them. Of the two, *Stingeu* is less robust. You can utilize it to smother a fire similar to the intensity of the one in your fire box." With that, she flipped her wrist, and my fireplace turned cold. It was as if it had never held a fire.

"*Ustrina*," she said with another flick, and the flame returned.

I raised my eyebrows and nodded my head approvingly. Admittedly, it wasn't tough to impress me with magic.

"It is always easy to impress primitives," she declared, once again making me question her ability to read my mind.

"James, this next spell is dangerous. So before I explain it, cast your protection charms on both of us," Davi said.

"*Serverbaris*," I said as I clenched both fists near my chest before shoving them as they opened toward her. I saw the satisfying purple glow form.

"That will do," she said, nodding approvingly. "Now you."

"*Castellem*," I said, my hands starting in the same position. This time, one opened palm up and pushed up past my head. The other opened, palm down, and pressed hard to the floor. A red halo appeared around me before evaporating.

"Well done. You have been practicing," she said.

"Thanks. I..."

She cut me off. "Since you don't have a wand, neither of these will work."

I'm positive she loved the drama of raising my hopes before crushing them seconds later.

"Let me properly cast them for you." She did. A rush of wind enveloped me and tightened around me, as if the air itself were protecting me.

"James, you have correctly applied the theory of those spells. When you finally construct your wand, cast them regularly. It improves by adding layers of protection on your target. The more you cast them, the deeper your protection. You can develop a robust defense—not unassailable, but potent."

"Can I cast it on María? Will it build layers on her the same way?" I asked.

"When you are near her, cast it. Also, cast it over Ms. Doss and your friend Presley."

"Her name is Varde. If you can't remember her name, at least call her Kate," I said, exasperated. How is it she is so clueless about Katie's last name while criticizing my memory?

"Does it fucking matter if she is a puddle of goo?" Davi asked.

"Good point. Back to the lessons," I said.

She grinned. "*Extingeu* is far more dangerous. While *Stingeu* can extinguish small flames, it can also kill small, rabbit-sized creatures. *Extingeu* will quench a woodland fire or kill hundreds in the blink of an eye."

"Nope! I don't need to learn that spell," I yelled.

"In fact, James, you must understand this spell. Dahl is powerful and knows powerful protections. Only a powerful VIS spell will defeat him." She went on explaining, and I decided I'd fret about the morals of using the spells after my family, friends, and even my world were safe.

I spent the morning and much of the afternoon learning spell groups, specific spells, and repeatedly practicing each one. We only paused for Davi to make me lunch: venison meatloaf, smashed potatoes, corn, and rolls. She also put a tangy brown gravy over my meat and potatoes. She may be a butt, but she knew what food I enjoyed, even if I hadn't ever tasted it before.

It was near three o'clock when Davi called an end to our practice.

"James, Dahl is drawing closer. Make certain the manor is secure."

I didn't hesitate before I rushed outside, saddled Constellation, and trotted him to Eldritch Manor.

26

MARÍA

his time of year, the hospital's doctors spent their days touring the county, helping people too sick to come to Metaterre. Since the physicians were male, they wouldn't let me accompany them. They also informed me I could not travel alone.

"It may not serve propriety for a youthful woman to proceed alone, nor is it fitting for her to attend a gentleman not her relative," Doctor Barry Crusher said. He refused to look at me, and hurried away once the words were out.

As he ran away, I closed my eyes, restrained a huff, and stepped into the fresh fall air on the veranda. When I was alone, I stamped my foot, balled my fists, and leaned forward, stifling a scream, which came out as a half-groan half-squeak. I tugged my smock into place with a jerk, then tossed my head before returning to the hospital floor.

His behavior was common among people in my profession—typical, but frustrating nonetheless. Fortunately, these fearful ones mitigated their chauvinism by leaving me in control of their clinics during their periodic absences.

Los tontos!

During my internship here, each doctor spent time instructing me about their specialties. If I had questions, some would volunteer the information I sought freely. Others were too stupid to teach me to help them.

Growing up in Spain, I had been trained by the finest tutors, including many superb physicians. But knowledge in medicine is ever-evolving, so having some of these men continue to teach me was indispensable.

Since training females to become physicians was one of my most-cherished aims, I required training materials. I kept detailed lecture notes in the healing arts. My intention to educate nurses was, unfortunately, restricted except in confidential settings. Still, when the rooster's away, the chickens will play.

I used my governance over the institution as an excuse to gather the nurses secretly in the hospital while the doctors were visiting patients.

Shortly after my first class, nurse Terry spoke to me privately. She said, "I don't agree with what you're doing. It's against the rules, and you know that women aren't as smart as men. You will cause patients to die."

Blinking rapidly for a few seconds, I gathered my thoughts, then said, "*Que estupido! Yo no creo ustedes idiotas! Como! Las védicas no tienen sesos!*"

Throwing up my hands, I pivoted and left her in my dust. I am sure she remained in place with her mouth agape. This was a typical expression of hers. She never challenged me again.

Later, I was approached by Doctor Crusher. His advice was to continue the training, but to remain discreet.

He said, "Some physicians here don't appreciate you taking these matters into your own hands. I won't give you explicit permission. However, no doctor will listen to that, um, nasty nurse Terry again."

Either I had convinced them of my purpose, or they were too frightened of me. As long as they let me tutor, I did not care. My primary aim was to improve patient results. To do that, I needed better-educated nurses.

Nurse Terry attended the next lesson, but remained at the rear of the room, and did not cause further problems.

My latest lesson was about treating frostbite. Our clinic treated dozens of these cases each winter. I had just finished describing how to apply a cocaine-soaked cloth to soothe pain when, over the heads of the gathered women, I noticed James Byrne moving hurriedly toward me.

He was carrying Kate Varde.

James

I LAY my red-headed friend on the wooden cot nearest María, who was running towards us.

"What happened?" María demanded.

If she were suppressing ill feelings from last evening, her professionalism wouldn't stop her from helping Katie.

"She was upstairs in..." I hesitated and glanced around the chamber before I caught María's eye. She acknowledged my overt omission with a quick bob of her head.

"She was just lying there. After I found her, I got her straight here," I said, out of breath from carrying Kate.

María leaned her face near mine, her hot breath brushing my cheek, seeking with her eyes what her lips couldn't express.

"I didn't look. I was in a hurry to get her here," I answered her unspoken question.

"Was the floorboard lifted?" María whispered.

"Yes. But I don't think she...she was leaving the room," I said.

One nurse helped María examine Kate while another tucked several blankets around her. Both assistants glanced between my intended and me. Neither of them said anything––they didn't have to.

I took María's elbow and escorted her away from her new patient, and the nurses' prying ears, to a vacant spot in the ward.

"Listen, you've got every reason to be angry. But I didn't tell you everything because I didn't want to scare you. You'd have said I was a raving lunatic if I mentioned everything that's happened at Eldritch, much less the spyglass. You'd have knocked me stupid, and we'd never have spoken again if I said we needed to marry. I just hoped we'd get acquainted..." I trailed off, tilted my head, lifted one corner of my pursed lips, and shrugged.

"What? Get to know each other and what? Your overstated belief in your irresistibility is charming, Mr. Byrne." I didn't see her, but she must have rolled her eyes, as the scorn dripped bitterly from her tongue.

"Please, María. That's not it. You'd already experienced enough, um, peculiarities. I didn't want to add to them," I implored.

She didn't respond. At least she wasn't saying I need to plunge off the cliff near Eldritch Manor, so I went on.

"There's a lot I need to tell you. I guarantee I'll explain everything if you permit me. You won't believe me. But I'll still tell you."

She said, "*Que imposible!* If you lie to me again, purposely or by omission, I will beat you silly. Then we will never speak again."

She crossed her arms over her, ummm, chest, and glared at me, her chin lifted defiantly. But those enormous brown eyes pleaded for my approval.

Of course, I promptly obeyed. "Agreed! Come over tonight. We'll talk," I said. Then I offered my most charming smile.

It didn't work. At least, not like normal.

"You had better spell out the unadorned truth. Not some bullshit story to mollify me, either. *Entiendes?*"

Her grasp of the English language constantly impressed me. She was a native Spanish speaker, yet she spoke better English than me. Seriously, who uses the word mollify?

"Oh yes, I'm listening. I'll cook supper," I said, and then realized I was staring at her, mouth open, with a stupid grin on my face.

Kate stirred. I shut my mouth and rushed to her side, sat with her, and picked up her hand.

She opened her eyes, saw me, and smiled weakly.

I asked, "Kate, what do you remember?"

"Help me up," she said as she raised herself to an elbow.

I hauled on her hand, then stuck my arm behind her back in case she was groggy. When she reached a seated position, María gave her water. She took a few sips, then inhaled deeply before answering.

"James, I fell asleep at home. I don't even recall being tired. But I had an unusual dream."

"What was it?" I asked as María chased away the nurses so we could talk openly.

"A man. He was different—hunched, and covered in tattoos. He ordered me to get him a dagger. He said he would kill someone at the manor if I didn't give it to him. But that was just a dream, right?"

"Sure, hun. It was just a dream," I said.

"*Roja*, did anyone know you went to Eldritch Manor?" María asked, peeking at me. Her eyes were narrowed and her brow furrowed.

"I'm not sure. Maybe," Kate replied, coming out of her haze.

"Katie, I'll leave you in gifted hands. María, make sure she gets home safely. I didn't lock the door at the old manor. I'll see you both tomorrow."

My last word trilled as panic gripped me, thinking of Presley or another friend being harmed at the manor.

Luckily, María understood my subtle message about seeing her tomorrow instead of the agreed-upon tonight and merely acknowledged me.

Her half-hearted grin was the only reassurance she offered before I turned and hurried back to Eldritch.

27

JAMES

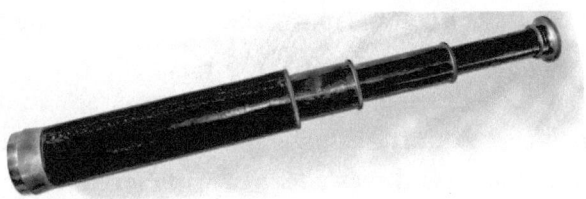

By the time I entered Eldritch, it was nearing five o'clock in the evening. Before I rode onto the estate, I checked for any storm clouds forming on the horizon. I was unclear if storms brought Genosqwa or the other way around. Since the horizon remained an azure blue, I rode onto the land.

I trotted Constellation along the U-shaped carriage way, past the marble colonnade, and to the front door. I hopped off my ebony steed and landed lightly beside him. There wasn't a spot to tie him, so I dropped his reins nearest the two sixteen-foot alabaster columns guarding the grand entrance. Besides, I'd taught him to remain within a ten-foot circle of where I left him. He'd stay there unless something hurt him.

Unlike what I told the ladies, I was positive I had locked the front, back, and both side doors. Thankfully, they remained closed.

The steps leading to the mansion were striking. The Verde Lago granite steps were an exotic crystallization of gold and tan coloring the deep-green backdrop. I'd seen this stone once before, at a certain Lady's villa in Rota many years ago.

The stonemasons' artistry was superb. If I survived the coming battles, I'd do my best to restore Eldritch Manor to its former grandeur. Its bones were still sturdy, and, despite its neglect, it remained magnificent.

I'd been casting *Castellem* on myself at every opportunity since I grasped it, and I shaped it again as I climbed the stairs. I hoped Davi was correct that it formed layers of protection.

The heavy front door creaked as I nudged it open. The room was murky and silent as I slipped into the immense hall. I needed light to investigate, so I lit a fire and as many pot lamps as I could locate. Still, despite lighting twelve pot lamps, the ceiling remained drab, and shadows trembled on every surface.

Since the clock loomed large in my nightmare, I studied it first. Someone had carved thirteen large circulating emblems in its olive-colored wood. Each swirl was adorned with seven delicately carved golden angles. Monstrous figures were chiseled into the burnished bronze minute and hour hands.

The hunchback minute hand started. A cog slipped, bracing for a chime. In the corner of my eye, a light blinked. My heart raced.

Kate had alerted me the clock was older than Charles Doss. Oddly, I didn't recognize it from my childhood.

I inhaled, held it, and slowly exhaled. My heart slowed. I turned from the perplexing timepiece to the figure dominating the room's heart.

Kate had prepared me. "Jimmy, this statue is a copy of my granny."

I examined its alabaster surface and instantly saw the family resemblance. Ms. Doss was as remarkable as her granddaughter.

A voice wheezed, soughing ice into my ear. "Keep Kathrine away." It was as unmistakable as a clanging church bell, but as weak as a sigh.

Have you ever seen a cat fall? It twists and turns in what looks like an uncontrolled fashion until it lands gingerly on its feet.

Yeah, that was me. I jumped several feet into the air, performed a complete one hundred-eighty-degree twist in mid-flight, landed, and braced to fight—or run, whichever seemed reasonable. Speaking wasn't an option I'd considered, but somehow, I replied.

"Pardon me?" I asked. It was a dumb question, but I couldn't think of anything else more rational.

"Keep my granddaughter...from..." This time, the sounds drifted past my ear. I had to work to understand them, so I leaned nearer the sculpture.

Its eyes fluttered, and a frigid chill enveloped me. I watched my breath as I exhaled. The raging fire inside the firebox had warmed the massive chamber well above freezing; I shouldn't have seen my breath.

"I'll keep Kate away. But I need your help. How do I stop Riaan Dahl?"

Davi had said Dahl was my greatest threat. I hoped that whatever was whispering to me through this effigy could help.

"No...ing... Dahl...witch kill me."

Each time the figure spoke, another storm of frozen air streamed past me. It was as if this thing speaking used the room's energy to interact with me.

A sudden inspiration caused me to gasp. "*Vis Indi*," I said as I forced two open hands toward the sculpture and felt the drain as I pushed energy toward the image.

Too late, I hoped I hadn't given it all my energy, causing me to die swiftly and carelessly. Yeah, I know I should've considered that issue before I cast the spell, so leave me alone. Davi would holler at me later––if I didn't die––again.

"I know nothing of a Dahl. I must hasten, or the witch will slay me. My granddaughter is in danger. Keep her away from this place. B... husband...help...with...th...witch."

The sounds were stammering and weakened the more she spoke. Although I didn't hear everything, I got enough. Ms. Doss, or someone speaking through her likeness, had requested me to bring Charles Doss here. I hoped it meant he could help with the monster stomping through my life.

"I understand. Is there anything else I should know?"

I didn't want to cast the energy-transfer spell again. At least, not before I chatted with Davi.

"Basement," was the one-word answer. It seemed final, too.

I knew where the basement was and headed directly to the stairs.

As I sank into their inky blackness, bile pushed its way into my throat, and my mind flashed to the storm when the waves had washed me overboard. Staring at the fathomless blackness of Davy Jones's Locker was no more frightening than this.

This basement didn't have ambient lighting, and the meager luminosity of my pot light did little to keep the darkness at bay. A lengthy, blackened corridor threaded the middle of the space. Four doors opened on the right and three on the left. I zig-zagged through the hallway, forcing open door after door. Each revealed only shades of blackness and desolation. Each latch click screamed for me to run.

The middle door on the left was tagged "Ice House." It was the widest of the seven and opened outward. I placed both hands on the handle to tug it open.

The clock upstairs rang out. It reverberated through the corridor. I wanted to run. Instead, I tugged with all my might. The groaning hinges mimicked the shriek of a captured beast as the door scraped along the stone floor, squealing through each inch. Finally, I'd moved it enough and stepped around the hatch.

I gasped.

This room was lit by a curious glow splashed onto the floor, walls, and ceiling, saturating the entire area in its ultramarine shimmer. The blue light was blinding, and my eyes took precious moments to adapt. Squinting through the brilliance, I saw centered in the room a portal nearly indistinguishable from Davi's.

My blonde tormentor's portal was crimson, while this one was a vortex, spinning wisps of white and orange through the sky-blue backdrop. A giant black blob bubbled angrily inside the revolving doorway. Besides the colors, this ebony stain was the only difference from the one I'd seen Davi create.

"Bloody hell, this complication is bigger than I can solve," I said.

I had to tell Davi.

I sprinted up the stairs and to the front door. Terror coursed through me as I recognized that this may not have been the sole portal on the manor grounds. I only slowed long enough to drag the giant door shut and latch it.

"Away, boy," I howled when I hopped onto Constellation's back, then slapped his reins against his neck and booted his haunch. I'd trained him from a yearling to respond to either. If I used both, he'd race. We shot toward town and reached its edge in less than two minutes. Inside the township, we slowed, since our speed would cause a needless commotion.

I'd learned this lesson from a childhood buddy of mine, David. He saw a bear once, and it frightened him, so he ran along this same street, arms flailing high above his head, shouting, "A bear! A bear!" He had to have yelled it two dozen times. It had been priceless, and I badgered him relentlessly.

Yes, that's the public commotion I avoided—that and uncomfortable questions. Still, if I needed a chance to act like David, this was it.

I roared, "Davi, where in the bloody hell are you?" as I dashed through the side door of my home and slammed it behind me.

I tossed my coat onto the counter in the galley and hustled through my house.

"Davi, answer me!"

Only now did I notice the three women peering at me. Two had puzzled expressions, while the third wore a decidedly impish smirk.

While I had known María was coming over for dinner and answers—mainly answers—I wasn't prepared to see her right now. It was totally my fault, but at least I made up for it with my scintillating comment.

"Uuuummmm..." I stated. I delivered it with determination, though.

I was further dismayed when I recognized Kate. My eyes darted to her, then Davi, then María, before I cycled through again and finally fixed on my tiny tormentor.

But it wasn't she who spoke. It was María. "James, I asked Kate to come with me. She deserves answers. Besides, she claimed she paid you to perform an inquiry into *her* family's former home. You agreed to keep her advised."

The Spanish beauty sat watching me with her arms crossed and a self-assured smile that dared me to challenge her.

I glanced at Davi, who shrugged. "You may as well fucking tell them both. Silence does not cause you to sound less like a doofus."

Her capacity to dream up new insults was vast, but tested my patience just now. Deciding it wasn't worth the fight, I sighed and began. "Fine. A voodoo witch and a murderous Iroquois created a demon that's haunting a relic hidden inside Eldritch. You both were looking for it." I hesitated and pointed to both ladies. Their eyes were wide as they focused on me.

I went on, "You two thought it was a dagger. Only it isn't anymore. Years ago, someone in your family remade it into a spyglass." I halted and gazed at my redhead friend.

Her green eyes sparkled in the firelight. Or maybe that was lightning bolts she was preparing to blast out of them, searing me to a crisp. Luckily, María came to my defense.

"Kate, I don't know what to believe either. But something is happening with that spyglass. I had the same dream as you."

María spoke at length about her vision and what transpired with her. She described Dahl's yellow eyes and twisted nose. By the time my brown-eyed beauty ended, Kate sat slack-jawed.

She wasn't a fool and didn't intimidate easily, though. She quickly regained her composure. "Okay. I'll bite. What else?" Kate asked.

"That tattooed guy has a name. It's Riaan Dahl. He's hunting for the spyglass. He tried to get María to take it to him. I'm thinking he did the same with you, Kate. The thing is, Dahl isn't from this world." I paused again and glanced between the two ladies.

If shock had a face, a painter could depict it using these two as muses. María took it better. But still, her eyes were wide and her mouth formed an O. Kate had the same wide-eyed, wrinkled forehead. She even carried the same O on her mouth. Where Kate differed was in her skin tone; she had gone sheet-white.

That shifted with my next remark. "Davi isn't from here either," I said, cringing as I spoke.

Kate's face flushed red and María's eyes went even wider than before. Both women swung from me to Davi and gaped.

Neither woman spoke as the little blonde told her story. I gauged their response as their breathing sped and slowed through Davi's telling. Everything was going well as she recounted how Dahl needed the artifact to return home, but terror built as she explained what he'd do to acquire it and how he'd unleash demons and beings from thirteen worlds if he gained possession of the spyglass.

Both ladies stared at me as Davi explained, "No matter how fucking insane it sounds, James is the one person suited to stopping Riaan Dahl, and thereby saving your families and friends."

"Why?" María asked.

She peeled her eyes from Davi and turned to me. I puffed out my chest. My mentor was finally going to offer me a measure of credit. Finally, my Spanish queen would see me as an equal. Then Davi stomped on my dreams.

"James is a wizard too," she said.

Their demeanor shifted, and both women shut down. Their eyes narrowed and their lips pinched together. Kate's cheeks blazed red and María's eyes burned white-hot. They scarcely glanced at one another before they rose and stomped out of my life without uttering another word.

I stared at the door after it boomed closed behind the two women. I looked at Davi. An enigmatic smile was all she returned.

Instead of yelling, I went to bed without saying another word to her. I slept as badly as ever since that blonde demon invaded my life.

JAMES

*B*y the time I woke the next morning, I was as drained as I was irate. I scarcely noticed the she-devil sitting with her food bowl as I stomped passed her. I slammed the door behind me hard enough that I heard something crash onto the floor.

Today the *Monarch* was getting four new thirty-two-pound cannons, which was a big deal, because cannons had been difficult to acquire since the war started. But the Federalist Governor of New York, John Jay, had personally requisitioned these cannons so we might, "Continue to torment the entire British Empire," as he said.

Yeah, it was over the top. But he ensured we had the vital munitions to go on raiding enemy merchant ships.

I recognized how badly the Continental Navy was equipped, so I was thankful for my embarrassment of riches. I suppose it didn't hurt that we had been abundantly successful in exploiting those riches. Just this year, we'd taken twenty-seven ships and burned twelve others while losing only one man to enemy activity. By a sizable margin, we were the most successful privateering crew. My friend Presley Varde captained the only other ship to come close to our success.

I once believed I was an able seaman. But, since meeting Davi, I knew I'd caused our luck with my wizardry. I'd unwittingly been practicing it to sail faster and fire my cannons more precisely and from a greater range.

Our new cannons were the finest produced in the colonies. They rivaled any in the world for range and accuracy. When we sailed again, I intended to employ them to their fullest.

But before I could use them, I needed to take them aboard the *Monarch*. I decided to stop by my best friend's ship, the *Aquilon*, for some advice on placing the new guns. Presley's ship was a merchantman, but he'd cut his teeth on warships, and could fight one as well as any Captain.

I found him on the docks near the supply house, closer to town than my own vessel. His ship was scheduled to take provisions to a small town north of us that the Brits were blockading.

"Hey, Presley," I called out.

"Jimmy, how are you, my friend?"

We greeted each other with a brief hug, despite it not being customary. We rarely cared about what society felt was proper. We were in a line of work where either one of us could perish in the next storm, so if someone thought our hug was silly, it was their problem.

"I'm bringing four new guns onboard the *Monarch*, and wanted your opinion on their final placement."

"Sure. Whatcha thinkin?"

"These are the finest cannons in the Colonies. Is it better to have them ready for fighting a Man-O-War or for chasing down hapless merchantmen?"

If I stuck a cannon at the bow of my ship, I could use it to induce a fleeing ship to drop sail quicker, minimizing risk to both our ships. However, with that cannon on the bow, it wouldn't be available in a straight-up fight with a warship off our beam.

I didn't need to explain this. Presley knew.

"Jimmy, you can take most ships in a straight-up fight. But that puts your ship at risk. The redcoats can afford to lose a few ships. We can't. You, your crew, and your ship are far more valuable to our effort than a score of British warships. You should always run from a 'fair' fight."

He made physical air quotes with his fingers around the fair. Neither of us believed in a fair fight. We always took every advantage in any engagement.

"Yeah, I know you're right. I trust your opinion, and wanted to check before I did something dumb," I said.

"My friend, you never have to worry 'bout checking with me before you do something stupid. You know it's our job to support one another when we do the idiotic act." Presley laughed and slapped me on the back.

"Hey, Cap'n!" someone yelled.

We both turned. Presley recognized the man and said, "Jimmy, I've gotta go. Let me know if you need any more advice." Then he hustled off to deal with whatever duty demanded.

I turned my attention to my own ship. I knew my men could load these guns without me. But why should they have all the fun? Besides, I was a hands-on Captain. That approach was especially critical during these types of armament upgrades.

The early morning fog hadn't burned off by the time I entered the docks, where the *Monarch* was moored. I thumped my way along the wharf toward a grouping of men near her bow.

"Mr. Dawson, show me the new ordnance, please," I said as I neared them.

"Ya sir," exclaimed the familiar voice of my First Mate.

I grinned and signaled for him to lead the way. Near the end of the berth, at the stern of my ship, rested four spanking-new cannons. I tracked my palm along each ebony barrel, marveling at their construction.

I came to the last cannon and crouched to inspect it closer. A large quad-wheeled wooden carriage held the heavy gun. My heart skipped when I noticed the gleam—its hazy golden sheen covered the entire rear axle. I'd spotted another part to my wand.

I breathed a giant sigh as relief flooded through me. No matter how trivial, this was progress.

"Mr. Dawson, have this axle replaced and transfer it to my home. I believe it's defective," I said, eyeing Kia Dawson and pointing at the butt of the carriage that bore the cannon.

"Ya sir," was his prompt acknowledgement.

My men held me in high regard, and they'd follow my orders, even if they didn't understand them. Before I'd met Davi, I thought they sailed with me because I was an outstanding commander, but she showed me I was capable of magic, and that knowledge convinced me that my *gift* was what made me a splendid sailor, not any innate skills in seamanship.

I simply wasn't as great a seaman as I'd imagined. That recognition was deflating. Yes, I realize this sort of self-doubt was harmful. Regardless, I couldn't resolve the negative thoughts, no matter how hard I tried. I dipped my head and decided to shake the negativity out. Kia saw me and spoke.

"Ya's all right there, Cap'n?" he asked.

I'd forgotten he was with me and startled at his question. I recovered and rubbed a knot in my neck to hide my reaction. "Outstanding, Kia. Outstanding."

Then I left to inspect my ship.

The shrill Bosun's Call piped me aboard, and the senior petty officer cried out, "*Monarch*, arriving!"

It was maritime custom to address the ship's captain's arrival or departure with the name of his ship. When I stepped off the gangplank, I recognized his honor and returned it with a crisp salute.

Only the duty crew was on deck when I arrived. The rest of the ship's company was busy cleaning, painting, performing repairs, or loading stores. Even in port, a ship was a busy organization.

After I'd answered the Officer of the Deck, I spotted a heap of debris staged nearby for offloading. The detritus was wooden scraps —broken railing, planks, and such. Laying atop the pile was a wooden spar broken from the *Monarch*'s wheel. This wooden piece featured the same golden hew as the steel axle. I snatched it from the stack and hardly glanced at it before I tucked it into my belt. It was too much to expect, but I hadn't been seen.

"Cap'n what you need that old billet o' wood fer?" asked Ron, one of the 106 crewmen on the *Monarch*.

Seaman Apprentice Ron Wolf was a cranky old fart whom we nicknamed Chief. He earned the moniker because he couldn't pass up an excuse to tell a person how they were making one mistake or another.

"I figured I'd take up a bit of scrimshaw and I wanted a piece to practice on," I said.

"Hell, Cap'n, ya's should'a told me. I can lay a pattern ta pert near anythin'. I was jus' tellin' John…" Given the chance, Chief would chat for days. I didn't have time, so I excused myself. Besides, I had just spotted Kate Doss on the pier.

"Seaman Ron, I have matters ashore. Excuse me, sir."

"Well, tain't no skin off my nose, sir. Ya jus le' me know when ya be need'n them teaches," he said as he doffed his cover to my back.

The Bosun's Pipe acknowledged my departure before I reached the bottom of the gangplank. Once there, I hustled to my best friend's wife.

"Kate! Good morning." I hoped she'd reflected on the disaster of yesterday and was ready to talk to me.

"Good morning, James. Can we speak privately?"

She hesitated for several moments and her eyes looked anywhere but at me. I noted she eventually decided on staring at the *Monarch*.

"Sure. Let's go to my cabin," I said.

I escorted her aboard and through the door of my cabin. After we went in, I shut and latched it behind me.

Here's an entertaining fact—redheads can turn on the fire at the drop of *any* hat. Kate practiced her waspishness, whetting it so she could cut your legs out from under you with a single glance. She'd done so many times over the years.

"James, you son of a bitch. How dare you not explain what's going on at Eldritch. You were supposed to be my friend."

Her face was bright red and her chest heaved as she fought both her anger and tears. Katie cried when she got mad, which made her angrier. At least I knew she was still furious about last night's revelations, but she was speaking to me.

"Katie, I couldn't have explained much, and you know it. You already think I'm insane, and maybe believe I'm worshiping Beelzebub himself. Besides, much of what Davi said, she'd just told me. And unless you expect I should rush to you with every extra detail, you'll have to stay content with imperfect knowledge," I said.

She ducked her head aside, another of her physical idioms. She hated confrontation and only acted when she was especially peeved about a specific issue.

I dragged a wheeled chair over beside her. She kept her eyes averted, but sat with her hands folded in her lap. Good. With them clasped, she wasn't likely to punch me.

I turned another chair around backward for me. Noticing my own affectation, the one where I hid behind the seatback of a chair, I flipped it around correctly before I sat and faced her.

I reached out a hand, tenderly touched her chin, and applied the slightest push. She lifted her head and her eyes found mine.

"Katie, I agreed to explain what I learned out there. I'll keep that commitment, no matter how bizarre it is. Trust me to keep some things confidential, though," I suggested hopefully.

"Like you worshipping Satan," she said, then glanced at me with one of her many coy glances. I took this one to mean, "If you are, I will murder you to save your soul."

"No. Information that could help Dahl. And to be clear, I am not worshiping the devil. But if I were, wouldn't I lie about it?" I asked.

She laughed. Thankfully, this crisis had passed. Kate and Presley were my nearest family...so to speak. I'd hate to have anything sink our relationship.

"Jim, my grandfather is demanding to visit the estate to collect his belongings. He is adamant that he goes today. May I take him?"

I noticed she'd called me Jim, and not James or something worse.

"I must be absolutely clear: Charles Doss may go. But you cannot. Under no circumstances are you to set foot on that land. Do you understand me?"

"I do. Honestly, I'm relieved. I wasn't looking forward to visiting that place again. Will my grandfather be safe?" she pleaded.

"I'm sorry, hun, but his mind is already lost. The spyglass can't harm him further. Based on what Davi told me, he should go soon."

"I'll consider it," she murmured.

With that, she stood and left.

JAMES

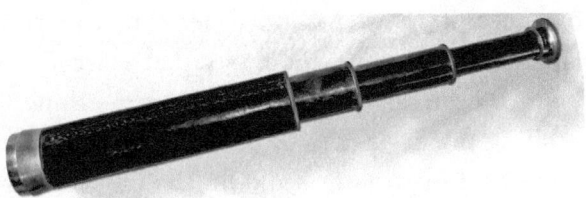

*D*avi infuriated me with how she'd stuck herself into my growing relationship with María. In one breath, she told me to marry her. In the next, she sabotaged our rapport. Even my giddiness at discovering two more segments of my wand wasn't enough to settle my nerves sufficiently to return to my home...and Davi.

No—tonight, I wanted no part of that tiny blonde villain.

Instead, I'd catch up on work aboard my ship. For too long, I'd invested all my time with María, Katie, and Davi, not to mention the two evils trying to wipe out everything.

Since Davi had planted herself in my life, I'd been ignoring *my* ship and crew. That needed to change.

My crew was exceptional in every phase of their duties, but they were like a finely honed blade—with use, they'd need the whetstone. My task was to apply it as required. I needed to examine every detail of every trip. Preparedness was key in that. Besides, even the finest crew need guidance.

I'd fill today with ship-wide inspections. I'd peer into every crevice and cranny, beginning with the crow's nest. For you non-nautical types, that's a platform built high on our forward mast.

I clambered up the rope ladder and started my inspection. I hollered out my repair orders to the yeoman on duty, Anna Akhmatova. She was a Russian who'd boarded the *Monarch* six months ago and primarily acted as an interpreter and my personal valet.

I'd never met someone as linguistically gifted as her. She spoke six languages, including English, French, German, and her national language. In addition, she prepared me for any shipboard duty, constantly having at hand a cloak, coffee, and her quill. When she wasn't tending her duties, she devoted her time to writing. I'd been told her adventures were quite good. Not that I'd read any of them. I could have, but I'd been busy… working—leave me alone.

After spending my day going through the ship, I retreated to my quarters, where I ate—yes, alone—and finished my log for the day. By the time I retired to my bunk, I hoped I'd sleep like the dead, although not literally, yet.

I know, so stop whining about my off-colored analogy. I love it, chiefly because…well, you know. I'm dead.

That night, another nightmare woke me several minutes after four a.m. This dream started as my last had, only instead of me standing in the blizzard, I was inside Eldritch Manor. The residence was in immaculate condition, complete with furniture, fineries, and even food on the dinner table, which was arrayed for thirteen. Fires glowed in every candle and firebox. Shadows danced on the walls.

I didn't worry about searching for signs of activity inside the house. If anyone was here, I knew specifically they'd be on the second floor, at the end of the hall, inside the master's bedroom.

And that's precisely where I discovered Charles Doss. He was relaxing in his rocker, scanning the storm as it raged outside the enormous French doors. In the minutes it took me to walk there from the entry, the storm grew powerfully. As the thunder reverberated, he swayed back, hitched, then moved forward. His actions developed into a sort of clock.

Rain ticked against the window, adding to the rhythmic beat. *Tick, tick, tick…*

A blinding arc flashed across the sky and red eyes glowered

through the broad glass doors overlooking the front of the house. Genosqwa lurched toward us.

The alarm in the great chamber below bellowed its chime.

Gong!

Charles Doss stood. Neither age nor senility held any power over him. When he rose, he did so without pushing with his hands. He rolled his shoulders once forward, then thrice in reverse. His only confirmation of my presence was a brief glimpse in my direction when he bared his teeth. I swear he growled. This man was preparing to fight.

Gong!

Thunder rolled. Genosqwa roared as it lumbered toward us, dragging a log the length of a tree.

From the air, Charles drew a sword. The blade burned blue in the storm's light. The hilt was decorated. I needed to squint to see it clearly. It was a skull-and-crossbones with the number 322 carved below.

Gong!

The giant demon raised its weapon and delivered it hurtling to the ground. The manor shook, and I needed to grip the wall to remain upright. Plaster cracked and tumbled in chunks from the ceiling.

Charles pushed open the doors to the terrace and stomped into the teeth of the seething storm. He flung his arms wide and roared as powerfully as any living thing I'd ever heard. He was embracing this battle.

Gong!

Genosqwa stomped closer. It sent its heavy wooden weapon crashing into the ground. The splendid facade inside the chamber collapsed. The brilliant alabaster greyed as the gale extinguished the candles.

Charles thrust his blade into the stone deck. Its blue light leapt toward the sides of the balcony, as if the sword were reaching out. Somehow, the weapon was much larger now; it stood several feet above me, despite being impaled deep into the terrace.

Kate's grandfather tore off his cloak and tossed it aside, letting the wind carry it to the ocean below. Without so much as a glance in my direction, he wrenched loose the giant blade, stabbed it high above his head, and surged from the porch toward the horror below us.

As his blade fell, Genosqwa raised its enormous wooden club to fend off the blow. As the two great weapons clashed, lightning arced, blasting rock from the colonnade and balcony.

The eruption was so powerful, it jolted me from my dream, and I bolted straight up in my bunk, breathing hard and clenching my chest.

I didn't sleep for the rest of the darkness. Instead, I recounted the remarkable, nightmarish events in my journal. I knew I'd need to relay this dream to Davi, despite my simmering anger with my guide.

After finishing the journal, I dressed and headed for the galley. "Anna, please see that Constellation is fed and saddled. I'll depart as soon as he is ready," I ordered without looking. I knew I'd find Anna in the galley before sunrise. She'd be arranging my breakfast before she readied my clothes for the day.

"Yes, my Captain. Err you certain? Err breakfast ee's not fini." Just because she could speak six languages didn't mean she was free of any accent. Luckily, I was versed in French, so any time she faltered on an English word, she defaulted to French for my benefit.

"It's alright. I'll eat at home today. Thank you, Anna."

She smiled cordially and bowed as she left. Moments later, I heard her requesting the watch to fetch my stallion. Less than ten minutes later, Connie was waiting at the foot of the pier. Anna must have predicted I'd need my horse and already ordered him fed and saddled. In any case, the sun was just sliding above the horizon as I began my ride to town.

As I entered the market, I hopped off and led him. Less than a minute later, I'd regret that choice.

As I edged my black stallion through the market, I noticed Kate walking arm-in-arm with María. My heart soared as the redhead disentangled herself from my Spanish princess and marched toward me. My heart sped further as anxiety coursed through me when her march turned into a stomp.

Her little feet pounded through muck and puddles, spraying debris in every direction, and soiling the bottom third of her blue-and-white dress. Kate didn't lose focus for a second. Her eyes never left mine.

I should've seen her hands balled into fists. Unfortunately, I only recognized the hazard when she snatched my shirt and yanked me to her. As my body bent, her other hand punched me dead in the mouth. She didn't say a word before she whirled, tramped back to María, and pulled her around to walk away.

Women had slapped me before. It's an occupational hazard when courting. I had a satisfactory reputation for having a lady in every seaport. Most of them knew and didn't care and I didn't keep it secret. A few took umbrage and left a record on my face revealing their disapproval.

Kate didn't slap me though. She punched me. To be precise, Kate was pissed, and had concluded I was the burr under her saddle.

I stood tall and brushed a hand across my mouth and chin, swinging my jaw from side to side. A few fellows in the market laughed. A few others shook their heads playfully basking in my discomfort.

After a few moments, my brain slowly engaged and determined I needed to discover why Kate was...impassioned. I tore after the two women.

"Kate! Wait, please. What's wrong?" I yelled at her back.

She leaned toward María and said something to the Spanish noble. My heart soared when the delicate genius glanced at me. It ached when she turned her nose up and tramped away toward the hospital. It raced when Kate paused, then stomped toward me, her little fist balled and raised, bracing to punch me again. This time, I took her swing on my side and pinned her arm there.

"Let me go! Let me go or I'll get Presley!" she yelped.

Again, I noticed the gawking crowd whispering and laughing to one another.

"Kate, please talk to me. I don't understand why you're so heated. Well, besides being a flaming redhead," I said as I freed her. My joke fell flat, and she drilled me again, this time in the arm.

"How dare you laugh?" Tears were rushing down her face.

"I'm sorry. I shouldn't have teased. Please tell me why you're mad. If you don't, *I* will get Presley."

Kate solved her own disputes. Her threat to bring her husband had been hollow, and I realized it. She wouldn't want me to summon him to sort this out, either. I knew that too.

She dropped her voice so I was the only one who could under-stand her. "You told my grandfather he could travel to that Eldritch house. I don't know where he is, and you won't let me find him." As she whispered, the tears fell faster and harder.

"Hun, I didn't realize he went. When? Why didn't you come tell me?"

"What do you mean? You suggested he go. I overheard you. It was yesterday, an hour after I left your ship," the diminutive spitfire said.

"That doesn't...I mean, what are you...I didn't...I didn't leave the *Monarch* until this morning," I explained haltingly. Bile had clambered from my gut into my throat. Was that mansion capable of inducing hallucinations too?

She studied me, her eyes narrowed, and repeated, "James, I saw you. You came to my home. Presley saw you."

She seized my hands. On some level, I understood she was touching me. On every other, I'd penetrated a mist among the reefs. I had surrendered all contact with the truth of my situation. The bitter-ness in my throat was nearly making me wretch. Panic constricted my rib cage. I battled to breathe, and I was positive that had I already eaten breakfast, I wouldn't have kept it down.

"Dang," was all I could stammer. I was bent over. My hands forced my knees to stay locked, or I would have collapsed.

"Jim, are you saying you weren't at my house? You didn't visit my grandfather?" the redhead stick of dynamite asked as she leaned near to my ear.

"Not that I remember." I shifted to stare into her eyes.

"Shit," she replied, glancing away.

We both recognized the ramifications of our conversation. Either I'd been a marionette, manipulated like María and Kate, traipsing around town talking to people, or someone was impersonating me. Or was it a some*thing* impersonating me?

"Kate, we need a secret code word. Ask me for it from now on. I'll ask you for it too."

"Okay, but I'm telling it to Presley and María, too," she said.

"What should it be?" I asked.

Kate paused, rose, and lifted me upright with her. "I had an acquaintance in Ireland named Nollag Dallas. Presley knew her, so let's use her name," she said.

"Okay, but just make it Dallas. Her given name sounds very much like a prison," I said, adding a feeble grin. "Kate, I need to talk with Davi and try to explain this. Will you please tell María for me?"

"I will," she said as she raised up on her tiptoes, hauled me down, and pecked my cheek. "I'm sorry I punched you. Find my grandfather, Jimmy."

"I'll do my best," I said as I patted her arm, which was still locked in mine.

She released me, and I collected Connie and turned for home.

UNNAMED OMNISCIENT PRESENCE

*I*t had been weeks of travel, but Riaan Dahl had finally reached the outskirts of his destination.

The first building was a spacious residence. Through a lighted window, he viewed two people eating their evening meal. He doubted they'd offered a penitent admonition of the homicide they had carried out for their meat. He remembered the slight red-haired woman as one he'd mesmerized to fetch the artifact for him. The larger dark-haired male he did not recognize.

Dahl turned away and proceeded into town. Cloud cover brought on a premature twilight and an icy drizzle. Nevertheless, he sought to evade attention, so he moved to skulk through the shadows.

The eerie familiarity of Metaterre terrified him as much as it reassured. He had experienced its different incarnations across a dozen Earths. As he crossed between the hospital and police post, he recalled the ghastly wounds healed by the kindly hospital personnel after the drones of the temple police inflicted them. On his left, the towering stone battlements of the castle reminded him of the persecutions he'd suffered within their frigid walls.

He crouched among the vacant stands of the market and slunk

between them toward the library and school. Their construction differed in this world, but he felt their function.

There were other buildings inside this township—fewer than in some realms, more than in others. The details always varied.

Dahl knew he must discover the owner of the artifact. He perceived from his dreams that it was the same individual who currently occupied the estate commanding a view over the ocean.

He retraced his steps through the market, past the temple, along a bluff overlooking docked ships, past the harbor, and raced for another mile. His path was unambiguous as he pursued the dim light charting the artifact's energy signature.

After a journey that spanned twelve worlds and untold time, he had arrived. His destination and destiny were at hand.

Tears cascaded down his scarred and tattooed face as he peered through the immense wrought-iron gate. His breathing came in gasps as he struggled to reclaim his dignity. Precious minutes passed as he gaped at his target.

The building's former greatness was unmistakable—not that this pitiable degenerate had ever looked inside such a stately mansion, but even he noted stylistic beauty and appreciated it for what it previously was. In a window above the central door, he saw a single flicker of light. This small glint brought him from his melancholy.

Finally prepared, he trod through the open gate.

But his foot did not settle within the property. It simply turned aside. This wasn't an assault; it was a nudge, as if an invisible entity had pushed his foot onto another path. He tried repeatedly, with the same results.

Undeterred, he clambered up the rock wall, seeking to jump inside the fenced land. He did leap, but was again rejected, and crashed violently onto the heap of rocks he'd used to mount the barricade.

Every try at countless locations ended the same. Dahl did not have another option. He left this manor to seek its owner. He knew where to search for knowledge: in every town, it was the library.

The crooked creature returned to Metaterre's library. Again, he held to the shadows as he picked his course through the municipality. The rain kept people inside, so it made his task simpler.

Dahl pushed wide the sturdy wooden door and shuffled toward the sole individual inside.

"Who is the landowner of the large manor north of town?" Dahl rasped.

Not realizing anyone else was inside with him, the curator startled with shock as Dahl spoke. The librarian gawked at the living goblin, gray in coloring, with long, spindly arms and hands. Its fur cloak covered its bulbous head, so the only part of the face he could recognize was its sharp nose.

The curator breathed faster. His heart quickened, and he pointed a shaking, arthritic finger toward the gray goblin.

Dahl flashed to the road and the old woman —"...demon..."—and her murder. His heart raced; phlegm clogged his throat.

"The documents are there. Please..."

Only then did he recognize the man was not pointing precisely at him, but toward a shelf of volumes along the wall behind him. He relaxed, turned, and walked away.

An hour later, Dahl found his information. The proprietor of the mansion, a place called Eldritch Manor, was Charles Dwane Doss II.

Dahl's singular mission was now to meet Charles Doss and compel him to turn over the spyglass.

Or to ensure Doss could no longer own it.

JAMES

*a*fter the events of the morning, I bolted home. As I arrived through the galley door, I spied the back of Davi's silver-blonde head resting in her armchair. As I rounded on her, her typical indecipherable smile dissolved.

"James, what has happened?" she asked sincerely, with the tufts of steam from her porridge brushing the blackened porcelain of her cheeks.

"This morning, I had a nightmare about Charles Doss fighting Genosqwa. I was coming here to tell you about it when Kate stopped me and claimed she and Presley saw me talking with Charles Doss yesterday before dinner. Davi, I didn't leave my ship. Well, at least, I don't recall leaving her," I added, crossing my arms.

"Fuck," Davi said unhelpfully.

"What does that mean?" I demanded, knowing what the word meant. I just didn't recognize the current context. In fact, to my ear, Davi used several pejoratives incorrectly. I rarely pointed out her inaccurate usage because I realized it would provoke another round of taunts. Besides, I didn't care.

"More to the point, what does your frustration mean?" I asked hurriedly, before she could disparage my intelligence again.

"James, I am as mystified as you. Possibly, Genosqwa fooled Kate and her husband into letting Mr. Doss visit that wretched place. Hell, maybe Dahl tricked them. Or it was you, and you do not recall. Have you inquired of your crew whether you left your ship?"

I rocked my head and answered, "No. I ran here after Kate confronted me. She and I set a code name we can utilize so we recognize one another," I said, with a bit of puffery oozing out. I used big words too, hoping to impress her.

"That would be a smashing idea if you were not confronting a powerful magical creature like Dahl. What, you expect an entity who can corrupt minds from many miles away could not deceive either of you into revealing your delightful little code word?" Her contempt was unmistakable.

"He has to know we've got one before he can try," I said, undeterred.

"Also, do not use sophisticated phrases. You sound ridiculous," she said.

My shoulders slumped. I couldn't win an argument with her because so often she refused to participate.

I opened the sideboard, removed a fork and plate, and sat at the table. "Could ya help a sailor out?" I asked, jerking my head to my plate with a smirk.

"I am not your fucking maid," she grumbled.

Nevertheless, my plate overflowed with my favorite breakfast foods. Sausage gravy covered two large biscuits, and there were hash-brown potatoes with two fried eggs on top—oh, and blueberry jelly for the other fresh biscuits.

My mouth watered and my stomach growled as soon as I saw the feast. The galley filled with the scents, too, as the steam drifted from my plate. It was as if she'd cooked the entire breakfast in my kitchen. Was she that good at magic, or did my brain produce the smells after seeing the sumptuous meal? Davi would likely ridicule any question, so I ignored my curiosity.

As I ate, the two of us chatted. Davi conceded the code word may function briefly, but would fail if Dahl discovered it existed. She also promised to show me a spell to stop him from changing me or my friends into his puppets again.

"James, you can form these spells correctly, if you have your wand," she declared, as if I hadn't considered that annoying detail before now.

"I know. And I have excellent news. I spotted an axle from a cannon and a spar from my ship with the same glow-y quality as María's hair."

I watched Davi, expecting a smile, congratulations, or something. Nope. She remained frustratingly quiet, sipping her tea.

"Well," I started, stalling for time, "I have three of the four parts. Now what?"

"Create your wand, dumb-ass," she answered, lifting her eyebrows as a visual exclamation.

"You aren't helping. How do I make a wand? I've never constructed one. I've never even seen one. Well, except for your ring."

"James, you never fucking listen. As I have explained, they are all unique. You have the parts. Combine them into something you choose. Listen to them."

Maddening doesn't describe what it was like for me to communicate with her. Instead of continuing a fruitless debate, I finished my breakfast and cleared my mess.

I rose to go upstairs and retrieve the strands of María's hair. As I passed the third step, a fierce banging on my door stopped me. I reacted by preparing for a fight.

Davi smiled enigmatically, her eyes full.

A shout echoed. "Cap'n, you in there?"

I caught my breath and opened the door without responding. Ronald Wolf and his twin brother, John, stood at the bottom of my wooden steps. Beside them, laying in the mud, was the "broken" axle.

"Where ya wan'in us ta put this?" he asked as he pointed to the substantial piece of steel.

"Carry it to my workshop, Chief," I said.

"Sorry, sir. I tol' 'em that's where you wanted it. He's just no good at listening," John said.

"Am too," Ron hollered and nudged his brother in the arm. John punched him back.

"I'll talk to you later," I said to Davi, and I accompanied my two fighting crewmen to the workshop behind my home.

The two brothers hoisted the heavy section of steel onto my workbench and then, after I reminded Ron of his duties, left, still cussing and shoving one another. I needed the subtle order because Seaman Wolf had begun offering unsolicited advice on how to re-manufacture the axle and eliminate the cracks. I didn't bother pointing out that they didn't exist.

The axle had rings hammered onto each end. These rings fit into grooves on the carriage and held the axle in place. It was these two rings that showed the golden halo.

I heated the entire axle in my forge. I didn't need to get it excessively hot. The rings only required more heat than the axle. Once heated, I easily removed the pieces.

I collected the two spheres and grabbed a chunk of a meteor that I'd purchased from an islander off Spanish Florida several years ago. The meteor was large and weighed nearly a pound. The blacksmith had been badgering me to sell it to him for years.

I'd answer, "I want to use it for something."

"What?" was his continual response.

"When I decide, I'll let you know," I'd answer back warmly.

I'd always coveted a European-style dagger. Made properly, they were stunning. At least, that was my opinion.

I figured the meteor would blend beautifully with the axle rings and produce a fine layered Damascus-style blade.

I brought the items back into the kitchen and found Davi reading a text titled *Gargoyles—Magi-can or Magi-cannot: The Whole Truth*, by Kokkino Petra Magnus. She slapped it closed and plucked up her steaming cup of tea from her chair-side table.

"Davi, can the blacksmith work the metal, or must I do everything?" I asked instead of inquiring about the life-like red gargoyle on the cover of her book.

"You may have anyone aid you with any task. Just as those fellows brought you the steel, having the blacksmith perform some function is acceptable. You, however, must bring together all the items."

"Thanks," I yelled back at her. My grin was manic as I rushed out the door.

Deciding on the simplest path to complete my wand and enjoy the greatest quality, I set on a divide-and-conquer path.

I began with the blade. The negotiations with the blacksmith were brief. He was so impatient to have the meteor that he willingly put my project first in line. I described the style of blade I wanted and the details I needed it to have.

He agreed to form two Damascus blades on the condition he keep the excess folded metal and the unneeded meteor as payment. It was a reasonable compromise, so I settled.

As we shook hands, he added a degree of clarity. "If'n ya's want seven folds, I'll need two days."

"Thanks," I answered eagerly.

Next, I engaged Seaman Wolf to turn the wooden spar into two matching fluted handles. He'd even inlay a gold thread on the lip of the fluting. Say what you will about his capacity to boss around his superiors, but he was a master carpenter. He had shaped the giant butterfly figurehead on the *Monarch*. At the time, he had been frustrated it wasn't a naked female bust.

"Cap'n, ya's mak'n a mistake by not follw'n tradition," he told me years ago as he sculpted the butterfly figurehead.

"What mistake is that, Seaman?" I questioned. I didn't especially care, but it sounded important to him, so I took an interest. Onboard naval vessels, custom and superstition are powerful motivators. Up to that point, I'd put little stock into such notions. This was BD—before Davi.

"Beg'n ya pardons, sir, but it should be a fine woman head'n ta ship. She'll watch out for us. I've not seen a butterfly do that 'fore."

"How about we complete the *Monarch*'s figurehead the way I ordered? Then you can produce a masthead the way you wish. Is that acceptable?" I asked. I kept the humor from my face.

"Very good, sirs."

As usual, Seaman Wolf had created two fine sculptures that still watched over us at sea. Oh—in case you were wondering, I asked Mr. Dawson to ensure the female sculpture was dressed.

Chief offered many ideas for the handles. I quashed each of them, including the one in which he wanted to use freshly cut wood. Apparently, I hadn't chosen a grain fine enough for his tastes.

"Seaman, please produce them to my specifications. Oh—I also need them the day after tomorrow," I instructed.

I left before he could offer more advice.

With the blades and handles in production, I returned home to build the lion's-head pommel and the upturned quillons.

I'd seen a lion's-head pommel on a sword in England when I was a boy. Since then, I'd wanted one on one of my swords. It'd look just as grand on these daggers too. Since it was considerably easier to work with, I made mine from brass. Plus, its weight offered a nice counter-balance to the blade. On my wand, I paid attention to every detail.

I cast four lion's-head medallions as big around as a Spanish Dollar and a quarter-inch thick and gutted a cavity within each set. Thinking back, I didn't have a reason for creating the crater. But Davi told me to trust my gut, so I did. I drilled four small holes that I could use to pin the pieces back together when I needed.

I fashioned the quillons from a segment of a steel rod from my shop. My coal forge provided me with all the heat I required to define the metal, twisting and flattening it as I wished. I was finally enjoying one of Davi's tasks.

By the end of the day, I'd finished my small contributions to my wand. Since I'd skipped lunch, I was famished.

I went inside and ate another meal created by Davi. This one was lamb stew and cornbread. The only moment she peered at me was when she admonished me that she wasn't my maid. Otherwise, she focused on her gargoyle book.

Intrigued, I read the back cover.

"*Gargoyle magic is not well understood inside the Ceorfan world, or within the nomadic Hewn. While every gargoyle is capable of magic, as evidenced by their nightly transformation, every gargoyle cannot wield it at will. The...*"

Her hand covered the rest. But if I survived this, I was going to ask her about gargoyles.

I hadn't slept well the night before, and I worked hard today. When I laid down, relaxing and falling into a dreamless sleep was as easy as...well...as easy as falling asleep.

I told you I suck at analogies.

JAMES

*T*he next two days were frustrating and repetitive. I practiced charm after charm, as well as protections, VIS spells, and conjurations. I even created my breakfast the second morning, although I needed more work before I reached Davi's skill, as shown by the eggs on my plate. They were still inside an orange-and-black clucking hen. Yep, a living chicken rested on the red clay platter where I'd pointed the spell to create scrambled eggs.

Davi roared with laughter. The chicken flapped off the table and ran through my home, strewing feathers in its wake. I finally shooed the two-toed bird outside to live with the other chickens before uneasiness caused me to waver.

"Davi, that hen won't lay poisoned eggs or something?" I asked as I watched it run through my garden.

She was sipping her tea as I inquired. I believe she nearly sprayed it across my galley. She gulped before she answered. "No, you idiot. It has two toes, not some venom sack," she cackled.

"Oh, that's what I hoped. Just needed to check," I said.

I spell-formed the rest of my breakfast reasonably accurately, although my toast tasted more musty than toasted. I didn't eat it.

By lunch, I could essentially create any food I chose, although I still needed to work on its doneness. Sometimes I undercooked it, and frequently, I overcooked it. I reproduced the spell over and over until I cast it properly.

One spell I'd become adept at forming was a removal spell. Davi quickly tired of having to get rid of surplus food I'd created.

"James, you must learn to clear your own mess or live in the filth. I told you before, I am not your maid," she said.

As a reminder to you, I didn't truly spend my magic to shape the spells. Davi had fashioned one that allowed me to acquire her magic. So, in truth, she was the one producing spell after spell, mistake after mistake. That's what I jokingly told her.

Right before she zapped me in the bum with a miniature lightning bolt. Right—no further quips about her spellcraft.

During the two days, I was disturbed twice: once when Seaman Wolf returned with the wooden shafts, and again when the blacksmith delivered the blades.

Both men had constructed the pieces exactly as I'd solicited. The only issue was when Chief smelled the cooking and invited himself inside. He hurriedly turned away when he noticed Davi.

"I'ma sorry's, Cap'n. I didn't sees you were, um, entertainin'," he said.

"Yes, and thank you for the job. Good day, sir." I grinned as I locked the door. The easiest task I accomplished today was letting him think what he preferred.

Another day behind me, I flopped into bed and fell asleep with no difficulty. In fact, it was the smoothest slip to dreamland I could recall since we'd returned to port.

The sun was brilliant, and made me squint as I tugged open my eyes. A blur on the horizon, black and sinister, contrasted against the silvery tufts clouding the azure sky. This darkness was out of place, so it grabbed my eye. I gawked, captivated by its unusual shifts.

As it drew nearer, I recognized that this wasn't a cloud; it was a beast. By the time it hung above me, it blotted out much of the sky. As it hovered, its enormous wings threw tremendous blasts of air across me. I squinted, then shielded my face defensively behind my arms against the shower of dust and other detritus.

Finally, the leviathan settled a few yards away. I stood straighter and marveled at the behemoth as it tucked its great leathery wings away. This was a dragon precisely as depicted in the novels penned by that English gentleman…sorry, I forget his name. This creature's skin was blue, the color of the sea, and light rippled across its skin like lightning.

"Why have you hailed me?" it thundered.

"I didn't call you. I didn't even realize you existed," I replied, facing him.

"Who are you?" it demanded, each word a hammer blow to my chest.

"I'm James Byrne. I captain the *Monarch of the Sea*. What are you called?" I asked.

"Ikiyoka, Dragan Uisce, and even Wasserdrache. They are the same. They are each incorrect. I am Vatis, an ancient one, formed at the birth of our world. You called me. Again, I demand, why?"

"Vatis, I don't know why you're here. But I'm building a wand, and I require a magical element. Have you brought something?" I asked hopefully.

"To call me, you have proven virtuous. I will offer what you solicit. But know this: I keep absolute authority of its power. If you pervert it, I will stop you."

With that, Vatis reared back onto its huge rear limbs, drew in his front legs, and employed them like arms. Its massive claws ripped deep into the muscle of its own chest and wrenched open a vast wound. I pressed my palms to my ears to deaden his wretched screams, but my ears still pulsed in pain. Vatis clawed out a fragment of his still pulsing heart, then crashed to the ground as his chest closed.

I approached the giant. He was breathing in grunts. He shoved a massive, clawed foreleg toward me. When he opened his claws, an ice-blue segment of the creature's heart dropped from his grip.

I took it.

"Thank you, Vatis. I will not corrupt your gift," I said.

I reached out my hand to comfort the beast and withdrew it for fear of insulting instead of comforting. Instead, I walked away. I only glanced back after several minutes had passed. I watched him take flight. This time, the enormous dragon struggled as it climbed to the horizon.

When I woke up the next morning, I was energized. I knew the dream meant I'd earned my magical component, but it wasn't until I spotted my right hand balled into a fist that I understood I held it. As I deliberately opened my hand, I discovered a quantity of lanyard or cordage. Its weave was tight, and no matter how hard I worked, I could neither separate its braiding nor cut it. It undeniably belonged to my wand, because it gleamed with the same faint glow as the other parts.

Finally, I could construct my wand.

I bolted downstairs and discovered Davi relaxing in her flowered, padded armchair and eating some type of triangle-shaped biscuits. Her pink cup was painted with a green mermaid. Again, despite my interest, I overlooked the odd snack and mug.

"I got my last part," I declared proudly.

"Amazing! Yet you still cannot deliver a precise sentence," she retorted.

"Davi, I don't have time for your insults. I need to get my wand finished."

Apparently, she'd decided insulting me wasn't worth her time, because she started reading her book again, although this one was new. It was *Mysticism: Witchery or Religion* by Jericho. I guess this fellow was well-known. He only needed a single name.

Yesterday, I'd created a live chicken instead of scrambled eggs. To forestall any insults from Davi, I used my skillet and eggs from the henhouse for breakfast. I conjured the rest, although I must have missed a crucial step in creating my biscuits, since they were bland and so hard, they were inedible.

After breakfast, I went to my workshop, where I selected one of the blades to finish as a wand. To it, I added the dragon heart to the cavity I'd created inside the pommel. Then I folded in María's hair. I pinned the pommel together and peened it to my knife handle locking the fluted wood in place.

As I struck the final blow, the dagger blazed to life, not with flame or heat, but intense as the sun. Its brilliance was such that I turned my head, closed my eyes, and flung my arms in front of my face. The brightness still scorched through my shut and protected lids. Through it all, I could still see the shape of my knife.

When the light faded, I picked it up and felt its power surge through me. Then it spoke—not with words, but its message was obvious.

It was time to kick some ass.

JAMES

*T*hree days had passed since I'd begun constructing my wand. Every one of them Katie had pestered me about her grandfather's location. By now, she was furious that I wouldn't let her visit the manor.

"Katie, I'm sorry, but you can't go. Dahl would control you as soon as you stepped onto the land."

"Then you go, damn you!" she screamed.

"Davi has forbidden it. She said I'm not ready—at least not until I finish my...um...wand."

We had, essentially, the same conversation over and over. Her understandable frustration over my inability to mount a proper search was pushing my redhead friend to near hysteria.

"Davi, damn you, you go!"

Katie had given up speaking to me and had marched straight to the diminutive Davi. Kate's hands were fisted, and her face burned.

Davi regarded her sympathetically. I swear, her eyes were near spilling over with tears as she answered Kate. Only later would I discover why.

"My dear, your grandfather knows what he is doing. Give him that, please," Davi said.

I suspect she added a spell or two to finally calm her. Finally, Kate briefly tucked her head before spinning on me.

"Jimmy, finish your danged wand and find my grandfather!"

Despite Katie's demands and my wants, I hadn't left my property over those three days. I'd been focused on finishing my wand and training with Davi. I'd scarcely noticed that the weather had unmistakably shifted from autumn into a premature winter.

Many trees stood proudly naked, their leaves discarded against any structure that barred the steady northwestern breeze. The shorter days also brought lower temperatures, into the mid-forties, although the wind caused it to seem more bitter.

By any measure, I was prosperous, having a grand house and a wealth of foodstuffs and other necessities provided by the grocer. My surpluses were excessive, considering I lived alone. I never even wanted for fuel to keep my house warm in the frigid New England winters. Certainly, by any measure, I was successful.

My abundance of wealth allowed me to take pleasure in supporting others. Some would say I did this selfishly, guessing that since, according to Britain, I was a pirate, it was in my self-interest to keep the entire town on my good side. While I couldn't eliminate those judgments, the truth was, I'd learned I honestly felt better when I served. This sense of helping also provided insight into the needs and wants of my neighbors and acquaintances.

That trait proved invaluable as I sought to reach María at the hospital.

I'd given her three days to consider all that she'd learned about me and the evil that I needed to fight. I hoped, at a minimum, she'd consent to helping me battle Genosqwa and Riaan Dahl. Davi had persuaded me María was crucial. At least, that's the lie I told myself as I marched to the hospital.

Yes, I walked the thirty-five hundred feet. Why? Simple: I had no idea how to speak with my Spanish beauty. Every time I'd tried to talk with her, I became so tongue-tied I utterly lost track of my intentions. Possibly, during the walk, I'd figure out a way.

Little did I know, nothing I said would work.

One problem I needed to solve was with the hospital personnel. The few I'd interacted with when I carried in Kate Doss were plainly annoyed with my existence. If I hadn't been carrying my friend, I'm sure they would've turned me away.

Today, when I entered, the gatekeeper was a plump nurse named Terry. In truth, her name was Theresa Mary Bristol; she loathed the name Mary, but shortened Theresa to Terry. Yes, it confused every-one, but if you knew this wretched woman, it made perfect sense. Nurse Terry was recognized throughout Metaterre as a bossy know-it-all who struggled to mold everyone to her will.

Susan Bonds, my once-in-a-while maid, cautioned me that this nasty nurse had concluded it was her duty to keep me away from my Spanish queen.

The thing was, I knew Terry's vulnerability. Well, she had three––eating, gambling, and booze. I couldn't help her with the first two. With the third, I was uniquely prepared to accommodate.

Today, I carried a small cask of malt whisky I'd acquired the last time I was in Tennessee. This was the tonic I required, and Terry let me through.

Once inside the hospital, María was simple to spot. She was rather statuesque, and her tanned skin, hair, and amber almond-shaped eyes stood out in the expanse of white frocks, pale skin, and light hair.

María was an anachronism in the hospital—hell, in the country. She was accomplished at a time in which women were hindered from studying. She was industrious when most ladies were urged into domestic chores. Most notably, she was unusually curious when her peers were broken by zealotry and chauvinism.

Oh, and I'd be an idiot not to appreciate her remarkable good looks. The only other woman I'd known who could measure up to her was achingly devoted to my finest friend, Presley Varde. Also, I plainly perceived my own piggishness in the subtle comparison of beauty. I guess perfection has only been achieved by one fellow. No matter how hard the rest of us try, we continue to fail—miserably.

The brainy brunette noticed me as quickly as I saw her. I watched as those beguiling, cocoa-stained eyes inspected me, and I deflated when I noticed the augur of anguish. In the moment she took to recognize me, she measured me, then passed.

I overlooked her slight and plowed forward. She rolled those eyes at me when I continued toward her.

I suppose you could disagree with my philosophy of chasing a woman who had previously rejected me so often. You'd be right if it weren't María.

She stood her ground, and didn't glance up as I halted in front of her. To my side, a nurse stuck a beefy hand on my chest. I stared at the fleshy paw, then the woman who owned it. She drew a quaff from a flask and winked at me. I hadn't noticed Nurse Terry following me, although, by now, Grumpy Terry had evolved into Tipsy Terry. Score one for Tennessee whiskey.

"It is fine. Let him alone," said María. The nurse turned, teetered, then left.

"James, whatever you have to say, please do not."

"Give me a chance. I've got an idea to…" I hesitated and glanced around before I whispered, "…stop Dahl."

She jerked at his name, but quickly looked back at her table. I pressed on.

"Just allow me a half an hour so I can show you," I added.

"I am glad for you, Jim. I sincerely am. But, for me, this will conclude tomorrow. My Uncle Don Diego is taking his family to call on my mother. Specifically, she has demanded he return me to Rota while his family is visiting."

I don't show emotions, even during times of considerable stress. Therefore, she wouldn't have noticed the degree of anguish her remarks provoked. My gut knotted, and I wanted to retch. I locked my knees and gritted my teeth. Then I caught myself and forced relaxation through my body.

María touched my arm and said, "Jim, I am sorry. I pray you defeat that creature."

Then she turned her back. I watched her lift a hand to her face.

Her shoulders shuddered. I chose to believe she rubbed away tears at our impending separation. Perhaps it was wishful thinking.

It wasn't possible to express my despair at María's comments. Devastated, shattered, wrecked—all were proper. It was as if I were enduring insults from my schoolmates after being rejected by the prettiest girl in class.

Nevertheless, I had tasks to finish. Letting my hurt feelings sidetrack me was a recipe for disaster. Besides, after I finished off the duel-evil stalking Eldritch, I'd take the *Monarch* to Rota and see María.

Hey, it could happen. I'd served under a skipper who loved saying, "Troubles are naught but teardrops in the ocean." In other words, 'focus on what needs doing, not on what you can't control.'

It was time to let her go.

Behind me, I heard a clearly drunk Terry telling someone off. I quieted, and turned my ear to her, while I watched María from the corner of the other eye.

"Yah, I did hear-ed you! Nows, you just shut yer trap an stop spreadin' blasphemies 'bouts demons. I've 'ad four t'other patients who saw this creature. Thems all described 'em as a tattooed *man*. Presley Varde even stop 'em and spoke wit 'em. He ev'n promise me 'twas only a *man*. You've got nut'n ta worry 'bout. I bet em's from a faraway place. Maybe em's from Poland 'r some'n."

That she emphasized "man" every time didn't escape my attention. Clearly Dahl was making an impression around town.

The interruption subsided and I returned my attention to my Spanish beauty.

María turned and faced me after she rubbed the tears from her eyes.

I said, "I wish you nothing but the best. You are the most extraordinary woman I've ever met. When I've beaten..."

She interrupted me. "James, do not make commitments you cannot control. And, yes, you must defeat evil. I genuinely want nothing ill to happen to you."

She reached out, took my hands, and drew me to her. Her embrace felt like the warmest down-filled blanket. I could have melted. Unfortunately, I needed to leave. I was on a deadline, so to speak, and I needed to tell my guide what Drunk Terry was saying.

"Safe voyage, María," I said.

Her smile was gracious.

Regardless, I had to hustle home. I bolted from the hospital, all thoughts except for those of Dahl having fled my mind.

UNNAMED OMNISCIENT PRESENCE

*C*harles Dwayne Doss II relaxed in his rocking chair in a room furnished with spiderwebs near the top of a formerly grand staircase. The only articles in the chamber were the spyglass stand, several candles pooling their donations of wax into niches, an enormous mirror, and, in Charles's lap, an antique bronze spyglass.

It had been ages since Doss was rational. But today, he was enjoying watching the ocean waves smash against the cliffside below his once-proud manor.

As he swayed forward, a particle of dust caused a gentle *tick* to reverberate in the area. It recurred with the backward tilt of the chair, echoing in synchrony with the seconds measured by the old clock downstairs.

Its first chime echoed throughout the room.

The venerable old man smiled and continued rocking as he heard the thump at the front door. It scraped across the floor as it swung wide. Its hinges, twisted and worn by age, groaned under the increased weight.

Footsteps now resounded in the parlor below the stairs.

Below him, a heavier chime rang out from the clock, as if its bell were too large for the timepiece.

The footsteps shuffled to the top of the landing. A shadow slipped across the doorway.

Joy leapt into the waiting man's breast. Finally, the time had arrived.

Dahl stepped into the room.

The clock clanged for the third time. Its reverberations shook the windows in the spider-infested room.

"Hello, Riaan. I've been awaiting you for some years now," Charles announced.

The goblin paused for a heartbeat. A flash of dread that fled as quick as it appeared crossed through his gut. "Then you know why I am here. Give it to me and I will depart as your friend. Refuse, and I will slaughter you and any who stand in my path. Then I will still seize what is mine," Dahl answered.

Charles rose and clutched the spyglass to his chest. "Then take it— if you dare."

The clock chimed the fourth and final time. This clang was deafening. The mirror shattered and crashed to the floor. Its tiny shards splintered across the wooden surface.

The old man's grin turned barbaric as he charged the now-frightened interloper.

Riaan Dahl cringed. This abhorrent behavior surprised him, especially because an archaic silver-haired man had caused it.

But his fear didn't divert him from his objective. The small gray being pulled his blade and in one effortless motion thrust it into the thumping heart of Charles Dwayne Doss II.

He fell, still grasping the artifact, the very one that Dahl had wandered many miles and across many worlds to seize. Charles's blood pooled beneath his body and onto the bronze spyglass. Then his body melted away as his blood was assimilated into the spyglass.

The clock downstairs stopped ticking as the reverberation of its ultimate toll passed into silence.

This was the simplest and grimmest murder the little fucker had perpetrated. He did not care, because he would serve his penance this evening on his own world. He was alive with the elation of realizing he would finally reach home. All that remained was to take the ordinary bronze spyglass.

His eyes swelled as he reached for the tool to his final gateway.

But as his hand moved closer, the relic moved further away. Impatiently, he snatched for it. His hands passed through thin air as the artifact faded from view.

"No!" Dahl screamed.

He crumpled onto his knees, grasping at the spot where it'd disappeared. Once again, the universe had compounded his burden. Once again, *it* admonished, he was a despicable creature, and *it* would bar him from returning home.

"*Touye Lavi. Touye Lavi,*" resounded throughout the manor as if it were thunder.

He cowered in shock at the roar.

As he that understood the spyglass had absolutely disappeared, Riaan realized he had another task. With the death of Doss, it was evident Dahl's treasure in fact had a different owner.

"Tomorrow, I'll discover its successor. That life will permit me my prize, or I'll have another tattoo to commemorate someone."

The only sound inside Eldritch Manor was Dahl gasping for his next breath. Eventually, he would relax. In time, he believed he would hold this last relic and finally return home. Something he would never learn was that I had blocked his initial attempts to step onto the manor grounds, and I was the one who finally let him through.

UNNAMED OMNISCIENT PRESENCE

"*M*y dear lady. You are a marvelously bright woman, yet you are truly young. Love is more…intricate," Diego said.

He kissed her hand and continued. "James is an exceptional man. I was indiscreet when I allowed him to call on you. Your mother would stand me in front of a battalion of soldiers and execute me if you took a colonist for a husband. You should meet a handsome Spaniard—one of your mother's choosing."

"Uncle, I detest that life. I need to help this world. I cannot do that wrapped in an absurd gown with a stick up my ass!" She slipped to her knees and seized his hands.

"My child. I am sorry. I have no alternative. Tomorrow, we depart for Rota." He spun and left her room.

She crumpled onto the floor and wept.

James

THE MORNING of September twenty-ninth dawned with low clouds floating in the soggy gray sky. Two days ago, Don Diego José de Gardoqui y Arriquibar, the Chief of the Spanish Embassy to New York, had charged his staff with preparing for a lengthy journey to Rota, Spain.

Fortunately, the King of Spain provided Diego with the merchant vessel *Bay of Cádiz*. The seventy-four-gun *San Justo*, commanded by Capitán de Navio Francisco Ordoñez, would protect the *Cádiz* throughout its southern course along the American continent and to Havana.

While there was a measure of flexibility in his schedule, the *San Justo* had been ordered to join eight other ships under Admiral Langara. They were to cross the Atlantic for Gibraltar no later than November first. If they missed the rendezvous, the unarmed merchant *Bay of Cádiz* would make the perilous journey alone. It was a risk that Don Diego was unwilling to assume, so he'd resolved to sail at high tide today.

Unfortunately for Lady María Pauleta Francesca Rose Pimetel de Rota, he likewise was ordered to bring her to Rota. It was an errand he loathed because he knew his niece well. She would despise every moment living as a dutiful wife to a pumped-up, narcissistic chauvinist who cared more about her presenting him healthy baby boys than any of her other achievements.

Burlap tarps covered the ladened wagons and their contents of baggage and provisions, which the family would require on their planned eight-week voyage.

As they climbed into the carriage, the women kept their bright-red leather hoods pulled over their heads and their faces to the ground, away from the wet weather. The journey was hushed except for the muddy thuds of the horses' hooves and the wagon wheels splashing through puddles. Only a single voice disrupted the silence.

"This should be an adventure. I organized a stoppage in St. Augustine. We should enjoy…" Diego trailed away. No one responded, and he didn't speak again.

Did leaving hurt her like it did me? That's a question I couldn't solve, so I hid in plain sight keeping a discreet distance behind the procession of wagons. I didn't conceal myself from the drivers, just from María. I resolved to spare her discomfort. But I needed closure, and watching her board her ship and drift away may help.

My perch, high on the cliff above the small harbor, allowed me a perfect view as the family—Diego, his wife, his daughter Christina, and María—boarded the twelve-man dinghy that would transport them to the *Bay of Cádiz*. I watched her anxiously for any suggestion, any hint, that she may prefer to remain.

She never glanced up.

After the family clustered closely in the small craft, I drew my newly constructed knife from its leather sheaf. Before I crafted the spell *Serverbaris,* I clutched the hilt of my dagger with both hands. As I formed the thought, I shoved both hands forward, finishing with the tip of the knife pointed at the group inside the craft. I saw the vivid purple glow as it fluoresced around every person. The violet after-glow continued to light them as they rowed to the waiting Spanish ship. Fortunately, non-magical folks couldn't see this, so they remained blissfully unaware.

For more than half an hour, I sat on Constellation in the cold rain, waiting. When I saw the dinghy returning, I headed for the docks.

Kia Dawson met me there. "Didn't see fer sure, Cap'n. But I bribed the cook. He said 'twas her. Said he delivered her things ta her room. Said the family's been ordered back ta Spain. And that the Diego fella needed ta meet with some mukety-mucks or som'in'," Kia said.

"Thank you, Mr. Dawson."

I was saturated from the rain. My leather overcoat fought hard, but it was an unwinnable battle against the continuous downpour, and I was soggy from my hat through my boots. It was time to go home and slip into dry clothing.

I lifted my sodden cover and brushed my empty hand through my hair. After I bowed my head and shook the excess water off, I replaced my hat. "Kia, I have work at home. I'll speak to you in several days. Please continue to keep me apprised of the *Monarch's* repairs."

He ignored my order and focused on what he saw as my point. "Cap'n, ya shoul'na worry 'bout ta lass. I canna explain it. But 'fore we set out ta that ship, I knew not'n could hurt me. That lass'll be jus' fine. Don'cha worry."

Inwardly, I was gratified he'd noted the effect of my protection jura. Outwardly, I retained my reticent disposition.

Still, my foe was here already. And with my workload, if María wasn't here, I was happy she was far away. Across the ocean was a satisfactory start.

I rode home and put away my stallion, taking time to dry him and properly brush him out. I started a fire to warm his stable and offered him extra oats for the evening. Then I stumbled inside to whatever frustrations Davi had devised for me.

The rest of the day was exhausting. Since I'd finished constructing my wand, my tiny tormentor gave me no quarter. She took advantage of every mistake, no matter how trivial. Soon after I formed my personal protective charm, *Castellem*, she retaliated with an electrical energy spell that flattened me into the ground.

"What did you do that for?" I demanded, massaging a knot on the back of my head where I'd struck the floor.

"James, we are using powerful spells. You can shape a competent ward of protection around yourself. After Dahl attacks you, he will perceive it. He may not penetrate your barrier. But he sure as fuck will slap your miserable ass into the mud. I figured you should know," Davi replied smoothly.

"You could've warned me," I argued.

"Better to show than tell," she said.

The afternoon was a debacle. By the end of the day, I'd cast my protection jura so often I could detect the crimson halo surrounding me all the time. Davi assured me the goblin wizard could see it too, and would behave accordingly. I guessed that meant I'd have more lumps on my skull.

We continued practicing late into the night. Spell after spell, effect upon effect was shaped and scrutinized. I was bruised and bleeding after many of the attack spells cast by my guide.

Unfortunately, I hadn't been capable of casting even the most rudimentary healing spell. My last attempt had left me with festering boils covering my still broken leg.

Fortunately, Davi was as skillful at healing as she was at attacking. The she-devil took pity as several of the boils burst, discharging a smelly pus that further blistered my leg.

She prepared dinner for me before I went to bed. Tonight, it was turkey, sweet-potato souffle, steamed cabbage, and broccoli. Oh, and she produced a dozen sweet rolls. I buttered them, added turkey, and drenched them in turkey gravy. Now that was good eating.

I was ravenous and ate extra turkey. I didn't understand why, but I was always sleepy after eating this meal, and I hoped this time, it would help me fall asleep and stay there.

James

THE NEXT MORNING, the sun flooded through my window and warmed my face. I used my fists to rub them open before I rolled out of bed. I expected intense soreness from yesterday's practice.

Unexpectedly, I felt terrific. In fact, I felt no tenderness whatsoever. That was, if you didn't count my throbbing toes from kicking the stupid rocking chair. Funny, I didn't recall having a rocker in my room.

Finally, I understood something was amiss. I stopped to examine my surroundings. I wasn't at *my* home.

Dang it. Another dream.

I panicked and started looking for Dahl or Genosqwa. I saw neither—yet. The familiar taste of bitterness filled my mouth as I gagged.

The room was tall and nearly double the capacity of mine. It was painted a magnificent white, with blue flowers adorning the top of the faintly stained wainscoting.

I dressed and moved downstairs. The galley was vacant. A

steaming mug of coffee was perched on the dinner table. It was in my mug. I grabbed it.

Out of the open rear door, laughter rolled inside. I stepped through the opening onto a spacious, covered patio. In the grass beyond, a stunning brunette played with two small black-headed children.

The youngest child, still a toddler, wore blue trousers with a faint blue shirt. Tan moccasins covered his feet. A girl, a few years older, wore a white fabric dress with tan calf-high moccasins. Her black hair spilled into the middle of her back and swirled wildly as she whirled in the courtyard.

The mother was easily––it was María! My mind raced. My breathing quickened.

I yelled out to her, "María, good morning. When did you get back?"

"Whatever do you mean, James? I have been nowhere. Are you positive you should be outside? Have you had your breakfast yet?" the beautiful brunette asked.

"I...I don't know," I stumbled.

"You don't know if you have had breakfast? Maybe you should lie down. You were truly sick. You may yet need to reclaim more of your strength."

"Sick? No, I feel fine. I haven't had breakfast yet. Would you and the children join me?"

Suddenly, I discovered myself settled in a chair on the rear deck, although I didn't recall sitting. In front of me, a broad wooden table held my favorite breakfast foods: sausage gravy, biscuits, eggs both fried and scrambled, and blackberry jelly. My thoughts darted to a ham steak. When I glanced at my plate, I saw a piece of pan-seared ham half the diameter of my plate and a half-inch thick.

The little girl seated to my left asked, "Daddy, will you please help me with my jelly and biscuit?"

"Of course I will, young lady." Did she call me Daddy? "Wait, what did you say?"

She didn't respond; she just pointed at the biscuit on her plate and the jelly sitting near me. I took the hint and spread the black topping on both sides of her buttered bread before I passed it back to her.

"Thank you, Daddy," she said through a bite of her food.

"Not with food in your mouth, young lady," her mother scolded.

How odd. Are we the parents of these children?

"María, I may be ill. I think I need to go to bed after we eat. Would you mind?" I asked. Waves of dizziness swept over me. The top of my head tingled, almost as if I could feel my hair growing. Of course, that would be silly…but….

"Jim, will you please hand me the jelly," Kate Doss asked.

"Kate?" I blurted. "I didn't know you were here."

My eyes squinted; my head turned, searching the table for others.

"Oh, don't be silly. You invited us. Presley and I brought Grandpa from Boston to see the manor, since you rebuilt it. He's been looking forward to this holiday for weeks," Kate said.

"I'm sorry. My memory…I don't…Charles is here too?" I shouted.

This day's bizarreness grew. I suppose Charles Doss being here shouldn't have surprised me. Well, not until he strode onto the back deck. He dragged another chair to the table and settled next to his granddaughter.

"Mornin', Jimmy. How you doing, youngster? I declare, you've done an outstanding job restoring Eldritch. It feels like a home again," a strong, lucid Charles Doss said.

I sat gaping at him. I remembered him being a vigorous man. But in my recollection, he'd faded years ago, when his wife disappeared. He had never been the same afterward.

Charles reached into his jacket pocket and removed a bronze spyglass and placed it on the table. I stared at it in confusion. The discontinuities of the day mounted.

A sudden chill blew across the table as the crystal-sapphire sky vanished, concealed by dingy, roiling clouds. The pleasant breeze turned into a windstorm, and blinding snow swirled around us.

"María, take the children inside," I yelled above the howling gale.

In the distance, I noticed a sharp red light—no, not an individual light. There were two. As the evil glow drew nearer, the storm intensified.

María and Kate each held a child and ran into the home. They covered the children's faces, shielding them from the unusual storm.

My terror grew as I realized they weren't lights, but eyes––great red eyes. They followed my every movement. I eventually saw the rest of the beast. It was the same stone monster that had attacked me inside this old manor weeks—or was it years?—ago. I couldn't recall.

"Charles, get everyone to the protected area. It will shield them against that behemoth," I yelled as I shoved his shoulder.

I didn't remember completing any work on this house, but I was positive I'd set up a room to shelter my family.

"Jimmy, you go. Let me fight this battle," he said as he drove me toward the door.

"I'll not leave you here with that thing. Kate would never forgive me," I roared back. My sense was that I'd previously failed him. But, curiously, he was still here.

He seized my shoulders and spun me toward the home. He hustled me through the door and followed me in, banging it closed behind us.

Genosqwa drew closer.

I searched for María and the children. As I wobbled into the magnificent front chamber, I saw Riaan Dahl sitting on the sole scrap of furniture. It was a big rocking chair much too large for his twisted shape. He was swaying backward...then forward. A fragment of dirt caused an audible crunch as it cracked under the rocker. Nearby, a clock ticked in synchronicity with the chair. It chimed.

"Give me that spyglass," Dahl said.

"Come and get it, you fucking piece of shit," Charles Doss growled back. He bared his teeth as if he meant to rip the smaller man to pieces.

Bong! echoed second louder and much more distinct chime.

I saw the ladies as they rounded a corner. They were securing the children inside the stone-and-steel fortress. A single thick steel door guarded its entrance. Once locked, only someone inside could reopen it. They had the strongest shelter I could provide.

While I clearly saw the protected room, in my heart, I knew the real protection was my spell, *Serverbaris.*

Dahl continued to sway. The sound of time passing grew louder and more relentless.

The tattooed man said, "I don't care about the others. I only want what is mine: the spyglass. Give it to me. I will destroy its demon. You and your family will be free."

Clang! came the third exclamation evoked by the clock.

Charles Doss leaned forward as if bracing himself. He held one hand in front of him, palm up, and moved his fingers, motioning Dahl to come. His other hand held the spyglass tightly to his chest.

"Take it from me if you can," Doss said evenly as he smiled mirthlessly.

Clang!

Riaan Dahl flew at Kate's grandfather. In his hand, he held a sharply curved blade, like the kukris I'd seen in East Asia.

Charles didn't fight. The blade slashed into him, and he fell onto the floor, collapsing abruptly. I was certain he'd died before he hit the floor.

I drew my knife. It glowed with an odd fuzzy golden outline. I defended the fallen body and glowered at the killer. I dragged my friend's grandfather onto his back. He rolled over soundlessly. In his grip, he clutched the coveted artifact.

The front door crashed open, then tore loose from its hinges, and the roaring gale suddenly blasted open the back door. Blood stained the front of my clothes as splinters from the violence tore through me. I ignored the pain.

"Give me the spyglass now!" Dahl demanded.

"Doss wouldn't let you have it; neither will I. And Kate is safely locked away from you," I retorted.

I gasped as Charles Doss faded from view, still clutching the artifact. The bronze spyglass remained laying on the otherwise empty floor.

The red-eyed monster also dissolved, and the dust from the havoc it had caused settled. The clock tolled again and the storm broke.

I stooped to retrieve the bronze device that Doss had died defending, having resolved I'd protect it too.

As I reached for it, it faded from view.

Riaan Dahl fell to his knees and sobbed.

JAMES

I roused to the smell of coffee and pork. As I scanned my surroundings, I recognized my bedroom. It was the same darkly stained wood that I remembered.

I rose and considered my clothes. When I retired to bed, I'd put on my nightshirt. But I was now dressed, and even wore boots. My shirt was ripped and bloodstained. When I tore it off, several deep lacerations marked my rib cage.

I changed shirts and trudged downstairs.

Davi wasn't relaxing in her customary spot, but was standing at the foot of the stairs, waiting for me.

"Did you see Genosqwa again?" she asked.

"Yes, and Riaan Dahl. I think Dahl murdered Charles Doss," I said.

"I assume you are correct," she said.

"After Dahl killed him, I watched Doss fade. I'm betting he's inside the spyglass realm now."

"James, it is called Kaysan. He is there. That is why I advised you to keep Kate away from Eldritch Manor."

"I was stupid. I should've never let him go," I said.

"Charles Doss has arranged this for years. He determined that fate.

At least offer him the dignity of letting him own his decision," Davi said.

I nodded, but didn't answer. I needed to inform Kate. This would be a painful conversation. She cared for her grandfather as much as any person could love another.

I sat and packed my plate with the food that had appeared on the table.

"James, show me your wand. I have not seen it yet," Davi said.

"Sure." I took it from its scabbard, flipped it into the air, caught it by its tip, and passed it, hilt-first, to the small blonde.

"You know Merlin helped a man win a kingdom with a sword once?" she said.

"I'd settle for a woman," I muttered absently as I rubbed my biscuit through the gravy on my plate.

"Thanks for the fucking gratitude, shithead. Now pull your fucking head out of your ass before I kick your balls into your throat. There is a dimension-traveling, demon-gathering, portal-opening, murdering piece of shit in this town, and he is coming after you. He has already murdered a man you have known your entire life. You can continue to play pitiful me and whine about losing a woman too good for you to begin with, or you can get off your dumb ass and do something. Now, which will it be?"

I looked up and smiled. "Kick my balls into my throat, huh?" I chuckled lightheartedly. For the first time since I met this woman, I didn't feel lost. I had a target and the means to defend myself.

"I'll break the news to Katie later."

It was time to get to work.

Today, Davi taught me two new spells. The first hid my magical talents. The second was a spell to destroy Kaysan. We knew how to open a doorway to other worlds to visit their version of the demon realm. But to fight inside this realm required all of me, not just a projection.

Neither of us understood how to get inside without me, um, dying.

In truth, I suppose you already know we never did sort out that complication.

Obumbro was a reasonably simple spell to shape. The first time I cast it, I suspected I'd set the galley on fire. Sparks flew off me from every direction. When my vision cleared from the shimmering lights, the room was just fine. Other than the dramatic visual display, Davi told me I'd cast it properly and that it would cover my magic from any except the most determined adversary. Even then, they'd have scant understanding of my power—or limited instruction.

"James, you must shape this spell each day. It will only obscure your magic for about twenty-four hours. If cast precisely, it may last longer. Nevertheless, you should recast it each dawn and dusk."

AgerDeleo was the most difficult spell I'd crafted. It produced no visual effect. And since I am not inside a dimension that I can damage, even Davi couldn't tell if I'd shaped it accurately.

"Keep working. I am confident you are constructing it properly," she told me.

Lunch arrived, and I told Davi I needed a rest.

"It's time I tell Kate about her grandfather. Also, I must report his death to the authorities. I'll make up something so they won't search for a body," I said.

"I understand. But remember, we have limited time to get your pitiful ass ready for this war," she replied, as if she were analyzing the weather.

JAMES

"Kate, are you home?" I yelled as I pounded on her door.

"Coming," I heard in acknowledgment.

She opened the door, sighing heavily. "Jim, come in," she said.

I accompanied her inside without talking. I paused after I shut the door behind me. Its latching caused her to stop. Without turning to face me, she demanded, "James, have you located my grandfather?"

I explained my dream from last night and showed her the laceration across my chest.

"Hun, in my nightmare, Dahl killed him. When I spoke to Davi this morning, she said she expected it was real, or at least it was a version of what transp…"

She shrieked, charged at me, and repeatedly pummeled her hands into my chest. I let her. She was one of my dearest friends. If allowing her to batter her waves of sorrow against my chest permitted her to process her loss, I'd let her beat me bloody. She wasn't trying to injure me, though. I was simply a safe target that she could trust with her personal tragedy at this moment.

"You said…you promised. You said…you should have let me go."

Her implication was unmistakable, despite her failure to complete a sentence. She blamed me for her grandfather's murder. As the waves of grief passed, I took her by her shoulder and drew her tight. "Katie, I'm sorry."

She stopped punching me and wept. I quietly held her for as long as it took for her sobbing to ease. When it abated, I whispered, "Davi said he's been planning this since your grandmother disappeared."

She pulled away and studied me. Her emerald eyes still overflowed with tears, and her chest heaved. She didn't talk. I hoped the red shooting through her pretty green eyes wasn't redhead fire she was readying to loose on me.

I led her to her chair. She sat, and I knelt in front of her, holding onto her hands, mostly out of friendship. But, realistically, I also preferred to avoid a punch in the mouth. She was sneaky like that.

"Kate, maybe you should leave town for a while."

"No!" she exclaimed. She swung her head resolutely, then went on. "You're going to require help. And since you can't tell anyone what's happening without being burned alive, I'm staying. Besides, right now, Dahl thinks I own that spyglass. You need to defend me from him."

"Then come stay at my home. Bring Presley too. I'd certainly like to keep him out of this, but he's my best friend, and it might help. Let's gather some of your clothes. I'll carry them," I said.

She passed her fingers through her long red hair and shrugged, seeming to lose focus on our discussion. I recognized the traces of deception, and my friend was suddenly putting on a show.

"Jimmy, I need…I mean, Presley, wants me to go to the grocer for a roast. You know how he is about food. I promised him I'd cook one today."

"I've got enough dry goods and vegetables, and had a fine roast delivered yesterday," I answered suspiciously.

"Sure, but you know Presley—he wants it seasoned in a special way. I'll be over later today. You know I wouldn't go if it weren't important."

She was avoiding my eyes and not engaging in the actual conversation. I was discussing life and death, and she wanted to chew over the menu.

"More important than remaining alive?" I pleaded.

"Well, your protection spell had better work. Otherwise, your best friend will be pissed at you, too."

"Fine," I said, giving up. "I also need to inform the authorities. I'll say I saw him tumble into one of his mines. The police are so scared of Eldritch, they'll never go looking."

"Then I'll talk with his attorney about his will," she said.

I plucked a cloth from the sideboard. She took it and swabbed her eyes. I held out a hand to help her stand, and she grabbed it and hauled me to her for a hug.

"Thank you for telling me, Jim. When this is over, we'll hold a fine service for him," she announced into my chest.

"Yes, we will," I replied more confidently than I felt.

I saw Katie out and started home, passing through the market. I still carried the lacerations from my waking-dream. I wanted to stop and see Martha-Mary Bruce, our local apothecary. Maybe she could provide an ointment to treat my injuries. I didn't want to ask Davi to heal them because she'd already told me to quit being a whiner.

In any case, Martha-Mary was more than happy to accommodate. She supplied willow-bark tea and a poultice that would soothe my cuts and bruises. The good Lord above only knew what this woman put in her cream—she was well known for using unconventional cures, but they worked well enough.

unnamed omniscient presence

KATE SAT in the office of Mr. Robert Owensteine, a solicitor in Metaterre.

"My dear, I am deeply troubled by your grandfather's passing. He was a most-philanthropic man. He raised many souls from insufficiency. I fear his death is a tragedy for our colony. If..."

"Thank you, Mr. Owensteine. I already miss him more than I can say. Do you have his will?" Kate asked.

She wasn't trying to be rude by cutting short his remarks. She was simply completing tasks. Katie Varde was a master at compartmentalizing, a trait she'd need in the coming days.

"He last revised it two weeks ago."

"What? How? I didn't know."

The little redhead stared at the attorney, eyes wide and lips slightly parted, before she quickly slammed them together. Her mother would have been cross had she noticed Kate agog. Ladies do not let flies take up residence on one's teeth, she had been taught.

The old attorney nodded, apparently agreeing with her surprise. "His lucidity surprised me. I had not communicated with him in approximately thirty years. Well, not..." he said, trailing off uncomfortably.

He glanced away from Kate, fearing to face her after pointing out her grandfather's thoroughly documented mental disintegration.

He proceeded. "If you are desirous of concluding this matter expeditiously, I expect this knowledge will not reassure you."

"Why is that?" Kate asked.

She held her frustration with his tongue-paddling. He was the legal version of a quill-driver and enjoyed using an overabundance of words. "Why speak fewer words when expounding costs more?" seemed to be his motto.

"Because your grandfather left, and I quote, 'All my possessions, except my money, to those who have passed on before me.' I almost didn't release him to make the alterations. His language could be manipulated to demonstrate he wasn't of a rational mind. He admonished me—passionately, I might add—that his will. as prepared, 'Left everything to family members who were already dead.' Thus, he determined he was not making revisions. He also desired you understand he loved you dearly and hoped to not dishearten you regarding your inheritance."

Kate laughed and said, "Mr. Owensteine, my grandfather knew I didn't covet his belongings. I have more money than I need. I just want to tell him I love him and will miss him."

"He perceived that, and spoke so that day. He adored you, Mrs. Varde."

"What will happen to his belongings now?" Kate asked.

"Any funds held in trust, safe boxes, or any other place belong to you. I will draft the paperwork. As for his tangible assets, including Eldritch Manor, a trust will control them until the justice decides its status. Unless another heir makes a claim, you will ultimately receive everything. Unfortunately, this will take time to arrange," Mr. Owensteine finished.

"I understand. Thank you for your time."

Katie considered telling the attorney about the sale of Eldritch, but James had been clear with her when she sold it to him that she should not tell anyone. Instead, she stood and walked to the door. Mr. Owensteine opened it, and Kate stepped out into the sunshine. She lifted her head to the warming glow, paused, took a deep breath, and moved away.

Neither individual saw the beggar sitting under the window and holding out an empty cup to passersby.

Riaan Dahl heard every word uttered by the two. Anger flared when he learned the news of his spyglass. He'd had a flash of euphoria as he imagined that since there wasn't an owner, he could take it, so it was crushing to discover a trust owned it until a court ruled. What the little fucker did not know would hurt him.

Dahl would eventually find the new owner. Then he would try to force them to turn over the artifact or he would murder them. He would continue murdering until he discovered one who would turn it over to spare their own life.

Kate Varde's clan was virtually wiped out. The demon collected most of them. It was why he could exploit its power to open his final portals. Their souls, combined with the beast's energy, would be enough to open the final two.

Soon, he would return home—finally.

JAMES

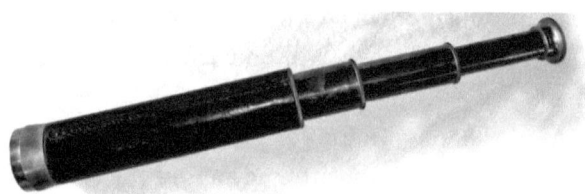

I returned home knowing Davi would have me practicing or studying from the new books she'd supplied. None of them reorganized or changed contents, unlike my spellbook *Down With Spells*.

Looking Back to See What's in Front discussed visiting other worlds to explore probable destinies. While another book's title, *Tips to Learn or Die*, sounded ominous, if not melodramatic, it was a useful read. Its first chapter focused on "the benefits and complexities of contrasting wand construction."

After reading it, I learned that many wizards built their wands into rings, bracelets, and other nondescript jewelry. This allowed them to carry their wand in hand—literally—whereas the chapter clearly listed knives as an awful alternative.

A knife, sword, or any dual-use weapon selection is not a recommended wand construction technique. When needed, drawing a wand-knife will command far more unwanted attention than——say——brandishing a stick. Generally, individuals are not murdered with blunt sticks.

While I was sure that in the history of humanity, some poor jack had been slain with a blunt piece of wood, I was upset that Davi hadn't let me study this chapter *before* I created my wand.

In any case, I was deep in thoughts beyond walking into my home. As I strode into my kitchen, I expected to discover the blonde she-devil sitting in her chair, lazily cooling a cup of tea and reading another book.

Ha!

"En guard, you fucking bastard!"

A torrent of sparks shot from her hand and pummeled my chest. I flew sideways, feet over head, and smashed into the cupboards along the wall. The dishes there shattered and littered the surrounding floor.

"What the hell are you..." I didn't complete my sentence as she launched another attack.

"Asshole, I am here to fuck up your day," she howled. Her eyes were dark and threatening. If they could've shot daggers, I'd have been dead...sooner. As it was, her spell lifted me from my prone position and drove me into the front wall on the other side of the house.

Luckily, for one, Martha-Mary Bruce's cure was in my room. For two, I'd piled cushions against that wall, so when I struck, it didn't hurt—badly. Unluckily, my favorite rocking chair was also in my path. It exploded as I hurtled through it, sending splinters spraying across the floor.

I've engaged in twenty-two ship-to-ship battles and taken part in dozens of hand-to-hand fights. One commonality was that I was skilled at all forms of combat. Events played out evenly and unsurprisingly. That happened as I plunged backward through my rocker.

Before I settled, I had my knife out. I didn't bother forming my protection spell. Besides, I'd cast it less than an hour ago, and reshaping it would've taken valuable time and wouldn't have helped.

"*Praeverto*," I screamed.

I hadn't previously used this spell and only read about it a few days ago. It was supposed to allow me both to divert impending attacks and better predict them.

"Shit, fuck, damn you!" she bellowed, teeth bared before yelling, "*Flattus.*"

She reached both hands behind her head and flung them forward toward me. The outburst of wind sent everything in front of her hurtling into the far wall of my home. The gust was powerful, but I only needed to lean into it to keep my feet.

"*Decipio. Ruina,*" I spoke one spell after the other. The first was meant to confuse Davi, and the second was a ranged destruction spell.

While I had little doubt about the outcome of the battle, I hoped I'd make her pay an acceptable measure for her assault.

Her eyes flew wide, and she swung both arms in front of her in broad circles. Then she smirked.

"Hello, James. How was your visit with Ms. Varde?" she asked, as if the fight and destruction inside of my home hadn't happened.

I rose and stared at her, wide-eyed and red-faced. If I could make steam shoot from my ears, the hot vapor would've been roaring out. I pointed at her and said, "You wrecked my home. You attacked without warning. Have you no honor?"

Okay, I admit the last part didn't matter. But I wanted to dig at her. I was pissed.

"You believe Riaan Dahl or Genosqwa will give you time to prepare? If so, you are as opaque as a black hole," she said. She must have noticed my confusion, because she continued. "I apologize, James."

Finally, the little demon-witch was apologizing for something she did. For a moment, I felt a bit of fondness develop for my guide. Then she continued. "I forgot you are a moronic super-dolt. If you had two brains, one would die of loneliness. I assume you do not know what a black hole is. Let me rephrase, then. You are as dense as a rock." She held out her hands, palms up, and bounced her shoulders.

"Fine. I needed to be prepared. Do you have any tips that may help, or are you content hurling insults?"

"I do not hurl insults. I disclose the truth. Insulting you is a fine reward, though," she declared without a hint of levity.

I chuckled and shook my head as I struggled to reclaim my dignity. Once again electing to not quibble with her, I collected myself and spent a few moments adjusting and scraping dirt from my clothes, then eventually glanced at her and beamed. "I did a good job of stopping your attack."

"Please. If flying across the room with your ass in the air is a good job, bend over, and I will fling you around again."

I surveyed the havoc her attack caused, my arms outstretched from my sides as I spun, scrutinizing the rooms. "Could you help with this?" I asked.

"You created the debris; you clean it."

I slumped and released my arms to my side. "At least repair my chair," I pleaded.

She didn't respond.

It took me the rest of the day to form the proper spells to mend my rocker. Still, it rocked with a slight wobble.

Cleaning the rest turned out to be more demanding. I learned to float objects to their proper location. My trouble was, I could only fly several light fragments or one large element at a time. It took hours of tedious effort before I was done.

Davi sat in her chair, drank her hot tea, and giggled the entire time.

39

JAMES

The morning of October first dawned sunny and freezing. Frost glazed the windows of my bedroom, and wind hissed through cracks around the doors. I added several chunks of wood to the cast-iron heater, and within a few minutes, a blaze warmed the area while I shaved and washed.

Today would be incredible. I could sense it. I donned a new golden shirt the seamstress delivered yesterday. It was another custom of mine. When I returned from a voyage, I'd pay the seamstress to produce several sets of new clothes, including pants, shirts, and socks.

Life at sea was rough on attire. Since a common voyage took between four and eight months, fresh clothes were a requirement, not a want. Besides, I appreciated looking my finest. You never knew who you might meet.

That thought immediately delivered a gut punch to my mood as I considered María. I finished dressing, crestfallen. Yeah, I know, put your big boy pants on and get busy. I got it. But you've got to cut me a bit of slack. I'd never met someone who made me weak in the knees like María did.

I trudged downstairs, my feet clunking a little too emphatically on the wooden treads. Davi was relaxing in her armchair, her porridge steaming away on the dinner table while she enjoyed her cup of tea. Her excited greeting startled me.

"Good morning, James. I trust you slept well?"

"Um, what's going on?" I asked.

"What, you dislike my cordial greeting? Fine. It is about fucking time you got your lazy ass out of bed. Eat so we can get to work."

I rolled my eyes.

She summoned a fresh breakfast. This time, she loaded my plate, although it contained far too many greens for breakfast.

"Davi, what is this green stuff?" I asked.

"For fuck's sake, James. You are going to become heavy if you continue eating like you do. That green stuff is edamame. Try it. You will enjoy it."

"Is that—"

Bang, bang, bang. Someone was knocking at my door.

Davi waved her hand again and two additional plates set themselves and more food appeared.

I glanced at her questioningly.

"Answer the door, dumb shit," she suggested. She wore that knowing smirk that frustrated me.

"Why is it you sit there circling your spoon in your tea with that stupid smirk on your face?" was what I tried to say. Unfortunately, my tongue betrayed me, and I actually said, "How do you always have that smirkle when you think you know something I don't?"

"You are dumber than I thought," she said and pointed at the door.

I answered. It was Kate.

"Mornin', Kate. I've made breakfast if you're hungry," I said, taking credit for preparing breakfast. Davi would give me grief after Kate left, but I didn't care. I stood aside and waved her inside. As soon as I did, I spotted another figure standing behind her. Although she wore a heavy cloak, it didn't disguise her.

"María!" I blurted, bouncing around Kate and jumping from the porch to the ground beside my Spanish queen.

"Shhhh!" they both hissed together as they scurried inside.

I tore after them. Once inside, María threw off her shawl and flung her arms around my neck. Her sweet lips met mine. They were hot as they parted for my tongue.

Then she hurriedly pulled away. I expect she remembered we were in front of company. Kate politely looked elsewhere, permitting us a moment of privacy. Davi, on the other hand, gawked at us unashamedly.

"Jim, remember yesterday, when I mentioned I had tasks to finish?" Kate asked.

I nodded.

"María's been hiding at my place since the Spaniards sailed away," she concluded.

"But I saw you board that ship. Kia rowed you away and loaded your belongings," I insisted.

"No. You saw Melodie Saddler's daughter, Maddie. She feigned being me and went out to the ship with them. Once there, she changed dresses, added a wig, and your Kia Dawson returned her," María said through a grin that could thaw an iceberg.

She was openly enthusiastic about this rule breaking. I'd have to needle her about it later.

"Then Presley and I smuggled her to my house. We couldn't have succeeded without Diego's support, though," Kate finished. She sounded content and remained watching me with a tooth-baring grin and palms on her hips.

"Presley and Diego both know? Your mother is going to be pissed."

My eyes must've gaped as the women snickered. Davi sat in her chair, sipping her tea and eating popped corn. The drama must have been riveting.

"No, Christina will take responsibility. My mother loves her dearly. She would never be cross. Our actual headache is that the Capitán of the *Bay of Cádiz* was charged with returning me to Rota. Eventually, he will realize I am not onboard. I am certain he will advise the fortress commander, who will take me into custody until another frigate arrives to send me home," María said.

Because her English is so perfect, I noticed that she pronounced Captain as Capitán, the way she would say it in her home country.

"Then we've got to keep this private. At least until we can figure out an approach to persuade your mother to let you stick around," I said, caressing her cheek.

"That's about it, Jimmy," my redheaded friend said.

"Are you positive you want this?" I said, tilting María's face to mine.

"I have never been more confident regarding something so preposterous in my entire life," she giggled.

"Marvelous," Davi said. Her palm slapped the table, and I spun to the sudden commotion. She continued, "Now, let him dip his wick so he can concentrate on genuine obstacles. Unless you think I should continue with my smirkle."

I turned brilliantly maroon and swung my head as I scanned the floor. Possibly, if I were fortunate, a void would open and devour me. At least Davi was dependable with her verbal assaults.

I pulled María back into my embrace and held her. Suddenly, an immediate inspiration caused my simple mind to engage, so I pushed her away. My heart raced and my breathing quickened.

"Are you suggesting you're staying—permanently?" I asked.

"My gosh, James. Not only are you a dumb shit, but you are also clueless," Davi said.

María only held my hands and laughed.

I disentangled my hands from hers and said, "Wait. I'll be back."

With that, I rushed upstairs to my room. I kept a modest wooden box with items I'd take if I needed to leave home in a hurry. I tugged open the pine box and emptied its contents onto my bunk. Besides gold and silver coins, it contained many of my most-cherished possessions, including the ring my mum had worn.

I snatched it and hustled back to María. Without hesitation, I sank to my knee in front of her and grabbed her hand. I didn't falter, because I'd never encountered a more straightforward choice.

"María, from the moment I set eyes on you, I've adored you. My passion for you is unlike any I've experienced. Will you give me the honor of becoming my wife? In the distant future, of course. I appreciate this is a rush."

I stared at her, my neck bent back, reading her captivating amber eyes in anticipation, her beatific beauty mesmerizing me. How could I not love this angel?

"No," she said, drawing her hands away.

Silence dropped like a barricade surrounding me. Kate looked away awkwardly. Davi sipped her tea, slurping and crunching her popped corn loudly. I glanced toward her while I was still on one knee. That she-demon had an infinite capacity to be an arse.

I forced myself to my feet. My gut turned and my face burned. María, recognizing my misery, reached and seized my hands again. "I am sorry, Jim," she said.

I couldn't form a rational thought. In one breath, the love of my life had come back to me. In the next, she'd yanked my beating heart from my chest and stomped it into the mud.

I pulled my hands away, as I preferred to escape the miserable room. María wouldn't let me hide, though, and she dragged my hands back to her, turning me around to peer into her eyes.

The ginger firelight gleamed in her flaxen eyes, and a naughty grin touched the edges of her mouth.

"The future is remarkably distant," she retorted slyly, tucking her chin and watching me through the corner of her amber eyes.

Kate roared with glee while María beamed and Davi crunched a mouthful of popped corn. I glanced at each of the women. I couldn't decide if my heart was racing because of bliss or embarrassment.

"Kate, is Presley busy this evening?" María asked as she tugged me to her lips.

I vaguely heard Kate's answer. "He is. Someone has requested he perform a wedding. It's some Spanish aristocrat who needs a hurried marriage."

Finally, like the clanging of a bell, my brain engaged, and I followed what the two women were suggesting. I backed away from the kiss, held her left hand, and pressed the salmon-colored sapphire onto her finger. Then I kissed her again, this time as her betrothed.

After the kiss, we remained close, and she sketched her finger along my jawline.

"Surprise," she declared.

"You two had this arranged?" I asked. Neither woman answered my foolish question because the answer was unmistakable.

"So, this is how it'll be," I teased as I caressed her chin and bent for a brief kiss.

"Davi, I need a couple of days off. Okay?" I begged.

"You must continue your study, James. Dahl will not fucking stop to celebrate. But you have displayed noticeable progress. After your holiday, you had better be prepared for work. We have until the end of the month," Davi stated.

"Great," I said.

"Jimmy, leave your house now. You can't see María again until the wedding. She and I have work. Go spend time with Presley. He'll fill you in on the marriage details," Kate said.

I kissed my wife-to-be one more time and vaulted out the door. I ran several strides before I realized I'd brought nothing to wear and neglected my coat. Realizing the temperature was well below freezing, I hustled inside, where María handed me my coat before shooing me out the door again.

Maybe the seamstress can sew me something nice to wear, I thought as I saddled my ebony stallion and rode to Presley's house.

He was watching for me, and jerked the door wide before I'd even knocked. He gave me a mug of coffee as he hauled me inside his home.

"Pres, how long have you known?" I asked as I drilled him in the arm.

"For a couple of weeks. Diego and I've been working on the details since you went to his house for dinner," he answered as he smoothed the spot I punched.

My mouth gaped. He sipped his coffee and smiled coolly.

Presley was as shrewd a man as I'd ever met. The two of us were perhaps too bull-headed to crew together, but we'd convoyed often. He operated his ship, the *Aquilon,* as a merchantman, and the *Monarch,* while it could carry merchandise, was made to seize other ships.

"Do you have a strategy if the Spaniards discover her?" I inquired.

"Well, step one is to delay them learning she's not aboard the *Cádiz*. At the same time, we keep her sheltered."

"You know Metaterre will be their first port of call," I suggested as I squinted at him questioningly.

"Yep. And our business'll be to mislead 'em."

"Pres, that won't work. We can't keep her indoors indefinitely."

"Well, I've been ponderin'. You own that Eldritch place. We could raise you a house out there 'til you get that manor all patched up. That's an extensive section of countryside, so ain't nobody gonna see her. Not to mention, everyone's petrified of the place. Besides, after the two of you have a kid, her mom's gotta leave you be."

"I can't," I responded, stalling for time as my brain played through options. I kept thinking of my vision when that stone monster came for María and our two children. I'd decided my dreams were variants of probable futures, much like Davi described, so my fear was reasonable.

"Jimmy, you just gotta play for time, that's all. You know María wants a family. She's been talkin' to Kate about it for the last two days. It's got Kate talkin' to me about startin' one, too. Once you have a child, it'll be *fait accompli*."

I nodded. I realized my friends would help keep María hidden. The townsfolk would, too. Between Presley and me, we counted everyone in this township as a friend. There wasn't one of them who'd trouble us or our families.

I guess if you counted Dahl as one of the townsfolk, they weren't *all* allies. I'd have to keep this marriage secret so that creature couldn't use my new bride against me.

Suddenly, Presley's door banged open and his pretty wife scrambled through. We both glanced up, startled at her abrupt entrance. A jolt of dread shot through me.

"Is everything alright? Is María okay?" I pleaded.

"Yes, Jim. Everything is perfectly fine. Davi's looking over your fiancée. Don't worry," Kate said.

"Hello, babe. What is it?" Presley asked.

"I need you to get the flowers and foodstuffs to the *Aquilon*. Jimmy,

I'm supposing you'll want this as secret as possible. But if you choose to invite Kia..." she paused. Kate was uncommonly perceptive, and María was a genius. Of course they'd talked about the need for privacy too.

"I expect I will. But you're correct: we gotta keep this quiet. Presley, do you need to tell your crew?" I asked.

"Nah, Jim. I took care of that yesterday. I sent some of the crew away. The ones there, I'd trust with Kate's life. The lot of 'em would crew with ol' Davy Jones before they'd let this secret out." If Presley stated it, it made it true. I didn't challenge it.

"But, ol' friend, we need to get you dressed. I had some clothes stitched together. They're upstairs. You get dressed and let's go to the *Aquilon*. There are a few consignments we have to oversee," Presley said.

Before we reached his ship, I paused at the *Monarch* to tell Kia Dawson about my impending marriage.

"Bout bloody times, Cap'n. You been a-pining for that young woman fur long 'nuff, now maybe you'll quit seein' broken axles on new cannons. The crew been a-wonderin' if'n you be needin' some of those spectacles." He laughed uproariously at his humor. I rolled my eyes at my Executive Officer.

Kia and I had met when I was a thirteen-year-old powder monkey on a Royal Navy warship, and he was seventeen and a captive in Costa Rica. Our Captain had heard of a pirate hideout and led a mission to destroy it. During that battle, we'd rescued Kia, along with dozens of other men. Kia had joined the Royal Navy and remained aboard our ship out of loyalty for being rescued. We became friends and had crewed together on the same ships since meeting.

Over the years, he'd become as disenchanted with the policies of the Empire as I. So, when I quit the service of fat King George, Kia joined me. He may have been my XO, but he was as rare a friend as you could imagine. He'd never miss my marriage.

Presley, Kia, and I boarded the *Aquilon* as the crew loaded crates of food and ornaments. The frosty morning faded as the sunlight thawed the day. Or maybe it was the fever from my heart.

A half an hour after I boarded, I saw Kate drive a wagon dockside. In the wagon was a wooden trunk spacious enough to carry a filly. In fact, several holes were drilled into the top, which I could only see because I stood on the deck, many feet above it. Kate paced back and forth in front of it, wringing her hands. I chuckled when one of the crew decided to shake the box to judge its weight. Kate exploded like an enormous cat seizing its prey.

"You'll give up those hands if you manhandle that crate again. It carries my best table and china," she said. Her face was flaming, and she leaned near her quarry as she lifted a clenched fist to just under his chin.

The crewman backed away, raising both hands as he moved. "I sorry, miss's. I don'na mean ta make an issue. But why's ya bringin' ya's invaluable's ta here?"

"Not that it's your concern, but I'm having repairs performed on my home, and I want these items out so they don't get ruined," she answered, relaxing now that the man was backing away.

Chuckling, I howled, "Hello, Kate. What ya got there?"

"Never you mind, Jim. You get my husband down here. And do it at once, or I'll get cross." She beamed.

I grimaced. Kate could wield her dual-edged smile as sharply as I could my saber. One facet showed a perfect cherub; an exquisite angel whose words offered harmony, kindheartedness, and tranquility on earth. The other was a wrathful dybbuk beauty. Anyone who'd seen Katie's pernicious doppelganger knew better than to cross her. I was no exception, and I shoved off to locate her husband.

Presley was below deck, tending to something less consequential than his wife waiting. His eyes flew wide when I informed him Kate had kindly demanded his presence. "Dammit, she's early!" He didn't delay, though, and hustled to the dock to haul the crate. I'd already guessed what was inside the container, but said nothing.

Presley also assured the festivities would stay secret by persuading the Harbor Master to close the bay to everyone except the *Aquilon* crew. His excuse was that he was unpacking a sizable load of explosives. Since this was a dangerous activity, the Harbor Master agreed, though I doubt he believed Presley's fiction.

It didn't matter, though, because anything either of us sought, the Harbor Master allowed. During our careers, we'd delivered that man enough port to float a ship.

40

JAMES

*W*e held the marriage ceremony in the galleries beneath the ship's poop deck. In the few hours since her arrival, Kate had decorated it with evergreen garland, stringers, bouquets, and plants from both our homes. There were, likewise, several designs I was certain Davi had magically produced.

For those of you who've been to a wedding, I won't bore you with the minutiae. For the rest of you, I won't bore you by recounting it. Yes, I'm flatly stating that this wedding, like all others, was exhausting. Why? Because the event forced me to gawk at this most exquisite woman without expressing my feelings. Feelings inappropriate to discuss with anyone but María, by the way.

Fine, I'll supply the highlights. But I must be brief, because that stone demon is practically through my defenses.

María wore a long yellow silken Regency dress. Frilly white decorations encircled her waistline, and the sleeves were puffy, with white cuffs matching her waist. Her veil was silvery and kept in place by a garland of blue, red, and white flowers. She told me afterward that she'd chosen those colors as evidence of her embracing the colonies and their cause as her own.

Presley mumbled something, then María spoke. "With this ring, I thee wed."

I stared at her, my mouth hanging slightly open. Presley kicked me.

Spurred back to reality, I followed with, "This gold and silver I give thee." Then I held my hand to her, pushing a leather pouch into her palm, which she raised to meet mine.

Like I said, María is a genius. She accepted the bag, scowled at me unflinchingly, and growled, "There had better be sufficient gold to purchase a horse, two donkeys, twelve chickens, and a goat."

Presley, Kate, and I roared. The rest of the gallery silently observed the four of us. My first mate, Kia Dawson, who was my best man, leaned close and blurted, "Cap'n, drinkin' 'fore ta weddin's bad luck." We laughed again.

After composing ourselves, María presented me with the gold ring. "James, my uncle Diego is the closest man I have to a father. This ring has been in his family for seven generations. He told me he would be honored if you would wear it as an emblem of my love for you."

I didn't realize Diego felt that way, since I'd guessed he only liked me because I'd helped him to compile a vast fortune. I beamed at the golden lion's head on my finger.

A hand on my shoulder spurred my return to reality. Presley was speaking to me again. It was my turn to give María her ring. After I'd set it on her finger, Presley said, "I pronounce you husband and wife. Now kiss your bride."

The guests cheered as we kissed and roared again when we faced them. Only now did I recognize my entire crew was here. I stole a glance at Kia, who only shrugged in response.

Kia and Presley led the men in setting up tables. I guess calling them tables would be a stretch. They used whisky barrels and laid planks across them. Invariably when they set one, Kate would order the men to move it to a new location. Finally, Kia and Presley threw up their hands, and stomped away in frustration.

While Kate wasn't fussing over the table placement, she busied herself with rearranging the flowers. She made sure the prettiest flowers were nearest María's seat. But, she made sure every table had a bouquet decorating its center.

Once satisfied, she allowed the cook to deliver the food. She had it set on its own table so each of us could follow a line to collect what meat and greens we'd want. No, there wasn't any edamame. But there was enough food to feed twice as many guests. Oh, and there was plenty of cherry pie. Mm mm!

After we ate, the men cleared away the tables. One of Presley's crew, a Greek named Darius, rose and led us through a dance called the Kalamatiano. According to Kate, María had insisted on this dance. She had been born and reared in Rota, Spain, but traveled frequently to Greece, and developed a particular affection for its history. She announced this dance was as ancient as the Trojan War, since Homer referred to it in the *Iliad*. To my mind, it was a merry dance in which people danced in a circle, hopped periodically, and tossed in random kicks for fun.

We celebrated until after nightfall, when it was time to take my bride home. With the sun having long left the sky, it was easy to get her there hidden inside the rear of Presley's buggy.

A squall was developing, and dropped tiny icy rain droplets. María lay in the back, covered by several blankets. It was early in the morning, so I doubted anyone would notice this buggy traveling through town, but I wouldn't take any chances on anyone noticing her, so she remained out of sight. The rain was frigid, but tolerable. Still, I didn't want my new bride outside any longer than necessary, so I trotted the horses.

As the rain began to freeze, ice pellets bit into my face and hands. By the time I stopped near my house, my fingers were numb and my eyes burned from the chilly wind.

As the horses halted, I hopped down from Presley's buggy, opened the door to my—*our*—house, and dashed back to my waiting bride. I folded the blankets off her to discover her beaming back at me. Her smile was a present I'd never take for granted.

"That was fun," she teased.

"Here, let me help." I dragged the blankets off and plucked her up in one fluid motion, then carried her across the threshold into the warm kitchen. I lowered her feet to the floor, then slammed the door shut behind us.

"Welcome home," I announced as I leaned to kiss her. She responded by placing both hands behind my head and pulling mine to hers.

I reluctantly drew away. "Make yourself at home. I need to secure Presley's mares," I told her before I hurried back outside.

I led the team of horses into my large pole barn. After I unbridled each animal, I led them to stalls and dried and brushed them before giving them buckets of oats. I didn't need to dry or brush them. They would have dried inside the heated barn. But a horse was an important asset, and taking care of these animals was a way of caring for my best friend's family.

I grabbed María's bag of clothes from the wagon. Before I hurried inside our house, I stomped the mud off my boots. Inside, I kicked them off one at a time and looked around the empty kitchen where I'd left my new bride. As I searched the room, I noticed Davi's chair, a permanent fixture in my kitchen, was missing.

Luckily, someone had lit several candles, so I easily saw a trail of clothes.

I followed it.

MARÍA

*T*made myself comfortable. The galley and living space were vacant. But I didn't choose to linger; instead, I began searching. I discovered the upstairs bedroom and decided to play a game of hide and seek.

I returned to the kitchen, tossed my shawl onto the middle of the floor, and deposited one slipper on the squeaky floorboard in the salon and the other at the bottom stair. On the stairwell, I dropped the veil I had worn during our marriage service. On a short bench at the top of the stairs, I draped my wedding gown.

When I strolled into the bedroom, a cluster of candles on an adjacent table lit. My stomach clenched, then softened as I grasped what had transpired. I appreciated James was a wizard, and days ago had decided I did not care. These were his tricks, and nothing for me to dread.

A slight fire smoldered in the stove. I added another split-pine log. The fire crackled as the wood dropped into the flames. Although this was plainly his bedroom, it was trimmed in an unmistakably feminine fashion.

"I must thank him for his inclusiveness," I said to the four walls.

A kaleidoscope of vases decorated every horizontal surface.

Dozens of them adorned the shelving, tables, and hearth. Most held red and yellow roses accented by blooms of miniature white, blue, and red, matching the flowers of our wedding. Others carried only either red or yellow rosebuds.

A steaming bath dominated the center of the chamber. A heavy, frothy white foam covered the surface.

The tub was built of cedar planks. Metal banding like that used on liquor casks held the wooden boards together. The cistern was lengthier than James and could hold us both. I slid my fingers along the arcing edge as I walked around its base, marveling at how silky the lumber felt to my touch.

I closed my eyes and leaned into the steam to take in its bouquet. Breathing in deeply, I detected a burst of spicy cinnamon tempered by rose. A base of what must be styrax added its vanilla undertone. The bouquet blended and left my nose searching for the lighter, more fleeting smells of rose and cinnamon. The whole of the bath intoxicated me.

I stood in the room simply wearing my undergarments. I slowly rotated to take in its sights and odors.

The few candles, along with the now-crackling fire produced a defused orange-and-yellow glimmer that danced across the brilliantly whitewashed walls. I wanted to encapsulate this moment in my memory.

Below me, a loud bang echoed as a door opened. My heart leaped as I heard it again, this time as it closed.

James

HAVING STAMPED my boots hard onto the floor, clearing the slush. I spotted the trail of clothes and realized what was in store.

I rushed to the stairs, my footfalls causing loud squeaks from the floorboards. The treads groaned as they took my burden. My head, then body, stepped higher and higher into the bedroom.

I was so focused on finding my wife that I neglected to navigate the dress-covered chesterfield placed outside my bedchamber.

"Ouch," I mumbled. "Who put that danged bench here?"

I knew full well it had been that blonde she-demon attempting to further sabotage me.

The modifications to my bedchamber were a curiosity. My eyes met María's. Her coy laugh was a celestial melody. "My husband, you have been a busy boy."

"I expect I owe Davi a thank you," I acknowledged.

"That candle lighting was an elegant trick," she said.

My mouth curled and forehead creased as I focused for a moment. I shrugged as I realized I didn't care about candles. Not while this divine beauty stood in front of me. Her décolletage was teasing and attracting my eye like a magnet.

"I love you with all my heart," I said.

"You, sir, are smarter than you look." She giggled, then said, "*Yo no sé te lo dije hoy pero yo te amo mucho mucho mi hermoso.*"

I understood what she'd told me, even though I didn't speak her language well.

"I've got a trick or two for you," I said, lowering my voice an octave. I crossed the room, dragged her to me, and kissed her on the mouth. Our tongues danced.

She drew away, softly pressing her palms against my chest, stepping back.

Finally remembering to breathe, I exhaled. My next breath was quick and hitched.

My eyes were glued to her as she raised one foot to the lip of the tub. She playfully slid both hands from the bottom of her toes to the top of her stocking, her fingers tracing the muscles along the way.

It bewitched me.

When she approached the top of the hosiery just above her knee, she freed the garter, then slipped her thumbs under and around the edge of the silky material before retracing her passage along her long, lean leg.

I followed, utterly absorbed in her every action. This woman accepted the force of her vivacity and the power of the voyage.

When the stocking was free of her painted toes, she tossed...

Wait! Never mind the rest. If you've been in this type of relationship, you know what happens. If not, well...never mind, I'm not saying anything else.

When the...umm, merriment was over, I lay on our bed with my eyes closed, my new bride by my side. The seconds ebbed our ecstasy away, and I opened my eyes to catch her watching me. At this moment, nothing else mattered; nothing except her.

"I don't want to sound silly, but that was extraordinary," I said.

She laughed, rolled to her elbow, and brushed my hair from my face.

"I cannot understand how I came to cherish you so quickly, but I am pleased," she replied and touched her index finger to my nose.

We chatted for an hour, describing our future. Then we... uh, participated in the merriment again. This time the fever burned less, but the reward was just as intoxicating.

Afterwards, we retreated to the bath, which remained hot, despite it having sat for hours.

The next morning, I dressed and left the room. While I was gone, María slipped into the tub. It remained as warm and frothy as it had been the preceding evening. She let it warm her body as she closed her eyes, relaxing into it until it touched her chin.

When I returned, I carried plates loaded with scrambled eggs, strips of ham, bread, and blackberry jelly. Two cups of steaming liquid sat on the tray, along with eating utensils.

"Is that a cup of tea?" She asked as she rose from the tub, her skin rouged by the bath.

"Yep," I answered as I set down our breakfast and snagged a towel to wrap around her.

She stepped into my arms and settled there. Steam rose from her bare shoulders and water dripped, puddling on the floor. She pulled away from my embrace, her amber eyes probing mine before glancing at the food, then back. Her face beamed.

"Mm-mm, that looks delicious," she said before asking, "Are you going to soak in the tub again?"

I looked to the tub, wishing to soak one more time with my new bride, when above the tub, in the wisps of steam, a message spelled itself out in large letters.

"YOU STINK, DUMBASS."

I shook my head. Davi never tired of insulting me. María giggled.

"I can't. I've got chores to get to," I said. We stared wide-eyed as the tub faded from view. I mouthed, "Wow."

"Did you do that?" she asked.

"Nope. But I'll ask that blonde she-devil how she did. I also need to find out if she's listening in," I continued, more than a hint of irritation creeping into my tone.

After she dried, I wrapped her in a woven robe and tied it around her waist. We sat on the bed and ate our first breakfast as husband and wife. Our simple conversation left no opportunity for awkwardness. Finally, since meeting Davi, I was relaxed.

It was a feeling that, unfortunately, wouldn't last.

JAMES

The forty-eight-hour reprieve that Davi had granted went in a blur. I lost both mornings feeding my animals, cleaning pens, chopping wood, and doing the dozens of other chores required on my homestead.

My farm was as self-sufficient as I could make it. I relied on others for remarkably few tasks. Sure, I'd buy clothes, food, and even have my horse shod. But if I could carry out a project myself, I would. I reasoned that by caring for myself and those dear to me, I'd be better prepared during emergencies.

Besides, taking care of trivial tasks informed me of bigger issues that I might not recognize if someone else did the work. You might suspect that, being skipper of a ship, I'd be accustomed to allowing people to finish insignificant chores. You'd be mistaken. On the *Monarch*, I received daily updates on work; plus, when I inspected the ship, I'd recognize other maintenance issues.

Unfortunately, since I considered this entire town my people, I felt an obligation to safeguard each of them. Now, I devoted too much time seeking fixes for every trouble I encountered, even ones I didn't need to fret about. This might be why Davi refused to tell me what to do.

When I wasn't working outside, I was inside studying, which was far more pleasurable. Why? Because I spent this time with my bride.

María was a remarkably trained woman and loved learning. She took it on herself to work with me, and rapidly became proficient in the jargon of spellcraft.

"James, have you mastered this spell called *Castellem?*" she asked.

Apparently, my spell book, *Down With Spells*, had decided to inform my wife of important spells. It would regularly reorder itself so she had the most powerful ones at hand.

"Yep. I shape it repeatedly. Davi said I'm decent with it. Still, it doesn't block everything. It handles moderate strikes, but only weakens the worst assaults. Mostly, it's kept me from being injured severely," I replied, hoping not to upset her unnecessarily.

"What do you mean, 'injured severely?' Did Dahl attack you?" Concern had caused her tone to raise an octave, and her eyes widened.

"Not at all, beautiful. Davi does," I answered steadily.

"Oh," she responded, calming.

"But she hurts you?" she pressed.

"Well, it kinda comes with the territory—training with her. She believes in a hands-on method of education. That frequently means she's shooting spells and tossing me around the room. When she's finished, I get to clean up the wreckage." I chuckled, hoping to defuse the anxiety she must be feeling.

I was hesitant to describe the specific interactions between Davi and me. Besides, coming to grips with the fact that I was a wizard must be challenging enough. I refused to add to my wife's burden.

"What do you mean, she tosses you around?"

"Just that. Literally, I fly and land somewhere inside the house. Sometimes, it hurts. She snapped my leg once. Don't worry, though. She's excellent with healing spells. She patches me up and we go at it again. Remember, Davi's an ancient, powerful magician. She's struggling to train me to deal with another potent magical being."

"So this Riaan Dahl is as powerful as Davi?" she asked. Genuine concern filled her words.

"She told me that in another realm, he could be. On ours, he's handicapped. That should permit me an edge when it counts."

"So why does she not just destroy him herself?" she demanded.

"She stated he's our problem. Specifically, he's mine. She'll guide me, but if I can't stop Dahl, she'll move on to help someone else with a different issue. I appreciate it sounds heartless, but those are her people's laws. She's got to adhere to them. Helping is ok. Doing it for us isn't. I have to win."

Tears filled my Spanish queen's eyes and she bowed her head and faced away. I tugged her to her feet and held her tight. She drew her arms to her chest and clenched her fists. Her fingers turned white at the exertion.

"Babe, I've got this. I realize I'm not prepared now, but I will be. I've encountered far more hazards in my life. I won't let a runt like Dahl stop us from enjoying our life together. These next four weeks will be rough. I've got a bunch to learn. But I'd wager I can get more accomplished with your help."

Having a prodigy like María on my team could only help. Besides, giving her a role should focus her on helping me win this battle, and off…well, pending disaster.

"How about that? You mind helping me work out this mess?" I asked.

She was an amazingly complex woman who could turn on a dime. That was one quality that attracted me to her. She shifted her face to me, her amber eyes squinted in resolve.

"I will help you, *mi amor*." I recognized she meant she'd do whatever it took to help me win this battle.

We spent the rest of the afternoon and evening practicing and examining various spells that my book deemed important enough to show us. By the time we reached our bed, we were exhausted.

Not that exhausted, though.

JAMES

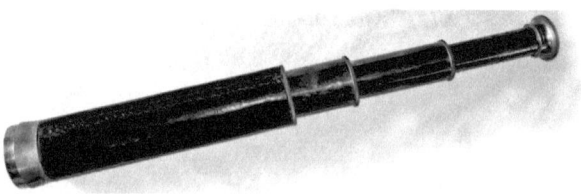

*T*he sunlight kissed the eastern sky and flooded through my glass window, waking me to scrub the sleep dust from my eyes. I drew a great breath and held it, fighting the desire to release the tantrum that longed to burst from the tired two-year-old boy inside me. I craved to linger in bed with my new bride, but Davi had given me a two-day respite, and it was over.

I slid my legs from beneath the rough woolen blankets. The chill in the room caused my skin to tingle as I fed the fire. In minutes, the flames licked the sides of the stove.

Contented that the blaze would warm the space for María, I dressed and started for the stairs. I didn't put on my boots, padding softly out of the room. My eyes on my bride, I closed the door quietly. As I moved forward to the staircase, I crammed my pinky toe into the bench once again.

"Holy…" I grunted and held my breath, proceeding down the steps.

I skipped the squeaky fourth stair, remembering just in time to crouch to avoid banging my head.

My mini-vacation had passed far too quickly, but I was determined to learn what was necessary to finish the dual menace of Dahl and the monster haunting Eldritch Manor.

Davi's pink overstuffed flowered armchair had returned and was in its place in my kitchen, where she sat sipping her tea and cooling a dish of gruel.

"Good morning, James. Did you have a suitable wedding?" she asked. The tilt of her head and devilish narrowing of her eyes told me the question was a tease.

"It was incredible. And thank you for the gift of the flowers, the bath, and the message. They were unusually gracious of you." I couldn't resist the urge to needle her back while simultaneously thanking her.

She closed her eyes and nodded once in reply, avoiding my veiled taunt.

"So, how did the tub know to dissolve when we stopped using it?" I inquired. I struggled not to be combative in my approach, but if she could overhear, I needed to know so I could stop her.

"Are you fucking kidding me? You cannot be that fucking stupid. Listen to me," she scolded. "Of course you can be that fucking dull. No, you dumb shit. That tub did not *know* to disappear. It was composed of wood. It perceived nothing. I placed a disillusionment charm on it. When you mentioned anything negative about it, it stimulated the spell and went *vacuefacio.*"

"*Vacuefacio?* You need to explain that one," I replied.

"No shit, Sherlock. It means it passed into nothingness. Its energy returned to the ether," she replied cluelessly, including two new terms.

"Do I care what a Sherlock or ether are?" I huffed.

"The first is after your lifetime. Ignore it. The second—let us wait for your bride. I prefer to describe this once, and she is more intelligent than you."

"I agree," I added truthfully and shrugged.

"It occurs when your blood flows to the wrong head," she explained dryly. I shook my head and shifted to cook breakfast for María and me.

"Do I need to ask what you are doing?" Davi asked.

"I'm cooking breakfast. And you claim I'm dumb," I teased.

"I recognize what you are undertaking. Why are you doing it?" she said. "I have demonstrated the correct spells for accomplishing that task."

"Sure. But I enjoy cooking for her. Just shut up and let me do my thing," I ordered.

Davi held her hands up in mock surrender. It was interesting. Every time she required her hands, they were empty. Otherwise, she held a cup of tea.

I overheard a delicate knock and a slight squeak, followed by footsteps. My bride was descending the stairs. If seeing Davi sitting in her chair with an "I know more than you" smile surprised María, she didn't show it. Instead, she beamed at my guide.

"Good morning, Davi. How are you today?" she asked as she stepped to the blonde woman and kissed her softly on each cheek.

A tingle shot up my spine. Something was off.

"Good morning, my dear. I trust you had a lovely wedding?"

"I did. And I cannot thank you enough for the generosity you showed with your magic. It was incredible."

Again, the chill tickled my neck. The smiles of both women seemed routine. But something was awry.

"It was nothing, my dear. I am pleased you appreciated it."

"Davi, I must get this off my chest." María said.

Oh no, it was here. I kept cooking, hoping to evade any shrapnel that may fly from the coming battle.

"My dear, I expect straightforward, open paths of conversation, especially from a woman as rational as you," Davi countered smoothly.

If the compliment put off my wife, she didn't show it. "Thank you. But if I discover you have injured my husband unnecessarily, you will pay. Do we understand each other?"

I turned when she mentioned injuring me. My mouth dropped open, and the fried egg I had been flipping slid off my spatula, landing on the floor with a resounding *splat*. It was a contest that could further open my mouth or eyes as I watched these two women parlay.

Davi slurped her tea. If María's warning offended her, she showed no hint.

María didn't break her gaze. Her eyes didn't flitter around the room, and her cheeks weren't flushed. This was tigress against tigress.

"My dear, I appreciate your criticism. James is the love of your life. I realize what you have given up far better than he. I assure you, I am not hurting him spitefully. If I could instruct him without inducing injury, I would. The fact is, he should have begun training at eleven. Instead, I had sixty-one days, of which I have fewer than thirty remaining to prepare him. I am sorry, but his practice must be rigorous. It may be the only means of preserving his life."

I'd seen the blonde-demon's serious side. As ever, she was composed, and never broke eye contact. As Davi spoke, María's shoulders slumped. Clearly, she believed my guide.

After a couple of breaths listening to the sausage and eggs fry, Davi returned to herself.

"James, we are not creatures in a petting zoo. For fuck's sake, finish cooking already. We must return to your training," she said.

Aaaand just like that, the positive feelings vanished. My amber-eyed girl giggled. I turned to my cooking. I finished frying the eggs and sausage and set them aside. Then I mixed about a quarter-cup of flour into the still-sizzling sausage grease.

As I stirred, María asked, "James, what are you preparing?"

"I'm cooking sausage gravy," I replied.

"Why?" was her heathenish question.

"The Bible calls it mana. The Israelites ate it when they roamed the desert for forty years. This food comes straight from our beneficent Lord," I said proudly.

My stoic, rational, rule-following wife spit her tea as she laughed. "They did not eat sausage gravy. They didn't eat pork of any sort. It was considered unclean."

"That's because they're trying to keep the secret of mana to themselves. I refuse to let them," I rebutted.

Davi seemed to enjoy this little tit for tat. She blew across her tea, her eyes bouncing between the two of us, that same enigmatic smile never faltering.

María tried a different tack. "*Mi hermoso*, eating that much grease is unhealthy."

At this, Davi grunted approvingly. "I told the dumbass the same thing. Maybe he will listen to you."

"Neither of you uncultured cretins know what fine cuisine is. Besides, you can't knock it 'til you try it," I said as I splashed in fresh goat's milk.

"I would sooner eat cow shit," Davi said. I glowered. She ignored me.

I got my wife to try the sausage gravy over a slice of cornbread. She loved it.

Despite having twice as much food, I finished eating before my bride. I concluded I'd need to slow down. In my defense, rushing through meals was something I'd adapted to because I constantly needed to complete a chore. With Davi's practices added in, the pressure to be more productive had become even greater.

Davi ordered me to employ magic to clear the breakfast mess. I did, and my wife scowled.

"Davi, how can you be certain nobody can witness this?" She held her hands out to her sides to encompass the room.

"Wonderful question, my dear. I believe your husband should have inquired. Sadly, he did not," she concluded as she ducked her head and shook it in revulsion. "I set an enchantment on the entire dwelling to block anyone from snooping. Someone standing near the window would merely see an unused room."

My teacher seemed pleased with herself.

María persisted. "What about Kate or Presley? According to Kate, they are as prone to wandering straight inside as to knocking."

"Another astute observation. They cannot enter until I allow. The charm makes them knock. If I choose, they will forget the purpose of their visit and drift elsewhere."

The question-and-answer session continued as my new spouse delved further into magical theory. Her curiosity simplified my lessons, or possibly made them more straightforward.

My instruction continued daily. I only paused to tend my animals, eat, and chop wood for heat. Since María was in hiding and couldn't work at the hospital, she spent her time studying the intricacies of magic and the threat Dahl and Genosqwa posed.

In that regard, there were countless occasions I worried she'd break down. But my girl was composed of tough material, and she shrugged off the threats to continue hunting for solutions.

Unfortunately, I had discovered a path that would secure my family and friends. But I had to keep it secret. I'd only discuss it with Davi if I couldn't find another option.

One diversion for María was the All-Hallowmas festival. It was her favorite festival of the year, and she enjoyed decorating. That meant she'd need to be outside.

Davi taught me a basic illusion charm that I used to conjure a pendant for María. The spell made everyone except Kate and Presley forget they saw her. The only reason they could remember her was because Davi created another incantation for each of them to counter María's.

The exclusive purpose of her pendant was to allow her outside while maintaining her anonymity from the Spaniards and Riaan Dahl, although I was more anxious about the Spanish than Dahl.

44

JAMES

The morning dawned sunny and chilly. The previous few days had been pleasant, and allowed María to devote time outside, festooning the exterior with pumpkins and evergreen garlands for color.

She had also been investigating the annals of Eldritch.

"Dear, I am leaving to ask Kate to visit the library with me," she announced at breakfast.

She caught me mid-bite, and I wavered, my mouth wide and a biscuit shoved partway inside. I spotted her smile and bit down, chewing slowly. I needed to play for time. If I said yes, Dahl might see her, despite her necklace. It was conceivable he could see through the magic, or maybe it would collapse at an inopportune juncture. Maybe this, or maybe that. My mind darted from action to hazard. I was searching for the correct response when she interrupted my spiraling thoughts.

"*Hermoso*," she declared, holding her tea in front of her mouth and gently blowing the steam away.

Was that something women did to throw off their adversaries? More likely, it was something intelligent women used against idiots.

I gulped and struggled to say, "Yes." What came out was, "Yuuuh."

She smirked. "I was not seeking your approval. I was advising you. Please respect my decision."

How could I disagree? Besides, I'd realized she was strong-willed before I married her. That was one of her most alluring qualities.

"Sure. No problem," I intoned, drawing out the words.

She grinned again. This time, she realized she'd won a trivial victory—one where she'd made the only move.

"I need to form another protection jura first. Also, I want Davi--" I halted and glanced around the room. "Wait, where is that she-devil, anyhow? She's always here causing me problems. Now I need her and she's missing in action."

"It will be fine, Jim," my brown-eyed beauty said, placating my inner boy.

45

MARÍA

I bridled the mares and hooked them to the buggy myself. James insisted on helping. When I cautioned he had other commitments, he left me alone.

I drove the buggy to the front of Kate's house, hopped down, and knocked on her door. James had teased me the first time he saw me jump from the carriage before it ceased moving. I suppose he had never seen another woman, besides Kate, do that.

Our redheaded friend had told me that it was okay to enter without knocking. However, I was unaccustomed to that intimacy. In Rota, no one would enter any private area without approval. It would be a hard habit for me to break. Besides, I didn't mind enjoying the sun during the few moments it took for her to answer.

"María!" Kate exclaimed. "Good morning, beautiful."

"Good morning, *Roja*," I answered.

We exchanged kisses as she tugged me into her home. As I expected, it was in impeccable order. The breakfast clutter was tidied, and a pot of something simmered near the fire. The aromas of onion and garlic filled the air.

"Kate, I must travel to the library to determine how the disappearances at your family's manor began. I mean to help James defeat whatever caused it. I was hoping for your assistance."

Kate Varde was as accomplished a lady as I and did not recoil at my invitation.

"Of course I will. I kinda got James involved in this to begin with, so I suppose I'm answerable for helping him fix it," the redheaded beauty answered.

After leaving, Kate drove. She loves the freedom she feels when she runs her horses. This ride to the library was an...invigorating ride. It was made comical as I recognized the men running from the roadway when they realized who was holding the reins.

"One day, I want to race," she told me, her eyes narrowed in concentration, apparently imagining herself winning some prize.

Once inside the library, we set to work on finding any information regarding the manor. The librarian was a boon. He provided documents, including copies of old newsprints from many of the disappearances. The ones I was the most interested in were the early ones.

"This is all so confusing. It is not possible to form a stone effigy through an individual's death," I said after nearly three hours of work.

"I had a preacher whom I was discussing demons and angels with. His name was Edward Lorane Warren. He was the biggest man... never mind. He used to tell me, 'Kate, you can't be scientific in a supernatural world.' That's where we are now. It isn't logical at all."

She perfectly surmised my problem. I could not analyze these events scientifically. Doing so would stop my research before it began. That bit of insight, while blindingly obvious in hindsight, made my research easier.

I chastised myself for my shortsightedness when we found the news articles written after her grandmother, Peggy, disappeared. The article explained that Kate's mother, Margret, had been raised by her father. Peggy had disappeared when Margret was nine. Tragically, Margret too died soon after Katie's birth, leaving her grandfather to raise her.

Unfortunately, I was so focused on finding information to aid Jim that I'd neglected to consider the hurt it might cause my friend. I

noticed tears streaking her cheeks, but I feigned interest in a document. If it were me, I would prefer to drop my tears in privacy.

After several hours of work, we both agreed we had reached an
impasse.

Kate drove me home, insisting she would not leave until I was
safely tucked away inside.

"Have Jimmy put away the horses. I'll walk home. It's not far," she
said.

Of course, I asked James to take her home.

I cooked dinner. Unlike my husband, my meals included many raw
vegetables and a smaller portion of meat. Over dinner, I recounted
what Kate and I had observed in our research.

"Jim, a single commonality connects those who have a sculpture at
Eldritch."

I hesitated and caught his eye to assure he was genuinely attentive.
I should not have bothered. He hung on my every phrase, even if I
were discussing the hazards of sloppy roads.

"Each of them was sick or elderly when they disappeared.
According to Davi, every person who perished after being injured by
the blade simply evaporated. They left no trace. In your nightmare,
you mentioned Charles Doss bled on the spyglass. He does not have a
statue either."

"That's unusual, María. But I don't understand how it'll help us."

"I suspect those who bled onto the dagger or spyglass did not
render an effigy. It might not matter, but it could be significant. I am
sorry I did not discover more."

"Thank you for this. I concede, it might not be useful. But…"

He trailed off.

46

JAMES

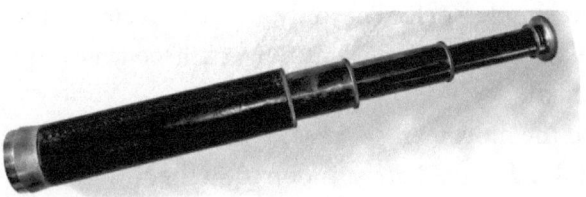

𝓜y dream was frustrating, since I could hear it distantly, but I couldn't comprehend it. My subconscious nudged at me, and I jerked open my eyes.

"*Necesitas instruir a Jim a combatir el demonio,*" María shouted.

"Oh no," I stammered.

I flung the blankets off and slapped my feet onto the chilly wooden floor before the blankets landed. This discussion had grown heated while I slept, and I needed to—to what?

I jumped to my feet and frantically began dressing.

"No, María. *Yo le enseñar. James debe determinar su manera,*" was the calm reply from Davi.

I threw on yesterday's shirt and grabbed my trousers.

"*Tu sabes como destruir, y tu preferiste mantenerlo secreto. Tu eres cómplice con Dahl's crímenes y el monstruo de la carnicería. Tu eres nada más como un mirador, y no un maestro a tu* assertion." María was clearly angry. She always deflated to her native tongue when she was riled.

I clutched my pants and slammed my leg inside. Unfortunately, I missed and thrust it through the seat of my trousers. I didn't have time to dig out a clean pair of pants, so I dragged my leg back through the hole and stuck it into the correct location. I lifted my other leg, missed again, and stumbled, falling onto the bed. While lying there, I finished yanking them up, tied the waist, and snatched a clean pair of socks as I rolled onto my butt. Okay, they were yesterday's stockings. But I was in a hurry.

"*Amada mia…*" Davi stopped short.

I tugged on my first sock. Now, I recognized I truly was a dummy and grabbed *Down With Spells*. It flipped open to *Percepio*, which I hoped would be the exact spell for the situation. I read through and formed the simple spell. The only hand movement required me to point my wand at the target and twirl it three times to the right and once to the left.

I shaped the movements and said, "*Percepio.*"

When I did, I immediately understood them.

"Do not condescend to me! I demand your cooperation, not your understanding," my Spanish bride warned, venom dripping from her remark.

I tossed aside my spell book and dragged on my second sock before snagging my boots.

"María, I do not mean to condescend. I mean to honor you. You must understand, I am restricted in my actions. James *must* choose his own path. Direction from me violates an indispensable law of my people. If we directed every civilization, we would recreate our culture in every world we visited, excluding their free will." Davi spoke her words tenderly, but I was certain a steely will delivered them.

I pulled both boots on and thumped them loudly, hoping to interrupt additional harshness.

"Even if it means a good man perishes? That is merciless, and makes you cruel. How can you live with yourself?" I felt the anguish as my brown-eyed girl's speech trailed off. I sidestepped the bench before I stomped down the stairs.

María didn't mean her last words, and I knew her well enough to realize she'd regret them and apologize later.

Out of appreciation for their privacy, and my own self-interest, I acted as if I didn't know what they'd been debating. "I think I need to travel to Eldritch Manor today. I want to find the spyglass and ensure nobody has tried squatting, either." As I talked, I nonchalantly conjured food for María and me.

Her favorite fruits were strawberries and purple grapes. I loved grapes, too, but they caused my nose to bleed. Odd, I know.

I added lumps of watermelon and cantaloupe to her dish and set it in front of her, along with a solitary shelled boiled egg. She grinned, but it didn't reach her cheeks.

For me, I conjured waffles, scrambled eggs, sausage gravy, and cornbread. It filled my belly and caused my wife to shake her head in despair over my health.

"James, I agree. You visiting that decrepit place is a wonderful suggestion," Davi said.

María rolled her eyes derisively.

"After breakfast, then," I offered, studying my bride for her approval. She nodded once, weakly, without glancing at me.

"James, take your friends Kate and Presley, too. You would have the freedom to reform your protection spell."

The recommendation wasn't what I was used to getting from Davi. She'd stubbornly refused to offer any suggestions in the past.

She simply smiled over her cup of tea.

I glimpsed a smile ghost its way across my bride's face. It was gone as fast as it had arrived.

I swept aside any other worries when Davi said, "James, your shirt has yesterday's dinner staining its front, the ass is missing from your trousers, and your feet smell like a bog. Perhaps you could do us a favor by freshening yourself."

My mouth carped as I hunted for an appropriate retort. Finding none, I slammed my lips together and rocked my head. María laughed.

After breakfast, I changed, then hitched the horses. María put on her necklace, which she'd named her *Necklace of Forgetting*. No, I'd never asked Davi why it didn't work on me. I cared, but candidly, I had so much else to learn, I wasn't interested in adding another element to the heap.

I walked the horses to the Vardes'. There, I helped my wife from the buggy and banged on the door. Presley tossed open his door, which almost knocked me over.

I regained my footing and, as he whisked María and me inside his home, asked, "Hello, Presley. How've you been?"

For now, Kate and I had agreed to keep him in the dark about what was transpiring. If it got worse or I required his help, we'd tell him.

"Mornin', Jim, María," he said warmly.

Kate rushed to receive my wife, then acknowledged me.

"Kate, how 'bout you and Pres go to Eldritch with us? I need to confirm it's secure, and I figured you'd want a peek around after... well, you know." I was referring to her grandfather's death, but I didn't wish to speak the phrase. I understood she didn't blame me, but I shouldered some part, nevertheless.

She narrowed her left eye slightly and turned it toward me, like it could examine my soul to determine the actual purpose of my invitation. "Sure, Jim," she said, drawing out the first word. Clearly, she didn't realize why I'd asked, but she'd play along.

The excursion was silent, since no one felt a particular desire to talk. I was as relaxed with these friends as anyone except María.

I let Kate and Presley take point as we entered the mansion, deliberately tugging María to slow with me. When they were far enough ahead, I tugged my wand from its scabbard and formed *Serverbaris* in my mind. I concentrated intently before launching the spell at my friends. Purple fluoresced around them. Neither noticed, though María's eyes shot open, along with her mouth.

She swung to me and seized my arm, excitedly mouthing, "I saw that."

Inside the enormous central chamber, I mounted the stairs, bypassing the shattered railing, while my wife kept our friends focused on the ground floor, searching for vagrants who may have taken up residence. I knew they wouldn't encounter anyone. But their exploration afforded me a needed diversion.

Upstairs, I dashed through the corridor, swung right, then went into the master's bedroom. Thankfully, the door remained sealed.

Likewise, inside, the door to the anteroom where the spyglass rested was secured. Inside the dimly lit room, I tugged up the covering floorboard. A glimmer from the bronze glass caught my eye. A second or two later, the spyglass came into focus.

I was relieved to discover it, and I promptly secured both doors as I left to investigate the rest of the upstairs for any unwanted guests. Finding nothing amiss, I trudged downstairs and declared, "Upstairs is secured."

María knew I meant the spyglass was safe in its hidey-hole.

"Kate, would you like to nose about?" I said.

"Jimmy, I realize you have a reason for us to visit this place, but for the life of me, I can't fathom it. No, Jim. I don't need to explore. I'm sorry, this place churns up too many ill feelings."

Now that I'd found the spyglass, I too wondered why Davi had suggested they come.

We departed and returned my friends to their home. I was still puzzled over the suggestion to take them.

Unfortunately, my day didn't improve with age. My training seemed to have plateaued, and I struggled to decide which spells were essential to practice and which wasted time.

As my clock tolled four o'clock, I requested an end to the exercise.

"Davi, I'm devoting the rest of the day to my bride. We've been married for over three weeks, and I've predominately spent it training."

"James, your spellcraft is deplorable. You suffer an appalling inability to concentrate, and most conspicuously, you cannot shape a proper healing spell. You require as much training as you can get. So return to your studies," she said as she pointed to *Down With Spells*.

"What good will I be if I can't remember the reason to win?" I asked.

"You do not need the afternoon to realize that; you need a fucking brain transplant. You may be correct, James. Take this evening. I will withdraw until tomorrow." Even as she mocked me, her remarks were oddly reassuring. Then she finished her thought. "But you better fucking be ready to work tomorrow."

After watching Davi go to wherever blonde demons go, I headed upstairs, my step more energetic from the premature conclusion of my day. When I passed the landing, having successfully sidestepping the toe-eating chesterfield, I saw María reading *Down With Spells*—the unabridged, fully annotated version.

"Don't you find that tiresome?" I asked, not guessing why she devoted so much effort to learning spellcraft.

While she knew several spells better than me, sadly, none of them had any effect. Davi said her mana reserves were simply too small.

"No, *mi amor*. Since that woman will not properly assist you, I will."

"Thank you, beautiful. Now come here. I've got something I want to help you with," I teased.

Most of you can predict what happened. I won't go into the details...again. I will say, "It was amazing!"

James

WHEN I WOKE, my amber-eyed lady was fast asleep in the crook of my arm. She wasn't the cuddly type, but our room was freezing, so she'd snuggled to share body heat.

I tugged my arm loose and clambered out of bed. I leaned to kiss her caramel-cream cheek, then turned my attention to the fire. It took a moment to become oriented and find my stove. I sputtered out a snicker and silently teased myself. Ever since Davi had painted my room, it felt foreign.

I'd raised my home with the help of my ship's carpenters. We employed many shipbuilding techniques that held out water to block out cold. We milled logs flat on two sides to fit them securely together. The only draft that invaded my house entered through an unlit fireplace or cracks around a somewhat-shrunken seal.

It was a fact that snow couldn't blow in and dust the floor. But somehow, the snow was so thick, the dark wood floor was white.

Guessing I'd left the window cracked, I shifted to it. Suddenly, a frigid gust tickled my neck.

This wasn't a breeze...and my window was closed.

Another frigid gasp whispered across my collar. Bumps dotted my arms in mute, uneasy acknowledgement.

I jerked my head around and tensed as the sudden fear response commanded me to seek a non-existent intruder. Of course, I didn't see anyone behind me. Unfortunately, I observed something worse.

This room wasn't mine. Once again, I was inside Eldritch Manor, and this time, my bride was with me inside the master's bedroom. My eye tracked to the closet where the spyglass was concealed.

María sighed and tugged the covers under her chin. She lay on her side, but in an unrecognizable bed. It was a four-poster, with delicate white lacing across the top. The fabric trembled in the currents wafting through the room.

I'd learned from painful experience that these events combined both dream and reality. The cold was certain, so I hauled more blankets onto my wife. As I did, I noticed the transformation. It was subtle, but her face was rounder. Not so considerable that it was startling, but enough that I recognized.

The gale whirled through the barren branches of the trees outside the window. The limbs swayed and hammered against each other, a spontaneous cadence purposefully constructed.

Tick.

Through the frosted window, red eyes blazed, then fled. The driving snow outside fogged them from my view almost before I noticed. I scrambled to the glass and used my sleeve to clean a spot.

Tick.

Another flash. This time, they didn't ghost from view. They were dim, but remained detectable.

A gust pelted the casement. The detritus carried into the glass percussed in time with the rattling limbs.

Tick.

A high-pitched screech split the vibrations of the arctic tempest. As the pitch ebbed, a baritone ululation cycloned into the windows, shaking their wooden frames. The demon-ghost opened wide its blackened maw and marched closer.

Tick, tick, tick. The limbs timed Genosqwa's thundering stalk toward us as the lightning lit the blackness.

Each step was audible and more emphatic as its murderous red eyes grew larger. This time, the colossus wasn't treading dangerously to the front door. It was moving straight at me.

Tick.

"James, what is wrong? Why is it so cold?" María asked.

I turned to her and pointed a finger to the opaline window. No matter how much I struggled, I couldn't form a sound.

Still, her eyes followed my arm. She squinted into the frozen inferno and climbed from our bed to see farther.

I now realized why she looked peculiar. Lady María Pimetel de Rota-Byrne was many months pregnant.

Tick.

My insides turned to jelly, and I fell to one knee, suddenly power-less to support my weight. She rushed to me and grabbed my arm, steadying me.

"James, what is it? What is wrong?" This María didn't understand she wasn't where she shouldn't be. She also didn't realize she shouldn't be bearing a child—my baby.

Tick.

I rose and confronted the approaching cataclysm.

The demon's scream reverberated again, fusing with the booming thunder. The pitch seemed intent on shattering the pane of protection between us and the tempest. An itch formed in the recesses of my mind. A thought that I needed to reach.

Tick.

The leviathan arrived at the manor. The building rocked as giant reverberations shook the floor. Genosqwa pounded its fists into the mason walls and howled; a terrible threat formed without words.

Tick.

Protection…

I ran.

Tick.

The glass exploded.

María cried, "Not my baby. You cannot have her." She curled her arms around her swollen belly.

Tick.

Massive grey and black clawed hands tore the window wide and came for her.

I reached my wand, and in one swift gesture, pointed it and shouted, "*Serverbaris!*"

With every fiber of my strength, I drove my free hand and wand toward the sole life that mattered to me. A purple corona fluoresced, then blossomed violet as lightning bristled around its margins.

Genosqwa reached her. The flash was precipitous and exhilarating.

"Die!" I screamed.

"James, what is it?" My bride demanded as she shook me awake.

I started and sat up quickly. Sweat fell in beads, burning my eyes. My breathing came in gulps as I battled a flood of panic.

Slowly, it ebbed as I recognized I'd tumbled from the dream world and into María's arms.

JAMES

The night grinded an eternity of rationalizations as my brain shot from one incomprehensible complication to the next, each a concomitant growth forming one misery onto another. I snoozed in fits, dozing briefly before being startled awake each time.

I eventually climbed out of bed and sat, wearing only my night-shirt and a woolen blanket, in front of the stove in my bedroom. The orange flames devoured several logs before the tangerine sky lit the margins of my blanched walls.

I dressed quietly and carried my boots downstairs. María was dreaming, and I didn't want to wake her. I padded down each tread before leapfrogging over the squeaky floorboard near the bottom.

Of course, Davi sat in her place, a dish of porridge cooling on the table and a cup of tea near her lips. A roaring fire crackled in the hearth behind her. She blew across the fiery liquid before she spoke to me.

"Good morning, James." Admittedly, this was a subdued greeting for the slight woman. She must've read my dour expression, as her forehead creased.

"Davi, we gotta talk."

"Okay, James. What shall we debate?"

"I had another 'dream.'" I formed the physical air quotes with my fingers. "In this one, María was pregnant, and Genosqwa was struggling to reach her. Why?"

I knew that neither demands nor anger affected her, so I didn't bother with any brickbat affectation and ignored her "debate" question.

Davi sat straighter, squirming in her overstuffed chair, uncomfortable with my query.

"James, you know I visit versions of your past and future?" she questioned, raising a single eyebrow and trailing her voice upward at the conclusion.

"Sure. I don't understand how, but you've demonstrated it, so I believe it."

"James..." The interval was marked, and provoked me to cease tugging on my left boot. My heartbeat ticked up.

I said, "Y—"

She cut off my premature response as if she'd never hesitated. "I cannot divine how, but I suspect you visit other variations of your destiny too. I consider these 'dreams,' as you call them, your consciousness taking you to separate realms. James, take these visions seriously."

"I won't bother questioning, or even trying to understand what you're saying. What matters: is María pregnant?"

"James, I suspect she is."

"So why's that beast after her?" I shook my head at my rhetorical question, not expecting my guide to respond. Yet she did.

"If I had to speculate, Genosqwa is after the baby."

Her claim was so vacant of sympathy, I didn't realize her explanation at first. Then, as my mind whipsawed through the ramifications, I reeled and collapsed onto a nearby bench.

"Why does it want my child?"

Unfortunately, I perceived the answer before I asked. In hindsight, I asked many questions to which I'd already identified an answer.

"By possessing the child, Genosqwa could be reborn, independent of its self-created prison. James, under no circumstances may you allow this to occur."

Her warning passed over me without registering. My mind rushed through the implications of my baby being possessed by the demon Genosqwa. Then it hit.

"I will not let you harm my child or wife." The threat carried by my words was absolute.

"James, I am your counselor. This is your battle to win, not mine. If you fail, your world will suffer, not me, and certainly not mine." Her measured words and tone were reassuring.

"Okay, okay...sorry. I just...I'm not sure..." I trailed off before I peeked at her.

She replaced her beatific grin with one of courage. "James, you must keep her safe. You realize keeping her from Eldritch will not work?" she asked, her lips pursed.

"I do. But I don't know..."

The floorboard behind me squeaked, and I sat up and struggled to strike a vague expression.

"Well, I suppose we've got a hectic day planned, Davi. Let me have breakfast, and we'll begin," I said.

"Good morning, *mi amor*." María's dulcet lilt drifted through the kitchen, the assuagement a comforting blanket.

I spun, feigning surprise. Since she didn't interrogate me, I guessed I'd succeeded.

"My queen, sit and let me struggle with my spellcraft and summon you breakfast. What is it you desire?" I bowed to her and tugged a chair from the table for her to sit.

"Just tea for now, please." She patted my hand away from her chair playfully.

"Well, that'll be simple. Davi already has the water boiling." I tipped the scalding water across the tea strainer and passed her the steaming mug, then set the sugar in front of her and handed her a miniature spoon.

"I am going to eat with Katie. Before you ask, we will be watchful of our surroundings, and I will also wear my *Necklace of Forgetting*. You have nothing to dread," María said.

"Sure. Davi and I've got a long day planned already," I lied.

Almost as much as I enjoyed sausage gravy over biscuits, I enjoyed soft-boiled oats, a spoon of butter, and a tablespoon of sugar—oh, and copious amounts of sausage crumbled atop. By the time I conjured the sizzling sausage and set my dish of oats onto the table, my bride decided she required a bowl of strawberries, melon, and grapes. Simple enough. I waved my knife, and it presented itself in front of her.

Weeks ago, Davi had taught me the spell to generate food ingredients. But she'd warned the mana I used consumed more energy than the meal provided me. Still, I could employ it to feed another person.

Sometimes, it seemed magic was more science than...um, magic.

In any event, I didn't conjure food. I magically combined and cooked ingredients from my cupboard. In effect, our feasts were as ordinary as any other. I could simply cook it faster using magic instead of fire.

After I quizzed María on her condition for the third time, she demanded why I kept enquiring. "Jim, you speak and act purposely. Always. Even in hostility to your intentions, your actions have relevance. So, why focus on my stellar verdure?"

I held my gaze level as she spoke, despite wishing to shoot an eye toward Davi. When María stopped, I shrugged. Fine—I shrugged because I needed to infer what verdure meant. Nevertheless, I overreacted, and made up the first lie that leaped into my tiny brain.

"Your health's important, and I'm feeling overprotective. Probably worried about your Spanish police coming to recover you."

I switched the subject and started discussing differing protection juras and how to exaggerate their effects with Davi. Since these spell types could shield me or others, my much-more-intelligent wife joined us. She concentrated on the ones to keep me safe, while I turned my instruction to the ones safeguarding her and others. Davi found the bouncing around amusing.

The clock tolled twelve times, and my amber-eyed beauty rose.

"Jim, will you ready the buggy? It is time for me to eat lunch with Kate." She pecked me on the cheek and went upstairs.

I watched her leave and caught her wink at me just before her head ducked out of sight.

"Davi, I'll be back."

It took me only a few minutes to get the horse and buggy ready for my bride. As I brought the mare to the house's front, she glided outside.

"Be safe," I said before I kissed her lips. I enjoyed it a beat too long. She noticed.

"Do not be silly, my love. I will be fine. Besides, I have seen your bruises, remember?"

She poked me in the arm, then hauled me close.

"*Yo te amo, mucho mucho,*" she said through the hug.

Then she spun, clambered onto the buggy, and hurried the horse too fast along the carriageway and around the stand of trees marking the border to my––our—property.

MARÍA

$\mathcal{M}$eeting Katie was pleasurable, as ever. She and I directed our visit on what Jimmy called "lady topics." I merely thought of them as matters.

Before James and I wed, Katie and I had spoken mainly of either her home life or my daydreams of living away from the Spanish gentry.

Kate was one of the few women with whom I could depart my pretensions. Since she was from old money, she did not need to advise me of my luck to have wealth. She realized I sought to prove myself able in a world uncaring of a woman's needs. We, Kate Varde and I, were women bound together in that commonality.

Kate rarely spoke of James's actions involving Eldritch Manor. The entire subject was distasteful to her. She loathed discussing her family's well-publicized disintegration. Pressing that point was a powerful means of learning another of her personality idiosyncrasies—her acerbic temper. When inflamed, her smile could fluctuate from congenial to malevolent in a breathtakingly transitory moment. Fortunately for all, stirring her irritation was challenging.

"*Roja*, you appear to be bearing up well. How have you…"

Crash!

The report was precipitous and vibrated through the room as the dishes that the proprietress carried smashed onto the wooden floor beside and onto Kate. A mug topped with honey-mead struck her head, spilling its contents across her front. A dish stuffed with Shepard's Pie landed upside down on her lap.

Kate let out a pained yelp and bounced from her chair to scrape the scorching food from her legs. Blood streamed from a laceration on her forehead. Several patrons rushed to her aid and assisted with the mare's nest.

The proprietress raced away, returning with a handful of fresh cloths, and whirled to Kate.

"Oh Katie, I'm sorry. I dun know what hap'ned. Twas as if a gust sun-edly blew 't all from me grip."

Kate glanced at her and said, "Susan, it was a mishap. Don't concern yourself. I'll be fine."

I knew my redheaded friend sufficiently to detect the slight interruption in her remark as she choked back tears. The laceration and burns surely hurt, but combine them with the circumstances unfolding at Eldritch. . . in her mind, this tiny disaster must suggest a catastrophe well beyond the cut or minor burns.

I grabbed a towel from Susan and put pressure on my friend's injury while I helped tidy her. I detected the sheen in her eyes as tears overfilled them. Kate Varde was a proud woman who would never permit others viewing her laments. I extended the cloth across her eyes, affording her the momentary privacy she required.

A precipitous and putrid stench nearly induced me to retch. Then, as fast as it had arrived, it disappeared.

A male voice hollered, "You lot, tend ta yer own affairs, or I'll give ya sump'n else ta worry 'bout!" It was Kia Dawson, who was pressing the cluster away from Kate.

I mouthed, "Thank you." He bowed in response and swung aside.

After helping with the clutter, Ms. Bond placed our food into a basket, releasing me to take my friend home and away from the prying eyes of spectators unkind enough not to return their awareness to their own interests.

She did not speak as we traveled to her home, and I did not press her. When we arrived, I carried her basket to the door. She presented her cheek, so I countered with a brief peck to each side. Then I drew her to me and held her until I felt her relax.

"Katie, you have a better evening," I said as I turned to my buggy.

The ride from Kate's to James's—I mean, *my*—home was brief. My horse knew the direction, and I offered minimal instruction. The last was when an undersized man wearing fur boots and a cloak ran in front of my horse.

"Please be careful, sir. I would hate to have unintentionally injured you," I announced to his retreating back.

The man dashed away without addressing me or my warning.

The rest of the ride was uneventful, and I tugged the horse to a halt near the side entrance. Davi and James were engaged in a spirited conversation when I went inside.

"That spell isn't powerful enough," James insisted.

"By its-fucking-self, it is not. But you are not fucking listening to me, you fucking dumbass. You are fucking meant to fucking combine it with two fucking other spells. They fucking work together. Have I fucking made myself fucking clear?" Davi countered without mirth.

I attended the grin stretched across James's face. He enjoyed this, and would not allow Davi to bully him, especially since he wished to make a point.

"I understood you. I'm saying I want a stronger option. This one isn't good enough." His response was unembellished, and through heavenly interference, he kept irritation from his expression. Davi, exasperated, threw her hands into the air.

James saw me and drew me into the kitchen. "*Hermoso,* help me explain."

"Yes, I will. But you first owe me a kiss."

"You're right. I'm sorry," he said before kissing me firmly on my mouth.

"So, how was your visit with Kate?" he inquired as he plucked a portion of smoked beef lying on the buffet.

I explained, and their earlier debate faded. When I finished, I requested, "Dear, will you please check on Kate before we eat?"

"I'll ride over there before I put away the buggy. I'm certain she's fine, though."

James and Davi continued the verbal sparring, and before they resorted to dueling, I withdrew upstairs to avoid unintentionally being flung across the room.

JAMES

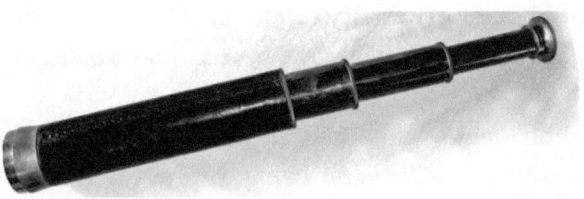

*D*avi and I finished training before dinner. In truth, I cut off the practice so I could check on Kate. María was worried about her, and as she was one of my most cherished friends, I was also concerned.

"James, you butthead, we do not have time for you to continue behaving like a rooster with his dick cut off," Davi said.

"I assume you mean, 'chicken with its head cut off,'" I countered as I snatched my coat.

"With you, it is the same phenomenon."

"Jim, I wish to go with you," María yelled from upstairs.

"Alright, grab a blanket for your legs. The sun's just above the horizon, and the temperatures are dropping 'cause of a front blowing through," I hollered back.

She padded down the stairs and perched on a bench near the door to tug on her boots. To lessen the slush, dirt, and other detritus carried on my shoes, my bride had outlawed them inside our home.

When explaining her motive in enforcing her new policy, she'd said, "This home is not large, Jim."

She was correct when measured against the magnificent estate where she was raised. But in Metaterre, there were only three larger:

Don Diego's, Presley & Kate's, and Eldritch Manor. The Vardes' home was only larger than mine by a single room.

"It will keep our home cleaner," she concluded. I couldn't argue. Besides, I'd never win a debate with her, although I had gotten efficient with an object-manipulation enchantment.

Once, I'd spelled the broom into sweeping the floor while a mop followed. It was an entertaining little dance to see, if you ignore the time when I lost control and a dancing brigade of mops and buckets flooded the kitchen. After that accident, Davi said I should call my enchantment *Vagabond*, because the objects had wandered more than I intended.

María didn't enjoy this skill as much as I did. "The first time someone sees it, you will regret using it," she advised when I proudly exhibited it a few days ago.

That girl was extraordinarily skillful at deflating my ego. Still, as usual, her logic was impeccable. I pledged I'd refrain until I mastered an illusion spell to obscure everything inside our home.

María tugged on her elk-hide boots and I helped her out the door and into the wagon. I let her take the reins. She enjoyed driving, and I didn't care. I could control the horses whenever I wanted. For her, this was a novelty.

She drove them faster and more recklessly than me. An abrupt turn guarded the entrance to the Vardes' tree-lined carriageway. She took it at a full gallop, sliding the buggy around the corner and almost bashing into one of the towering hemlock trees. My logical, rule-following wife giggled the entire time.

I hopped out of the carriage, landing softly, as she drew the horses to an aggressive stop. She engaged the brake and extended her hand for me to help her, though she didn't need my assistance. I believe she allowed me to support her because it made me happy.

Knock, knock, knock. I rapped my knuckles on the enormous, glistening crimson wooden door.

"Yeah, keep yer shirt on. I'm coming," Presley yelled.

He shoved open the door, causing María and I to hop backwards. No matter how often I visited his home, I never remembered he opened it outward. Presley said it discombobulated potential burglars and made it simpler to exit in an emergency.

He smiled, first at María—smart man—then at me.

"María, Jimmy! How ya doin', my friends?" he asked.

"Good, good, Pres. Listen, we wanted to check on Kate. How's she doing?" I asked.

My wife bobbed up and down on her toes and peeked around Presley, clearly wanting to check on her friend.

"Hey, Katie, it's María and Jim. Where ya hidin', woman?" he bellowed.

Presley and his wife had a remarkably rich relationship. They'd teased each other since the day they met. Him calling her woman was only one of the many endearments they used.

He stepped aside and invited us inside. Unlike mine, Presley built his home with an immense kitchen and dining room dominating the first floor of the building. Kate had demanded it because they enjoyed entertaining, which she usually centered in the eating area. So, when we entered, it was into the kitchen.

"Katie?"

A cast-iron pot swinging over the fire in the simmering heat. The liquid steamed and crackled. Presley rushed over and dragged the dark kettle from the blaze, letting it cool, dangling on the same hook.

"Um, I don't know…"

María grabbed my arm, startling me.

Presley alerted and said, "What is it?"

"It might be nothing. But, after the…um, mishap, I smelled something rotten. Then, after I dropped her off here, an unusual man wearing a shabby fur cloak stumbled in front of my horse," María said. I recognized she didn't suggest who the man might be.

Despite Davi's relentless attacks on my intellect, I was generally keen to recognize connections. Here, I hoped I was adding two plus two and summing twelve. Unfortunately, I was sure my gut reaction was correct.

"Babe, you wait here with Presley. I've gotta go to Eldritch." I bowed my head and hurried to my carriage.

"Wait, damn you! She can stay, but I'm going with you," Presley said.

"Neither of you *cabrones* are ordering me to do anything," my spunky wife hollered at our tails.

I didn't know what a *cabron* was, but I figured it meant she was coming with us.

Presley helped her into the buggy, then clambered in beside her. I lashed the reins, launching the horses forward. The rapid acceleration rolled all three of us backward. Both turned to me, startled at my rush. I avoided their wide eyes.

"What in the hell has you in such a rush, Jim?" Presley demanded.

"The night's closing in, buddy. You've experienced Eldritch as well as me. I want to check to see she's not there. That's all."

I abhorred lying to him. But I needed to limit information sharing, reasoning Dahl couldn't drag it from those who didn't have any. Besides, the stakes were too high.

I contemplated free-walking the horses through town because of the risk of injuring passersby should they be in the path of our fast-moving buggy. Hurrying also created an unwanted commotion on the town's roads. But both issues were penny-ante compared with the peril Kate faced alone at Eldritch, so I galloped the team through town, howling at anyone in our path, hardly slowing to swing onto the manor's carriageway.

As I drew the team to a halt, Presley leapt from the wagon, landing before it rolled to a stop near the front entrance of Eldritch Manor. I passed the reins to María and bolted after my friend. She finished stopping the carriage and clambered after us.

I drew my wand and gripped it as if I were girding for a knife fight, the handle in my palm and the blade near my forearm. Presley saw me and aped my actions. I didn't know if a physical weapon could injure Dahl, but it couldn't hurt to try. Plus, it made my friend ignore my wand.

My Spanish queen rushed to catch us, and I lightly pressed her in front of me. I shaped a protection spell and watched the purple fluoresce around them both.

María glanced at her hands and body before swinging to me and mouthing, "*Yo te amo.*"

A slight breeze bore the boundary of the polar front as it struck out its icy tentacles. I needed to locate Kate, if she was here, and bring her home before the storm hit. But, since I had the worst luck in the annals of luck, and I was at Eldritch while it was cold, I knew a monster was nearby.

Presley pushed wide the enormous front door and we hurried inside the immense empty front chamber. I shouldered the giant door shut and latched it behind me.

A fire smoldered in the hearth. Someone was here.

Tick, tick. That damned clock still ticked as it observed its otherwise-empty surroundings.

Presley looked over his shoulder. I shook my head, showing I didn't know who was here.

BOOM! The burst of lightning and crash of thunder was abrupt. The three of us startled. A low rumble growled through the evening for several seconds, an atmospheric drum roll created by the streak of lightning.

Tick, tick.

"You two check downstairs. Pres, check that room in the rear. It's difficult to locate if you're not watching for it."

I pointed to a series of rooms at the corner of the mansion. They weren't any harder to spot than other places; I'd simply told Presley that they were to commit him to a destination. That's what he required, and I preferred he not follow me.

They both acknowledged, turned aside, and headed in divergent directions. As I neared the summit of the crumpled stairway, I heard the *tap tap* of another set of feet. I didn't have to turn because I knew it was my wife.

If Kate were here, she was probably upstairs.

Tick, tick.

We ran.

When we approached the master's bedroom, I extended my arm to stop María from entering the room first.

Tick, tick.

Boom! Another flash, accompanied by raucous thunder powerful enough that my brave wife covered her ears. Another concert of drums beat through the sky.

I entered the bedroom and noticed the anteroom door ajar. I flew to it and shoved it wide. It screeched to a halt before reaching the wall.

My redheaded friend sprawled on her back, her arms folded across her chest and her legs tucked underneath her. It looked like she'd collapsed, like a marionette with her strings cut.

Tick, tick.

One thing was certain: when this was over, I'd be getting rid of that danged clock.

María was at Katie's side in a rush. She probed for a pulse, then leaned her head near to the prone woman's mouth to watch and feel for breathing. My wife glanced at me and nodded.

An icy breath washed across my neck.

"*Lavi, vang...* Charles," The echo fell from the passageway outside the chamber. My startled wife stared at me, eyes wide in disbelief. She dropped Kate's wrist and bounced to her feet.

I watched something tumble from the little redhead's fist as it dropped to her stomach. The item rolled onto the floor and was clearly illuminated by the next outburst of lightning. It was a miniature figure covered with a fur cloak and boots. I reached for it.

Tick, tick.

"No!" screeched through the room. I jumped, bracing to fight. I turned toward the sound and observed that both the bedroom and hallway remained empty. A stink of new leather and spiced rum filled my nostrils. I recalled the aroma, but couldn't place it.

"Jim," María warned as I bent and reached for the figurine again. This time, there wasn't any supernatural sound-effect.

As I retrieved it, a red fluorescence blossomed enveloping my hands. María's eyes flared wide, and I could see the crimson light flicker across the obsidian of her pupil. She slid away from me scooting away on her backside.

My wand glowed a brilliant vermillion and a tingling sensation crept along the fingers of my wand hand, then through my palm as my blade glowed brighter, encompassing my entire lower arm. A sudden flash caused me to blink as the miniature figure I held burst into flames.

The blue-and-white fire that erupted didn't scorch my hands, but I felt the heat, so I tossed the odd figurine into the nearby fireplace, where the mysterious flames consumed it.

I swung to my wife, thinking to ask what she'd witnessed. Her mouth was open, and she clutched both hands to her chest.

"*Lavi...*" The sound wasn't loud; but it was unmistakable.

The thud of footsteps resounded from the darkened hall—Presley was running towards us. María slid beside Kate and quickly lifted her head onto her lap. Presley rounded the corner and flew into the room, dropping beside his wife. I was just able to slide out of his way and avoid being flattened.

"What's wrong with her?" he demanded as he scooted to a stop beside her.

"We don't know," I replied honestly.

"We found her this way," María said.

"Who yelled 'no' earlier?" he asked. He'd taken his wife's hands and was checking her pulse.

Before either of us answered, he added, "That smells like Charles." Presley looked around the room for his older relative.

María and I shared a glance. She started before I could.

"We don't—" Another flash and boom of thunder cut the rest of her reply short. These weren't as loud, and the drumbeat took longer to reach our ears after the lightning lit the darkness. The edge of the storm had passed us.

A stiff wind rattled the windows. "Let's get her home and away from this creepy place," I said.

Presley picked up his unconscious wife, carried her downstairs, and lifted her into the back of the buggy. Without pausing, he climbed in beside her. I helped María into the wagon, where she set about helping to cover her friend.

Since riding in the carriage's rear was more jarring than the seat, I didn't gallop the horses. When I turned to check on my passengers, I'd see their lowered heads bounce like tiny boats in a storm.

"Jimmy, where are we going?" Presley asked as I passed the turn to his home.

I was taking Kate to Davi. If anyone could help, it'd be my little blonde friend. I ignored Presley, acting as if the noise of the wind and wagon had blocked his question. He didn't repeat it.

When we arrived, I was out first, hustling to the rear of the buggy. Presley handed his wife to me, and I rushed inside, not waiting for him.

Inside, Davi was waiting as if she knew we were coming. She stood in the middle of the parlor beside an unusually constructed bed. I didn't hesitate, and laid Kate down. The bed cushion, while firm, formed around her like a protective cocoon.

Presley bustled in and took her hand. If he noticed the unusual bed, he said nothing. "Alright, Jimmy, spill it!" he demanded. He did notice the incongruities. Presley Varde was one of the most observant men I knew. Of course he saw.

"James is a wizard, and you have entered a ghost story where the phantoms are legitimate, an ancient monster has murdered those at Eldritch, and another, more serious beastie is coming for your township," Davi said.

"Who the hell are you?" he asked.

JAMES

"**You** may call me Davi." She remained near the bed, her hands clasped together. She bounced once on her toes and beamed that same irritating smirk. I don't think Presley liked it either, but he said nothing.

Davi spoke for nearly fifteen minutes. No one dared interrupt. When she finished, my friend remained stoic, his expression wary. Then he declared, "Bullshit!"

"Not bullshit," Davi replied levelly. "This is a certainty. If Dahl obtains the device, he will form the culminating portal. Should he prevail, your entire world, not just your charming township, will be imperiled. Even if James stops Dahl, a beast lives inside that spyglass, and it wants out. You merely need to consider the events at the manor to recognize its capacity."

"Let's say I accept any of this...story. Why should I believe in magic? How do I know you aren't one of Satan's minions controlling all of this?" my skeptical friend asked.

"Let me," I said.

I drew my wand knife and pointed it at the broom, mop, and bucket sitting in the kitchen's corner. They sprang into action. Water pumped into the bucket as the broom swept across the floor. The wetted mop followed.

I regarded Mr. Doubting-Thomas, weighing his reaction. It went as well as I expected.

Presley Varde stomped across the room and punched me in the mouth. "You bastard. You should have told me and kept my wife out of this. Now look what you've done." He pointed a jittery hand at his wife, prone on the bed.

I straightened, rubbed my jaw, and stared at my angry friend. My wife moved to stand in between us. She wasn't having Presley's tantrum. Her expression dared him to attack again. He dropped his fists, and I moved María aside.

"Pres, I accept you're angry. Kate approached me about the manor the morning I got back. When I figured out what was happening, she was already involved. I took control of Eldritch as quickly as I could, and I've been forming protection juras over you two since I studied them. I'm sorry I couldn't manage to save Charles."

I peered at Davi, hoping she'd fill in details of Charles' death. "Mr. Doss had a strategy. You could do nothing to aid him. If it were possible, I would have saved him. I, too, am sorry, Mr. Varde," my unexpectedly kindhearted teacher said.

Why couldn't she treat me this way?

"Pres, I had to preserve these secrets. Tell me anything I would've gained by discussing this mess." I paused and waited for him to respond. He didn't, so I continued.

"You can't fight Dahl, none of you can." I gestured to everyone in the room. "According to Davi, I'm the only one who can. Besides, anybody who knows anything's at risk of being attacked, tortured, and murdered. I can only protect so many lives. Plus, that demon spyglass has been destroying Kate's family for decades."

Finally, I saw his shoulders droop and his eyes shifted to his wife.

"Sorry, Jim. But you'd agree, this is…disturbing. I mean, I've read tales of magic. But they were just that—stories. Now you say they're true and Kate's being attacked. Besides, it was a proper blow."

Presley deadpanned the quip as only he could while completing the delicate double entendre of comedy and fact, by erasing emotion from his voice and expression. Most folks couldn't recognize when he was serious, which Presley thought was uproarious. I noticed it and appreciated his jape. I rubbed my jaw again, this time for his benefit.

"Scarcely noticed," I retorted. María threw her hands up and flopped into a nearby chair.

"Presley, I need you two to move in here for a few weeks," I said.

"Why?"

"Because distance is critical in constructing my protection wards. The closer you, Kate, and María are, the easier it'll be for me to shape them regularly," I explained, swinging my attention to my guide.

"Davi, Katie had a miniature doll in her hand. It was decked with a fur cloak and shoes. When I grabbed it, my wand glowed crimson, as did my hand gripping the figurine. Then it exploded into flames." While I implied my question, I was hoping she'd figure out my intent.

Fortunately, she continued her serious line of reasoning. "James, I would surmise that it was a totem planted on Kate at the restaurant. Dahl must have arranged the accident as a diversion," she said as she shrugged her shoulders.

"So why did it burst into flames?" I asked.

"Because of your protection jura. It glowed when Ms. Varde held it as well, but your wand reinforced the spell on you."

"It didn't work," I said as I pointed to my friend laying on the nearby bed.

"That is incorrect, James. Dahl sent her to retrieve the spyglass. He failed. At some point, your friend resisted the totem's power. I believe she had help," Davi said, one eyebrow arched.

"Charles," the rest of us said together.

"Precisely," Davi replied.

"I'm withholding judgment on this whole magic business. Jimmy, I trust you, and I don't believe Satan's got you. But, if I find otherwise, I'll go to war. Got me?" Presley Varde said.

He stared at me as he rested beside his wife, who remained unconscious on the strange bed.

"I understand, my friend. Trust me. This isn't evil. It's only another form of energy. That's it."

"So help Katie, then, shithead," he quipped, although the plaintive look he gave his wife advised me he meant what he said.

It was a good sign he could joke. The casual expletive directed at me was trivial. Presley and I insulted each other constantly. We'd done it since we were kids.

I didn't answer because I didn't know how to help. I shifted and stared at Davi.

"Oh, she is fine. She is merely sleeping. She must have resisted mightily to remain away from the spyglass. Let her sleep. She will wake by dawn," Davi said.

We spent the evening talking through what had transpired. Presley grilled me on every detail, and by the time we finished, he seemed convinced I wasn't being manipulated.

"Jimmy, grab me a blanket. I mean to sleep here with Kate."

Davi stood and waved one hand. I caught sight of her ring as it spun. Kate's bed glowed blue and expanded until it was twice its previous size. Then Davi disappeared to wherever mean blonde enchantresses go.

Presley looked at the bed, then me, shrugged his shoulders, tossed his jacket over an adjacent chair, and climbed into bed with his wife.

"My queen, let's go upstairs," I said.

JAMES

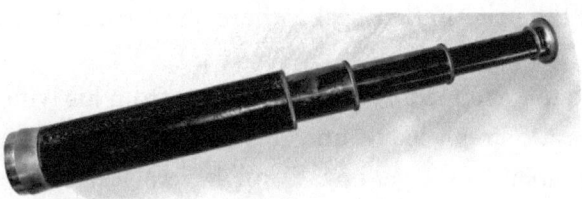

*M*y eyelids opened as if they were pieces of splintered glass. Brilliant light spilled through my window and rushed my passage from sleep to waking. The incandescence of the daybreak washed over my face, warming it, burning away the dread of yester-evening's events.

I tossed my covers aside. As my feet struck the floor, I noticed the stone under my feet. The question was lost before it formed. I moved to the wash basin to clean up.

"James, you are awake at last. Stay where you are, and I will help you downstairs to breakfast," María yelled.

I glanced up, my face wet. I saw her through the window, waving both arms above her head. Her ebony hair bounced as she gestured. She was a vision equal to any angel in paradise.

I slid the window open and yelled, "I'm fine. I'll be right there."

The inconsistencies of my room, the hitches in time blurred, and I lost their importance as I watched her. She hurried around the fringes of my perception, chasing two children before seating them at a grand French trestle table. I remembered the table as one I'd acquired when my crew seized our last merchant prize.

I rushed to finish dressing. When I got outside, the sun hung well above the horizon. The morning was oddly warm. The ocean breeze, salty from the waves crashing on the rocks below, mixed with the flowers on the table and formed a briny perfume. Its acridness burned the inside of my nose before the breath of the zephyr wafted it away.

I didn't recall walking through the house onto the rear porch. At the table, Katie sat, her head propped on Presley's shoulder. She was talking with María, punctuating her words with her hands. Her head lifted from her husband's shoulder long enough for her to bob it a few times, and then she settled back, where she'd rock it back and forth again.

"Jim," Kate exclaimed. Presley looked up from his wife, his expression of adoration replaced by one of friendship.

"Jimmy, great to see ya, boy. Come have a seat. Let's eat," Presley said, no longer mad at me.

I shut my eyes and drew in a deep breath before I exhaled, blowing through a count of five. At least Kate wasn't suffering any obvious ill effects from last night's misadventure. The spicy smell of the pork sausage joined with the malty, sweet smells of the rolls and filled my nostrils.

When I opened my eyes, I startled, discovering I was seated at the table. My plate was laden with biscuits covered by steaming gravy. Sausage patties sat in the gravy lake beside my rolls. My abdominal-brain took control of my hands and started scooping food into my mouth. It was delicious.

María leaned near my face and took my hand to place it on her tummy. I felt a shift. It was a kick—or was it a punch? My mouth dropped open in a broad grin.

I couldn't have felt the baby move...

Suddenly, I understood where I was. This was more than a dream. It was real. Somehow, I'd again traveled between dimensions.

Davi had taken me on several inter-dimensional trips. The many encounters with the beast, Genosqwa, had persuaded me I was dimension-traveling through my dreams—something that shouldn't be possible, according to my guide.

I jumped up, spilling my chair onto the ground behind me. I

swung in a circle; my eyes scanned the nearest edge of the horizon. There, I found it: the stone-monster stomping toward us.

I spun to my friends and shaped my protection over them. The spell fluoresced a purple corona around them. Six eyes stretched in astonishment. Then Presley discovered what I'd seen.

"What the holy hell is that?" he yelled.

"Presley, get them inside the house. I'll take care of this." After he'd ushered them away, I cast another spell, this time over the house. I'd never tried to form a spell to protect something as vast as this place. It might not work, but I needed to try.

The breeze grew crisp, and clouds led the monster toward me. The wind became a gale as a storm erupted. It grew stronger with each of the demon's crashing steps.

Lightning flashed. Thunder roared.

I'd seen this drama before. I was prepared for the storm and its frozen fury, but I didn't know how to defeat this creature. What I knew was that I could never let it near my wife or friends.

The giant gray creature didn't stamp toward the house, as it had in my other dreams. This time, its march carried it straight at me. I formed another protection jura over myself and waited.

My offensive spells were most effective near me. So I needed to let it get close before I acted. I brought a flat palm in front of my face, an ineffective attempt at thwarting the howling gale and pelting rain. When the demon was barely feet from my outstretched hand, I lifted my wand.

It paused and wailed. It was a dreadful groan, terrifying and demoralizing. How could I beat this thing?

"Puny man. You cannot stop me. I will have the child," it said.

Its declaration stunned me into silence. The beast had never spoken to me. I wasn't sure how to react.

It moved faster than I'd ever seen. Before, it had been a lumbering giant—slow, deliberate, and unstoppable. Now, it was a nimble dread behemoth. It reached a massive hand and swatted me like a bug.

Its blow knocked me backwards. I hit the wet, grass-covered ground and tumbled head over feet, but my protective spell guarded me from the worst of the beast's power. As I slowed, I rolled upright and ran toward the giant.

Genosqwa turned its awareness to the home that sheltered my friends and family, pounding toward Eldritch Manor and my pregnant wife.

I leveled my wand at the mansion as I slid to a stop, feet from the giant. *"Muras Ignis."*

A tremendous wall of flame exploded from the ground, climbing dozens of feet into the air. A thick, acrid smoke blew off the flames burning my nostrils. The heat was brutal, and I reacted by moving several leaps away, shielding my face with my arms.

Genosqwa raged, beating its great fists into the conflagration. Its massive paws glowed red as the heat scorched them.

"Liquefacta," I shouted as I pointed my wand at the feet of the beast.

The loam transformed into a carrot-colored pool of melted dirt, and Genosqwa sank into the roiling, molten earth. Its cries filled my ears.

In less than a minute, the creature vanished into the magma pool. The storm passed.

I collapsed. The effort of shaping those spells had utterly drained me.

There was a streak of light, then thunder followed, and another frozen zephyr knifed through me. I glanced up from my knees.

The gray monster stomped toward me. This time, its shriek was full of mirth.

I fell as it raised a colossal foot to crush me.

JAMES

I awoke with a start.

My crushing defeat at the hands of Genosqwa left me unsettled. I realized I'd never fall back asleep, so I dragged myself out of bed. My head sank into my palms as my feet touched the floor.

No time for self-pity or reflection. I had a problem that I alone could fix. Well, if I believed that she-demon Davi. Thinking of her made me chuckle. How could someone so maddeningly irritating hold such an honored place in my heart?

Both hands scraped sleep from my eyes, then moved across my unshaven face. I turned to gaze at my pretty bride. She lay sleeping beside me. I placed one hand on her tummy and caressed her face with the other. She moaned softly and snuggled into my hands.

Gingerly, I edged my body from the bed, dressed, and tiptoed from the room, hoping to let her sleep. The sunlight barely brushed the horizon, so it was time to wake, anyway. I skipped the squeaky floorboard and stepped into the kitchen. Davi sat there sipping her tea.

My recovered friend, Kate, was awake and standing in the kitchen, rolling out dough for rolls. She prepared the best sweet rolls and called them "angel biscuits." I agreed with the nickname.

"Good morning, ladies," I said. I included Davi in the "ladies" remark as a kindness. I was being cordial.

"Jimmy, I hope you slept well," my ginger-headed friend said. Davi only smiled enigmatically. Did she already know about my dream?

"I did. You?"

"Like a log."

She kept her back to me as she talked, so I couldn't study her expression, but her tone was firm and showed no hint of anxiety.

"Katie, how can I help?" I asked.

"Why don't you start the ham-steaks?" she said.

When I drew my wand, she cleared her throat. I glanced up, leaving the question unspoken.

"There's enough supernatural in my life. If you don't mind, just use the meat from the market," she added as she nudged her nose toward the table.

I twisted to where she was staring and spotted the ham. I carved it into slices, then cooked them on the cast-iron plate. Soon, the smell of the cooked ham mixed with the biscuits caused my mouth to water.

Katie was an Irish girl and had grown up eating potatoes. They were recent to New England, but Presley guaranteed there were plenty grown in his fields each year. Katie enjoyed them cut into thin slices and fried in oil.

The smell of the food must have stirred María awake, because it wasn't long after I started the ham that she padded downstairs. She pecked me on the cheek and said, "I love you." Then she shooed me out of the way and helped Kate finish. Today, María cooked my eggs over-medium—my favorite.

Everyone gathered for breakfast. Before we ate, I gave thanks and asked to defeat the twin evils nearing our city. Before I could finish my wife squeezed my hand. I hesitated, wondering why.

She began speaking. "Dear Lord, thank you for Davi and the guidance she has provided. Bless her in her travels."

She squeezed my hand again. I finished, "Guide, guard, and direct us in all that we do."

Everyone joined me in saying, "Amen."

We sat and began passing around food. Davi, who always only ate her gruel, conjured herself a plate and filled hers along with the rest of us, although she didn't eat the ham. She'd grumbled about eating animals in the past, so I didn't offer her any, either.

"My dear, that was a lovely sentiment. I have not had someone pray for my benefit in many generations. I thank you," Davi said. María smiled before taking a bite. I think she blushed, but it was there and gone so fast I could have misread it.

My wife had teased me repeatedly over the volume of food I devoured. I reminded her I spent considerable energy working the farm. And besides, I knew someone who ate much more than me. That caused her to laugh in disbelief.

At this breakfast, she got to see that someone eat. Presley Varde could out eat any man I'd ever met. He wasn't a big man, either. He was unusually tall and fit, full of muscle, but reed-thin.

The year before he and Kate married, he'd invited nearly two-score of the townsfolk to his home to celebrate the fall harvest. Most were impoverished or didn't have family nearby, so he'd welcomed them to pick through his fields after the harvest. His standing rule to his pickers was to leave behind one-tenth of each crop in the field. All were welcome to the leftover crops. It was one of his means of watching out for others.

That day, he'd cooked a dozen turkeys, several hams, and two rib-roasts. The fascinating part was that I saw him eat a twelve-pound turkey...by himself! It wasn't just the turkey, either. He inhaled more than a dozen rolls, cornbread stuffing, baked corn on the cob, beans, boiled greens, Marlboro Pudding, and more slices of cherry pie than I could count.

Today, he swallowed four large ham-steaks, seven eggs, and a half-dozen biscuits.

As he dined, my wife's eyes grew as she observed the vast amount of food he could devour.

"Is anyone gonna eat that?" he asked as he pointed to the last biscuit. My bride laughed, and the rest of us shook our heads.

"What?" was his answer through a mouthful of food.

I cleaned the dirty dishes, employing magic, of course.

Presley shook his head in astonishment before criticizing. "Why haven't you been using this stuff before now? There've been several scrapes we could've avoided if you'd only…"

He nodded to my wand. "…you know."

He seemed baffled about how to discuss it.

"Sorry, Pres, I didn't know. Besides, we survived fine without this stuff," I replied.

Our wives declined to watch Davi and me practice and fled upstairs. Presley stayed and observed, but he eventually grew bored and went to my workshop.

We shared many common interests. Knife making was one. I figured he'd noticed my dagger and wanted to create one of his own.

JAMES

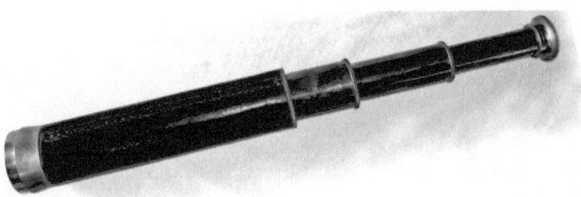

*T*he days bled one into another. Eat, practice, eat, practice, sleep...*cum taedio in sempiternum*, forever tedious, as my Latin teacher would instruct me. If it weren't for María ensuring I ate, I'd have missed most of my meals.

Davi's training turned brutal. If I didn't create the spell perfectly, I'd end up battered and bloodied. In one day, I broke both legs and arms while sustaining a concussion. María angrily interjected that we were spending more time mending me than training. She also added that Davi needed to back off.

The injuries subsided––somewhat.

Presley and the ladies spent their days decorating outside for All-Hallowmas. As usual, I expected to have the town's children visit my home, hoping for some sweet. I wanted to have it ready for them.

María, too, enjoyed giving sweets for the Spanish celebration *Todos Los Santos*, or All Saints' Day. They observed it the first of November. My wife, never one to compromise, prepared for both festivals. She insisted on preparing one of her favorite traditional foods, which she called *huesos de santo*, or saint's bones.

I enjoyed the confection so much, I asked her to prepare it for my birthday in June.

JAMES

*J*don't know if I was fortunate, because time glided by. The dawn of the final day of October broke bleak and drizzling. Distant thunder rolled through the house as I slogged downstairs in the unenthusiastic footslog I'd perfected over the last several weeks. When I greeted Davi and Kate, I spoke without looking.

"Morning, ladies," I grunted.

"Just me," a perky voice returned.

My head shot up and my eyes swelled as I saw only Kate in my kitchen. Davi's pink overstuffed flowered armchair, which was an enduring component in my galley, was missing.

"What?" was the unthinking response that slipped from my tongue. I followed it with the profound, "When—wait."

Finally, my brain engaged, and I proposed the germane question. "Where's Davi?"

"Not sure, Jimmy. She claimed you're properly trained, and the rest was up to you,"

Kate continued cooking breakfast, looking away from me, although I spotted her shoulders near her ears. She understood what I faced, and I suspected she realized I wasn't prepared.

I collapsed into a chair. An enormous weight left my shoulders, only to crash back as a terrible betrayal.

I realized I was wholly responsible for defeating Dahl and Genosqwa.

Even though Davi had continually reminded me she was here to instruct and advise me, I guess I was hoping she'd stay and help. She must have known that I hadn't discovered a means of killing either the demon or Riaan Dahl.

Kate made coffee and passed me a mug. I sat, brooding, in my rocker, which I dragged from the parlor to where Davi's armchair had held station for the last two months. In front of me, I heard the gentle patting as my wife slipped down the stairs. First her feet, then her pretty face came into view. I pasted on my best smile.

"What is wrong, James?" María asked.

I'd never play poker against her. She was naturally talented at deciphering my expressions, even when I was positive I'd hidden my feelings. Come to think of it, Presley complained about Kate discerning his thoughts too. Maybe it was a woman thing.

Kate said, "Davi's gone."

"Where?" my wife inquired. She sounded earnest in wanting to know the actual location.

"She's gone to wherever condescending, ornery demon teachers go, I'd guess," I said. My Spanish queen laughed. It was elegant and musical, and buoyed my spirits.

"She believes I've mastered everything I needed to learn," I finished, shrugging my shoulders. It was a foolish decision made tactile as the movement sloshed hot coffee onto my shirt. I flopped forward and tugged the now-steaming material from my chest. Kate tossed a towel over my shoulder. I used it to soak up the coffee before I remembered I could work magic.

"Do you not believe you are trained?"

"Honestly, I'm not sure. No matter what Davi said, I was sure hopin' she'd stay and help."

As I brandished my wand over my shirt, returning it to its precoffee spill condition, the door lurched wide and a burst of frigid air rushed into the kitchen. Presley stomped twice, cleaning the mud from his feet, then slammed the door behind him. He lifted a foot to move toward the table and María raised an eyebrow, looking at his still muddy feet. Presley stopped, dropped onto the bench beside the door, and tugged off his boots.

"What's wrong?" he asked as he took in the group's demeanor.

I guess it's not a woman thing. But I should've expected my best friend to gauge our mood. Especially since it was an occupational demand for us both.

"The blonde hobgoblin's gone," I deadpanned.

"Davi? She wasn't that bad. You're just sore a lady of her...um, stature could toss you around," my best friend replied.

"Pigeon-head," I retorted. He laughed and patted me on the shoulder as he strode to his wife and stooped to kiss her cheek.

"Jimmy, I've known you for years. You've got a natural feel for discovering ways out of scrapes. This one'll be no different. Once you quit obsessing over it, you'll spot a solution. You always do," Presley offered.

I stared at the fire, not meeting the gaze of the most important people to me. One fact was certain: my bride and friends supported me. I only needed not to fail them.

"I know, I know. But I've got sort of an idea."

"You going to let us in on it, Jimmy?" Kate pressed.

"Sorry, guys. This one's gotta stay with me. I can't let Genosqwa or Riaan Dahl have any idea what I'm planning."

Then I spotted María staring at me, her forehead scrunched together.

"Besides, today, the paper will publish the ownership change of Eldritch. I'm sure Dahl will be searching for me. Today, I'll let him find me," I finished as I let a ferocious grin slide across my lips.

"We will prepare breakfast while you scrub. You will not display your slovenly manners while you are my husband," María said, playfully punching me in the arm and shooing me upstairs.

"Ouch," I whined.

"*Pobrecito*, did that hurt? *Debería besarlo?*" she asked as she puckered her pouty lips.

"Knock it off, you two. You're makin' me sick ta my stomach," Presley said as he grabbed his abdomen, pretending to retch.

While the three of them prepared breakfast, I went upstairs and washed. I hadn't lied when I told them about the beginnings of my plan. I simply hadn't told them the whole truth.

Surely there was a reason Davi had insisted I learn how to destroy a realm, despite not giving me a way inside.

At least, not one that didn't force me to do something stupid.

DAVI

*T*he miserable little fucker you'd recognize as Riaan Dahl woke early. He'd devoted the last weeks to monitoring, repeatedly forming a simple *Diskaver* spell, enchanting a *Gudiya* for the redhead, and most notably, awaiting today.

For, this day, Dahl was positive he would uncover his artifact.

Since the individuals who occupied this realm celebrated this day with a remembrance that included costumes and ornaments, they would perceive his typical fur cloak and boots as such, allowing him to strut openly. Although this was a paltry advantage, it was one he would use.

He recognized that the township's population identified him as an interloper. He likewise noted they referred to him as a curiosity. While he didn't care about festivals or judgments, he would not be diverted from his target.

To turn these beings aside, Riaan cast a simple distraction enchantment on himself. It would confound all who ventured near him. Afterward, they would ramble away, forgetting him.

When he arrived in this world, I'd locked away much of his magic. While I realize I should not be involved by leveling risk for all parties, I judged I'd remained within bounds of my people's edicts.

The little shit did not fathom why he could merely perform a few of his most basic spells. The reason was as transparent as the twisted, pointed nose on his face. He was an irredeemably vile being, not deserving of his extraordinary abilities. I granted him magic to mend himself, detect and recover his object, and cast minor wounding. Still, these spells were not potent enough to overpower a powerful wizard like James Byrne. Yes, he was a nitwit, but he was also astonishingly caring.

If Dahl wanted to prevail, he would have to avoid direct conflict and plead for pity, an act the contemptible creature was incapable of performing.

Even with me blocking his magic, his mana reserves were so vast that most spells could not permanently injure him. If confronted, all he required was escape. Once alone, he would restore himself and begin his plots anew.

Dahl wandered through the familiar town of Metaterre. If you have not paid attention, he has existed here since he remembered anything. Well, not strictly this version of Metaterre, but they were all similar enough that he recognized their design.

Today, his destination was the library. Yes, the same location I'd found James many weeks ago. Dahl knew important notices were announced in the town's newspaper. Often, those remarks would be republished as each month concluded. Since today was October thirty-first, the final day of the month, Dahl hoped he'd discover a reference as to who owned the spyglass. Technically, he was seeking the landowner of Eldritch Manor, but in his single-mindedness, they were differences without contrast.

Days ago, he had worked to compel Kate Varde to fetch it for him by provoking a waitress to spill her tray. In the tumult, he'd slipped a totem into Kate's pocket. If she had been the legitimate owner of his artifact, the token should have obliged her to relinquish it. That she refused was the sole confirmation he required to prove Kate was not the owner of his coveted target.

Dahl looked up in bewilderment. He stood at the entrance of the familiar library. He had not been paying attention during his journey.

Instead of his destination, he had been fixating on matters he could not change. He could not echo this mistake if he wanted to avoid prying eyes.

Sure, his spells caused humans to veer aside and ignore him, but they only functioned when someone moved too close. Others would recognize the wandering. This was emblematic of the mistakes that had made returning to his realm so difficult.

Dahl shoved the door open. The library was badly lit, and the outside chill permeated the chamber, despite the roaring fire inside the hearth. A lone person attended the hall.

"Where are the day's advertisements?" Dahl snarled.

The man, balding and hunched by age and arthritis, jerked his head toward Dahl's sound. He had not realized another individual was nearby. Riaan grinned at the fright playing across the pockmarked and creased face of the hoary librarian.

The man raised an unsteady arm and pointed a single bony finger. Dahl followed the gesture across the room. His eyes locked onto a facade dotted with several racks of wooden dowels, over which large sheets of paper were draped. The little fucker grunted a *harrumph* and shuffled his fur-covered feet toward the spot.

Not understanding where to begin, he withdrew the top-most paper and began scanning. Sheet by sheet, he studied, deliberately replacing each before removing and reading the next. His analysis took more than an hour.

It was on the final page of the day's news.

Under the heading Real Property Sales was the following:

"The freehold title to Eldritch Manor, as surveyed for the 1762 tax roll, has transferred from the registered proprietor, Mr. Charles Dwayne Doss II, to Mr. James Byrne, a resident of the State of New York, for the valuable consideration of $750. This transfer was registered on September the 21st, the year of our Lord 1781, and approved retroactively to the same date on September 22nd, the year of our Lord 1781."

Dahl had discovered James's deception.

His mangled heart soared. He folded the paper before stowing it into his sack and shuffling to the exit. He flung it wide, banging it against the wall. The crash startled the elderly curator, who did not realize anyone was there. As usual, the shithead did not care, nor did he notice when the door rebounded, striking him.

The damned goblin had never met the new owner of Eldritch Manor, but knew of him. Riaan had heard many townsfolk speak well of Byrne.

The turd set out to locate my student at the mansion overlooking the great ocean. The little shit had no imagination and assumed James must be at the manor.

Before he set out, Riaan removed the spell he had shaped on himself. After all, he could not have James Byrne wander off as he sought to speak with him.

On this adventure, he held his misshapen head high as excitement buoyed him. Each footfall was gentler, as if gravity had lost its influence.

As he approached the threshold of Metaterre, a rather striking gentleman astride a stallion black as midnight passed. The man tipped his head and Dahl started. Fortunately for him, he was an expert in disguising his emotions, and seemingly remained indifferent, though his heart galloped as James glanced at him and said, "Hello."

He tapped two fingers to the brim of his hat and bobbed his head once before continuing on, acting like nothing remarkable had just transpired.

"Stop!" Riaan yelled.

"Excuse me?" James said.

Dahl noticed there wasn't any fear in the response. In fact, it lacked any emotion.

"What I mean is, please stop and chat with me for a moment," Dahl appended.

"Sure thing. What can I help you with?"

"I learned in today's news that you are the legitimate owner of Eldritch Manor."

"Yes, I acquired it several weeks ago. It's a lovely home that I intend on renovating and using as my family home. Why?"

"Well, my...my sister left a family heirloom...before she—disappeared. You realize many have perished while working there. My relative was a cook...in the kitchen." Dahl stopped talking, realizing that he was rambling.

"I'm sorry for your loss. What was this heirloom?"

James's curiosity surprised the vile creature. "You see, I don't...I mean...well, I don't remember what it was, though I'm sure I'd recognize it if I saw it. If you'd permit me to travel with you, I'll recover it and leave for home."

"Let me get this straight—you demand I allow you to search my property for an item you can't specify, and I merely have your assurance that you own it?" James's demeanor had turned glacial.

"Um—" Dahl began before James cut him off.

"Listen, *sir*, I have commitments, and if you'll forgive me, I'll be on my way." James doffed his hat and turned away.

"You shouldn't ignore me. You'll discover that...unpleasant," Dahl growled.

"I don't take your meaning." Steel crept into James' tone.

"You don't appreciate what I am or what I'm capable of doing."

"You're mistaken. I understand *exactly* what you are."

The emphasis James placed on the word "exactly" surprised the twisted fucker.

Byrne knew. But how? It was only this morning that Dahl had realized who owned the estate. And he was certain the two of them had never met.

His thoughts churned and flew from question to question. Nary an answer supplied itself. Shaken, the shithead watched as James rode away, as untroubled as he had been the moment he arrived.

Later that evening, Riaan Dahl warmed himself beside his campfire. The flames were intense as they devoured the kindling and split pine. The log popped and a small ember burst, landing on his leg. The ass-wipe did not react. He was used to much greater misery than a small ember. Because he used a continuous healing charm to tend such trivialities, the ulcer would restore itself.

Besides, after his run-in with James, he required another technique —one that would let him return home.

Tonight, he would meditate over his impasse. Tomorrow, he would respond.

Dahl shaped his spell. It was unnaturally weak, a condition he denounced as an improper structure of this Earth—stupid little fucker. Still, this conjuration allowed him to search energies, which he exploited to reveal anything coming near.

The small animals scurrying shone a vivid tangerine, fading into lighter shades of green. The insects haloed innumerable hues of pink and blue, while the surrounding vegetation added an emerald flush to the radiance of the narrow gulley where he camped.

Sure of his surveillance, Dahl sank into a meditative trance. When he awoke, startled, a mass of energy far larger than a single man had entered his field of detection.

The color was a vivid amaranthine, its purple so deep, it bordered on red. The tone was so perfect, it must be a protection spell produced by a powerful wizard.

Dahl smiled as the savor of triumph swelled in his mouth.

JAMES

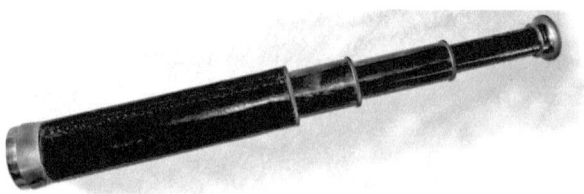

I rode into the encampment of the creature Davi had tasked me with killing. I still didn't have a wholly formed strategy for handling the creature, but I was confident I could permanently hide the spyglass from him while simultaneously protecting my wife and friends.

The wildcard in my plan was the giant stone monster Genosqwa. I couldn't defeat it. It attacked from a reality I couldn't access. No matter how often I conquered it in my realm, it would only reform from its own created existence and attack again. Still, I could only fight one battle at a time.

Dahl didn't react when I rode into his small clearing. His only recognition of my appearance was when he tossed another split pine log onto the already furiously burning fire.

"Mr. Byrne. I sensed you'd return," Riaan lied.

"Your perception isn't that powerful. I recognize your capabilities and your limitations—and your lies. Riaan, I'm not here to listen to your threats either. I'm here for one thing."

"What is that?" sneered Dahl.

"To offer you your one and only warning."

"Warning! I—" Dahl roared, amplifying and resonating his voice before I cut off his reply.

"I *will* shatter the artifact if you so much as look at my town again," I answered coolly.

Dahl froze. His hesitation only flitted by, but I recognized it. He rose, his slight frame further diminished by the bulky furs of his cloak and furry footwear. He twisted toward me, the expected sneer and loathing missing in every essential form.

His tone was gentle and his words full of empathy. "You have a baby developing inside the ebony-haired woman."

Hate and terror warred inside me. My desire to act pressed my hand to my wand. My instincts forced it back onto the saddle.

He recognized the conflict. I expected to see victory spread across his face.

No such expression appeared. Instead, compassion prevailed. If I hadn't realized how many beings he'd slain, I may have believed it. I didn't trust myself to speak, so I stared at him.

"I can read energies. You have three linked to you. I'm confident you reduce yours purposely, so I believe yours is the smallest. The woman's khatra is the most intense. Still, it cannot camouflage the second energy within."

"I'll destroy the artifact if you––

His interruption was calm. "I'm not threatening you. I'm suggesting an avenue for us both. There is a stone giant who occupies that artifact. I have felt its strength. That energy is what I can use to open a passage to my home. When I use it, I will consume the giant before it can take your infant as its vessel. You already recognize that's its intention."

I bounced once in my saddle, pressing up with my feet before relaxing into it again. "What do you want?"

"My only desire is to be home with my people and face my eventual destiny. Is that such a threat?" He hesitated, but his words were reassuring and his tone was gentle.

"I assure you, I will destroy that artifact, and your household and friends will be safe. I will leave you in peace," Dahl finished.

"Someone informed me your passage would allow other portals to open. I've located one such rip already. It's inside the manor house. I can't let you open them. It would wipe out this realm," I said. I was only playing for time. Time for what? I didn't have an answer for Dahl.

"My passage has left open doorways. I've left them open because I've had no reason to close them. You only have my word, but I'll seal them on my passage. I'll also take the artifact with me so that the misery within cannot escape, even if I don't waste its energies."

Dahl's proposal was simple, and would fix every headache. But could I trust him? The vicious acts of murder he'd committed, and the equally vile tortures perpetrated against him, made me doubt his sincerity. Could any creature inflicted with such bitterness, who committed such acts of depravity, keep a promise?

My shoulders dropped in acknowledgment; I didn't have a choice.

"Give me an hour. I'll meet you at Eldritch Manor."

I turned and began my ride home to use the one advantage I held. After spending my life working on the edges of the law and doing what I thought was right, despite the technical legalities, I now needed to pin the fate of my family, my town, and my world on a technical legality.

I'd already ordered Mr. Owensteine to document my wishes. Now, I only needed the guts to follow through with the plan.

JAMES

I entered my home empty of any burdens or apprehensions. I'd cast every spell I learned to erase any negative image or energy before I stepped through the door. Unfortunately, two things I couldn't expunge were dread and loss.

"Hey!" was my single word hello to the three most essential individuals in my heart.

"*Mi amor*, where have you been?" María asked.

"I needed to practice constructing a last couple of spells, and Davi suggested I move away from anyone I liked. So..."

I grinned as I brought my arms wide, encompassing the kitchen. María took it as a suggestion and settled into them. Her embrace supplied the conviction I lacked when I arrived.

"Listen, I've got more to finish. I don't need any of you to wait for me. This may take me the better part of the night," I announced as I selected one of Kate's angel biscuits and bit into it. I expected the bread to bury the knot swelling in my throat.

"What's goin' on, Jimmy?" Kate and Presley asked simultaneously. They snorted, and the pint-sized ginger punched him lovingly on the arm.

"I've one last piece of magic to perform before this complete mess explodes," I mumbled through the biscuit.

"Do you require my assistance, *hermoso?*" María asked.

Not trusting myself to speak, I crammed the rest of the roll into my mouth and swung my head. Instead, I looked at my friend Presley and talked around my food. "Presley, could you help me with Connie? I believe he threw a shoe. I don't have time to repair it, and I need your opinion on his feet."

"Sure thing, Jim." He hopped up and started to the door, tugging on his coat.

I swung to my beautiful wife and cupped her face in my palms before I whispered. "*Mi amor*, I *will* see you again. Don't give up on me, no matter what."

"Jim, what is wrong? What do you mean, 'no matter what?'" Her eyes narrowed, and she tilted her head. But in them, I didn't recognize the same dread now gutting my innards.

I'd properly cast my charms, so I shrugged off her concerns with a quiet wink and a peck to her lips. "It's excellent discipline to trust me. That's all." I laughed as I fled the room. She slapped my backside on my way out.

"Go on then, you pirate," she bantered at my rear.

"I'm a privateer."

Bang! The door closed behind me.

"Hey, Jimmy, his shoes look perfect. You wanna explain why I'm actually here?" my childhood friend asked.

"I can stop Dahl, but you gotta protect the ladies and keep them away from the manor tonight," I said. I put one hand on his shoulder and the other on his arm while my eyes scanned his for any hint he may doubt me.

"Sure thing, buddy," he countered. It was as if I'd begged him to feed my animals for the week.

"Though you owe me an explanation," he finished. Presley held Connie's reins, and I realized he wouldn't drop them until he chose to.

"Presley, the demon knows María's pregnant. It's coming for our baby. Don't ask me how I know. Just trust me."

"All right, I believe you," he announced with the same tone he adopted when we discussed strategies for trapping some English merchantman.

"The only way I can stop the monster is from inside the spyglass realm. I can fight it there. But here…" I waved my arms as if to involve the Earth. "Out here, I don't stand a chance. I've already challenged him many times, and I've failed every time."

"Jimmy, I don't understand. You haven't fought him. At least, not any fight that I've seen. Besides, how do you get inside that spyglass?"

"Pres, trust me. I *have* fought it, and it utterly defeated me every time. Out here, I can't prevail. Inside, I have a chance. To get inside, Dahl's gotta kill me."

Leaves blew in the gelid breeze and tapped against the glass. A distant howl caused me to scour the gloom. It was a response ingrained through years of defending my livestock.

Presley thudded against my house and dropped to the ground—his method of separating himself from me. He required time and distance to think.

Finally, he spoke. "Jimmy, there's gotta be another idea. Maybe if I helped. Maybe together—

"My friend, even when I killed the demon, it only reformed in another location. The new creature was as powerful as the one I'd just defeated. It's not possible to kill it here. This must be why Davi taught me to eradicate a dimension."

"How can you be sure?"

"I haven't told Katie, but those who disappeared weren't murdered. The demon inside the spyglass captured them. Some souls have resisted and moved on. That's why those sculptures have fallen apart. Others were caught and are being depleted by the demon. Those are the worn, ancient-looking statues. Other souls are struggling and winning, so theirs still look new."

"Jimmy, I appreciate you believe what you're…um…but it all sounds so unlikely," Presley said. To underscore his remark, he firmly shook his head. I noticed he stared at the mud between his folded knees instead of me. I knew my friend well enough to reason he'd be facing me if he believed me, although I now questioned my rationale for bringing him in on my plan.

"What? As implausible as my magical abilities? That type of improbable?" I asked sarcastically.

Presley laughed. "I guess you've got me there."

"Pres, the spyglass collects souls of those it slays. If it doesn't kill 'em, it's got nothing to expel to create a statue. I appreciate this makes little sense. But when it is time, tell María. She'll understand. Tell her to listen for me. I'm more capable than any of you realize. I can't say more. The risk is too great. But this is the single chance I've got at winning both battles. Or at least gett'n a draw."

Presley Varde tilted his head and looked at me, then stuck out his hand, and I tugged him to his feet. He flung his arms around me, and we hugged like brothers.

"Just promise me you'll keep María away. She doesn't need to see this. None of you do, but especially her," I entreated.

"I will," he mumbled. He released me after he slapped my back.

I hopped onto Connie, swung him toward Eldritch, and spurred him forward.

Speed was my ally, as I needed to arrive before Dahl.

JAMES

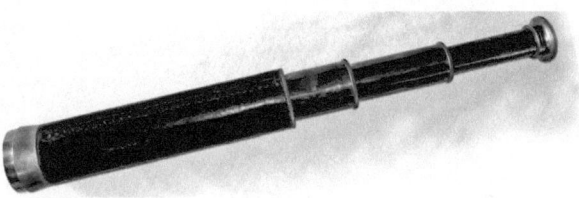

*T*he manor was dark when I arrived. It was also clear of any energies except for the baseline life. That meant I'd beaten Dahl here. Step one--check.

My plan was about as simple as you might believe. Its key was my death. That was the only way inside. Getting inside was easy. Stopping Dahl from taking the spyglass and destroying the souls inside it, including mine, or opening a portal to thirteen alien worlds, or letting the demon free on this one, or destroying Genosqwa, or…

Never mind. Fine, I was inventing this as I went along. Happy? You bunch of jerks.

Sorry--I didn't mean that last part.

Tick. Gong!

The wooden clock still echoed its march on the far wall. I swear, I'm going to burn it if—I mean when—I win.

I lit a fire in the hearth and conjured a split cord of pine to feed it. One thing was sure: no matter what I said, María, Presley, and Kate would all be here before the night was done. The least I could do was have a supply of wood ready for them.

Gong!

I conjured a grouping of chairs and even a cell to hold Dahl. If

Presley could capture him. I was pretty sure he could. After what I was about to do, Dahl should be an easy target. I was betting he would quit fighting at all, at least for a time.

Gong!

The cold wind rushed through the swinging door as it scraped its way open. Turning, I saw the diminutive Dahl pushing through it. He didn't bother to close it. He just walked to me, his hand extended.

Gong!

59

UNNAMED OMNISCIENT PRESENCE

Susan Bond blew out the last lamp lighting her restaurant and rounded to bolt the door. She offered scant concern to the boots' scruff as they tramped across the boardwalk in front of her establishment—until the sound stopped, and a fist pounded on her door.

"I am closed fir ta ev'nen," she shouted at the imposition.

"*Señora, no quiero nada.* I have knowledge. You must help James Byrne and his bride," came the accented reply.

She opened the door and confronted a Capitán from the adjacent Spanish garrison. Susan held her lamp to the man's face before recognizing him. Her eyes flew wide, and she seized his arm and snatched him inside, closing the door behind them.

Capitán Raphael Jenyn had once served as the First Officer of *The Inverness* under Presley Varde before being recruited to the Spanish Navy. He was from Rota, Spain, and had been close friends with Lady María when they were children. Their history was the lone reason he was posted at the stronghold. María's mother supposed he'd protect her daughter, while his faithfulness to the rule of gold—meaning whoever possesses the gold creates the rules—would motivate him to snoop on María for her.

Her first hope was a certainty. Capitán Raphael Jenyn of the Spanish Navy's Infantería de Marina, or Marine Infantry, would protect María with his life. Her second hope was nothing but a dream. His loyalty was, and always would be, to his childhood friend María, who had helped him flee the poverty of his birth and secure a position as cabin boy on *The Inverness* when he was thirteen.

"*Ellos vienen*. They know María is here. My commander will arrive by morning," Capitán Jenyn said as if his last task on Earth was to provide this information.

"I un'tersand. I'll tells 'em."

Raphael checked the darkness for anyone following. He turned to Susan, nodded, and then charged into the blackness.

The tavern owner grabbed her cloak and a wicker basket. She loaded the basket with bread and the leftover roast duck and dashed out the back door.

It took her less than five minutes to reach her destination.

She thumped on the door, and Kate Varde opened it. Susan drew her outside and revealed the Spanish Officer's message.

"Take dis food. If'n anyone be watchin', they's'll tink this be why I came." Then she bowed to the pretty redhead and spun away.

Kate returned to the kitchen carrying the basket and strode in to the wide eyes of her friend and the somber face of her husband.

"You both heard?" she asked.

"*Pinche pendejos*," María said.

"Yeah, we heard," Presley replied, grumpier than necessary.

"What, then? Should we interrupt Jim?" Kate asked.

"No," María said.

"Yes, and I'll tell him," said Presley. He spun and disappeared, shutting and latching the door before either of the ladies could challenge him.

They glanced at one another. Kate bolted the door and listened as Presley galloped away.

"Do you understand any of this?" María asked as she grabbed her cloak and gloves.

"You're not leaving without me," Kate stated flatly.

They hustled to hitch the carriage. Then María raced it toward the edge of town as if a demon were hunting her.

Unfortunately, one was, and she was rushing into its waiting arms.

She didn't slow as she moved through Metaterre. If she survived the night, she would apologize to anyone she'd frightened.

"Where are we going?" Kate hollered into the wind above the pounding of the horse's hooves.

"Eldritch!"

60

JAMES

"*S*urrender it, and I will keep my commitment," Dahl said evenly.

Gong!

"Riaan, you can't keep your word, and you know it. You can't shut those portal doors, nor can you destroy the artifact or demon. You know you can't," I countered.

Gong!

"Your belief is not relevant. You have no alternative."

Gong!

"Ah, my friend, you're wrong. Kill me and my power will multiply. Kill me and you'll never control this."

I drew the spyglass from under my cloak and clenched it against my chest. My heart pounded wildly. The brass instrument bounced away and back.

Gong!

Dahl's eyes flew wide at the sight of his cherished prize.

"Kill me and you'll never determine the owner. I've obscured its ownership from everyone," I boasted.

Gong!

"I will murder everyone in this town. Then I will find all you have known and kill them. Ultimately, I will discover the owner, or none shall live, and I can take my prize. You can spare them that suffering," the small grotesque man growled.

He advanced toward me, seeking to pin me against the wall. I stepped aside, putting the grand entrance near my back. I was consistently conscious of proper footwork when using a cutlass. This fight was no different.

Gong!

"Please, Mr. Byrne. This solution is your last opportunity," Dahl pleaded.

The appeal didn't rattle me. I'd guessed he'd do this. Davi hadn't. It was one of the many subjects over which we'd sparred. Pleading or not, Dahl was resigned to his plan.

Gong!

The door shot wide, crashing into the wall. Presley rushed through, his shoulder leading the way. I heard horses and a wagon racing along the carriageway, and I realized who'd be driving it.

"Shit!" I blurted.

I saw Dahl's hand flash, and a gun appeared. Its report was jarring, and I followed the musket ball as it sped toward my friend.

Gong!

My protection jura deflected the ball into the wall, saving Presley. The confusion on Dahl's face was the first hint I'd seen that the introduction to my plan could be effective.

The curse that struck me was fast. I never saw it shaped. Only then did I realize I could've never defeated this creature. Davi should've warned me. Maybe she did, and I didn't listen.

The expected pain never occurred—possibly because of the stunning abruptness of the attack. The wound was deeper than I'd counted on, and my crimson life flowed readily. I stumbled, then fell.

I didn't want her to see me this way, but it overjoyed me when I heard my love yell.

"James!" She collapsed to my side and pushed her hands onto the wound to staunch the gush of blood. The damage was considerable, so she started tearing parts from her dress to act as a bandage.

"James, I am here. You are safe."

María cried as she bent and kissed me. The heat of her tears as they fell across my face ripped my heart. This was what I'd sought to avoid. But having her here with me at the end made it easier...at least for me, anyway.

"I warned you. All you had to do was give it to me," Dahl whined.

"No, Riaan, I warned you. The strength of my magic will be unbreakable when I'm gone. You'll never injure my friends. You'll never recover this spyglass. I've won, and you've failed."

"No, James," María cried. "You must fight. Do not give in."

"I love you more than I can express. You've been the best thing to happen to me. Don't forget what I told you at home." I drew the spyglass to my wound, and my blood covered it, then absorbed.

Darkness crept in from the fringes of my vision.

"Huh, there literally is a tunnel of light," I said. Or at least I tried to say.

The sounds of crying faded, as did the light. Darkness enveloped me. Then nothing.

María toppled onto my chest as terrible sobs of loss heaved from her breast, a vocalization of her breaking heart. Her tears fell, wetting my cheeks, obliging both of us to weep—me by sharing her tears.

Kate settled her hands across her friend's shoulders, and after a moment, she relaxed her head against her friend's. Neither woman commented as the bronze spyglass, the object that had provoked so much misery, faded from view.

Dahl's sob was wretched, and only an evil man could overlook his unmistakable sadness.

--or a furious man. Presley seized the little being and flung him into the cage I'd magically formed when I arrived at Eldritch.

Dahl didn't struggle. He only cried.

....

*L*osing the spyglass was as painful as any defeat Dahl had ever suffered. His home had been feet away. He must suppose James was evil for taking it from him.

"How?" he complained.

In truth, he did not care how James managed it, because nothing but his destination ever mattered.

"These creatures have no right. I have suffered. I have suffered," the troll mumbled under his breath. He left out the truth of the tremendous suffering he had caused.

Dahl felt the universe itself must be conspiring against his eternal right to return home. It furnished him the only answer to how anyone could have stolen the relic, his transcendent target, from him.

"It must be the universe...because of my sins. Yes, doubtless my depravity. For the transgression of birth, I am forever denied. Regardless, I will return home. It is my right, through my life of suffering, that I finally rest with my kind."

"Stop your damned mumbling!" Presley growled as he lifted the firearm he'd plucked from a pocket inside his jacket.

"One individual here must own the spyglass. I will observe, listen, and determine who."

He observed the tears of the ebony-haired María continue to fall, and believed it was pointless for her to be so tormented. "She does not understand unending pain. Hers must be the pregnant energy whom Byrne sought to obscure from the absolute evil that lives inside the spyglass."

Dahl never studied the wreckage of his murders. He never desired to understand the product of his carnage. He never hated those he murdered, just as he despised none here. Hate was a vessel without a dimension inside him. "I simply wished to return home."

María's grief was so potent Dahl could read it bouncing above her, a powerful conflagration of lavenders, its base the stain of an orchid and its tips shaded pink. He had never encountered that type of energy. Certainly, her anguish was more than fantasy. It contained a visceral component that he did not realize existed.

"If I could console her...I would not tolerate the smallest creature I slaughtered, even those who sacrificed themselves for my boots, or my cloak, to suffer the anguish of this woman."

Dahl could not remove her grief. But he could consume a fragment of the terrible energy. "I can provide her that comfort. Besides, it would rebuild my reserves. Reserves drained because I have been deprived access to the entire magic of this realm." He shaped another energy spell. This time, he joined a siphon, which drew the iridescent lavender into his reserves.

The effect was awful and instantaneous. Her grief became his.

As it flowed away from her and Dahl absorbed its blazing violet energies, he experienced pain unlike any before now. "I have led a wretched existence. I have foisted misery upon misery onto any creature, great or small, that rose between me and my target. So much suffering, and I have accomplished nothing. This woman did not deserve this."

Dahl reached an arm toward her. A flash of light threw him away, crashing into the far side of his iron cage. His cell transformed from iron into untouchable energy.

Through the blinding light, he saw another figure. Her dark skin stood in striking contrast to her platinum hair and her blazing ice-blue eyes.

I faced Dahl and laughed. "They have caught you, haven't they, you little fucker?" I questioned.

My laugh lacked mirth.

"For fuck's sake, put that away, Presley. You will put your eye out," I suggested as I faced Presley and the two women.

JAMES

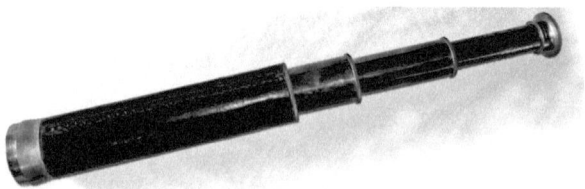

I opened my eyes. Or at least, I opened what I assumed were my eyes. The blackness was total—almost.

Tick, tick. Tick, tick.

That damned clock. I couldn't escape it, even in death. I heard... wait...I felt. Frigid rain beat down, soaking my clothes. I found it interesting that I was wearing clothes.

"Impervio."

The drops of water beaded off, and I no longer felt their icy touch. I chuckled. I couldn't construct that invocation when I was alive.

Tick, tick, tick, tick... danged incessant noise.

Lightning flashed and thunder rolled. I reeled and scoured the gloom for the massive gray beast. The ground quaked, and I found it. It was gigantic. In retrospect, I figured it should've been obvious it'd be larger, more powerful here. After all, it created this place.

"Shit!" I exclaimed. Yes, I recognize I'd let one of Davi's words slip. But, if I ever had the right to use one, it was now.

The next surge of lightning backlit the behemoth clearly. Oddly, watching it march toward me in this realm was less distressing than in mine. I was dead, so I suppose it sort of makes sense, too.

Genosqwa stomped toward me, causing the ground to reverberate and the puddles from the storm to echo the quake.

My initial plan, if you could call it that, was to locate as many captured souls as feasible, then ally myself with them before battling this demon. Since I'd only just appeared, I didn't have that chance.

It still didn't matter. I couldn't destroy this domain without helping them escape first. Doing otherwise would utterly destroy their immortal beings. I'd consider that option purely as a last resort, and only to keep the monster from taking my child and entering the earthly plane to wipe out humanity.

No allies, no problem, I hoped. Another key facet of my plan was the notion that if I could consume a dimension, I should also be able to establish one—of a sort, anyway. But, like forming other magic inside the demon realm, Kaysan, these spells only operated here. That meant that no matter how regularly I practiced, I'd never be confident they'd function until I was *inside* Kaysan to try them.

I shaped the spell and smirked as I watched the shell form. The demon's club smashed into my tiny protective dome. The resulting flash was brighter than noon as it slipped off and crashed into the ground. Whatever the ground was composed of dusted up in huge plumes before settling on my newly constructed barrier, then sliding off, along with the wintry rain.

The lightning arced and blasted into my dome. The effect was brilliant. I was exultant as the beast wailed. Its cry was deafening.

The defensive barrier shrugged off multiple bolts of lightning, which curved through Kaysan. Genosqwa raised its tree sized club and forced it plunging down. The hammer blow, combined with the force of the lightning, caused my little dome to flash.

Well, heck, no plan survives contact with the enemy, and I can't fight hiding under my protective dome. I suppose it's time to develop a plan...um, C. No, D.

D—for dang it, I've got no freaking idea what to do. Fortunately, that's how most of my ideas developed, anyway. None of them ever went the way I intended. I only succeeded because, at the perfect moment, I discovered the correct path when my adversary couldn't.

Another hammer blow. This time, the dome shrank. It wasn't much. But I noticed.

Come on, James, pull it together.

Blow after blow, my world actually was shrinking as the edges of my dome crumbled. I decided my sole chance was to run. I'd wait for the next stroke, drop my shield, and run. Maybe I could locate help or invent another location to hide. Other souls here must've discovered how to fight, so it must be possible.

The giant raised its club. Its scream was primal as it brought the weapon down.

Another great eruption of lightning—only this time, it was above my shield. The burning flames above me lit the surroundings, granting me an unobstructed view of the events.

There, standing as towering as the monster Genosqwa and holding a blade nearly two-thirds his size, was Charles Dwayne Doss.

"Hey, Jimmy, you want to help me out, or you just going to stand there fucking gawking at me?" Kate's grandfather demanded.

JAMES

Together, Charles and I formed an impenetrable defensive barrier. The stone monster finally abandoned its assault and lumbered away.

"Jimmy, why the hell are you here? I urged you to stay away. Why the fuck didn't you listen?" Charles demanded as if he and I were discussing the evening's rain.

"Mr. Doss—" I started.

Tick, tick...

"Call me Charles or even Charlie. After all, we're both dead. Leave the ridiculous titles for the living."

I laughed and shook my head, then conceded. "Yes, si...I mean—" For the first time in nearly two months, I didn't feel the burden of the universe resting solely on my shoulders. Then I thought of María and our baby.

"Charlie, I came here to eradicate this realm. It's the one and only means of beating the demon who lives here. I need help getting everyone here to safety first," I answered.

Then I hesitated, hoping he had a solution.

"So, we're on the same mission. Son, I came here to recover my wife and to keep this fucking beast from harming anyone else."

"Did you find her?"

"No." His eyes dropped as he swung his head. "The others claimed she discovered her own path a ways back. I suppose it shouldn't surprise me. She always loved the Lord. I'm confident that's how she escaped. But I've not worshipped in decades, so I guess I'm stuck here. Besides, inside here, I *can* stop the monster from attacking Katie or anyone else. If that's my eternity, I'm content."

"You can't beat it?" I asked.

"I don't know." He rubbed his chin in thought. "I can keep it from injuring anyone, at least for the foreseeable future."

His words gave me pause. Clearly, he wasn't confident in how to beat the thing, so I was glad I came to help. "Do you understand this place?"

"Fucking sure do. I explained it to you when you came to visit. I thought that's why you agreed to let me return to the manor after you bought it."

"Nope. A blonde demon suggested it. I didn't understand your meaning at Kate's. It was only later that it made sense."

"Ah, I see. Davi can be a little off-putting while you're getting to— appreciate her," Charlie answered with a wink.

"Wait. You know Davi?"

"Sure I do. How the fuck do you suppose I figured how to get inside here?" Charles reached his arms wide to encompass the whole of the Kaysan realm.

"When did you meet her?"

"Right after Peggy, my wife, died. We worked closely for many years, and even married," Charlie stated, as if explaining water was wet.

"Married," I blurted.

"She's rather attractive, and a hell of a lover," he said, a devilish smirk widening across his face.

"Well, that's a mental picture I'd like to expunge from my mind," I said.

Tick, tick, tick...

Again, we shared a laugh before he spoke. "Son, a portal opens at each four o'clock every day. If someone's touching the spyglass when it opens, they get yanked inside. Since this is an unusual dimension, only their soul enters. It leaves the rest of their body, and it's why everyone has a stone effigy after they disappear."

"That's the way I understood it. So, it didn't suck you in at a four o'clock?"

"No—I forced Dahl to kill me. I let my blood soak the glass before I died. I came in at four o'clock because the pathway was easier. Davi buried my body on the manor grounds. You should've found it."

"Yeah, I did the same thing, except I opened my own door. And sorry, sir, I didn't look."

"Ahh, no matter. She did it for herself, anyway. I assuredly didn't care what happened to that old husk."

"Charlie, that four o'clock doorway, goes both ways, right?"

"You already have the answer to that, my boy."

"It was just after midnight that I, well, died," I said.

Tick, tick.

"I swear, I should have destroyed that damned clock before I arrived." I complained.

"Son, you sure as fuck will be happy you didn't," Charlie said. I stared at him, puzzled.

"My boy, I enchanted it as both a warning and an anchor. The anchor is what ties it to our version of Earth rather than floating between universes. Besides, I heard the ticking whenever the monster changed planes to come to Earth. The chime told me it was near."

Charles shrugged his shoulders as if I should've discovered these facts long ago.

"A letter may have helped," I replied, frustrated at missing the unmistakable link between Genosqwa and the clock. Unfazed, he shrugged again.

I pushed on. "I've got a plan. But I need to get everyone—everyone except for that monster—to me. Can you do that?"

"No problem," Charles Doss said confidently.

"Great. I'm tired of getting my butt kicked by this thing. I think it's time we kick some of our own. What do you think?"

Charles bared his teeth. His growl was savage.

DAVI

"For fuck's sake, put that away, Presley. You will put your eye out," I said. Presley glanced at the pistol in his hand, shrugged, and tucked it back inside his jacket.

Kate glared at me as a flush rusted her face. She rose, stomped to rest in front of me, flaming indignation, and drilled me in the mouth.

"Don't you dare come here and start issuing orders," Kate stated matter-of-factly.

I hardly noticed the blow. Centuries of discipline had prepared me to take a punch. Millenia of evolution also made me resistant to any form of secondary physical assaults.

"My dear, I appreciate that you believe you understand what is occurring. But you must listen," I said. I understand the hurt of the four individuals here. Besides, I restored the minor bruise on my lip before I noted the discomfort. They deserved their moment of grief, and I would not deny them that dignity.

"What do you mean, we don't understand?" María asked coolly, not glancing up from James's body.

"Pretty much exactly what I stated. None of you realize what or why matters are proceeding. As an illustration—Kate, did you know your grandfather and I married many years ago?"

I enjoyed dropping minor explosions into my remarks. Doing so granted me control of the discussion. Curse words, at least the pathetic excuses for curse words from this race, released me to speak of scarcely believable topics. My cussing diluted the intensity of the contentious subjects and facilitates fucking understanding.

I assessed their reaction. It was what I expected—disbelief.

Except for María. Her veil of grief endured.

I proceeded. "It was two years after your grandmother disappeared. I arrived intending to aid Charles with the demon at the center of the spyglass."

"Why would you help my grandfather with the demon?"

"Your grandfather had the same ability as James."

On hearing his name, María's head jerked up, and she snapped at me—unfairly, from my viewpoint, but from hers, fucking appropriate. "Do not speak his name. You do not have the right. You could have spared him. Instead, you let him…"

María's voice broke as she glanced back at him and brushed his cheek. More tears slipped from her eyes. The spectacle was heartbreaking. But, since it was their world that would permanently change due to their efforts over the next hours, these three humans needed to make their decisions swiftly.

I proceeded. "I encouraged him to recognize his capabilities, and later began treating his sorrow. During those efforts, we fell in love, and…well, there you have it. We practiced together for many years, until I could teach him nothing further. He made choices too. They were his to make and own. He elected to locate his lost spouse and free her soul. It became his preoccupation, his undoing, and ultimately, it will be his triumph."

"He's dead, too. Are you saying you let him die in your game of pawns?" Kate suggested.

"Kate, it is not a game. It is deadly serious for your entire planet. It is likewise not mine to handle. As I told James and Charles, if I corrected every dilemma, no culture would flourish. They would order as I chose. I do not have that right."

I appreciated that my response was correct, but most individuals personalized it and turned it against me. Shit, I understood their misery. What feeling creature would not? Still, many lifetimes had taught me that I was *not* answerable for their decisions.

"Say what you must." Presley growled. I nodded once to him.

"Charles and James are fighting a beast that, if they fail, will eradicate all of humankind. If they prevail, they will stop this wretched creature from returning home." I pointed to Dahl.

"He killed James. I have no sympathy for him," María said.

"No, my child, you should not. But before you cast him aside, appreciate his history."

I devoted the next hour to recounting the tortures Dahl had suffered at the hands of his kidnappers, those so-called priests who had betrayed his trust and beaten his soul into submission.

"His life has taken all that he was, everything he could have been, and distilled it into a single mission—an inexhaustible longing to return home," I finished.

As foreseen, my analysis of Dahl's history of suffering moved María, Presley, and Kate. But, with James' recent death, I did not predict any of them would grant him absolution, either—particularly the widow.

"He murdered my husband. I will never let that betrayal rest," María said. While she may have spent her anger, she was resolute.

"That is one decision you must make," I said.

"María, let me move James's body onto the bed," Presley stated.

The intelligent ebony-haired vision quietly rose, supported by the redheaded Kate. María's dress was darkly discolored and her hands sticky from the blood of her lover.

"Davi, will you please help clear this?" Kate pleaded, nodding to the sanguine pool on the floor and covering her friend.

"I am sorry, dear. I cannot aid you. This is a task to which you three must attend." I realized my comments were unfeeling. But their efforts, even the slightest, must determine the day, not mine.

"Bitch," Kate blurted.

María placed a blood-covered hand on the redhead's arm. "Thank you, Katie. I will clean it," María said. Then she set about clearing the gore.

Presley laid the corpse onto the bed James had conjured upon his arrival, then shoved it into the blackness on the far side of the chamber near the antique clock.

Gong!

Gong!

JAMES

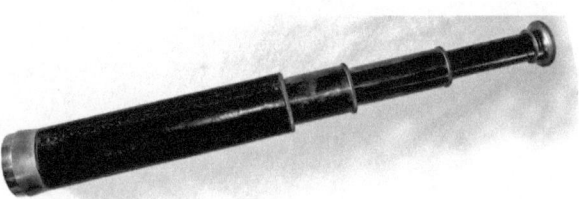

*T*he spirits huddled near me were akin to breathing people. It wasn't unexpected, because what endured was their distilled essence. Most craved word of their family or friends. After that, they simply wanted out.

"I'm positive I can eradicate this plane. But doing so will also destroy our consciences if we can't slip away. Charles, when I cast the disintegration spell, Genosqwa will counterattack. I will add obstacles to delay it. Can you engage it long enough for the spell to drain this domain?"

"For fuck's sake, boy, you realize that's why I'm here, don't you? How thick can you be?"

"According to Davi, pretty dense. Listen, sir—I mean Charlie—your vocabulary is gaudier here. Did Davi coach you?" I quipped.

"Who the fuck do your think trained her?" Charles deadpanned.

I shook my head. "Alright, Charlie, you delay Genosqwa. The rest of you remain behind the barricade until I instruct you the portal's open. I'll mark it so you can find it. Once inside, you can move freely, either toward Earth or to whatever's on the other side. Know this—returning to Earth cannot restore your lives. Your bodies are dust. But it is your decision to make."

"What about you, son? Which path will you travel?" Tedene Varde asked.

"Ma'am, if my body survives, I'll return. If not, I'll follow you."

66

....

*M*aría jumped to her feet and flung down the sodden rags she'd been using to clean up the spilled blood. They splatted to the floor in a gory echo of liquid slop.

"Davi, did you tell James that if he perished, his spells would break?" María chirped. Her tone was intense, her movements quick as she scrambled to her husband's side.

"I did," the blonde woman responded, an impish smirk flitting into the edges of her mouth.

María yelled, "The bed—it is still here."

Kate and Presley looked at one another, bemused expressions fouling any other response.

"María, what do you mean?" Kate asked as she rushed after her friend.

"If he is still bleeding, it means his heart is beating," María whooped. "I stupidly assumed..."

She tore open his shirt and pressed a bundle of bandages onto the wound, mopping away all traces of the blood. She withdrew her hands and stared as, slowly, a paltry dribble of blood spilled. She seized his hand and pressed his index finger. The skin under the nail turned white. She held his hand and waited.

"What are you doing?" a confused Presley asked.

"Wait," she hushed. The smile that stretched across her face was unequivocal.

"Yes!" she shrieked. "He is alive!"

"How?" Presley and Kate asked together.

"I do not know, but when I pinched the blood from his finger, it refilled. It can only do that if his heart is beating." Her words raced from her lips as fast as she could manage them.

Kate and Presley rushed to her side. Presley pressed more bandages into the wound, while Kate gathered the medical supplies laying on the end of the bed.

"James said, 'Do not give up on me.' This was his intention to get inside to combat the demon." María said as she fought her growing excitement. She bent and kissed his face. "Hang on, my love."

"He told me the same thing. I didn't understand. But he claimed he needed to fight inside the realm. He also claimed he was more capable than we knew," Presley replied, his excitement adding to the room.

"What do we do?" Kate asked no one and everyone.

María, James, and Kate all glanced at Davi, who turned aside from their gaze.

"Help me get this stitched up, Kate," María said.

"We do not have time to wait on the she-devil," she decided as she began helping her husband.

It took María almost an hour to stop the bleeding and sew the wound. When she finished, she wrapped James's body with every blanket she could locate, including from the bed upstairs. Experienced doctors had taught her that injured people grew colder because of their trauma. Keeping the subject warm improved their chances of survival.

JAMES

ick, tick...

Any expectation of postponing our attack awaiting the portal opening ended when I saw the first flashes of lightning. The groaning thunder caused vibrations underfoot as the demon stomped toward us.

When I first arrived inside Kaysan, Genosqwa had attacked almost immediately—an attack I wasn't prepared for. Now, it was attacking much earlier than I'd expected. Clearly, the demon would fight this battle on its terms.

Every soul here had encountered the monster at some stage during their imprisonment. Most had only escaped after Charles appeared and released them. Every soul also notified me they'd rather I dismantle the demon realm, along with their spirits, than suffer the future awaiting them should Genosqwa win.

Tick, tick...

My strategy was as simple as peeling an onion. I'd executed it many times in my head before I got here. I needed to flay the layers of offensive and defensive powers of Genosqwa until we weakened it enough for me to destroy the dimension it had spawned.

In theory, this was simple. In reality, it would be tough to accomplish, because I could only end the domain after the portal opened. Otherwise, none of the souls could move on, and I'd never return home. Also, while the portal was active, we needed to keep the demon engaged so it couldn't follow us out.

My first decision was to select the proper time for the battle. I believed that our joint attack could collapse the demon's energy in fifteen minutes or so. If needed, we could stretch it out to twenty-five minutes, but if we tried to go longer, the demon would recharge faster than we could drain it. And unlike Genosqwa, we couldn't recharge.

I was confident in my plan for many reasons. Primarily, I maintained a decent window to strike and weaken my quarry. I would attack at four, when the portal opened. Since it would close one hour later, that would be how much time I had to win the battle.

Secondarily, Genosqwa didn't want to kill the surviving souls within its territory. It merely craved mine and Charles's elimination. Since it had seized the others once, Genosqwa must be positive it could again. This was a fact I was counting on.

Tick, tick...

The outset of the battle played out like every one of my waking nightmares—lightning flashed and sleet blocked our visibility. I constructed spells to defend us, then further abjurations to keep us dry and warm.

Genosqwa tried to hide, but the beast couldn't stay hidden, since every flash lit it like cannon fire back-lighting a ship at night.

"Charles, when does the portal open?" The torrent of wind coupled with the resounding thunder leading the behemoth made speaking difficult, so I yelled to be understood.

"Half an hour," came the booming reply. Clearly, Charles had learned a trick for speaking above the din.

Tick...

"Everyone, back away. Let me take the lead!" I bellowed.

Tick...

"*Liquefacta.*"

The ground between us and the demon dissolved into an ebony magma pool. The creature roared.

Tick...

"*Muras Ignis.*"

A tremendous wall of flame erupted and soared into the substrate of the realm, leaving an acrid smoke billowing from where the flames met the ground. The smoke and heat were as tactile as when I'd shaped them in my dream-walk. My nostrils burned, and the heat was blistering. I flung my arm in front of my face as protection.

Tick...

Genosqwa raised its club and brought it crashing into the wall. Lightning and flames burned across the blackened void. Repeatedly, the ancient monster beat its tree-sized club against the flames. The barrier crumbled as I fed less and less of my mana into supporting it.

Tick...

"Time!"

"Fifteen minutes," Charles boomed back.

"Just a little longer," I shouted into the cyclone.

Tick...

The wall of plasma weakened as I eased feeding my strength into it. I'd already spent a hefty fraction of my magical reserves, and the battle was hardly underway. At this pace, I wouldn't have adequate power to forge a path through the void and into my body. It'd be disastrous to return simply to drift unattached from my physical form, a phantasm left to roam the Earth.

"Better make it count, James."

"What's that, boy?" Charles yelled.

I didn't respond.

Tick...

I waited until Genosqwa brought its club crashing down before I abruptly ceased supplying the blockade. With nothing to strike against, the monster over-balanced and tumbled forward— straight into the pool of molten void. Its cry was far more terrifying than it had been in my waking dream, its hatred significantly more immense.

Tick...

Unlike my nightmarish vision, this time, Genosqwa didn't reform in a new position, but worked like a swimmer struggling for shore. It took valuable minutes, but it reached the boundary of molten and solid void and climbed out of my ambush.

"Jimmy, you'd better get this ship underway," Charlie announced.

Tick...

"Everyone, now!" I yelled.

After their death, each spirit had been distilled into a singular essence of the most dynamic energy imaginable. According to Davi, this force was a basic framework within creatures in every dimension, linking life and death. Love was the only power capable of surviving death.

At my command, every spirit in the void rushed forward and poured forth that singular force. The realm bloomed with the fury of dozens of suns as each spirit energized their love for their family, friends, and their god before dumping it onto the demon.

Tick...

Genosqwa stumbled, then fell to one knee before crashing onto its huge, clawed hands. Its head tucked before lifting and blasting a dreadful roar. It rose, utilizing its tree-sized club for leverage. It screamed the entire journey. Once set, it raised the club and delivered it plunging into the ebony ground.

The resounding blast of sound percussed like a hammer blow. The resulting explosion threw every spirit aside, provoking them to surrender their assault. I'd compensate with another shield.

Wait—one remained. As the others discontinued their attack, this one fought harder. She poured even more onto the enemy, intent on crushing it alone. Tedene Varde never faltered in her storm.

The others saw and rejoined the struggle. This time, the weight of their charge was so fierce I feared they'd cause us to win before we were prepared.

Then, as if every move I'd made to win this twin battle came into focus, I heard the single sound I'd been preparing for.

Gong!

"Charles, now!"

The monster's wail was horrifying. It swung its great club in giant circles, struggling to fend off a force it couldn't understand. Charles's sword smashed into the club with the power of a million charging elephants. Nothing could have withstood the blow.

Gong!

The giant wooden club slipped from the grasp of the evil demon and crashed to the ground with a thunderclap. The powder of this plane plumed out in giant waves.

My onion was peeled.

I entered the fight with one last spell—a spell I'd never truly cast, using reserves I didn't know were adequate. Fortunately, I had the same boon available to buoy my reserves as did Tedene and the other spirits. For me, it was my yearning for my María and our unborn child.

Gong!

"*Disevocation.*"

I cast the spell as a breath. I was so confident of its result, I didn't need to vocalize it.

All sounds ceased. The great riots of lightning stopped arching through the blackness. Even every soul stopped pouring their poisonous joy into the enormous beast. That is, all except Tedene.

"Ms Varde, we won. I need you to lead the others out. Go now," I urged as I marked the doorway.

"James, tell Presley I love him, and I have a star to find," she said before she shot off, the others following her.

"I will," I said to her fading flare.

Tick...

"Charles, it's your turn."

"No, son, it's yours. I'll stay until I know this beast is really and truly dead," he informed me, his great sword held high, a guarantee of necessary violence.

"Charles, if the void is consumed before you get out..." I left the suggested meaning unsaid.

"Don't you fret, Jimmy boy. Davi taught me a thing or two that you still haven't learned. I've got my own way out. Now skedaddle before I whoop ya!"

It was only now that I recognized I didn't have the strength to reintegrate my soul and body.

JAMES

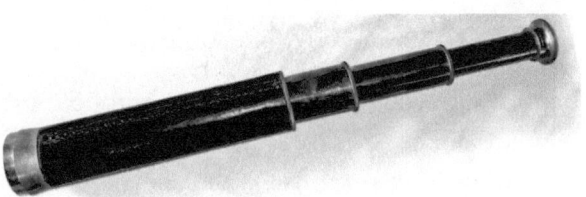

*M*y transition from the void into the sphere of the living was quick. It was black outside, but it was especially well lit inside Eldritch Manor. It was heartening to see María and my friends as they stood staring at...

"Well, darn, that didn't go well," I announced.

I remained calm, since I'd resigned myself to this possible fate.

"Yes, you fucked it up proper, did you not?"

I spun. Standing behind me was the spectral form of Davi, her smirk still beatific. That was, if you didn't account for her being as cranky as a trapped possum.

I just shook my head. "At least we finished the demon and kept Dahl from opening the final portal," I said.

"Yes, at least you did."

"Say, Davi, could you help a fella out?" I asked, turning my head and lifting my chin to my body.

"I should force you to float there, holding your dick. But since it would not be fair to your wife—for her, sure, why not?"

She flicked her wrist, and my vision went black again.

Dang it, why can't this she-devil do anything easy?

"James, open your fucking eyes, you dumb shit."

I did. María screamed and fell onto my face, kissing me.

I raised my good arm and held her, kissing her as if it was the first time we kissed in the market those many weeks ago.

Then she pulled away and drilled me in the arm. While she didn't judge our kiss—at least not obviously—her punch found my uninjured shoulder, but she followed it with a verbal onslaught, balancing her lovely kiss. It was a tide of Spanish cuss words, insults, and, I'm certain, general attacks on my intelligence. I allowed the untranslated assault to sweep over me as I quit struggling to follow it.

This was love!

"Baby, I appreciate you're angry. But can you hold off a moment? I've got to handle Dahl."

She kissed me again in response. Then she and Presley tugged me to my feet.

I faced Dahl for the first time since he'd killed me. This time, he didn't have any measurable magic left. I could destroy him. Still, I'd seen portions of his torture, and wanted to grant his wish.

"Riaan, I won't let you open your final portal. But I've cleared a passage inside the demon's sphere, which you can use. You merely have my word that it'll work. To access it, you must cut yourself and let your blood flow onto the spyglass."

"Jimmy, you can't," Kate said, her forehead creased and her eyes narrowed.

"Jim, don't," Presley said with her and in the same manner. His expression only differed with the tilt of his head.

My friends doubted my intention to let Dahl out of his cage, even to return to his own planet. Still, because they were smart, compassionate individuals who understood his misery, they doubted themselves, too.

"Our other options are to execute him or keep him secured until he dies," I said.

"And I sure as hell don't want 'em on our planet, so our only actual choices are to kill 'em or send 'em home," Presley said.

"Jim, are you sure this doorway won't open the others?" María asked. She held a vice-like grip onto my arm and tugged me around. She needed to see my answer in my eyes while I spoke.

"Guys." Kate rolled her eyes at my use of the word. "I can't be sure. But I created that gateway inside a detached dimension outside our universe. I don't understand how they could connect."

"First, don't call me or María 'guys.' It's sexist and demeaning," the redheaded spitfire said. Presley turned away, smiling. He'd heard the same opinion from Kate before today. His view was that the term guys included everyone and wasn't suggestive of gender.

Hers was, "Fine, adopt the term 'gals,' then."

Presley would counter, "I don't speak to girls often. Besides, my audience is normally my ship's *male* crew. It's nothing more than common vernacular."

"So, you prefer discussing the sexist policy of excluding women on your little boats. The one that supports the notion that because we don't have a tiny trunk between our legs, we're bad luck. And don't call us 'girls,' either."

Wisely, Presley had learned to not use either word. I bet my wife would eventually teach me the same lesson. But not today.

"Second," Kate added before I could defend myself, "why don't we ask Davi?"

The four of us, including Riaan Dahl, turned to Davi, who was relaxing, perched in the same pink padded flowery armchair that had decorated my home for the last two months. She quietly sipped her tea, then blew across it before she rose and spoke.

"I have visited many similar histories of this event. Never did James successfully open a channel through the demon realm to Dahl's home, though, from a magical perspective, he established the passage perfectly. My short answer, then, is yes."

"Yes! I—at least this version of I...or me...whatever—created an option that none of the infinite number of other Jameses discovered."

I was justly pleased with myself for having executed the unparalleled task of rescuing my friends, town, and world, while affording the tortured murderer Riaan Dahl a path home.

"Please, most of your separate selves were too stupid to survive this long. Something you will realize in a few moments," Davi said.

Crash!

The front door scraped loudly across the floor and smashed against the facade behind it, and a dozen men from the Spanish garrison poured into the chamber, shouting orders to remain *inmóvil*.

I didn't need a translator. Their intent was unmistakable as they formed a semi-circle protecting the front exit.

Another thump, and Capitan Raphael Jenyns rushed into the room from the rear.

"Lady María, I am pleased to see you, if not somewhat amazed," the garrison commander said. María faced her soon-to-be captors and smiled.

"Commander, you are on private property. Property owned by Mr. Byrne. You are in a foreign country, and are uninvited inside this building. I suggest you leave before you cause an incident," my bride said. It was clear she wasn't intimidated.

"A situation I, too, wish to avoid. However, I am sworn to follow the directives of my superiors. They have ordered me to take you into protective custody until suitable transportation is available to return you to Spain."

"You'll not be holding anyone," I said as I pulled my knife—something I realized quickly didn't carry the intimidation I'd intended, as the assembled men pointed their weapons at my chest.

"Please, sir. That tiny knife would not even slow us down should we decide. James, we are friends. Do not make this difficult," the sharply dressed officer said.

I realized my options were rather limited. I could use magic to defend us. That wouldn't help, because the soldiers would simply tell everyone I was working for Beelzebub.

I looked to my guide for any help. She rolled her eyes and said, "Your forgetfulness is fucking amazing."

When I didn't answer, she continued, "You really are a fucking moron. I weep for your species."

"Muck-spout," I retorted. Then inspiration hit me as I realized the importance of forgetfulness. Forgetting was the effect I needed.

"*Depergeo!*" I mumbled as I formed a sphere using my pinky finger and thumb, pointed my other fingers at the garrison's men, and moved my hand from my left to my right.

The effect was instantaneous. They fell asleep and collapsed to the floor.

"According to Ms. Constance Goodwin, that spell should keep them out of our way for several hours, and they won't remember the last five minutes," I crowed.

Then, just to be certain, I conjured *Down With Spells* and opened it. Sure enough, Ms. Goodwin confirmed I'd selected the correct spell and shaped it properly.

Finally, since returning to my body, I heard the clock again. It wasn't the annoying and terrifying *tick* that had haunted me for the last months. This time, it was a simple shift of mechanics as it readied its chime. A single minute remained before five o'clock.

"Dahl, you're out of time. Make your choice. Live in prison here, die here, or risk the demon's doorway." I tossed him my knife—my other knife. It stuck in the floor beside his cage.

He reached his hand toward the edge of the cage, wary of the spell Davi had placed on it because it'd already hammered him once. But, when he reached the barrier, his hand passed through. He tugged loose the knife and turned it toward me. At least if he tried to attack, I wouldn't regret killing him.

In a swift move, he flipped the knife around and cut his palm open. Dark-blue blood poured from the incision. The edges of the wound started healing almost as soon as they split apart.

I hurried to him as I cast the retrieval spell to return the spyglass to me from its home at the top of the stairs. Tears streamed down his cheeks as he placed his injured hand on the artifact he'd chased across all of those worlds.

"Thank you, James," was all he said as he faded from view.

I was rightly proud of my day's accomplishments when I looked up. Unfortunately, I didn't notice the smiling faces of my friends. I only noticed their wide eyes and open mouths. Only then did I see the object of their concern: Capitan Raphael Jenyns.

His mouth opened and closed like a fish out of water while his gun raised toward my chest, before falling as he saw María.

"*Depergeo,*" I mumbled as I shaped the spell.

"Dumbass," Davi said as she shook her head and pinched the bridge of her nose.

JAMES

*B*y the time the Spanish awoke, María was gone and in hiding at Kate and Presley's home. The Spaniards thoroughly investigated the manor grounds after I grudgingly gave approval. Don't misunderstand—they would've explored the estate with or without my approval. But my part in this charade was to feign displeasure. Anything less, and they'd suspect my involvement in hiding her.

I shaped several illusion charms, their yellow glow only obvious to Davi and me. The others simply saw tattered tapestries hanging on cracked walls. That kept them from exploring areas that might have open portals. Fear of the history of Eldritch cut short the outside inspection.

Davi placed a charm on Presley's home, causing anyone who happened by to veer away. She explained, "This petty grievance between two cultures is hardly something to alter the evolution of your realm." Yes, she was stretching sincerity. But I didn't care.

The five of us assembled for dinner at Kate's after the four of us took well-earned naps.

Dinner was one of my favorites: roast beef, potatoes, carrots, cornbread, and blackberry cobbler. Kate prepared the vegetables separate from the meat, respecting Davi, who was a vegetarian.

"Davi, did Charles escape?" I asked, casting an eye toward Kate. At his mention, the little redhead stopped mid-bite and stared at Davi.

"I could not be certain, James. But Charlie was a powerful wizard. If he claimed he had a path out, I believe him. Charles never boasted." Kate's shoulders dropped as the anxiety she'd developed waiting on the answer was released. Presley patted her arm, and a lone tear stained her freckled face.

"Jimmy, how d'you get back inside your body?" Presley asked. The two of us had been friends since childhood, so the boldness of his question didn't bother me.

"Presley, I didn't. I'd consumed so much of my reserves, I didn't have the energy. We've got a friend to recognize for that deed," I replied, nodding to Davi.

"So much for not becoming involved," my wife said. She was still resentful that Davi hadn't simply fixed the mess.

"María, did you realize it was Dahl who granted you the capacity to recognize James remained alive?" Davi asked. She was skilled at dropping verbal boulders into the conversation and altering its dynamics.

My Spanish bride stopped eating and stared at the blonde in disbelief.

"True, it was also selfish, since it allowed him to regenerate his mana reserves. But he deliberately shaped it to remove a quantity of your burden. Riaan was a complicated being. He did not induce pain deliberately. He simply no longer cared who or what he hurt. But, when he recognized your bereavement, the aspect of him capable of empathy made him extract a portion of your sorrow," Davi said.

"You mean he could still form spells inside your jail?" Presley asked.

"No, Presley. He shaped this spell before I arrived."

Presley shook his head knowingly.

"Jim, your preparations for the room were excellent. The fire, wood, bed, blankets, medical supplies—without them, I do not believe we would have saved you," María said.

"Um...I remember the fire, wood, bed, and blankets. I didn't remember medical supplies," I said.

"Well, for fuck's sake, the dumbass forgot. I could not have Maria become a widow because of his stupidity, could I?" Davi asked.

"Thanks for that," I said, raising a glass in salute.

"Davi, is that portal in the manor's cellar still open?"

"I am afraid it is."

"Dang it!" I declared, before more helpfully asking, "Do you know how many are open?"

"Eleven."

"I don't expect you'd be amenable to closing them and ending this mess, would you?" I asked.

"For fuck's sake, James, you better be joking. I will guide you for a time, though."

"For a time? Why can't this get easier?"

"James, this builds character," Davi said.

"And we can all agree, you need help building character," Presley added unhelpfully.

"Great. So I assume these are world-ending catastrophes if I fail?" I asked, glaring at my friend.

"Some are worse than others. Indeed, you may choose to leave some open. Their races are as benign as your own. Others are terribly incompatible with yours, and you should close them before something dreadful occurs. In any case, you have your wand and books. Other accoutrements will present themselves when required," Davi concluded.

"Accoutrements? Is that like shit and caboodle?" Presley asked. The rest of us stared at him as if he'd sprouted a third eye. He rolled his eyes and continued, "He'd have all the tools, but still crap his pants over how to help everyone."

Everyone, including Davi, groaned at the absurdity of his jape.

"What?" Presley whined.

"Have I got anything to do tonight?" I asked.

I needed to relax and spend some quality time with my wife. Maybe we could take a visit to Rota, Spain, after the baby was born, and possibly convince her mother to let us live in peace.

"Tonight? No, not tonight," Davi said.

"Great," María and I said together.

JAMES

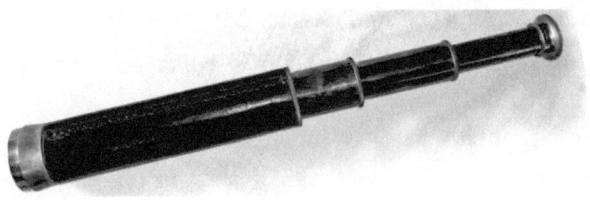

*I*t had been a remarkable number of days since I climbed into bed without the proverbial Sword of Damocles hanging metaphorically above my head. María glided up the stairs, and the door thudded as she closed and latched it behind her. Then she stood confronting me, an expression of frustration spreading.

"Jim, you recall, the wound is on your right shoulder?" she inquired. It was her upturned tone that warned me of my obliviousness.

"Ummm…" I started, carrying the delay for a beat too long.

"It means you must sleep on the other side of the bed," she finished.

The "dumbass" remained unsaid, but suggested. Her impish grin also let me know she was having a bit of fun with me.

"Babe, it's my duty as your devout protector to sleep nearest the entrance. How else could you expect me to preserve your delicate personage from plagues and evils in and beyond this world?" I exaggerated.

"Jim, if something can harm me simply because I am on the improper side of your body, you cannot defend me the way I deserve," she taunted.

"Ummm," was the finest response I could manage. Dang it, how did she continue to do that?

"Besides, what if something attacked through the window instead?"

"Okay, but you've got to scribble a note, so if they discover our bodies with me on the incorrect side of the bed, I get to be right," I suggested as I slid over, allowing her to climb in beside me.

"It does not matter what I write. If our bodies are discovered, Davi will continue to mock you in death." My bride had a point. I'm sure that if the blonde she-devil could, she'd bring me back to life to make fun of me before she let me die again.

My wife snuggled close, laying her head on my uninjured shoulder. This was the most comfortable I'd been in my entire life.

Blissful sleep came quickly. I was evidently more tired than I'd known.

TEASER

The Vampire and Eldritch Manor
James

The snow was light and fluffy and drifted lazily from the darkened sky. This snow was the kind you got when the cold sucked moisture from the air, crystalizing it before it fell. There was almost no wind, but the chill forced me to tug my coat up around my ears and stuff my hands deeper into my pockets.

I'd been walking for more than an hour, and still didn't know where I was or where I was going. I only knew this was the right direction. I guess, I didn't *know* for certain, but it *felt* correct.

I stopped, turned around, and looked back along the path I'd just trodden. My footprints mashed the white snow into the muddy ground, leaving a distinct path of minor valleys surrounded by the mud pushed up by my weight.

I still dragged my left leg, leaving a clear drag mark. The wound hurt, and the splint forced me to keep my knee unbent. The broken bone hadn't healed, despite my numerous sorcerous curative attempts.

As I watched, my footprints faded, beginning with the ones

furthest away and *walking* toward me. Within seconds, the only prints that remained were those under the soles of my shoes. It was as if I'd been dropped onto this spot.

An owl hooted before it took flight. Pine needles and accumulated snow dropped from the branch as it shook from the disturbance. The orange moon was full and sat fat and low on the western horizon. This was the second full moon of the month, so it was called a blue moon by those like me who cared about such things.

Navigation was a critical skill for any seaman. Using the moon and stars as a reference was intrinsic to our success. Tonight, I followed the moon as my only hope for rescue.

I stood, staring at it, and forgot why I was here. I focused on my surroundings until I remembered.

Then I restarted my trudge.

I hadn't begun the day hopeful of my prospects of success. No, I'd begun it sure that today was the day I'd be recaptured and tossed back into prison. This trudge was the baleful slog of a wretched creature certain of its inevitable doom.

Dogs barked in the distance, and I heard men yelling. I quickened my pace. The pain was sharp and excruciating. I stumbled, then fell. I was near a placid pool of water and pulled myself to its edge. The reflection that greeted me was the same terrible monster that had awoken inside the prison yesterday.

I'd once fought to protect the very men who now hunted me. I'd protected them from the beast's attack. But my victory came with a cost—a broken leg and a flesh-rending wound that had altered my body in ways I'd never imagined possible.

It was the smell of my blood that the dogs followed. It was this same blood that had changed me into the monster now running from civilization. It was also the sanguine fluid that I'd grown to crave after the attack.

I looked up from my place at the edge of the water and saw the cave I'd been searching for. Presley was waiting there.

"It's about time you got here," he said, as if this were a meeting for a meal instead of a hastily thrown-together rendezvous after my prison break.

"Sorry, Pres. Got here as fast as I could. Have you seen her? Davi, is she here?" I implored.

"You bet your ass I am here. Now what the fuck have you done this time?" Davi asked.

Her hands were pushed firmly into her hips, and her expression was a mixture of her typical mocking countenance and plenty of "I told you so."

HELP AN AUTHOR?

Thank you for reading my book. I worked incredibly hard to transport you to a fascinating destination while moving you through an exciting tale.

I have a favor to ask... will you please take a minute, click the link below, and leave me a review. I recognize you don't have a reason; but, consider this, reviews drive sales more than a brilliant cover, well-written blurb, or any ad copy. Without reviews, my readership plummets, as will my royalty. Most importantly, I can't judge whether my book is meeting your high standards.

Please click the link and leave me a quick review. Thanks!

https://www.amazon.com/review/create-review/?ie=UTF8&
channel=glance-detail&asin=B09GRDGNYS

Thanks for your time, and I hope you enjoy one of my other books listed on the next page.

OTHER TITLES BY GARRETT WARD

The Ceorfan Gargoyles RH Series
Carved
Etched
Hewn

Ceorfan Gargoyles Novellas
My Tormented Mage
Ceorfan Teens

The Shivers a YA RH Paranormal Series
We See You
Double Mirror

Elser Books are Fantasy Stand Alone
Flesh & Bold

GLOSSARY

Places

Aquilon: Presley Varde's Ship.

Ether: The magical construct that provides all magical energy.

Eldritch Manor: Charles Doss' generational land and home and the center of this mess.

Kaysan: The realm Tituba created as she was murdered. Later, Wáhta and her converted it into a demonic realm.

Metaterre: James' hometown.

Monarch Of The Sea: James Byrne's ship.

SPELLS

Amori: Love spell

AgerDeleo: Immediately deletes a realm.

Castellem: Protects yourself. Remember to move your hand above your head, dumb-ass.

Deannix: Dimensional transition. Allows me to walk different pasts and possible futures.

Decipio: Confusion spell. Confuses a target.

Depergeo: Sleep, forgetfulness spell

Diskaver: A discovery spell. Used to search for something.

Disevocation: This spell will disentangle all energy contained within the volume of the radius of the caster's wand movement.

Extingeu: Extinguishes large fires or kills up to hundreds of people.

Flattus: Sends a strong burst of wind at a target.

Key-see-us: Invisibility.

Kinno Antim: Clears my mind so I can concentrate on what I'm doing, instead of María.

Liquefacta: Turns a specific area of ground into molten liquid.

Muras Ignis: Wall of Flame

Mortus Exerptum: Gives the caster access to the energy of the deceased.

Osteaendo: This spell tracks the energy of Kaysan across time and distance.

Ruina: Ranged destruction spell.

Serverbaris: Protects others

Spaceum Deleo: Destroys a realm.

Soporium: Causes your target to sleep.

Stingeu: Extinguishes a small fire or kills small animals.

Ustrina: Lights a fire.

Vacuefacio: Disappearance spell.

Vis Indi: Allows the caster to give energy to the dead.

CREATURES / PEOPLE

Akhmatova, Anna: A Russian linguist who boarded the *Monarch* six months ago. She's both an interpreter and acts as my personal valet. She and I share the same birthday, June 23. Although, I'm six years older.

Bond, Susan: Proprietress of *The Old Crow*. A wonderful dining establishment.

Bruce, Martha-Mary: Our local apothecary

Byrne, James: That's me!

Christina Rosetta de Gardoqui: María's Cousin, and Diego's daughter.

Crusher, Barry: The doctor in charge of the local hospital. He's also a man born under the stars, trekking through darkness.

Davi: That blonde she-devil who claims to be my guide.

Don Diego José de Gardoqui y Arriquibar: María's uncle.

Doss, Charles Dwayne, II: Katie's Grandfather.

Doss, Peggy: Charles' first wife and Kate's grandmother.

Genosqwa: The demon who wants out of its self-created dimensional prison.

Capitán Jenyn, Raphael: Sent by María's mother to watch over her and report anything he deemed important. Primarily he was supposed to spy on her. But they were friends and he only reported things that impacted her safety.

Jericho: He's one of the most powerful mages and a member of the Ceorfan people. He was also the headmaster of the Colonial Magical Education Society.

Juliana Valentia de Gardoqui: Diego's wife.

Kokkino Petra Magnus: Kino is an author and magical gargoyle and a member of the Ceorfan people.

María: Lady María Pimetel de Rota. AKA the most alluring woman to ever grace this or any other world.

Owensteine, Robert: A crotchety attorney.

Riaan Dahl: He's a dimensional traveling, shape-shifting murderous creature who's searching for an artifact with enough power that he can use it to open a set of portals to return to his world in a different universe than mine. Did I mention he was a murderer?

Saddler, Melodie: Proprietress of Below the Salt. It's a fantastic restaurant that I highly recommend.

Tituba: A former slave, convicted of witchcraft in Salem, Massachusetts about a hundred and fifty years ago. When she got out of jail, she moved father north and married an Algonquin man who was murdered in a mourning-war by a group of Iroquois. Their child died after she was captured.

Varde, Kate: My best friend's wife. Okay, that description will make her angry. So, let's say she is a friend of mine and married to my best friend. She's also the redhead most responsible for this entire mess. She has several nicknames, including Roja and Hun.

Varde, Presley: My best friend.

Varde, Tedene: Presley's Grandmother.

Vatis: A powerful and ancient dragon who gives part of his heart to me for my wand.

Wáhta: He's a hate-filled, Iroquois chief who was killed seconds after he murdered Tituba. This man has no love in his life, only hate.

Wolf, Ronald Seaman: Called Chief by his shipmates on the Monarch because he's forever offering advice on _every_ subject or task.

Wolf, John: The quieter twin to Ron Wolf.